EDSEL

By Karl Shapiro

EDSEL

by

Karl Shapiro

Published by

BERNARD GEIS ASSOCIATES

To Teri

Among the Just
Be just, among the Filthy, filthy too.

Auden

CHAPTER I

Seven miles over Labrador the ice had melted in my martini. I skulked in my Pan Am armchair, my eyes glittery with fatigue. London was a couple of hours ago, a bit of Ireland, a hand's-span of Atlantic.

"Ladies and gentlemen," the captain crackled, "we are now situated over Goose Bay," and began his thank-you speech. The word "situated" made me start. Did the pilot have the right to use that word? Was it a nautical term or what? The poet in me reared up in challenge. I hated the captain, hated the summer weeks of Rome, Urbino, Frankfort, Hamburg, Berlin, hated the lectures I had given about American poetry, and hated most of all the debriefing session I had to attend next morning at the State Department. I gazed out of the window, then into my dying drink. You can't see a goddam thing from an airplane anyway.

We were flying over Maine; we were flying near Boston; near New York; near Baltimore. My eardrums registered the downward miles. I craned my neck to find landmarks but missed. I wanted a landmark desperately, but, hell, what difference did it make. The big ship breasted down over green farmland, Maryland-Virginia land, and small chimes sounded in the cabin. Lights went on to do and not do. The mighty

3

aluminum wing sped along the concrete slab of Dulles International Airport, slowed, turned many corners, coasted. An announcement or two, then Muzak leaked preposterously from the sound-vents of the cabin.

Minutes later I lined up with the other passengers before a huge poster of a President Johnson which said, Welcome to the United States. A Negro customs officer had me open one suitcase, fingered through dirty laundry and let me go. Home, James.

Home? And where exactly was that? Somewhere in the flat-ass Middle West in the little university town where I, Edsel Lazerow, campus bard, earned bread to pay my alimony and buy booze. And that's where Wanda lived—primarily on her back, I ranted to myself. I'm going home for punishment; I haven't had enough, I thought. Back to let that whore cut off my balls again. Back to convince myself that I'm impotent, between the legs and at the typewriter, above and below the neck. More punishment, more, more! I clenched my teeth and my partials and looked at the rich Virginia countryside and the big slow-moving American cars. Vast hideous-hued machines staying within the speed limit. Not like Europe. Europeans drove to the death, all of them killers. Americans had accidents, yes, great brilliant screaming accidents, but accidents. As if there were no accidents and every accident *was* an accident. The childishness of "It was an accident!" Apologies, law-suits, fender-benders, chipped paint. How dare you chip my paint! Not like Italy or the Autobahn where every driver is a murderer.

Back in the land of the child, I thought. I'll go to the State Department for a mild spanking, then back to Wanda to be whipped within an inch of my life. I couldn't wait to get to the hotel to call her. I knew in advance her line would be busy, either at the Fountain of Beauty Salon, where she worked, or at home, where she played. The telephone was always off the hook, to me. Busy-busy-busy was her standard answer. And fool that I knew I was, I prayed her line *would* be busy or that one of her men would answer. I breathed a sigh of relief;

4

I'm back where I can feel, back where it hurts, back in the telephone hell.

The taxi entered stately, magnificent, mindless Washington, the architectural circus of the world.

Wanda's line was busy. I ate a cold turkey sandwich in the moistly cold hotel room and drank warm scotch. I would keep calling.

At the debriefing I was made to feel important and welcome. I had cultivated an offhand charm which permitted me to say practically anything which is not said in polite or official society. I was seated at the head of a vast ovoid conference table and was asked to recount my visit to the foreign universities I had been sent to, a day here, a week there, during the summer. I held my own. No, I had not sided with U.S. Foreign Policy when the Commies baited me. Yes, I *had* insisted that I was merely a guest of the State Department, not an officer or employee. And so forth. *Und so weiter.* I thanked the assemblage for having sent me on the tour, and then the questions began with greater specificity (one of the company dropped that word in). I entered into the discussion while my mind played back the actual tour, the experience rather than the abstractions.

I had left Wanda one evening in June, after she refused to spend the night with me. "I hate goodbyes," she growled, and then bombed off to somebody's bed. I had left Milo Airport the next dawn and bumped my way on prop planes to Chicago. I had left Washington after my briefing and spent one night in New York during a cab strike. I took scab cabs to visit a poet or two. And the next day I took a half-empty Pan-Am monster albatross to Frankfort, daylight filling the cabin all the way. Frankfort, where grandpa wasn't made into a lampshade because he got out of there in 1880. All the way, coming and going, I would ask myself: what the hell am I doing here? But I worked well, did my duty to God and my country, and bombarded Wanda with letters of my wanderings.

5

First stop: Zagreb. I had a holy terror of going behind the Iron Curtain. Part of my poetic paranoia told me that the Communists were going to ax me one of these days, the way they did Trotsky. After all, I had been fighting the Commies since the existential Thirties, and I merited a comeuppance. Wanted and feared my just desserts. But "State" had given me leave to go to the Poets-Essayists-Novelists International Convention in Yugoslavia (they called it the PEN Club and I never really knew what the initials meant) and I intended to drop in, as it were, at the close of the meetings to chat with literary wheels. Not that I really cared. I did and I didn't. Once their annual meet had been held in Tokyo and I had been sent on a clipper plane with a planeload of U.S. writers, the most famed and anthologized. I was the only poet aboard. If that plane had slambanged down in the blue Pacific, American Lit would have stopped for two generations.

I sat down on the terrace of the Esplanade Hotel in Zagreb at seven o'clock in the evening and ordered a beer. A scattering of people, some drifting in from the PEN Congress, intelligentsia, by the crook of their heads and their hot eyes; real potted oleanders looking fake, hot dusty sunlight and the humidity of Washington, D.C. Frankfort had been cool and there I had felt superior. Now I was behind the Iron Curtain, a figure of speech which I despised as Churchillian trash, yet a fact which I attributed to Churchillian rhetoric. Without that cheap and poisonous epithet there would be no Iron Curtain; I was convinced of that. The Russians would never have thought of erecting their great wall except for the Englishman's jeer. And yet it was necessary. Historical consciousness insisted on those metaphors which were next day manufactured into tanks, barbed wire, and TV "check-points." "Checkpoint" was another expression that made my heart turn rancid. Another Madison Avenue Churchillism, part of the vast shit lexicon of the "modern world." "Modern world" was one that made my gorge rise.

I drank my beer slowly, uneasily. I hate eating or drinking in public alone. I always feel watched and am myself a watcher who has suffered from staring all my life. I know for a certainty that eyes are ray guns, that anyone can make anyone else turn around to meet a gaze. I got up, took my beer, and moved to a table closer to a little low wall, closer to the oleanders. I sat facing the stage—there was a stage against the hotel facade with placards announcing the "entertainment"— some American Beatles would perform (when, to whom). "Entertainment" is a word I loathe.

Alternately I watched the entrance from the terrace to the interior of the Esplanade for newcomers, and two lesbian-looking delegates who had just sat down—no doubt from the Writers Congress. I had flown maybe 800 miles to the Congress, wanting to miss it and knowing I would. On my own money, I thought with sour sweetness. I wondered if the lesbians could possibly recognize me: I felt that I radiated "writer" to those who could spot one. Then Spencer Day, the international poet, emerged from the door and cringed gigantically toward a table. He sat six tables, more or less, from me, facing the empty stage, thus providing me with a view of his back and his huge, delicate gray-white head. Day studied the terrace for acquaintances or strangers perhaps, swinging the beacon of his head from left to right, almost turning 360 degrees at times, now and then putting on his glasses and taking them off (still vain, I thought, and why not, a handsome seven-foot-tall international cultural wheel, never in the same capital more than a matter of days). I watched him drink white wine, order, eat rather elaborately, from the gestures. It was getting dark and little terrace lights went on and sometimes off (Yugoslavia, Jesus!) and I also ate. I ate a huge and stinking fish and created a cairn of fishbones bigger than the original bulk of the animal. All the while I was deciding not whether but *when* to accost Day. I waited until there was nothing on my table but coffee.

Day flicked his tongue quickly over his lips (an English habit?) and answered the Yugoslav journalist before I could open my mouth. Question: I did not see you at the Congress, Mr. Edsel. Day: "He didn't get there," and laughed—meanly, I thought, pleased with the *mot juste*. It would have to be *meanly* because there is nothing in the world more important than a Writers Congress. To miss an important one would be the ultimate dereliction. And to arrive too late could only signify idiocy. Purposeful idiocy, I consoled myself coldly.

In the morning I raced from the hotel to the nasty little airport in a cab, back to Germany. The once-grand driveway of the Esplanade was choked with little black cockroach official "limousines" each flying a Yugoslav flag and a red flag on the fenders. My cab had to hold in the dusty street. I burst into it. Oh, God, get me back to Germany, I more or less prayed. West Germany, I amended to the Almighty. I hated Germany but understood the German selfishness, the thickness, the stupidity. In Germany, or what was left of it, if one just looked like an authority or a free body or soul, the clods fell back and cringed. Behind the Curtain every minuscule clerk, official or proletarian sneered at every Westerner. To the drones of the drone world any suggestion of individuality was high treason. German stupidity was refreshing. Stunned like oxen by a thousand years of well-deserved defeats, they eyed the individual out of the corner of their eye with adoration and awe. The German adores nothing but a conqueror, the one who crushes the universe in his jaws. The Russians and their millions of slaves adored nothing, nobody, no man. *History*, they spat, was what they adored. All are slaves *to* history, they sang. We are all slaves, they preached. I prefer tyrants to slaves. I'm a visiting tyrant, I said to myself. So be it. Fuck the slaves. Give me a hot bath in a cold city, a bottle of scotch and a whore.

I flew into Hamburg righteously.

What I remembered of Hamburg was the whore; no relevant subject for the State Department. Why bore them with that? What I remembered of Hamburg was a Käthe Kollwitz show, an avenue where every shop window was stocked to explosion with cameras, and crowds around each camera window—imagine a Kraut without a camera. I remembered a Chinese restaurant where I ordered some egg-roll, a minor deal, and got as an entree an egg-roll fit for the World's Fair, a foot long and 3 inches thick. I thought of ordering two gallons of Coleman's Mustard, which they had forgotten, but I didn't. I remembered a walk through a Buchenwald, just an innocent birch forest, not a real Buchenwald, beautiful but frighteningly clean and foresty. And I remembered a visit to Bismarck's grave and chapel with a Jewish guide from the U.S.I.A. and his little daughter. The Americans had had the poetic insight to bomb Bismarck's estate to rubble—or was it the British? I didn't care—but the chapel where the holy body was, was either undamaged or rebuilt. At the entrance of the estate was a Bismarck Museum. Sol Bluestone (my guide) and I were awed by the size of Bismarck's boots, probably the largest boots in the world. The Bismarck furniture was also Texas size, hideous, Victorian. The curatress was charming without being deferential. There are more things, many more, she trilled in unimprovable English diction. Sol and I were sure of that but went our way up the little knoll to the shrine. It was a shrine, so what. Bismarck's dust and little knots of Germans moving around in catatonic worship. Start it again, I thought, as you sure as hell will goddam have to. We tiptoed out of there.

Next morning I walked out of my hotel and caught a cab. The driver spoke English, as cab drivers do in seaport towns. Where is the nightclub district, I asked. The driver turned and looked at me. "The Raper-Bahn, yes?" And took me there. Good word, Raper-Bahn, I thought, though I would never learn to spell it. We drifted down to the waterfront, through monuments and medieval buildings, apparently all replaced since the latest holocaust. The taxi swung into the Raper Street and cruised slowly against the curbs. Blocks of strip joints with uniformed hawkers outside at ten in the A.M. The cab stopped. I paid the driver and tipped him well. The driver said carefully and proudly: you are to be careful. In these places, careful. They push you and take your money. Thank you. And drove off.

I walked six or eight blocks up one side of the street and six or eight blocks down the other. Then I crossed back. The hawkers too spoke English. A hawker lured me inside a vestibule. I sat down in the dark. One light somewhere on a little platform and a thick waistless fraulein standing there with the light on her. She was dressed, just standing. There was no one else anywhere, no music, nothing. Suddenly a man appeared at my elbow and I ordered *ein bier*. Then everything happened at once. The waistless fraulein was sitting next to me and said in English to move up against the wall, where there must have been a booth in the dark. We went there and she jammed me against the wall. Simultaneously the barman brought what looked like a bottle of Seven-Up and said *champagne* and presented a bill for sixty Deutsche marks. "Do I open it?" he asked. I was in the process of saying I didn't order champagne, much less for fifteen dollars a squirt, while it was being opened. The barman sat down across the table. I didn't drink while the stuff was being poured and the fraulein drank hers. "You are a nice man," the fraulein kept repeating, squeezing against me, while the bartender was asking to be paid.

How I weaseled out of there I'll never know. I took my passport wallet out and emptied its contents. I had stashed about a hundred dollars in my watch pocket, those sartorial holes which are never used except for such purposes, but I emptied only about five American on the table. I emptied my passport, TWA and Hertz credit cards on the board, my A.A.U.P. card, my group hospitalization card, my voter's identification card (what a fucking bunch of cards, I thought to myself) and said that is all I have. That is what I have. This is it. The woman continued to crowd me, saying Nice Man, and I wondered what that would be in German. The bartender pounded the table a few times. I continued to look and act meek and mild. All at once the man grabbed my five dollars' worth of Deutsche marks, the woman removed her bulk, and I walked out free and unbattered into the Raper-Bahn.

I sailed back to my hotel and wrote Wanda an account of the A.M. I ended by informing her that tonight I was going to find the legitimate whorehouse district. I figured it was near Rape Street. It was.

I followed the crowds from the main strip up one side street after another. Nearly all the joints seemed to feature female impersonators, something peculiarly German, I thought. I steered clear of the hawkers. Suddenly I stood before a high green wooden wall that blocked the entrance to the street. On the wall was painted in white and in German simple enough for me to read: FORBIDDEN TO YOUTH. Two doors were cut neatly into the high wall. Men were coming and going through the doors, and I entered.

The solid block of houses was blazing with lights on both sides of the narrow street. The sidewalks were so crowded I could hardly move. The whores sat in the open windows, laughing, bargaining, cursing when they saw a woman in the crowd and slamming down the shade. There were old men, sailors, toughs, soldiers, respectable-looking men, sightseers, youths with grim leers on their faces. Half of the mob must have been drunk. The pavement was slick with vomit. The entire street had a coating of slime. I brushed against a man pissing against a wall and recoiled. I milled around, getting as close to the windows as possible, studying the faces of the women. I believed in the Hoor. I didn't think of whores as fallen women, women led into corruption as children, but as women with a definite inescapable calling. I thought they loved their situation. True, they usually hated men, were frigid, insatiable, and vicious, and that was their service to mankind. They ate men with their cunts. They burned away the sentiments and left lust pure. I began to romanticize: theirs was a sacred function, almost a religion, their street was a temple dedicated to animality. The money transaction was a sacrament, the putting on and taking off of the rubber a ritual blessing of the prick. To a whore there are no men, only pricks. And to the whoremonger there were no whole women, only the parts of the woman, sometimes only a particular part, a foot, an armpit, a mouth, the buttocks. The vagina itself was only a part. Each whoremonger has his particular delectation, as at a banquet one man will choose the leg of the bird, another the liver, another the neck or the back. I was convinced that man contained a vestigial brain in his genitals, a highly sophisticated brain which thought for itself and lived a life of its own. As I searched the faces of the whores I asked myself:

11

what am I looking for? The answer came from my groin: impassivity. Feelingless lust. The arctic lay. Joylessness. My upper brain replied: and at the bottom of lust lies murder. Every fuck with a whore is a double murder. I began to get an erection but had already decided that I would come back next morning, slightly drunk, when maybe the street of vomit would be empty. No crowding in waiting-rooms which were like doctor's offices or bus stations, men coughing and spitting on the floor or impatiently leafing through grimy magazines. I wormed my way back through the green door, went back to my room and drank myself to sleep.

At noon next day I wrote Wanda.

Dear Wanda,

I've just come back from the Street of Vomit, my tail between my legs. Tell it to the girls at the Fountain of Beauty Salon. Put it in headlines: Regents Professor Gets Fucked. Second headline: Big Deal. Well, as I am now an habitué of Rape Lane, I got a taxi to take me straight to the Green Wall. Remember the song, Green Door, What's That Secret You're Keeping? The secret is out. I had three scotches for breakfast, hid fifty Deutsche marks in a secret part of my passport case, another fifty loose in my pocket.

The street was empty except for three customers in the distance, searching the windows. I walked slowly down the sidewalk. At about the third window I spotted Irma (all I got out of her later was her name). A hefty blonde with Slavic cheekbones and possibly blue eyes, more a deliquescent green or tawny. Or did I imagine that. She was reading a magazine, her legs propped up on the window sill. Sandals. Had on coarse white cotton panties. She held one hand on the back of her neck, exposing a rich crop of hair under her pit. Corntassel. A regular brute of a peasant. Barely glanced at me. I kept sauntering on down my side of the street. Most of the windows were empty. A couple of scrawny black-haired ones gave me the smile. One gave me a dirty look, I guess as some kind of come-on. About three-quarters down the block I turned back to the Slav. Stood in front of her window and said in my English "Where is the door?" She pointed to her right and got up.

I trailed her up four flights of narrow stairs. On two flights women were scrubbing the steps. There was a little apartment at the top. *"Bier?"* she asked. Yes. Someone brought two bottles of beer. Irma disappeared into a little bathroom and did something or other. Then she put on a phonograph record and we sipped the beer. She told me the price. Seventy including the beer. I fished the money out. She undressed. It was suddenly freezing in the room and I was afraid if I put my hand on her thigh it would freeze there. Motioned me to undress. My penis had shrunk down to a medium-price mushroom. She stroked it and I played with her pussy. When she managed to build me a passable erection she went and got a rubber out of a drawer and rolled it on me. My prick was still soft and she kept squeezing and coaxing it. I grabbed her tits which were big and rubbery and cool. No heat there. Nipples asleep. Her armpits stank and I leaned over to smell them. She closed her hand harder on my penis and all of a sudden I came. She knew I had come from my breathing and she leaned back and looked at me in surprise. Then came the scolding.

It was a pantomime with the word *kaput* as frequent punctuation. Not here, she was saying, opening her palm. *Kaput. Here!* she was saying, grabbing her pussy. *Kaput.* "Broken," I said. "Broken," she answered. *Kaput. Ich bin kaput,* I ventured in daring German. *Kaput* she replied with a mock-reproachful smile. I started to get dressed. It was then I asked her her name. She repeated her name thrice, pointing to her breast. I even got a little autobiography for my seventy. East Reich. Escaped from there. She led me down the four flights and we shook hands at the door. Thank you, ma'am.

Went home, took a drink, tried to sleep but jerked off instead. Some of her stink was on me.

Greetings from Edsel Lazerow.

I stitched back and forth across West Germany, lecturing on the U.S. poets, dissidents and regulars, on the American Jewish writer, and such things. The latter was a favorite topic for me in Germany. Never had I heard deader hushes or seen more controlled faces. Questions were few. Sometimes I felt that they weren't even listening, just drinking in the sight of a real live Jew, a creature as fabulous as the unicorn, straight out of the Dark Ages. At the Berlin Wall I looked with love upon the ruins, but unfortunately they were all on the Red side. I tried to imagine the entire city still smoking and crashing into rubble. I summoned up the image of the Nazi armies, a hundred abreast, goose-stepping up the Unter den Linden to the Brandenburg Gate, the largest mob of pure murderers in history. I felt superior to the Germans, *racially* superior, you might say. German women make good American wives, I sociologized. The German motto, I thought, trying to bring it down to my level, is Kitchen, Kids, and Kunt. Even Tacitus had written about the fidelity of Kraut females. Though Krafft-Ebing hadn't!

In a little university town near Frankfort I was taken under the wing of a wifely widow who had made my living arrangements and fixed my schedules. We were immediate friends. Uta began to talk about her husband straight off, as if to get that out of the way. He was killed in the Nazi army but had not been in uniform. He was an engineer and *refused* to wear the uniform. A likely story, I thought, wanting to fall into her big wifely arms. The uniformless Nazi had been killed in a motor accident in Italy. Okay, I thought, I'm not the Nuremberg Trials.

They stashed me in a medieval inn or hotel, more or less. It was nice, unconfusing. I felt a kind of Amerigo-Semitic superiority to the place. And I felt comfortable—in Germany! I knew I had this particular village eating out of my hand. For a couple of days anyhow. Uta was eating out of my hand from the word go. Good girl.

Still there was nothing in it. I felt sorry for all the female Krauts her age who advertised in the German papers daily to find husbands, describing in minute detail their charms, their property, and their sacred honor. What a wife she would make! The bosoms alone would be worth the price. With boobs like that one has psychosexual security for life. She

14

was solid in all directions, a bit wrinkled but not beyond the call of duty. Energetic as all get-out. And highly educated of course. Nothing happened. No happening. I was living by the clock. I counted the hours between planes, lectures, cocktail parties. I was working, working well in fact, doing what "State" expected of me.

Uta and I walked through the rain uphill to the castle of Frederick III, a slob king to build such a dreck. Bourgeois through and through, no divinity of the regal there. A restaurant now, just what it must have been designed for. And the food only so-so. But Uta by instinct had ordered U.S.-type martinis on the terrace, and I was as grateful as a cat.

Next day when the brutally black plain American Plymouth came for me to take me back to the airport she kissed my hand through the window of the car. Had I made a conquest? I wanted to jump out and accept her invitation to spend a weekend somewhere in the something mountains. Instead I drove on down the gentle slopes in a state of exhaustion and blankness. Frankfort, where grandpa came from, looked peaceful and prosperous, modern as hell, clean as a whistle, the Standard Oil barges crawling up the Main to the Wagnerian Rhine.

The plane skipped over the trees and new tiled roofs, glass office buildings, the gleaming ever-forgetful rivers. I loved Germany and wanted to vomit. The plane made a long slow bank and pointed its pewter jets toward Rome.

Boarding the Rome plane, I was handed a manila envelope. My schedule, I thought, and opened it in the air. Instead there were two letters from Wanda. I had a fleeting thought that they began, Dear John. I tore open the earliest one. My eyes began to itch and I trembled with rage and insult. Letters about her latest crush. *Crush!* She had the effrontery to use that diaper word on me. The words of her letters blurred in my head. I raged all the way to Rome, to the nasty little hotel off the Via Veneto, the royal sewer of the modern empire. After dinner that night I bought a fifth of scotch for three times the price, even the Italian price, and sat down and drank and wrote her in cold bile. A long knifey letter which she told

15

me a few weeks later she destroyed. She would. Didn't want that one in her guts. It was in there anyhow. I almost wished I'd made a copy of it. She sure as hell kept the letters she liked. What cunt didn't. A few days later I followed up with a coda, from Fabriano, where I had gone to buy great heavy sheets of paper for an artist who had made me promise I would. I reviled and cursed her again, reminding her that it was my final letter. And amazingly it was. We would see each other again and love-hate in the usual manner, but the beautiful silent words on the page—no more. Quoth the raven: Basta-basta.

And so it was. For me not to have a writing relationship with a woman was a Liebestodt. Words on paper to me were as flowers are to women. No letters, no love. No tickee, no laundry. At home, in Milo, even when I returned and was at it with her daily or nightly, each grinding the other down in the hopeless, mutually destroying dependence we had erected, a scaffold from which we were hanging our daily lives, at home I would always open my mailbox on the porch to see if she had perhaps left a note. A note about anything. She would come or telephone; we were together, not together; always within reach, in red blood or black blood. But yet I demanded that she put pen to paper to say something for me to find. That was the realer thing at that time when we were splintered and debased and evilly eating one another's hearts and guts and genitals out. But now, and that was the sad part, there would be no more putting pen to paper; no more of that mystical intimacy of the sealed note, the heart leaping up at the handwriting, or raging against it, no matter what it said within. Even the trick of the blank sheet of paper in the well-addressed envelope would have sufficed. Even the Mallarméan expanse of nothing on the beautiful empty page—which emptiness I had begun to love. I fondled blank paper, looked through it up to the light for the watermark, crackled it in my fingers, if it would crackle. Then suddenly I would think: the horror of that waste. The waste, the waste! The words of love all gone down the toilet or into some goddam tomato juice or beer carton of some rotten slut in a closet littered with

pissed-in or bloodied panties. And just as suddenly I would
think: the paper is to write on and I will write—no, I will find
someone I can make it writeable for. I will write when I find
who to write to. Wanda is dead; paper won't keep her. Maybe
I still kept thinking of kinds of paper that would attract her
beautician's eye. Like what—Kleenex? Puff-Puffs? Waldorf?
Kid stuff. All that paper in the world. Glorious paper, beautiful soup. No, I would stick by my right to paper and the grave
secret of it, the sanctity of love in writing on the white ex-
panses.

In my anguish I thought of writing Marya, but she had forbidden it. Besides she was back with her husband. I had met
her only twice and had fallen in love with her with a crash.
She was in the process of a divorce at that time and I went to
her house the morning after the backyard party she had gone
to, weaving slightly, unused to being unescorted. But I had
frightened her with my morning beer-drinking and my loose
reputation which had preceded me. I was at the end of my
own marriage and to make matters worse, some neighbor had
called my wife and spilled the beans about the visit to Marya.
When I warned Marya on the phone that my wife threatened
to name her as corespondent, she panicked and summoned
her husband home. He came, blubbering, and bearing a load
of dirty laundry, the bastard.

Molto triste, the Italians said of me in front of me, the professors, the students. I let it out that it was because of my
pending divorce. That was why I was *molto triste*. In a pig's
ass it was. It was Wanda who was battering me to death. I
couldn't wait to get back to good old Milo to go at it ham-
mer and tongs. I would beat her to death with a French wig
or an electric vibrator or shellack her with hair glue. Italy was
beautiful and sad, *molto* sad, *bellissima*. Urbino, San Marino,
Rimini, but I couldn't wait for my last lap to start. England,
my England.

How do you get something like England out of your system?
I had long forgotten when England had died in my heart and
in my mind, but I suspected that it had to do with those days

17

when I had become famous (if a poet can be). England had been when I had latched onto books, Literature; England had been home, mannerliness. The manners of the poem, manners of language which exist only in poetry, good and bad manners, but the game with the rules that everybody in England at least, in the Quiller-Couch Oxford Book, played and played to the hilt. And English is beautiful and dead, like classical Greek or Sanskrit. I must have gone through a period of mourning for my dead love of England but I couldn't remember when. When would it have been? I still trembled at the thought of ever *going* to the sacred land. And then the war itself had murdered the England of my dream, the England where my English would be appreciated! No more, *pas encore, finito,* shot to smithereens. Socialism finished off what was still a reminder. Was it meeting the Great Tom Eliot that gave my England the coup de grace? What difference did it make? When I began my poetry trips to Europe I always managed to avoid England.

Once I had landed in the almost finished postwar airport in London, but that was just a shuttle on the way to India, of all places. It was late at night. I listened to the announcements of planes for Beirut and Capetown in the quiet, arrogant upper-clerkly English of the female, still efficiently amazonian, warlike, war-as-usual diction, stiff-upper-class crispness and no damned nonsense about not getting on the plane to Zenobia in the proper seat, quickly but politely, while somebody steps crashingly on your foot, which is an old English custom that proves seriousness. I had no feel of my old love that time. Was trundled in a truck from one part of the new airport to Qantas Airlines, which would take me to—I forget. Ever after, my trips took me past or over or nowhere near England.

Tonight the Thames amazed me with its breadth and its brilliance. It was four o'clock in the morning on the weekend commuter plane from Rimini. How about that, I thought. Those London business guys fly their chicks down to Rimini (the Atlantic City of Italy, I would say, if anybody asked me) for the weekend, shack up at a big hotel, buy some semi-precious jewelry, and take off in the wee hours for London.

London, thou art of cities a per se. Jesus. The plane was loaded with them and their brassy voices, tired, happy swine who would burst into their offices five hours later boasting of their exhaustion. The secretaries on the plane were young and fleshy, guttural-sounding and loud. Okay. Introduction to London. Even with the lights off in the cabin they barely toned down. Still hopped up from the safari. I didn't care a shit or criticize them; but my nostalgia and romance for England didn't want it that way.

I stood behind one of the loud youngish businessmen in Customs and had to listen to a questionnaire about the semi-precious necklace, a necklace that could be seen for two blocks, a kind of charm bracelet for the neck and bosom with real semi-precious stones garnished all over it. I turned my head away. The Customs let me through without examination; I was only going to be in England for three days, my destination, yes, was Oxford and the scorn in my heart must have been reflected in my smile. I took a taxi for Paddington Station as dawn broke. And the ride, that was heartbreaking. Dirt and drab, all the brummagem of bad English domestic taste. Brummagem, brummagem kept drumming in my head in the cold gritty bad-taste dawn. Brummagem means Birmingham, I remembered, where the junk jewelry came from. So this is Brummagem, I said to London, this is the flower of cities, this is where—I didn't want to do an anthology of English Lit at the moment. Then big glass Mies van der Rohe office slabs came into view. That's London? Looks more like Indianapolis. How do you like London, someone somewhere would ask. Indianapolis, I would answer. Now and then there would be curved streets with the tiny front gardens and the heavy Assyrian architecture of some fin de siècle, restored I guessed from the bombings and burnings. More twisting and turning, then Paddington Station, confusion of Italian and American money, getting my two heavy bags toted to an empty train, along with directions about how to change for Oxford. The station filthy, grim, and chill under the great streaked glass roof.

The filth of Paris was not noticeable, I remembered, maybe

19

because it was expected. The shabbiness, the unwashed look of London, their pride in it, made me angry. Muddling through the mud. The puritanism of the dirty. Oh yes, we aren't the spick-and-span London of the old days but we are equalizing our losses. Equalizing dirt. Socialism. Taking the joy out of life. I was by turns anti-socialist and Tolstoy egalitarian and something approaching fascist. I paid the porter who had led me to a second-class carriage, in spite of my first-class ticket—the deliberate insult of the—I hesitated to think the word—*bounder!*

The train was icy in July and musty. It was empty but I was shown into a compartment where a man slumped down asleep in a kind of short overcoat. The train sat. I sat in a trance of dejection, *molto triste.* The train moved, moved through the usual limbo of gaspipes and tenements, billboards, factories, junkyards, all the large intestine of the modern city that provides the exit of the human from the inhuman.

The door screeched open and the conductor cheerily bade good-morning and shook the sleeper to collect the ticket. The sleeper slowly unwound and stood up and started through his pockets. The conductor watched a while and relaxed to see the show. People without tickets always put on a show. The conductor and I watched from the front row while the pocket-act continued. The sleeper finally muttered something which was not even worth being inaudible. Conductor: Do you have any money? (Act two is the search for the no-money.) I had money and wanted to do something—how? My real problem was whether I could lend the man—gentleman—fellow. . . ? The trouble was that I didn't speak *English* and didn't know how to express myself, so I sat through the third act. That's where the conductor says a little speech about people without tickets and money and informs the fellow—gentleman?—that he will be put off at Reading. I wondered what happens at Reading. Reading? Jesus Christ! *The Ballad of Reading Gaol!* Oh to be in English! Each man kills the thing he loves. Oscar standing on the platform of—was it Paddington Station—handcuffed—was he handcuffed?—for three hours—was it three?—while the crowd gaped. His crucifixion, his crowning glory. If

20

I were queer, I thought, what more thrilling place to be than jail. Like a stud condemned to live among women convicts. I didn't even see Reading when the train slowed. The man got off alone and walked straight and at medium speed toward the barrier. Would they nab him there? I never knew.

The conductor had said to me after the ticket show with the penniless man: Your ticket is first class. The car to the right. Or did he say carriage? I lugged my two weighty American suitcases into first class and sat in the first compartment, depressed and cold. My heart was cold. It was like passing the grave where English poetry had been buried—and spitting on it. I would have emptied my pockets for the Sleeper had I known how. No I wouldn't anymore. But I would have paid the man's fare, the fifty cents or whatever it was. I loathed the idea of someone being in the twentieth century without fifty cents. Why keep up the pretense of not having fifty cents. That's what was stinking about England, my England. Socialism stank because it took the last fifty cents. Why do you have to pay to ride on a goddam train, especially one owned by the government. Soon they will be charging for the amount of oxygen intake. Had the porter who had looked at my first-class ticket put me in with the Sleeper because of the obvious? I was glad I had let the bounder go without recognition. Let 'em humiliate each other, but leave me OUT. Let 'em destroy the world over fifty cents. Great England rolled by out of the streaky window, England exposed, now just a greedy little island with ordinary farms and ordinary sheep, nothing beautiful about it whatever. Grim green grimy ungrate ingrate no-longer-great England. A slum. A dream. Bad dream. A nightmare. At a place the name of which I later corrupted into Discoteck I dragged my two bags out of the compartment and waited for the Oxford train. When it came I dragged them back into a first-class compartment. It was still the small but not wee hours of the morning, but there were people all over the station. A distraught girl about fifteen, haggard and wild-eyed, scared shitless, ranged up and down in front of the train, stopped in front of me on the platform and asked if this was the train for Chumblylygong, or something that sounded similar. I said I didn't know but to ask the man in the uniform up the way. A minute later into the compartment she climbed and with a look of pure terror said: Is this *first class?* and reeled back as if she had stepped into a Bethlehem Steel furnace. Fifty cents, fifty cents, was all I, now on the way to being Dostoievski's idiot, could say or think or feel. I sat down. More little green hills and sheep, distant steeples. England must be emptier than Wyoming. It must be six in the morning by now. In minutes Oxford rolled into my view. Nobody said it was Oxford but it was the only place that looked like pictures I had seen in encyclopedias or on postcards—those postcards that always lie. I knew it, for Christ's sake. It *was* Oxford. Suddenly my love of England burst through some weak wall in my loathing, like good blood mixed with pus, and I saw the beauty of it, the spaced towers at those perfect distances which no longer existed, where a thing of beauty was set apart in its own sweet distance, to keep its pride. Where it was not just a shrine or a monument but the greatest university in the world, and which was still. It was still alive and hadn't been slimed over by modern educational garbage, not completely anyway, but even if it had, it still pulsated with an indestructible will. Genius? Stupidity? Views of the Oxford Colleges, said a thousand modern poems in their titles. Yes. Now I had the view. The brain of England, once and often the brain of the earth.

Twenty minutes later I passed the porter's gate of "my" College where I was to spend the night, and was fast asleep in a good bed, near an electric heater (in July!) dreaming of Rimini. Three hours later a secretary of the Conference on American Literature shook me by the shoulder and woke me up. I charmed her with drowsiness and said I would be ready for the luncheon in no time.

I left the debriefing with a feeling of elation that I had finished my tour and justified my journey. Mostly I was relieved at the idea of getting back to my bed of nails, or rather my cross. I had shaken hands with about half the officials (some had left with a slight urgency about leaving), signed a few vouchers, and grabbed a cab for the airport.

Over Ohio or Indiana or somewhere I toyed with my two empty baby martini bottles. Land of the child, I hummed. Back to the professoriat. Back to the Wanda-child.

There had come into the debased speech of a certain breed of American college student the word *plus—at the beginning of a sentence!* I was sitting behind a soft-spoken motherly woman on the plane, who was sitting next to a fat college girl. "I don't like to go home for every holiday," said the fat girl. "Plus I really love it when the school is so quiet." My blood began to boil. The fat girl piled on philistinism after philistinism, idiot cliché after idiot cliché. She loved and approved of discipline, chapel (compulsory kind), "limited dating," heavy assignments. I wondered whether the fat was a cause or an effect. When she got up to waddle to the john I marked that she was good-looking and had massy dark hair. I studied her with hatred as she waddled back to her seat, a smug sad face that spewed out safety-zone signs like bubble-gum. Poor sorority sister, deeper in the fat than a nun. Plus she didn't know a goddam thing except what the textbook said. One doubt would have cooked her like a tub of lard at Hiroshima. Plus her mind had been rendered thin and rancid in her eighteen obese years. Riding first class in the plane like me, I seethed. She wants a mop in one hand and a chaw of tobaccy in the other. And if they use *plus* as *also* or *alors* or *allora* or the beautiful *and yet* or *still—*if they use *plus* to start a period, then why not minus. *"Minus* I don't like to go home." Or *equal:* "Equal he isn't exactly my type." I turned my eyes back to an editorial in *Lux* magazine where all that toilet rhetoric came from. A new propaganda term had just been invented by the machine cerebellum: *Vietnik.* Yes, Vietnik. Soon the fat girl would be saying to someone else: *"Plus he's a Vietnik; I certainly wouldn't date that type."*

The plane cruised silently, obliviously, mightily over the high clouds of Lake Michigan—one of those delays—cutting downwards through the heavenly haze. The handsome Gold Coast of Chicago shot into view like a memory, back of it the brick-red wilderness of mixed old houses and factories, then the new miles of suburbias, then the thick arteries of white highways with massed vehicles slowly speeding in both directions; then grassy area and the square black outbuildings of the great air-port. Then the rumbling "touchdown"—I had accepted that word in my vocabulary waiting room. I unclicked my seatbelt quietly while the plane was still doing about 150. Like cocking a pistol, I thought, looking at the dense waves of the fat girl's hair. *Go home, child, and stay home,* I thought to say to her, but said it only to myself. What's the point. What's the point of anything in the *Lux* world. How can you fight that. They've already won. She'd cut my throat the way she'd slice a radish.

I walked through the Fallopian tube of the covered gang-way that had telescoped out to kiss the exit of the plane. I walked swiftly past the plus-girl. Our Father Which Art in Heaven, I prayed. Never let me sit behind her again.

In a Victorian bar, shallow, nice to fade in and out of, in Chicago, at O'Hare International Airport, at eleven o'clock in the morning, I stopped for a martini on the rocks. I didn't know what time it was, though I cared in a way. It was the equinoctial time screw-up in America when anybody flying from east to west or west to east sets his watch in all directions till the governor snaps. It could be anywhere between ten and twelve, even one or nine. All I knew was that I had missed my connection to Milo because it was putrid weather in Chicago.

"The traffic is very heavy," said the invisible captain in a marvelous gravelly fuck-you voice, and then went into great boring detail, boring for him and eventually boring to his au-dience. There was a ceiling of 600 feet and visibility of a mile; no sweat (he would have said in his own lingo); no difficulty in landing except a delay. If he's so goddam sure of every-thing, I thought, why have a delay. What amused me was that nobody was nervous or even concerned; in fact they were all pleased that the weather gave them a little more time to re-arrange their lives and morning appointments. Two hand-some, lean, and sunburned lawyers across the aisle from me had been rehearsing a brief during the trip from the capital. Would the court wait? I wondered; or those other lean, sunburned, and old fat dragons high up in the Loop where some vast sum of loot was about to be chopped up, trundled off, and swallowed. They wait, they wait; I knew that much about business. A twist in the weather; waiting is great. Excitement, poetry. I now had *three* hours to wait in O'Hare. I had only a slight destination home, to be with Wanda, who would be waiting as much for me not to arrive as to arrive.

I entered the Victorian bar. I liked that hole in the wall, a piece of interior decorating dreck with genius. Phony red embroidered velvet (printed on a printing press in a minute, I knew) and pasted on the walls; three deep curved mirrors with milky globe-lights in between, making four lights and three mirrors. And a framed print in color of three red apples; as a matter of fact there were two of these, duplicates, one stuck into a minute corridor which led behind the bar, almost as an optical illusion—but they didn't have to go that far, I thought; maybe two had been sent by mistake and some joker had hung the second one on the only available wall.

There were three people at the bar, standing because there were no barstools. Too shallow the niche and the time too fast. Two young Marines in browns stood in the center, close together. At the far left, as on a stage set, was a young woman in black. At eleven o'clock in the morning. I took the far right, to keep the ship from capsizing. The nice mirrors, however, reflected everybody; everyone could sip and watch and of course listen. Presently the two Marines took off, and as if by a signal two well-dressed civilians about the same age took their place. They kept their heads turned in the direction of the young woman in black at about 30 degrees instead of banking her off the mirrors. They kept to the center and said nothing, now and then sipping their beers. The bartender, schoolteacher type, was standing in front of the female. He spoke gently but in a tone which I could only describe as "objectively" though there wasn't a goddam thing either objective or subjective about it. The barkeep said, "Where did you say you were from?"

To my amazement she spoke with an accent, German at that. "I am from Germany originally. I never want to go back there."

I suddenly caught that exciting tone of insistence of the Kraut woman, something clumsier than the edgy shine of the French female in public but a hell of a lot more appealing. The voice of the woman who is for man and man only. She was turning it on for this practically nonexistent bartender because he had addressed her, and in a split second dredged up the Rhine-maiden, the Lorelei, the Beast of Belsen, and the yellow-haired Valkyrie written about by Livy. Or was it Tacitus? "I am full of penicillin," she said, sipping something that looked like a whiskey sour, something cloudy. "My husband is in South America; I have just come from New Mexico." Mysterious words perhaps. "He is in the American service. This cold is terrible." She ordered a second drink and started working onto her arm a long black glove. Or maybe it was white. She was pretty with her baggy eyes and throaty voice and slim solid figure. Who wouldn't take her for a whore at eleven o'clock in the A.M. in the shallow Victorian bar at O'Hare between towns. The bar lay near the international corridor; she had come from a foreign country, not New Mexico, I guessed stupidly. The bartender—it was hard to tell whether he was interested in her or in the fact that she was there—asked her about Germany.

"It's just like America," she said to the assembled company, "only smaller. The people are more polite and less friendly." I almost jumped out of my skin. She hadn't said it like she had rehearsed it, though it was obviously one of those clichés of the exile which can turn the wind. She chatted along, pulling on the other black-white glove, and merrily bade goodbye. She picked up a female-heavy satchel-pocketbook (it could be expensive) and walked almost elegantly out. The four hearts of the men felt sadder and fuller as she walked away. Nobody made a dirty crack or even thought of one.

CHAPTER II

Flying across the Mississippi my heart began to pound. One more river to cross, I thought grimly. Wanda had made a reservation for me at a motel I'd never heard of. It sounded like the edge of town, the farthest point from where she lived at the other edge. What was that all about? I bought myself another martini for a buck. I was back in paying territory.

At Milo, to my surprise, I was met by one of my graduate students. (And what was *that* all about?) He was one of Wanda's friends—she had quite a few on the string from the U. Wanda was working late, or words to that effect. Spoof Thomas (reputation for practical jokes) drove me to the motel. There were no cars in front and the proprietress was an aged hag who appeared to be stone deaf but kindly. I asked if there were a telephone in my room. There was.

I hadn't forgotten her number, the number on which I had wasted God knows how many thousands of dimes, and got the busy ring. At the Fountain of Beauty the line was busy, though one time I got through, only to find that she was "washing up." I didn't believe she was there anyhow and called her apartment; nobody picked up the phone. I called the Thomases several times on various pretexts; I had a hunch she was there with a friend. No satisfaction in that quarter.

I got a new frisson every time I dialed and got a busy signal or a no-reply or an evasion. I had my Scotch bottle by my side and what with the martinis was well on my way to commit murder, indecent exposure, and assassination of tenure. Suddenly, at midnight, I began to boil over, slammed down the phone and poured a deep glass of the whiskey. I timed myself during the non-phoning period. Maybe two hours. Then I must have dozed, then drowsed, then slept. I jumped up with a start at a knock at the door. "Who is it!" I bellowed. I wasn't sure what country I was in. There was a corny clock on a wall; it had two ears of fake gold corn hanging down phallically. It said 3:30. I lurched to the door and opened it.

Wanda stood there and said, "Do you want me to come in?" She reeked from brandy. Brandy yet. Nothing but the best.

"You can sleep with me if you want to," she said in the tone that little girls say, "You can carry my books if you want to." Or "I'll show you mine if you show me yours."

I couldn't get an erection but I came.

A bird twirped and Wanda dressed hurriedly and left.

"I don't know how I'll get through work today," she said. "I'm glad you're back," she said. I heard her start her Volvo and shoot up the street. She drove at top speed even at a standstill. She had so many places to go. I had nowhere to go but bed.

Wanda lived in basements like a rat. She preferred it that way. Her flesh was the color of fish-belly. Her eyes were big and soiled-looking. Her teeth had a bluish cast. She had heavy calves and tough buttocks. She always wore something black, either the sleazy black uniform of the Fountain of Beauty Salon, or black nylon stockings. The nylons accentuated her bulky calves. She had feet like a man but smallish carefully tended hands. Her favorite nail polish was what I called silverfish. Her complexion was more than lightly pocked. Her forehead jutted slightly. Her hair was colored ash-gray, a la mode. Sometimes she wore boots like greaves; my penis stirred when I saw her striding in leg armor. Her lipstick ran from white to iridescent orange. All in all she resembled a negative Maybe that's why she lives in basements, I once decided.

Her mind was clear but lazy, totally lacking in curiosity. Being a poet and professor I was always bringing her books. She liked to keep them but never read more than a chapter or two. The poems she never touched. I didn't feel that I had a mission to educate her, but I had to have something to gain her attention. Naturally, I plied her with erotica, everything from the more salacious girly magazines to the poetry of Martial, the *Kama Sutra,* and the Earl of Rochester. She had a stack of Grove Press items which I had reluctantly selected from my own library. Deep down I thought of her as a lesbian. Considering myself sexually busted at the age of fifty, I would stimulate myself with the phantasy of Wanda as dyke or anal pervert or sadist. Our relationship was purely autosexual. Each insulted the other's body, so that the pair of us were constantly glowing with wounds, blips, cuts, scratches, swellings and bruises. I was never sure whether all the marks of the beast had been made by me. Fidelity was not her strong point. And the greatest gift she gave me was humiliation. I wanted to crawl into deeper and deeper basements, through thicker and thicker slime, till death did us part.

Frequently I would ask her to marry me and she would laugh. "You *are* married," she said. (I had been separated from my wife for two years and more or less postponed the divorce because I didn't want to marry Wanda, only to torment myself with the idea.) I told her that if we were married she could continue her whoring to her heart's delight. It was intended as a filthy proposal and was accepted as such. I even had daydreams of pimping for her, not that she needed any assistance from me; I just wanted to be in on it.

She put up with my acts and artifacts and debasements because she was endlessly puzzled by me. A famous writer, a Full Professor (I had taught her the hierarchy), a person whose picture was always in newspapers and magazines, who was sent around the world by the State Department. It didn't make sense. There I would come crawling to her, slavering like a cur or a masturbating idiot, spewing out more filth than she had heard from twenty cab drivers.

I was her Dirty Daddy, that was all. She needed me to be that.

I had met her through my wife just at the time the marriage was nearing the great barrier reef at full speed. Wanda was my wife's beauty operator and I had picked the wife up at five at the Fountain of Beauty. It was the beginning of a blizzard and she offered Wanda a ride home. The offer was accepted. I drove, shivering at Wanda's gravelly laugh. Wanda spoke to me. That night I rang her doorbell.

I had prepared for a night out, hoping the beautician would come across, by turning a minor domestic hassle into a major engagement. First, I walked into the living room from my study swinging a bottle of rotgut sherry. The sight of a liquor bottle turned my wife into the president of the WCTU. Nasty exchanges about drunks, livers, anatomical and metaphorical; whereupon recriminations, followed by imprecations, followed by obscenities and concluding with blows. I got more than I bargained for. After some cliché I mouthed, such as frigid bitch, I felt a blow on the temple and saw my eyeglasses disappearing from vision across the room. I scrounged for them, grabbed my overcoat from the minuscule hall closet (I already had my keys and wallet safely stowed in my trousers) and slammed the door as hard as I could. It didn't slam at all actually; the snow was already whipped up to two feet on the front slab of "porch."

I ploughed gaily and expertly through the snowdrifts. I love blizzards, the only interesting thing left in the Milo world. I love getting stuck, getting pulled out, and getting stuck again. Catastrophe, I love you, I wailed with the wind.

I made my way to a liquor store and bought a gallon of gin. "For my car," I said to the grogshop keeper, and we both laughed.

Wanda was awed and uneasy at the size of the bottle. She made a mild drink with a gin mix. We sat on opposite sides of the room and discussed the storm. You could see it and hear it piling up in the windows above the little apartment. In the dark the snow took on the glow of pearl, at once soft and comforting and deadly. I wanted to snuggle in this basement and never come out.

At the second drink I made a pass. Still reeling from my wife's haymaker, I stepped back when Wanda said in stentorian tones, "Goddam it!" and then followed up immediately with, "I'm sorry." We resumed our neutral corners.

During the third round I sparred with her over the subject of my wife. We questioned each other about her. Was she easy to get along with? Wanda asked, Did we love each other? Was the marriage okay? Tell me all the places you've been. From this the subject drifted to good looks and bad looks, figures, hair-dos, manicures, pedicures, superfluous hair, and customers we might know in common, university wives for instance. Gossip time, leading to snickers.

Somewhere between the fourth and fifth gins the trap door opened and we fell through. I never really remembered what happened.

We were rolling naked on the basement carpet, rolling and fucking on broken glass, bleeding and grunting and cursing, biting and punching, burnt with cigarette ends, crawling to the bathroom like wounded animals, slimy with anger and lust, lower than hogs strung up by the hocks for the kill. The nightmare must have gone all night. Light grew in the windows above where the wind whistled like razors. Still we drank and wallowed in our muck, too anesthetized by alcohol to feel our cuts and lacerations and toothmarks. I remember mostly that we cursed each other, each calling the other pervert, queer, bitch, bastard, fink, communist, dyke, cocksucker, until we ran out of that vocabulary. It was a hate-fest and a good one.

I managed to get my car out of the snowdrifts by sheer stupidity. I put the car in reverse when I thought it was in low and smashed into the car behind me. The blow, which crunched the headlights of the other car, dislodged me from the snow bank. I slithered to my neighborhood and my own house before I looked at my watch: two in the afternoon.

My mouth was swollen. I was covered with blood. "Had to shovel out," I told the wife, and brushed past her. I took a searing shower and dove into bed.

That was how the long nightmare began.

CHAPTER III

When I awoke I knew without confusion that I was back in Milo. Naked I walked to the window and opened the drawstring of the fibreglas curtain. Milo. The light had bronzed, summer had had it. Brightly enameled cars tooled infrequently by. Everybody in this burg has a new car, I thought. *My car!* I've got to get my car. With no place to live you have to have a car. I had left my car in Spoof's garage all summer, hiding it for some reason, and generously offering its use to the Thomases. They'd shrunk back from the idea, and I wondered how many hundreds of miles they had put on it before locking it in the garage with its coating of farm dust, as a "practical joke." As a matter of fact it *was* sprinkled with dust when I picked it up, clouds of it. "It sure is dusty in here," I said when Spoof opened the garage doors, and we both laughed. No sense checking the speedometer; I didn't remember what it said when I left, and it would have been turned back anyhow. Practical jokers are born mechanics. Besides, hadn't I said to *use* my car? I had a beer with the Thomases and began cruising the Milo streets looking for FOR RENT signs. Half a century old, it was the first time in my life I had looked for a place to live all by myself. Not only didn't I know where to begin, I didn't even know what I was looking for. Something very private, no landladies, no smiling neighbors, quiet on the inside, busy on the outside. A place where no questions were asked. In Milo?

The thought of living within seeing distance of Wanda's building I vetoed straight off. What, to sit up all night and watch who was coming and going from her pad? In two weeks I would have been a raving maniac. I toured the two blocks of the Negro ghetto but it was a disappointing slum. Milo was too lily-white and WASP, too unimaginative for an honest-to-God slum. The Negroes were wraiths, ghost-like creatures with the usual quota of befinned Cadillacs and smoking Pontiacs. True, there were a couple of sagging picket fences with even more sagging sunflowers behind and before; a tabernacle or two shouting in outlandish paint the living presence of Jesus. There was even a phrenologist's hovel. It all made me sad. It was such a dismal attempt at a slum. All the same a few professorial colleagues lived there, marginal homos mostly who carried on their "marriages" in safety in that section of town because few whites had reason to come there, except occasionally to take home a maid who had sprained her ankle. If anyone asked the professors why they chose to live there, the reply would be that Blue Town, as it was called, was within walking distance of the campus. True enough. I stopped my car in front of Oscar Darling's house and sat for a minute examining the sidewalk from the steering wheel. Still unrepaired. Oscar, I theorized, refused to have his rotten sidewalk fixed because he enjoyed the accidents of his guests. Or maybe the potholes discouraged intruders or nosey acquaintances? Oscar had enjoyed more than one law-suit over his pavement; he always lost but gladly paid. I mounted the steps gingerly and opened the screen door without ringing or knocking.

"Are you there, Darling?" I called. There was no answer and I sat down on a sofa that proceeded to eat me up to the waist.

Oscar reveled in the surname of Darling. Rumor was that he had changed it from McGrath, for euphony, so to speak. Phony name or not, it served Oscar well. Even if a clerk in a post office asked his name, Oscar could reply, "Darling." The intonation would convey the rest. And without fail, there would be a meeting of eyes. Oscar and Darling were interchangeable, and with intimates there was always an audible comma between Oscar and Darling. Quite a moniker, I thought. I started wandering through the rooms, looking for a drink first of all.

"Damn good Pinch-Bottle," I said out loud. I examined the Mojave rugs on the walls, the crystal on the cupboard shelves, the Magritte reproductions, the copper kitchenware, the books —the whole red and green Loeb Library which I wanted to steal, the entire *O.E.D.*, not to mention the *Encyclopédie Française*—but these were just for reference: the real library was in the bedroom, all Pathographies. I had seen it before, a modest but frightening collection of sub-literary Confessions and other graffiti, all well thumbed and annotated. Darling had gotten his doctorate on Mario Praz and had printed his dissertation privately under the title of *The Evil Eye*. Once I had asked Oscar to show me his whip collection. It was the kind of bad joke which is not only forgiven but rewarded by loyalty and respect. There was, of course, no such collection, and Oscar replied by reciting a stanza of Swinburne's *Dolores*.

> By the ravenous teeth that have smitten
>   Through the kisses that blossom and bud,
> By the lips intertwisted and bitten
>   Till the foam has a savor of blood,
> By the pulse as it rises and falters,
>   By the hands as they slacken and strain,
> I adjure thee, respond from thine altars,
>   Our Lady of Pain.

"Swinburne disgusts me amusingly," he remarked after his recitation.

I was peeing in the bathroom and drinking at the same time and simultaneously admiring the walls (all papered with different size reproductions of Piero's *The Flagellation of Christ*—a bit much-too-much, I thought) when Oscar appeared in the mirror. My urine shut itself off automatically. I

35

deposited my member behind my zipper, emitting a long dark streak down my pants-leg.

"Edsel, you cunt!"

"Hi, Oscar."

In the livingroom we had a new drink, this time tinkling with ice. I described my trip for the State Department and recounted a few anecdotes, cultural and erotic. "I did see the original of the *Flagellation*," I said. Oscar twitched. "It's the blues," I said, "the blues of the color, the Italian blues, the stasis of it, but the blues." And I added, "Blues, just like the nigger blues."

"Have you seen Wanda?" Oscar crooned. I had brought Wanda to Oscar's a couple of times and they had hit it off. Kindred spirits. Ballcutters.

"She came to my motel round about dawn," I said.

"Sopping wet between the legs," Oscar said.

"This *is* an Army base," I replied, immediately sorry that I had underlined *is*. "Listen, Oscar," I went on, "I'm looking for a little apartment. Do you know of anything around here?"

Oscar studied me for a while, humming.

A thing that fascinated me about Oscar was that he never answered a direct question, or a question directly. There was always a fugal structure to his replies, almost as if he were the maestro of my score, or at least the one who did the instrumentation of my thoughts.

Oscar said, "Milo, unfortunately, isn't exactly Naples or Istria or even Cicero, Illinois. In that shambles across the street live two of the eleven whores of Milo. One is a darkie, the other Simon-pure Aryan Ozark. They are amassing a small fortune, with the aid of the football team and the Teamsters Union. There are four apartments for rent in the block, one on that side and three on this."

"That is," I said, trying to be at least witty, "there is one whore per football member?" And added, "Have you had any of the team lately?"

"All," said Oscar mildly. "Look," he said, and, reaching under his chair, opened a folio of glossies of the team in full regalia. The slippery photographs slid off his lap onto the floor.

I got up and said I had to continue my cruise in the search for living quarters.

"Bring Wanda over," Oscar said at the screen door, knowing I intended to.

I found a two-room apartment on a silent leafy street and moved my suitcases. The place was furnished, even well furnished. What property I had left, following the murderous financial settlement with my ex-wife, was in my office at school. The books I needed to teach from, my files, a few knickknacks were all. I bought a small FM radio to listen to the FM music, a few hours of Real Music and the rest Muzak. I would have perished without at least one dose of Mozart a day. They would have taken me away, a sack of shattered nerves. I'm baroque, I would say to myself, let's face it.

I bought flowers for my new apartment, daffodils, which was about all Milo had to offer, except roses, but roses were loaded with conjugal conjugations. Daffodils I bought, and stalks of wheat, straw-colored or stained red or blue. From the front yard I cut a few grim marigolds. From the one Japanese florist in town I acquired six small pots of cacti, green and mean-looking, waiting for some hand to come within sticking distance. I love cactus, I would say with a kind of conviction. I already had a huge grafted cactus in my office window, a spiny spindly ugliness which reminded me of Texas and broken glass. Maybe I would bloom under the sign of the cactus.

I lay down on the sun-drenched livingroom sofa within an inch of the telephone. The telephone was lit by daffodils. With one hand I caressed the dead black organ of communication and with the other opened the zipper of my trousers and shoved my hand over my privates. Ice-cold and almost non-existent. "It's that trip, the goddam trip, it's catching up with me. I'm cock-stricken and cuntstruck—dead!" I rose and went to the minute kitchen and made a bourbon and water. It's a fine thing when a man of my accomplishments can't even masturbate. I had a small fit of laughs which didn't quite rise to my throat. Wanda was due to call within an hour: would she?

All at once I forgot her and went to rearrange my books. In a week I would meet my new students, nests of crossed legs and adolescent ignorance, still redolent of bubble gum. Maybe there would be a few older women, even a popeyed nymphomaniac, the hysterical wife of some physicist or philosopher. Maybe some stinking Cuban doll who would look up the only local poet as a sine qua non and a quod erat demonstrandum. Maybe a Negress from Martinique who left jet-clouds of musk even on a windy parking lot. I began to enjoy the opening of school. But I lay within inches of the phone and toyed with my drink. I knew I had lost the initiative. I dozed for a minute when the phone rang and my body jack-knifed in the air.

The throttled voice said, "Hi, it's me," and waited.

"Hello," I said.

"You can come over after midnight. One would be better. Park around the corner where you used to. I'll leave the door open, I mean unlocked. Oh shit." And she laughed ("meaningfully" was the word that popped into my head).

"What are you drinking?" I asked.

"Courvoisier, you dope. (Pause) I need it for my cooking." Another masculine giggle.

"Fine," I said, and had the strength to hang up the phone and collapse.

I would have to get to the liquor store before ten, when everything closed in good old Milo. That would give me almost two hours to rusticate in my new apartment and plan the assault. What assault? I knew she would lay, so what was the problem? The problem was not getting laid, it was getting loved. No, it was either the problem of getting loved, which I knew would never come from that quarter, or getting fucked *on my own terms.*

I asked myself: How do you get fucked on your own terms?

Answer: By making a whore know she is. Honesty is the best policy. To do this, I thought in my comfortable monologue, you have to degrade degradation a notch at a time. Sex has nothing to do with it.

I went for another bourbon. I am a sexual-intellectual who warms to his subject. To break Wanda down, I moralized, I had to get her to rockbottom, down there somewhere her amateur whorishness would come to its own dead end, *là-bas*, down there where she would have to face either the fact of love or the Void. I began to be sententious, my mind inventing such epigrams as: An amateur whore is more evil than Judas Iscariot. And: Christ forgave a whore but whores can't forgive Christ.

Then, instead of taking a shower for my evening out, I sat on the toilet and burnt the shaft of my penis with a lighted cigarette.

Once upon a long-ago time I had gone on a voyage to the Society Islands, L'Etablissements Françaises in fact, otherwise known as Tahiti. I went on a broken-down New Zealand steamer, the S.S. *Mongonaui,* making its last trip to the Antipodes, with a stop-off at Papeete. The iron of the boat was so rotten that no one dared lean against the ship's railings. White paint was all that held the long-gone tubing together. Bilge rose throughout the carcass of the hulk; the sea was calm but everyone gagged or vomited as soon as they entered a hatchway. The entire population of the little stinker lived on deck, even in the rain. Passengers and crew became a happy company of flotsam and jetsam. Screwing abounded under the stars, supervised by coarse Australian women deported from various continents, along with bona fide refugees from Middle Europe.

I loved to lie in the extreme bow of the rusty steamer, leaning my head over the glorious aquamarine water, watching the prow rise with such serenity, breathing its way through the pacific Pacific. I waited for the burst of flying-fish that scattered like rabbits from the sea into the air, dividing into squadrons starboard and larboard, and now and then one or two of their number lighting frantically on deck. They were all colors of many rainbows with their stiff little wings, soaring away from the steamer rigid as dragonflies, then making a slight splash-down and disappearing again into the light-lit water. Hours and hours I stayed there watching for the fish to burst from the surface and sail away and make their escape.

The bow, sharp as a knife, had a rusty iron plate at the top, where I clung, and a tiny bit of flagstaff which I held onto as the ship plunged down into the smooth blue and reared majestically up again with the same tempo. I would lean far over and watch the Roman numerals disappear and reappear, for on the knife-edge of the prow there were I, II, III, IV, V, VI, VII, VIII, IX, X, XI, XII, and God knows how many more numbers marking the penetration of the ship into the waves.

One of the crew, a man named Jepson, also sat under the prow, sewing. He was there every day with a needle a foot long and what I took to be sail-cloth or canvas. He did have a piece of sail on his knees, a tarpaulin of sorts. I paid no attention to the man until one afternoon as I got down from my perch I had to step over his legs. It was then I saw what Jepson was up to. He was holding his penis in one hand and the needle in the other and he was probing at its head.

"Careful, boy," said Jepson without looking up.

"What in the name of . . ."

"Almost finished," said Jepson. I started to keep moving but changed my mind and half-squatted down, not too close to the sailor.

"When we get to Papeete that will make 'em leap and squirm. The niggers. Stay away from the French cunt." He turned his penis over in his hand. There were drops of blood on the foreskin where Jepson had made holes with his needle. He picked up a heavy wax thread and worked it through one of the perforations. Then he took a monstrous belt knife and neatly slit off the ends of the string. Finally, he returned his genital to the inside of his trousers and buttoned up.

"It's for the hoors," he said. "I'll have four knots on my prick when I shove it in. They scream blue murder but later they admit they like it. Ever try it, boy?"

"I'm circumcised," I said panting, without knowing why. Jepson got up and wandered off between the winches and disappeared down a hatchway.

'Down the hatchway," I said to myself as I opened the outer door to Wanda's apartment. I had almost dropped the bottle of cognac getting out of the car and had it tucked under my arm like a football. I descended the carpeted stairs guiltily, as if I were forcing entry. I pressed the button and heard the chimes. Chimes, I thought, gritting my teeth.

Wanda opened the door hurriedly; she was on the phone. She gave me a bluish smile and said, "I'm almost through, Ed. Make me a drink, okay?"

She had on a hairy avocado sweater and a black skirt sleazy with age. Wanda had feet like Stonehenge and was barefooted. Her legs were bare and were the color of gutta-percha. She squatted back on the floor where she kept her telephone. It had a twenty-foot wire, twisted into a thousand knots and actually cracked in places. It would never have occurred to her to unwind it. Rather have the telephone man fix it. Once or twice I had untwisted it myself. I could hear the coda of her conversation while I emptied an ice tray and took the seal off the bottle.

"You've just got to read that book about President Harding," she said. "This book says he was a nigger. Not only that, he kept a mistress in the White House. It's pretty ripe." A long pause while I poured the brandy to cover the ice cubes and added just a little water. "Damn right I'm going. Listen, Milly, I don't care if they're red, white and blue. They can dance you right out of your panties." Another pause, a sort of laugh, then, "Sometimes."

I bent to hand her her drink and she winked at me. I sat down on a fat brown chair opposite her, where I could look up her thighs. I thought she spread them a little.

"Hey, Milly, I've got to hang up. Eddie just came in and we're drinking pure French alcohol. He just got back from that Europe trip. I think he's a goddam spy." She paused again, laughed again, and hung up.

I tried not to say it but said, "What's that party you're going to?"

"It's more like your party," she answered, taking a wicked draught of her drink. "Those Jamaicans you bring to your college are all coming to that crazy sociologist's house Saturday night. You're coming, aren't you? Why don't you take me?"

"You going to get danced right out of your pants?"

We had a toast over that and I agreed to the date.

The sociologist was married to a sociologist. He was a sweet conspiratorial man with a handlebar moustache and he drove a crazy Citroën that collapsed on its haunches when he got out. He wore turtleneck sweaters and had the only interesting parties among the faculty. His wife, who had published more than her husband, was convinced that President Kennedy was assassinated by the CIA; she had even been visited by the FBI. But because she spoke only in whispers and to only one person at a time, and because she always laughed when she made her horrendous accusations, she never became a scandal. Her name was Karen, his Brom; Janiczek was the last name. As soon as either heard a rumor of an exotic person coming to little Milo they immediately began to build a party. "Exotic" could mean anything from skin pigmentation to a criminal record. Visiting firemen were frequent. Homosexuals were gently encouraged to bring a prostitute, could one be found. Mentally ill students thrown off Greyhound buses to and from Grinnell, Reed, or Sarah Lawrence were more than welcome and sometimes housed for days. Karen would say on the phone to a total stranger, "Come to the settlement house," and give the address.

The Janiczeks were waif-lovers. There was only one requirement for admittance: exoticism. But that covered a lot of territory. The curious thing was that the parties, however ear-splitting with rock and guitar groups, were decorous. There were never any fights or even ugly little scenes. You could have an abortion in the bathtub while someone was shaving: no sweat. Coupling was simply not seen, no matter where you stumbled over it.

Wanda had been to the Janiczeks' in various capacities. I knew that all Milo knew (or was I flattering myself) that I was one of her men. It was odious to me to be in that shabby

42

entourage, but necessary. I could already see her on the darkened sunporch clasped in the arms of a swaying Jamaican. Once she had told me after a similar party for six Negroes from Mississippi: "That Brutus Jefferson, he's got a tongue as big as a ham."

I had waived the cross-examination and my penis shrank into its shell.

Along about the third or fourth brandy Wanda said, "Let's hear some gut-bucket," and started fingering through a stack of record albums. When she played that kind of jazz I knew she was on her way. I took a flyer.

"Play the record with the bedsprings," I suggested.

She turned and looked at me for a time. "If that's your kind of aphrodisiac. I'll get it." Her vocabulary wasn't bad.

That record she kept in a closet underneath some hat boxes. It was one of those more or less illegal recordings of the noises of lust, and the two or three spoken words were in Spanish. Wanda would shrug when I asked where she got it, certainly not in Milo. The recording was a kind of Ravel's "Bolero" for real. It started with a slow rhythmical squeak of bedsprings, a deep grinding rusty sound with now and then a woman's low moan or heavy breathing. I was positive the recording was authentic and marveled at the ingenious degeneration of the human mind. The only thing that disturbed me about the "authenticity" of the recording was that somewhere along the first inch of record tomtoms began to be played softly.

"Must be a third party in the room," said Wanda.

"Maybe he's playing them with his feet," I said and took off my shoes.

Now the tempo of the bedsprings began to increase, and intermittently the woman let out a little scream, a true scream but muffled and definitely a cry of pain. Pretty soon the squeaking was going at breakneck speed and the tomtoms grew louder and faster. Now it was the man's turn to emit sounds and these were truly amazing. He let out warwhoops like an Indian on horseback. I wondered if he was using a riding-crop. But there was no grand climax; apparently no orgasm. Only a sudden stop, a pause, and a return to the original rhythm.

"Sonata form," I said. Wanda gave me a dirty look. She hated to be reminded of my education.

The bedspring sonata rose to a new climax. The woman yipped, cried out and even wept, suggesting rape or a too-large penis. Too good for acting. The man whooped and whispered and cajoled, the tomtoms twittered and smacked out messages of love and then in the *allegro vivace,* springs, drums, yips, yells, groans, pants and grunts all joined in the orgasm. The first side of the recording came to an end with *a capella* breathing returning to normal. Beethoven couldn't have done it any better.

"Halleluia," I said, while Wanda turned the record over.

The flip side was more of the same except that there now seemed to be three inhabitants of the rusty bed. I thought the third party was another woman, deep-voiced. Wanda said it was another man. We held a psychological discussion about it.

"If it was another man," I argued, "the woman of the bedsprings would do a hell of a lot more yelling and crying. All she's doing is grunting like a contented sow. Besides, the man is the star of this performance. He's riding one mare and breaking in the other by the short hairs."

"Maybe he's sucking her off," said Wanda, now firmly in her cups. I began to get an erection. I stretched out my legs and began to stroke my zipper.

"It's a man," Wanda went on, "and the bitch is getting it you know where."

"Let's go to bed," I said.

"Frig," she answered in the negative. When Wanda got ugly I got hot. When she began to talk like a sailor my member rose to the occasion.

"You talk like a goddam sailor," I said, encouragingly. "You ought to join the navy and give us a trip around the world. Okay, so it's a man. She's got one in her twat and one in the tar-pit."

"Like I said," she answered. She got up and went to the

kitchen. I heard the refrigerator open. Good Christ, I thought, she's going to eat again. I took the record off and put on one of the gut-buckets she had laid out. In a couple of minutes she ambled back carrying a long fat cucumber. She tossed it to me. I barely caught it.

"Do you think it's hard enough?" she asked with a mean twist on her face. I tossed it back at her.

"You stay where you are," she said.

I sipped my drink and watched her with a bloodshot blur in my eyes. She sat in another fat chair opposite me and lazily lifted a shark-belly thigh over one arm of the chair. She had on one of those striptease triangles of black nylon instead of the usual panties. A G-string no less. With one hand she gnawed at the raw cucumber, or rather scraped it over her lower teeth to get the skin off. She spat the skin stuff on the floor. She stuck out her tongue and licked the white of the cucumber. With her other hand she scratched her triangle of silk, or whatever it was. I could see it growing wet under her nails. Her breath began to come faster and I thought I could detect the beginning movement of her thighs, tightening and loosening to the music, the licking of the cucumber, and her hand which was now stroking herself inside the G-string. I released my prick which sprang out like a hungry dog. Wanda's eyes were closed or half-closed and she took no notice but only increased her lucubrations.

I was unprepared for what was coming but was good at suggestion. "Suggestion box" crossed my mind.

"Stick it in your cunt," I said.

As if hypnotized, she gave the cucumber a last lick and ran it slimily along her thigh. She moved it closer and closer to her vagina and pressed the blunt white end against the silk. Suddenly she gave a heavy heave and unsnapped the G-string, which fell to the floor.

Got to have that, I thought. I would steal it later.

Naked below the waist, she threw her other leg over the other arm of the chair and began pushing herself against the cucumber. She reared her ass up higher, giving me a chance to make a scientific study of the yellow stains around her anus.

"One of those rotten books you gave me," she started to say but was unable to finish the sentence.

"I didn't have any on cucumbers," I said, masturbating slowly.

". . . said, having a baby is like shitting a watermelon."

She was holding the vegetable in both hands now, twisting it back and forth like a spindle, trying to force it in. The lips of her vagina were purple and opened to receive the lunch. It was in about four inches. I was beside myself, terrified that I would come before she would release me from the chair. One move, and the jig would be up. Her fun, her way, that was it. In this game of double-degradation-or-nothing, I was waiting for her command. I would have to crawl like a dog and do something that even dogs don't do. I was anticipating the command with as much curiosity as lust.

All at once she snapped the cucumber out with a sound like a popping cork.

"Come here," she said with closed eyes. I lurched to her side of the room.

"Bite it," she said in a low voice. She held up the cucumber. I leaned over in the way one would make a mock-bow to kiss the hand of a mock-lady, say at a dress-up party, and knocked it out of her hand.

"Give it back. It's mine," she said. "Get down and lick my ass," was her next request. I opted for handing her the cuke.

She started in again with the multilated and humiliated dildo. A moment later she let out a weak snort, and dropped the cucumber. She let herself slide to the floor, lay on her belly, and to all intents and purposes fell fast asleep.

I scooped up the G-string and shoved it into my back pocket. I went to the bathroom and peed without lifting the seat. I *aimed* at the seat. I noticed her cosmetic department, uncorked a small bottle of perfume and poured some on the G-string. This I returned to my pocket. Out of habit I flushed her toilet and then wished I hadn't.

Wanda lay on the floor, her shirt around her shoulders. I stepped over her and went to the door. I heard her say, "Bugger me," as if in her sleep. When I unclicked the door she leaped up and yelled, "Where the hell do you think you're going?" She grabbed my arm with a black-belt judo grip. Her voice softened.

"I got to be browned. Brown me off. Give it to me. Here, here, here!" She had her index finger in her anus. Her nails dug through my coat into my flesh. Tears ran down her destroyed face.

I raised my gripped arm slowly and she released it.

"I'll call you," I said, and went out. I closed the door so quietly, I went back for a second to see if I had closed it at all.

CHAPTER IV

୬ A university just before it opens in the fall is exciting, depressing and nerve-wracking. The great machine is having its final dusting-off, bewilderment fills the halls, doorways are choked with registrants and professors still without ties, corridors are hard with wax, desks are piled with purple notices and accumulated mail and books which should never have been written, much less published. Youngish instructors are telling each other about the summer in Corfu, Edinburgh, and Aix-en-Provence and looking greedily over their shoulders for greetings.

I rushed to my cubby-hole, let the door close—it was one of those doors that won't be rushed into shutting—and drew the blind over the glass panes. I hoped I would not be interrupted by a knock, that I had not been seen by the voyagers or the students. But I hoped that my phone was connected.

I stared out of the window at the parking lot and noted various faculty notables by their walk, their car. I watched the bacterial colonies of bright-colored students pausing and moving uncertainly in all sorts of directions. I looked around the room, about six by eight feet but with an enormously high ceiling, thank God, a room built in the days when at least ceilings were lofty. Stacked on my desk was a pile of books in cartons or in those spongy brown envelopes made apparently of rats' nests. I looked away from the pile. There was also a neatly aligned foot of unopened letters which someone had placed between two bookends and in front of this construction a note. Not wanting to touch it, I leaned over and read:

Mister Lazerow: (Mister was underlined and I could determine the contents of the rest of the note without reading it.): *Foolish as it sounds, it was a joy to share your office this summer, your books, your shall I say artifacts, your cacti. Thank you. I will be here this year. Sincerely.*

It was signed Bruce Binder. I stared at the signature and said to myself: It's one of those people who are named after their names. Then I stared at the dusty black phone and said aloud: "Should I or shouldn't I?"

I dialed 9 to get "outside" and then dialed the Fountain of Beauty Salon. Wanda, I was told, had taken the day off and no, she wasn't ill. I was positive that Milly, the "operator" who answered the phone, had been primed for the call. I swiveled in my ugly blond oak chair for a couple of minutes, opened three books which I glanced at gingerly and deposited in the clean olive-green trash can.

"I love you, big green trash can," I said, again aloud, "for you are so big." Then I dialed again.

To my surprise, almost to my disappointment, Wanda answered.

"I thought that would be you, Ed," she said.

"Are we still going to the Janiczek thing?" I replied.

"Well, of course, well Christ, why not. How are you feeling after all that Simon-pure French alcohol?"

"I'm still breathing it," I said. "Why don't I drop by for some coffee."

"Can't be done," was her answer, and her voice dropped an octave. "I'm just taking the morning off by prearrangement and then back to the curlers."

"And tonight?"

But tonight she had promised to go to a barn dance in West Milo where there was going to be an illegal cockfight and money flying around like green feathers. I made my goodbyes, swiveled some more, and began to leaf through my summer's mail. Or rather, I shuffled it, opening nothing. If you open a letter there is always the temptation of answering it. It's like opening a wound. I studied postmarks, dates and return addresses, then scattered the letters over the empty part of the desk and began making designs with the letters. I looked at my crazy cactus plants; Bruce had moistened them all right. I looked at my wall of books, all poets, all poetry, and swiveled back again. Abruptly I got up and headed for the parking lot.

I drove aimlessly out of the campus, through the Eleusinian mysteries of Rush Week. Crowds of girls in red sweaters and practically skirtless skirts were lined up on the neat lawns of sorority houses, chanting God knows what gibberish. On the other side of the street the fraternities were also out in force, white shirts, ties, jackets, going through their own jactations and middle-class middle-western voodoo. I had always refused to let my mind find out what these rites portended. I've got enough garbage in my head already. I had a sneaking suspicion that the brain could only assimilate so much before it turned into a rotten cabbage; I excluded much information which I was dying to understand. Rush Week was high up on my taboo list. Let Janiczek handle that one. Anyhow, I thought, as I drove away from the fraternities and sororities, it's only cunt-practice. The phrase pleased me wryly and I smiled as I drove up to a drive-in liquor store. I had decided without knowing it that I was going to Spoof's house to find out where the cockfight was going to be. I bought a quart of imported Chianti in its wicker dress. Poggibonsi, I noted on the bottle, the cutest word in the world.

Spoof was out in the garage but his wife Helena was in the apartment. Spoof called her Hell, characteristically. Everybody called her Hell except me who, also characteristically, called her Helen. Just to be different.

I presented the bottle of Chianti and Hell laughed and thanked me. "Come on in," she said. "I'll yell for Spoofy." She disappeared into the kitchen from where I could hear her calling her husband. When she returned she carried the opened bottle and three lotus-shaped wine glasses on a wooden tray.

"That's a lovely tray," I said. The Thomases acquired things of taste. They really did have taste. I admired and resented that at the same time.

"Danish," she said. "Daddy gave it to me. The old great Dane."

It didn't make much sense but I knew that there was a definite Nordic thing about the Thomases. Nothing anti-Semitic, mind you, just northern. Ex-European. Hence the taste, I thought.

When Spoof came in he was carrying a carpenter's level which he sat down delicately against the wall of the living-room; he had been refinishing some farmhouse antique picked up at the Good Will.

"Vino, vino!" he said first, and then grabbed me by the shoulder in greeting. "Did she fuck, Ed?" he added to the salutation. The Thomases kept an interesting balance of propriety and lewd language. Their apartment was gracious, even beautiful. They loved and cherished *things* and distributed them wisely and without making any particular thing conspicuous. As graduate students they already had amassed a sizeable library. In ordinary grocer and tenant dealings they were as proper and friendly as pie. But within the purlieus of the apartment they talked like pimp and whore. But it's only talk, I had convinced myself. I knew enough to fall into the idiom with them. What's more I was their elder and sometime professor and the one thing I refused to let happen was an impression of a stuffed shirt.

"So she fucked. So what," I answered.

Spoof guffawed and Helena giggled. We all drank the Poggibonsi and talked about courses and degrees and Comps. I knew I was going to be used for my inside knowledge of Comprehensive Exams but I was ready to trade information for clues of Wanda's campaigns. A tricky business. I decided to take a plunge instead of beating around the bush.

"She's going to a cockfight tonight," I said. "I've got a different date but I want to see it." I leaned over and pulled out my wallet from my back pocket. "I'll bet you this against Helen that you know where it is."

Spoof loved to draw maps and he did know. Any action within range of fifty miles from Milo he knew and usually had a hand in. What was a guy like that doing in graduate school, in English at that! He should be running heroin in Naples, I thought.

"Who are you taking?" Helen wanted to know.

"Grace," I answered, though I had just thought of it.

Grace was a tall, pretty, silent female graduate student from St. Louis. She claimed to be amoral and dauntless, and boasted of her frigidity. Her chest was as flat as Kansas but she wore beautiful expensive clothes and was the only female under forty in the English Department who was an expert in face makeup. She had a long neck which made her head toss when she walked. I associated this with a line I had read in Walt Whitman about prostitutes, something about a pimpled and bobbling head. It was something like that anyway. Rumor had it that Grace was the "protégée" of a mean, inverted brilliant and God-struck professor of Middle English. In any case, he was her advisor.

Grace lived in the little Negro slum section, Blue Town. Because, she apologized, it was only a small walk from the university, and her daddy insisted on her walking to and from school, even though she had a tomato-red small Buick, spanking new. But that was only to drive to St. Louis in, she had said. But what amazed me about her little apartment, which was above a grocery store, no less, was that she had no livingroom. The kitchen was the living room; the other room was the bedroom, filled with lacy curtains, flowers, and decorator bedspreads. There was a Degas dancing-girl picture over the bed. Nothing added up.

I had asked to peek in the bedroom once and she said of course. I never laid a hand on her, for some reason. But in that kitchen-livingroom, the biggest item of furniture was the *refrigerator*. It sat facing the sofa. I was so fascinated by this piece of symbolism that I never mentioned it, any more than I would mention a crucifix on the wall, had there been one.

"I want to use the phone," I said to Hell, and went to call Grace.

She was home. She was always home, another thing I couldn't figure about her. Was it because her father, as she claimed, was a prison guard and had somehow infected her with the idea that life is a prison?

She greeted me effusively and sweetly and asked about Europe. I said I was glad to be back and added, "Listen. I just heard about a crazy thing on the outskirts of town. Have you ever been to a cockfight? A real illegal cockfight?" I waited. Her answer surprised me, though it shouldn't have.

"What should I wear?" she asked, skipping the acceptance.

"Feathers, I guess," I laughed, but added, "Anything farmy and inconspicuous. How the hell do I know?—bluejeans. Bluejeans and makeup."

I waited to see how that settled and we decided on the hour. According to Spoof's map it would take a half hour to get there, but in case of errors in the dark you should double the time. The barn was going to be dark, you had to avoid state highway patrol cars, if any; you had to drive the last half mile without headlights, park behind the barn if you could see it, then walk with a flashlight to the west door and knock before entering. That sort of thing. I told her all that and she laughed pleasantly and said she'd be ready.

When I came back to the livingroom, Helena said with a kind of compassionate glance, "It's not far from the Happy Hour. Let's have a bourbon. Ed, why don't you have supper here."

I declined the supper but accepted a bourbon and water. Spoof said, "Sure, sure," and went to make the drinks. Hell looked preoccupied and I asked her what was on her mind.

"Oh nothing, Ed. But you must know that Wanda is going to that stupid bird fight with Kaz," and looked at me sheepishly.

"So," I answered, "it's a free cockfight." I laughed and then we both laughed and she began to look serious again when Spoof came back with the drinks and pretzels.

"A cock is a cock," I pronounced idiotically, baiting Spoof.

"And that's all there is to it, Edsel," Spoof said, giving me a serious look for once. "You take Wanda. She ain't a whore.

She doesn't even want to be one. But she's got to act like one out of pride. She's cold and ugly but she's growing something. She's cultivating a feeling. She's creating a person, herself."

"It takes two to play at that game," I said.

"If so," Spoof answered, slightly professorially, in a future role, as it were, "you're not the other party. Kiss it off."

I began to swivel my drink in my hand. I was afraid of being silent for long, lest I should fall into self-hypnotism, self-pity. I looked at Helena who looked down into her own glass.

"I think," I said, not knowing what was going to come out of my mouth next, "no matter what *she* wants or *she* does, I'm going to fight for a piece of that. And I don't mean poontang. She doesn't even know how to jerk off with a—cucumber!"

"That's the neatest trick of the week," Spoof said and started in on his wild indeterminate laugh.

Helena sat up straight and slammed her drink down on an end table. "Shut up your goddam loud mouth, Spoof," she yelled at him. He gave her a slow look. "You listen to me, Ed. You're my friend, you're our friend, but Wanda is our friend. And she's not *your* friend. She's your goddam foe. She's in love with Kaz. Leave her alone. Leave her the hell alone. You know you wouldn't touch her with a ten-foot pole outside of her bed. What are you trying to do, punish yourself to death? You've got her so screwed up she can't see straight. Why don't you pick on somebody your size?"

She started to cry and Spoof started to laugh again. I got up and said I was sorry. Spoof took me to the door, moving the carpenter's level gently with his shoe, touched me lightly on the shoulder, and winked goodbye. I started down the stairs to the ground floor and glanced at my wristwatch.

CHAPTER V

I found it hard to eat, though since I had been living alone I had become fascinated by cooking. I undercooked and over-flavored everything, used curries by the pound, cayenne pepper, white pepper, coarse ground black pepper, salt crystals and the whole range of spices which came in symmetrical bottles from Myron's, the best grocery in Milo. Instead of eating, I made fancy drinks which I invented, vodka and sauerkraut juice, which I named The Manifesto, vodka and borscht, The Wandering Jew, or studied out recipes for mulled wine, for which I bought special mugs (at the best hardware store in Milo). In desperation at my loss of appetite I drank raw eggs, to the horror of anyone who happened to be standing by. Sometimes I would beat up raw eggs with sherry, being careful to add plentiful splashes of cayenne. "I've got the rajas," I would tell people. "It's a mental disease of the stomach in which you don't have enough hot pepper or curry you begin to yodel." However, I swilled quarts of milk and whipping cream in between the drinking and felt fine, all in all. Except for the sneaking suspicion that I was neglecting certain of my vital organs and overplaying others. Only I didn't know which ones, and didn't really give a damn.

I drank four raw eggs and a cup of cream and then made a martini into which I dropped a Mexican pepperino. Then I took the martini to the bathroom and shaved. I decided on a pair of dark corduroys instead of bluejeans, a deep red Viyella shirt and an old gray Harris tweed jacket much too big, which I wore from time to time anyhow. At the last minute I decided' to wear my pair of raw leather hunting boots which I'd picked up in Colorado one summer. I figured I was overdoing the costume, but then I didn't really know.

Grace almost didn't open the door when she saw me. Her Siamese cat skittered behind the refrigerator. I had not forgotten to rummage in my suitcase for a gift and I handed her a Florentine cigarette box which I presented encased in a sandwich bag. I knew she didn't smoke, so I said, "I know you don't smoke, but somewhere, somebody does." She took it out of the sack and she wanted to know what the picture was on the lid. It had something to do with Pompeii; there was a stylized volcano with a few streaks of reddish lava on the hillside, then a heavy line underlining the volcano, underneath which were two symmetrical horsemen facing each other. In between them were a few minute figures on foot, a man in a toga sheltering a woman and facing them some kind of messenger.

"This guy is bringing them the news," I said, "but it's obviously too late. The atom bomb has struck." Grace made her thanks without going into ecstasies.

"I have some bourbon. What would you like with it?" she asked. She was dressed in a dark dress. No bluejeans, but she had had the foresight to avoid high heels, which she wore even to seminars. A weird one, I thought.

I had a stiff bourbon and water without ice. Grace took a weak one. We talked about our summers, each avoiding the summer's truths, whatever they had been. The Siamese cat had recovered from his initial shock and patrolled the top of the sofa behind my back. I had lived with Siamese cats for years during my marriage and feared and hated their guts.

"Siamese cats are the lost tribe of Israel," I announced, and Grace smiled. But instead of letting her say she would remove the animal, I picked it up deftly behind me without looking, and placed it on my lap and stroked it between the ears. It didn't purr but it began to relax, and having won this terroristic victory the cat stepped down and went to appear on top of the television, which was still warm. It was growing dusky outside and I thought we might begin to try to find the Graindorge farm, where the cockfight was going to be.

"I know," said Grace at the door. "Let's take my car. It needs the exercise."

"Swell," I said, "but I have to get the bottle out of my glove compartment. In case of a freeze." Grace was now wearing a black cashmere sweater which I suspected was not the right attire, but I said no more about what to wear at a Milo cockfight.

I drove, exclaiming about her car. "A tight little bitch," I said, glancing at her with a metaphysical grin. Grace showed a row of improbably perfect teeth.

I had laid Spoof's map on Grace's pocketbook, which was on her legs, and I drove slowly west through the frayed edge of Milo, which without warning became pure country. There was about fifteen miles of mere highway and autumn-rich red sorghum fields, yellowing cornfields, now and then a stand of Russian olive trees. Once I placed my hand on hers and wondered whether it wasn't her pocketbook. Her skin was as smooth and cool as patent leather and it was hard to tell them apart. She understood the map like an expert navigator and seemed to trust it implicitly.

I said suddenly, "You know that jerk Spoof. It would be just like him to draw a map that leads us directly into the largest hog-wallow in America—whatever a hog-wallow is." I was beginning to be suspicious.

"You really overestimate Spoof," said Grace. "He wouldn't hurt a fly. He plays jokes to make a point about a friend but not to hurt him. It's his way of talking."

"Self-expression," I answered, becoming even more suspicious. "He's a director," I added, "and I hate directors. We'll see if that map pans out."

Grace gave me time to slow down before we came to the

country road. The twilight had become blinding, indeterminate, and I blinked. To make matters worse, the dirt cut-off was orange with dust clouds. Grace suggested that this must be the road because of the amount of dust kicked up by cars. I decided to turn on all the car equipment. I rolled up my window (and she did hers), and asked her to switch on the air-conditioning, which I couldn't locate, and then I switched on the windshield wipers and pressed the squirter to wash the windshield. I could feel Grace relax, curiously, and imagined I felt a wave of warmth coming from her direction. We jolted through the crepuscular countryside while Grace clocked the tenths-of-a-mile numbers on the speedometer. You could only see ditches by the roadside.

"Stop," she said suddenly, and then, "back up when you can see."

I backed up without seeing, into my own dust cloud, when I noticed a tiny hand-painted sign on a huge tubular mailbox which said Graindorge. I turned left into two deep dry ruts.

"Your transmission is getting scraped," I said grimly.

"Daddy will get me a new one," replied the graduate student, and turned away with a flutter. I floated the car up the ruts to the farm. It really wasn't dark enough to turn headlights either off or on and I thought we must be early. But all of a sudden the rut-road came to an end and we were driving on a lawn and could make out the silhouettes of farm buildings. It was dark except in the west which was a silky washy blue high up, dimming down to a purple and splayed out with violet and gold flecks and toning down to blackness.

"Which building do you think?" I asked.

She said nothing but pointed ahead to a beveled shape of a barn, as certain as if she had grown up there. I moved the car over the lawn. It was as soft as if it were being carried.

"You're not offended?" I asked.

She gave her all-American smile and answered, "Offended! At what?"

And just as the map said, there were all those cars lined up at crazy angles behind the barn: pick-ups, new and old Chev-

58

ies, Volkswagens, and at least three Cadillacs. There was also a collection of Hondas and Harley-Davidsons. I thought I spotted a few faculty cars. In one corner was a Citroën.

We were getting out when I said, pointing to the Citroën crouched in the grass, "That must be the Janiczeks' crazy car." We went over to look at the windshield. Sure enough, it had the university sticker.

It was really pitch dark as we stumbled over the stubble to the back door. We hadn't time to knock. The door opened; a man stood there and simply admitted us, with the words—no smoking at all. It was a barn all right, squishy and crunchy with hay, manure, mud, the sound of collared animals grumping against wood stalls, and the overall atmosphere of great urine poured from God knows how many great organs of evacuation and procreation. Added to that was the yelling.

A corrugated iron lamp hung from a high rafter, making a perfect circle of light over the pit and the circle of men and women crowded around it. The rest of the barn was in shadow. I edged up to the crowd and got a glimpse of black feathers flashing high in the air and the glint of steel spurs. I thought I smelled blood but couldn't be certain. The yelling rose and fell around me. Grace clutched my elbow. I glanced at her and thought her eyes had a glint in them as we edged up closer. The man who had let us in the back door came up to me and said, "You forgot to pay. Ten dollars." I fished for my wallet and was surprised to find my hand shaking. I figured I was being taken but it was no time to argue. The farmer went back to his post at the door.

"Excuse me a minute," I said, "I want to ask that guy . . ."

She appeared not to hear me but kept her eyes fixed on the kicking, wing-slicing, beak-slashing birds. One had a hole in its head as big as a nickel and blood was welling from the wound; still he kept lashing out with his steel footgear. Their handlers at opposite sides of the ring leaned into the circle silently; everyone else was shouting for a kill, men and women both clutching loose bills in their fists.

I didn't seek out the man at the door at all but began to

circle the pit, looking at backs and when I could, the frenzied faces. I passed behind Brom Janiczek and his wife, he clutching an empty pipe in his teeth and she with an unlit cigarette dangling from her lips. They didn't see me and I passed on.

I had almost circled the crowd when I spotted Wanda sitting on a bale of hay. She was wearing a black motorcycle jacket with the usual stars and studs and was drinking something from a Coke bottle. I got into a shadow and watched her. She seemed to be alone but in a second Kaz materialized beside her and without looking at her took the Coke bottle from her hand and drank. Then he handed the bottle back to her, still with his eyes on the dying cock. I walked in front of the pair. "Advance and be recognized," I said to Wanda but really to Kaz. Kaz said nothing but nodded with a jerk of his head.

"You do get around, Ed," said Wanda. And added, "Bring somebody?" Her eyes roamed around the circle but she didn't see anyone she could pin on me.

"The cashmere sweater," I answered. "Next to the kid with the handlebar moustache." There was a centennial coming up in Milo and lots of males of all ages were taking advantage of the occasion to grow Wild West hair. In fact, it was being encouraged by the Chamber of Commerce. Next year the males would all go back to butch haircuts and business suits, except for the motorcycle fringe.

"She's pretty," said Wanda, swigging from the bottle. "Want some, Ed?" She handed me the bottle. I didn't relish drinking from the bottle that Kaz was also swilling but I took a slug to see what it was. Bourbon with a touch of Coke. I took a good swallow.

"Good," I said. "See you Kaz." I thought for a moment before I said to Wanda, "Good cocking." I thought Kaz twitched or tensed but wasn't sure. "That's what the game is called," I added, pointing to the ring. The cock with the hole in its head was finally dead and there was a silence while money changed hands.

"Keep your fucking education to yourself," said Wanda and put her arm around Kaz. I wandered back to my date.

The Janiczeks had spotted Grace between matches and were flanking her when I got back. We all hugged sociologically and conspiratorially. Karen whispered into my ear, "We can see about three more kills before the cops come," and scrunched up her face and smiled.

"Do you mean it?" I asked. I didn't relish a ride to town in one of Milo's 1945 paddy-wagons.

Brom added, "We're leaving at ten sharp," and looked at his wristwatch, which he wore on the inside of his wrist. I never can understand why anybody wears a watch that way. It might be a gesture of self-protection. When you look at your watch your hand is in front of your face. "You and Grace come by our dig for a drink?" Brom called his house a Dig, as if it were some archaeological find.

"Let's do, Edsel," Grace said, not looking at me. She must have seen me while I was lurking around the bale of hay.

"Give us the signal when you go," I said. "How do you know?" I asked Brom abruptly.

Brom shushed me and whispered, "Gimpy Slezak, the Chief. He's on my payroll." He nudged me to save the details for later.

I took this to mean that the local police chief was contributing information to Janiczek's celebrated and long-unpublished study of the Plains city. Brom had the confidence of all the city officials and access to all files as well as copious tip-offs and a warehouse full of inside dope. The clerks and political appointees trusted him as a lovable old university dope who eventually would put each and every member of the society on the map with flying colors. Brom subtly traded information from bureau to bureau, gossiping really, but no more than was necessary to keep his oar in. His knowledge of rape-murder cases, of which Milo had more than its just share, could have blighted whole suburban neighborhoods, had he wanted to use it. He didn't. It figured that Brom was really a collector, a librarian at heart, and that he would never draw the conclusions and lay the generalizations on the line which it was his profession to do. So Gimpy had tipped off the Janiczeks about the idiotic cockfight and the P.M. raid.

I slipped my hand into Grace's; it was cool as marble and as soft as tissue paper. I felt the chill but didn't let go.

During the next bird battle there was a fight between a man and a woman at the side of the pit. Graindorge dragged the man by the collar to the door and opened it for the man to leave. He left. Nobody took much notice. There was the same yelling, waving of paper money, flashes of black feathers and red blood and white steel cock-feet. I really didn't watch the fights but studied what glimpses of Kaz and Wanda I could get sitting on the hay across the circle. They must have had an endless supply of bottles of Coke; it seemed to pass back and forth with the rhythm of a metronome. He never touched her but she either leaned against him or lay her hand in his lap. Once I thought I saw her stroking his crotch but wouldn't swear to it. I felt a sudden queasiness and suggested to Grace a breath of air. It was her turn to look at her watch, a delicate platinum thing which seemed painted on her match-stick wrist.

"Five minutes," she said, looking at me with big clear eyes.

"I'll get the bottle," I answered. I worked my way to her car and worked my way back to the group. We sipped from the bottle and coughed. Nobody interfered, including the farmer-bouncer, who was now wandering back and forth.

"Time," said Karen in a low voice and nudged me. "Go casually," she hissed. Another nudge.

We peeled off imperceptibly and Indian-filed through the door.

"You go first," said Brom. "You know the house. Door's always open."

Brom had to pump up his crazy Citroën, which had some sort of pneumatic springs which let the car down like a balloon when he stopped. The red Buick floated around the barn, into the ruts, and out onto the dusty county road. I drove slowly to see if the Citroën would catch up. I saw the smoke of headlights a quarter of a mile behind me and decided it must be the Janiczeks, and I speeded up. And about a mile from the highway, sure enough there passed one state highway patrol car, then another, then the Black Maria.

"They really mean it, by God," I said. "Why don't they let the bastards kill their chickens."

"Gambling is supposed to be immoral," said Grace vapidly. I gave an empty laugh. "How is your friend?" she added.

"She's not my friend. She's not even my whore, Grace. She's . . . she . . ."

"That you think you have to degrade yourself . . ." she started, and looked out of the window silently all the way to the dimlit Janiczeks' Victorian bungalow.

When I had turned the Buick's motor off, I said to myself, "Degradation." I shifted in my seat and looked at Grace. "Since when do you preach?" I asked rhetorically.

"Please forget it, Ed," she answered, and added, "Isn't it a beautiful house?" It *was* beautiful, even in the dark. Huge old elm trees, already marked for slaughter because of the elm tree disease, guarded the lawn and shut out the moonlight. The house was brown and brown, dark brown trim on the lofty gently curvy windows and cornice and light brown the rest of the way. Brom and Karen had done the painting, and I felt a twinge of envy at their complicity, their coupledness. Tears came to my eyes but I kept them to myself.

"What did you make of the cocking?" I asked.

She fluttered again, looked toward the house and then back at me in the speckled shadow.

"I liked it," she said. "No, I loved it. I think it was honest. I don't mean the gambling." She faltered. I waited. "It was animal," she went on. "Or maybe I just admired it. Anyway, I'm glad I went. And I'm glad you went. And I'm glad you asked me."

She shuddered slightly and my hand sought hers, both of which lay primly on the surface of her pocketbook. Her hands remained palms down on her pocketbook but she edged her body a fraction into mine. Without thinking, I ran my hand

63

under her dress and up her thigh. If she had been marble she couldn't have felt it less. No muscle twitched, no limb stirred, the temperature remained the same.

I thought, Okay, Ice Maiden.

"They'll be here in a minute," she said, still as a statue, looking again at the lovely Victorian bungalow. Car lights announced themselves in the rearview mirror and jounced neatly up the street a couple of blocks away. They grew bright to the point of blindness. I gripped Grace solidly so she wouldn't open the door. The headlights turned majestically into the Janiczeks' driveway and coasted to a stop. But in the rearview mirror appeared new headlights. The Janiczek headlights were turned off when the new ones approached slowly and began to turn into the driveway. I leaned over to the dashboard and switched on the Buick's lights.

"Wanda and Kaz," said Grace, stiffening.

"How do you feel about some transactional psychology?" I said.

"In a minute, Ed. I want to fix my mask." She was redecorating herself in the dark. It didn't work and she switched on the top light. I watched the reconstruction in a daze. Grace was a master of the cosmetics department. I didn't feel that I had the sanction to criticize her but nevertheless thought, She's a live manikin, a store dummy, she's a clothes horse, she's a big-enough-to-fuck doll. And I thought, while she was biting on a piece of Kleenex to get the excess lipstick off, No, she's a human being person. She's intelligent, she's pretty, but she grew up in a Frigidaire. She's on an ice floe and will never get off. And me, I was born in the Sahara with a craw full of sand and all I want is a drink.

We got out of our separate doors and went up the walk and entered the hallway of the Janiczeks.

"Kiss the totem pole, darling," I instructed. There was a truncated totem pole in the entrance way. Grace kissed it obediently, leaving a little trace of lipstick on an eagle's wing.

"I'm patriotic too," I said, and ran my hand down the phallic symbol which topped the fragment. We entered the living-room, which was empty but which had a small table in one corner. On the table was a crowd of gallon-sized whiskey bottles, glasses, ice bucket, and an unopened bag of pretzels. We both took bourbon and ice and sat down. I found myself breathing hard. From another room flamenco music started up and a stomping of feet.

"Let's have our drink," said Grace. I smiled at her and sipped.

"Apologies aren't that bad," Grace said out of the blue. "You know, Ed, you don't make a very convincing savage. People don't really take your savagery very seriously. You're like a gentle civilized person who has discovered—well, Villon or Walt Whitman. But it really doesn't go with you."

I bristled, thinking I was hearing echoes from her religious Ph.D. padrone and master.

"I'm not a *sauvage*," I answered, listening to the stomping of feet. "I'm a barbarian. It's quite a different style. I don't want to see the idols fall from behind my tree. I want to topple them with my own hands. I want to push."

Grace sat silent and I went on with my idea.

"I want the idols to fall but not to be buried. I want them like Rome in the Renaissance, the Forum all silted up but visible and grown over with vines. Me, I'm strictly baroque. I'm the baroquest son-of-a-bitch in history—in Milo, anyway."

I snuffed pleasurably into my drink.

"Well," I went on, "of course, fallen beauty, Faisandage. Stink. Malaria in the Colosseum. Henry James. Oscar Darling. Astrology. You take Wanda. She digs astrology. Now, I ask you, what is better, the busted Victory of Samothrace or the whole one which I hope to God nobody will ever see? Who wants to see the Acropolis in all its vulgar glory? Not me. I'll take it after the Turks took it. Just like it is right this minute, crawled over by the little old ladies from Dubuque and the toothless tourists of London and Sydney. A bomb crater, but with the bones bleached and blazing in the sun in rotten little fascistic Greece, Anno Domini 1984. Your idealism is for the birds. It's pure Germanic monomania which you are being converted to by your saintly Tremaine Atwood. For the love of God, as Poe would say, how can you take anybody seriously who is named Tremaine Atwood. He belongs to the paleontology of English Departments. He wipes his ass with parchment. He screws his wife with gauntlets on."

"And you?" asked Grace. She was not given to dueling and I was tagged off base and gave her a grateful smile.

"Let's go see the party," I said wryly.

We wandered through three rooms of books and maps, statues, ceramics, spiny spears once tipped with poison, huge dark red urns, modern paintings from the Milo Art Department, batiks and laces on wall-spaces, and stunted Japanese trees in tubs, all dead but striking in their littleness. We found the Janiczeks and Wanda and Kaz in the bedroom of the son who was away at Antioch for his junior year.

Brom had yanked back a huge glowing Navajo rug and the floor of the bedroom was bare. Kaz stood in the middle of the room with arms folded, looking for all the world like a flamenco dancer. His black motorcycle boots added to the impression. Wanda lay on the bed as if she had been flung there. The Janiczeks were standing and clapping in rhythm and emitting *Olés!* at more or less appropriate times. Apparently Kaz was serious in his try to imitate the footwork. I, doing a slow burn, wondered where he had picked up his interest in this kind of thing. The guitar record buzzed like a giant hornet; in the background of the record could be heard the spontaneous plaudits of some audience who had once witnessed whatever the performance was. Grace went to sit on the bed next to Wanda. For some reason I admired the gesture. When the guitarist approached an unidentifiable speed toward the end of the recording, Kaz gave a motion of helplessness and stood still and listened.

"You've got what it takes, Kaz," said Karen. A lump of her hair, heavy and graying, had fallen to her shoulder from the clapping. "You'd be a natural in Andalusia." Kaz lit a cigarette and said nothing. He always said nothing.

I noticed that Grace was sharing her drink with Wanda. If Wanda was drunk she didn't show it. Her eyes were clear with the dull sparkle of iron filings.

"I listen to those records," said Kaz, "and I've seen Greco

66

on the tube. It's a real kind of dancing for a man. Nothing fairy about that kind of dance. Great stuff." And abruptly he walked out of the room.

The company reconvened in the livingroom, Kaz handing a new drink to Wanda and Karen one to Brom. Brom felt he had to give a small lecture about flamenco and told about the *cante jondo*, deep song, he explained, and the erotic gypsy style and the resemblance to the wailing chanting of the Spanish Jews.

"It's tragedy," said Brom, "the tragedy of the bitten-off peninsula, as Auden says."

"Therefore homosexual," I said, surprised that I had said it.

The sociologists were always ready and willing to entertain a far-out conclusion and looked at me expectantly. Everybody waited.

"I was in New Orleans before I went away," I started badly, "and some guy who was a friend of the English Department or something, who owned a nightclub on Bourbon Street—anyhow he and his wife were flamenco buffs and they opened a real flamenco club with six honest-to-God Spaniards from Spain. It wasn't taking on too well but he was going to keep it open, no matter what. I went there one night at the end of the show and when the customers had left and the door was locked he had them run through the entire repertoire just for us, about six people." I stopped. I took a swallow. "I'd never seen it before really and didn't know what it was but I was damn impressed. I always thought Spaniards were dead people walking and they convinced me. Beautiful and dead. Automatons. Fascists, I guess, to the manner born. It's like what Lorca said about the Civil Guard. Always dressed in black, silent as the tomb, armed to the teeth, with high heels, the better to stomp the enemy. The cool killers whose greatest art is being gored in the groin by a bull trained to do exactly that."

I felt I wasn't quite on the right track and might be building up to a head-on accident, but I lurched on.

"Naturally, the Roman Catholics have always called Spain Our Second Sister in Christ. If Christ came down from the stratosphere he'd head straight for Madrid. The first thing he'd do would be to buy the most expensive box for the bull-fights. He'd personally give extreme unction to Manolete. Maybe he'd heal his wound with his tongue. Why is it that black is the favorite color of the most blood-thirsty people? They kill so they can mourn. Then they kill some more. Then they dance it. Like the red and the black."

"What about the flamenco place?" Wanda asked in a dark voice.

I experienced a sudden wave of drunkenness and felt as if I were in front of one of my classes. I knew I was going to be pedantic and knew I couldn't stop myself.

"As Lawrence said, noli me tangere. The dancing was the dancing of untouchables. Above the waist the little black straight-jackets or the bare arms and ruffs of red for the fe-males. All the action is from the waist down except for the snake-arms and the castanets. It was just like that Rilke poem where the Spanish dancer bursts into flame like a struck match. Only they strike the match with their feet because their life and their sex have all been forced into their feet, or rather their heels. It's the art, if I may disagree with Rilke, of stomping out the fire which they can only imagine."

"What were the women like?" Wanda asked.

"I recall two. One was short and stocky and quick as a spider. The other was tall, with an El Greco neck and a beau-tiful expressionless face. She was the star. She was titless but well-haunched and danced like a machine gun. The best-resur-rected corpse I ever laid eyes on. She damn near drove holes in the stage with her heels but not a hair of her head even quivered. It was fantastic. The only live thing about them was the sweat under their arms. You could smell it. Incidentally," I added, "one of the best male dancers wasn't a Spaniard at all, but a Jew from Brooklyn. His name was Joel Spritz, or something."

I took a solid gulp.

"No, not homosexual. I take it back. The dances are asexual, one of the higher forms of jerking off. An attempt to resurrect Jesus, which in Spain is obviously hopeless." I wished that I

68

could stop using the word "obviously" because I always used it when it obviously didn't apply. I used words like that for "charm," charm being a trick for disarming the enemy or decoying an authority.

"But after all, Brom," I said, "it's that kind of desperate ritual which leads to the explosion of art. You come to a dead end when you are being pursued by Jesus H. Christ or Francisco Franco and you damn well break out into Art or die. I think the Spaniards die because they like it that way. When they get a real poet like Lorca they shoot him in the balls. Even if he's queer."

I had run out of gas and Karen picked me up.

"I know what you mean, Ed," she said with a half-serious laugh. "I think I know. I feel sometimes we only admire the dead, and the deathly."

"It's true," Brom added. He always added to his wife's thesis, or put in some documentation to show their solidarity. "If we could know the mystery of a dying culture we might be able to save something of our own. All us highbrows are toxicologists and taxidermists."

"Love on the death-bed," I said and shot a look at Wanda.

"Give me another drink, Kaz," she said.

As Kaz crossed over me, he said, "I think you got a point there," and disappeared into the kitchen. I wondered which point had been picked up, or whether the remark was some kind of response to my unconcerted attack on the Kaz-Wanda team.

We dropped the flamenco seminar and went back to the cockfight. Grace wanted to know whether the police had actually raided the Graindorge farm and Brom told the whole story, who was taken in and who wasn't, how much money changed hands, how much Gimpy Slezak pocketed, the reason for the state of the roads around the farmer's house, which college students were not arrested and why.

"But the whole motorcycle set are in the cooler," Brom finished. "They are very essential to policing. They are carefully arrested and attended, handled with kid gloves even when they have their teeth knocked out. Nothing is more necessary

69

and—esthetic?—to the police than a fixed sub-culture of amateur criminals. The cops couldn't possibly function without them. Of course, they are created by the cops, you know, Ed, the way a poem is. If the provincial public doesn't have a living example of the Wrong, the police die. They get tired of hanging around the public lavatory of the Pawnee Hotel waiting for some visiting salesman or some Milo professor to expose his penis erectus to the next pisser. They need a Group Enemy, just like the State Department." He laughed enjoyably.

"And what's so goddam funny about arresting people because they ride motorcycles?" Wanda wanted to know. She leaned forward pugnaciously. I started to answer when Karen took the ball.

"It's not motorcycles. Motorcycles used to be for cops and cops only. Cops—and couriers—in the First World War."

I sat back for a lecture which I was hoping against.

"Then the motorcycle racers took over, those guys who used to race in a wooden pit, like a cockfight. It was a big wooden saucer and when the racers got to top speed they rose horizontally around the walls of the pit. One spill killed or maimed the whole lot of them. It was great sport. Then there were the cross country cycle racers, leaping ditches and ploughing down corn and rupturing their spleens and other equipment. Then they took to the highways. But that was after the daredevil image was firmly implanted in the *public* mind by the films." She underlined *public*. "It was when the Public," and she capitalized *public*, "began to see the *evil* in motorcycles," she giggled, "that the cyclists became Fallen Angels."

"And just what the *Polizei* ordered," added Brom.

Sociology forever, I thought.

Kaz had given the drink to Wanda, *en passant*, as it were, and was again standing in the middle of the floor. He started to drum with his heels and made a neat circle, standing in place. There was no music and when he stopped he was facing me. I looked him in the eye and slowly stood up and gave him a push, saying to Grace, "Let's go."

I thought I might get a karate rabbit punch as I brushed by him but nothing happened. I wondered if the rhythm of my walk was slow enough as Grace and I went to the vestibule, followed by the Janiczeks. I waved goodbye to Wanda and smiled at Kaz. Grace used polite farewells to everybody. We went out to the tight little Buick.

CHAPTER VI

ᕙᕗ I pondered what to wear to my opening class and selected a black wool shirt with white buttons and a pair
of tan fatigues. I bought clothes at the Army Surplus and
Army and Navy stores and at the work clothes counters of
Sears. This gave me not so much a feeling of masculinity and
militarism or of woodsiness as it did a feeling of separateness
from my colleagues. I hated their uniform, tweeds and wools
and bowties and their English shoes. My own shoes were
buckskin or some type of unfinished leather. I even had a pair
of Hush Puppies, but the name revolted me so much I hardly
wore them. It was hot and I skipped the tie altogether.

In my office I brushed all my mail into the top drawer except the new class rosters which the secretary had laid on top
of my correspondence. I looked at the one called Creative
Writing. The number 20 at the bottom told me the bad news.

"Twenty students in Writing of Poetry! Even ten is six too
many. The bastards." I wasn't too sure who the bastards were.
When I had come to Milo U. my writing class was kept down
to seven. But then my main job had been to edit *Tracks West*,
the university quarterly, and they kept my teaching load to a
minimum. And after I had resigned the editorial chair, or
rather been fired for publishing an "indecent and irreligious"

story, I was told that my classes would be larger—unless I wanted to add a new course. I opted for the double-size classes.

I ran down the list of names to see what I could see. Two faculty wives. I raised my eyebrows. One was the Nisei, Irene Yamashiro, whose husband was a professor in Bus-Ed. Dainty and sly crossed my mind. Or you might say inscrutable. The other was Bumpy Harrington. I had met her at faculty parties but not at the Janiczeks'. The Harringtons were upper-class, blue bloods on the Plains. She had the Vassar whine and the horse laugh that went with it. Her husband, known to the local society columnist as Bean, was professor of orthopedic surgery. Bumpy and Bean claimed to have chosen Milo because there was plenty of room for their horses in these parts. Bean was president of the Saddle Club and every year came away with a few ribbons for jumping. He also personally operated on the crushed limbs of the football team. There was talk of Bean being made a Regent of the University; his love of the football team, his money and his social position, the best that Milo or even Chicago could offer, all pointed to his election.

"If they put any of those goddam athletes in my class . . ." I muttered, but didn't finish the idea. "What the hell do I care?" I decided. I had always made the deliberate mistake of letting anybody enter my classes, first come, first served. I figured that the caliber of student at Milo didn't warrant much screening and I took a masochistic delight in the asininity of the whole operation. I had even rationalized my predicament. "Anybody can write poetry, given the incentive. Anybody can be a poet if he wants to pull himself up by his jockstrap." I boasted to myself that I could make a Polack right guard write a double sestina. As for the housewives and Junior Leaguers, they added a kind of gamy aroma to the atmosphere. Like most teachers, I never talked to the class but either to myself, which was when I was at my best, or to a particular member of the group who had for a moment caught my fancy.

It was five minutes before the hour and I decided to wander into my classroom and look the newcomers over. All I would do was write my name and the number of the class on the board and then sit down to see who was there. The Junior Leaguers and professors' wives would be late; they always were. The athletes would come early and would sit in the back of the room, as they always did, either because they were taller than anyone else and had some animal shyness about their size, or (as I thought) to look over the girls and be in a favorable situation to cheat on exams. The athletes would think there were exams in Creative Writing.

Sure enough there were three tall specimens in the back row, one a Negro basketball player. I had seen him on television a couple of times. When the basketball player saw the professor take his seat, he came up and smiled and deposited three registration cards on the desk. I thanked him and glanced at the names. Devogue Henry, yes, that was the basketball fellow. Ap Koslow (I had been to a few football games and knew that Ap was known lovingly as The Ape. The Ape had been in three bowl games and was a quiet studious man. He wanted to be a dentist, a radio announcer had once informed the world). The third one was Wes Cawkins. I glanced at him, a wiry satyr-looking type. I had never heard of him, but then I was no sports writer.

Four sorority sisters minced by my desk and took adjoining seats in the second row. A white-haired fairy about sixteen and a half years old sailed into the room with head up and books clutched to his breast. He had a tiny face and huge eyeglasses and sank into an aisle seat and proceeded to open a book. A fat blonde girl followed. She had long streaky hair, partly peroxide, and wore a sweater filled to bursting. She sat in front of me and crossed her legs and lit a cigarette. There was a sign behind me in red which said NO SMOKING BY ORDER OF THE MILO FIRE DEPARTMENT. I stood up and detached the sign and put it in my top desk drawer and lit a cigarette of my own. The sweater with the blonde in it suppressed a giggle.

A sad-looking boy with black hair pulsated into the room in a wheelchair. He wheeled to the back of the room and sat catercornered to the athletes.

74

One with a red beard and a string of Indian beads sauntered in. A Jew, I thought.

Bumpy and the Nisei followed. "Anywhere?" Bumpy asked me, extending her arm like V. I. Lenin in bronze. Her grin was dazzling.

I stood up to welcome the faculty wives, asked about their husbands, said I was fine and hated Europe, the usual rot. They decided on seats next to the windows, about midway down the room. It was a small room with thirty seats and there was little opportunity for the luxury of avoiding one's fellow men. A bell rang.

I waited a minute and then started. It crossed my mind that it was important right off the bat to avoid proper-sounding English. I would find their level, however abysmal, by putting them at ease. I felt I was good at that. I wound out of my chair and moved briskly to the door and released the doorstop and then came back in front of my desk. I said:

"This is a class for writing poetry. That's all it is. I'm not going to keep you long today, just long enough to tell what the rules aren't. And the rules aren't that there aren't any." I stopped and went around to the front of my desk and opened the top drawer to see if somebody had left an ashtray. There was no ashtray and I snuffed out the cigarette in the drawer and closed it.

"You can smoke in here," I said, "but it would help the janitor if you brought a paper cup or something instead of using the floor." I went on: "There are no textbooks in the course. Lots of people have written textbooks about how to write poetry but I've never seen one that mattered. You can't teach writing from a book."

"Can you teach writing at all?" asked the fat blonde in the front row.

"No," I said, "that's what you're here for. You're going to teach yourselves. And I'm just going to look over your shoulder. Presumably, if you weren't here in a group, you'd never get around to the writing you want to write. Here you have a built-in audience and—a Controversial Professor." I laughed a short laugh, something between a cough and a smile.

"The text in this course is what you write, good, bad, or indifferent. Bad poems are easier to learn from than good ones.
It's very hard to analyze or criticize or dissect a really good,
finished poem. It's as hard as taking apart a seashell. All you
have left is sand. Your worst poems are more than welcome.
We will all need them. You will learn, not from any models I
will hold up, but from your false starts and errors and writers'
blocks and neuroses and your bad education."

Bumpy of Vassar held up her hand. She was a user of arms,
a waver to acquaintances.

"But you have to know the great models of the past, don't
you," she asked. "Why, I read poetry all the time and always
have, and always will, and I'm proud of what I know of the
greats. And how would I know what to write without those—
models, you call them?"

I bristled at her use of a word like "greats," which sounded
like something from *Variety* magazine or the Hall of Fame for
Baseball at Cooperstown, N.Y., where I was sure she had been
at some time or other.

"I didn't make myself clear, Mrs. Harrington," I smiled at
her. I wouldn't dream of calling her Bumpy in front of this
class, to allow any prescience of even the slightest intimacy.
"We'll get to this quite a bit," I continued, "but for now, well,
there is no connection between education and creativity. No
connection between scholarship and creativity. No connection
between the most highly cultivated sensibility in the arts and
the ability to write a poem." I made doughy gestures in the
air with my hands.

Bumpy was about to start in on something like a Junior
League Great Books Seminar, or so I feared, and I changed
the subject. I explained where to turn in their manuscripts, to
which secretary, where to pick up the purple mimeograph
copies, and gave them the option of signing their names or
being anonymous.

"In fact," I added, "if you want to hand in a poem by Shakespeare as your own—presuming I don't know it—or by some
obscure poet, say, William Alabaster" (here I rolled my eyes),
"that's fine. The point of this class is to let you find out what

it is, and possibly *how,* to write a poem. It is not very likely that anyone here is already a full-fledged poet with a recognizable style of his own. Or so I assume. I may be wrong. I hope I am. If you were already that, why would you be here?"

The hefty blonde switched legs. Her chair creaked.

I was about to dismiss the class when I said, "It would be convenient if somebody wanted to act as secretary or, like, courier, and see that the poems are collected and typed on the stencils and run off and brought to class . . ."

A tall bony boy with a hungry look raised his hand. He did some work in the English office part-time and would be glad to handle the poems. I asked his name. Hugh Gilchrist. The name was familiar. Gilchrist had been in and out of a Trappist monastery in Missouri and had led a Freedom March. He was in training for the new underground and the administration kept its eye on him. He was one of those gentle saintly characters who might someday blow a city sky-high. He dressed inconspicuously but was always surrounded by the few girls who wore the straight long hair and black stockings of the local hippie clan, and the boys with Jesus-sandals and wig-like coiffure. With his mild countenance and flickering smile he did look like a sort of young Jesus, which was his intention. The red beard with the Indian beads also lifted a hand. The two helpers nodded to each other. It put me in mind of my Marxist youth, when I felt naked if I didn't have a bundle of some kind of papers in my hands. The first and most important trick of the Revolution, I remembered, was to control the mimeograph machine, then the printing press, then the air waves, etc., etc.

"That's it till Wednesday," I said, and opened the door and propped it while the class brushed by me. When I got to my office around the corner I noticed a pair of female legs sitting in my red overstuffed chair. I always left the door open, inviting let-come-what-come-may. It was the leg-crossing blonde in the sweater. I wanted to be annoyed at the intrusion but instead enjoyed the sluttishness of her gesture, if that's what it was. The girl didn't rise and I sat down tentatively on my swivel chair and looked at her. I had bought the overstuffed chair at the Good Will because it looked like one I had once seen in a whorehouse. It had cost ten dollars, including delivery. An oak office chair stood beside it, and I thought I could tell things about the character of my students by who chose the straightback chair and who sank into the rubbed red throne. Oscar Darling, the first time he saw the red chair, said, "Wonderful, Ed, nylon frieze. *Campy.*" Oscar had sat down in it and bounced three times.

"I'm Inge Amen," said the girl in the red chair, as if that explained volumes. Funny she didn't say, "My name is . . ." She had a nasal twang which seemed too shallow a music for the size of her front.

"Yes," I said, without a question mark. She wasn't going to mince matters, whatever the matters were.

"I'm twenty-six. I've come back to school to take your course. I want to be a writer, not just a poet. I want to master the whole works, criticism, editing, fiction. I hate my husband and my brat and I'm going to be a writer. I'm starting with poetry but I know you can help me a lot more than that." As a non sequitur she laughed.

"Okay," I said, a little taken aback. "Poetry will help, I guess."

"It's a goddam shame you were bounced off *Tracks West*," Inge continued like an old acquaintance. "Do you think I could get some work on the magazine? I need every kind of experience. I'm going to make it. Can't I get on the staff and read some of the hick shit that comes in? Tell me what to do."

When a stranger, especially a woman, uses verboten language to me, I always accept it as an engraved invitation. Maybe, I thought, that's why I can't shake Wanda. I swiveled slightly in my chair, pretending to think.

"How do you pronounce your name?" I asked.

"Amen, not Ah-men," she answered. "*Ah, men* is another thing again. It's a Kraut name. I was raised with the rod across my backside. Inge is good enough. Do I call you Dr. or Professor or Mister Lazerow?"

"Mister is good enough for me," I said. I noticed out of the corner of my eye that Bumpy and Irene were coming toward my door. Suddenly I decided I would call her Inge.

"Well, as you say, Inge, I'm totally off that magazine and they're totally off me. If you want to try out as reader you'd better talk to Oscar. I mean Professor Darling. He's the editor, not me. They don't even send me a copy anymore, even though it's sent out from the office next door. Not that I want to *read* it." I hesitated; I felt I was on the verge of telling the whole shabby little scandal about how Oscar and his assistant editor had yanked the editorial rug out from under me while I was on leave the year before. Inge pushed her face forward and I leaned over to light her cigarette. I waved to the faculty wives who were chatting at the doorway.

"In a minute," I called to them.

Inge said in a perfectly audible and resonant twang, "You were royally fucked, Mr. Lazerow." I started slightly, not because of Inge's language, which was beginning to interest me, but because of the F.W.'s standing in the doorway. I couldn't manage a double-level conversation at all. I could talk to the F.W.'s on their level and with their level of charm, just as I could talk to Inge on the pseudo-sailor level, but only if there were no fugal complications. Women like Bumpy or Irene wouldn't be caught dead with a woman like Inge, unless Inge were a famous something or other; and vice versa. I began to feel annoyed and wanted to end the interview. I frowned.

"I really can't help you," I said. "Go talk to the editor." And I couldn't resist saying, "He just might take you on. Editors always have openings." I gave her a bland smile and made a getting-up gesture from my chair. Inge, instead of rising, settled back in the whorehouse chair. She spoke in a lowered voice this time.

"What I really want," she said, "is to work with you. Typing, filing, your correspondence. I've read all your books; I know how much you do. I even know you don't have a secretary." She anticipated my obvious objection: "No, I don't want to be paid. I ought to pay *you*. I won't push you to the wall about it," she laughed, "but I can help you and you can help me. I'll come back on Wednesday?"

I nodded and she heaved out of the chair and left. The faculty wives parted on each side of her like sentries.

"Enter the doctor's office," I called to them. They entered and fussed about who was going to sit in the big red chair. Bumpy ceded it to Irene, or rather insisted that she sit there, to throw her off balance, I thought. Bumpy took the straight chair and spilled over it. She wasn't fat, just large. No amount of contact with horse flesh, which her husband insisted she have, could reduce her. She wasn't muscular and she wasn't fat. She was—Bumpy.

With mock timidity Irene glanced at the empty doorway and asked, "Who was *that?*"

"A student with the improbable name of Ah-men," I answered. "She must have thought I was still on *Tracks West* and wanted some experience."

Bumpy screwed up her face. "Doesn't everyone?" she said.

We talked about our summers. Bumpy and Bean had gone all the way to Alaska and Bean had got his Kodiak bear and Bumpy had backed him up, Hemingway-style, along with two sharpshooter guides, and I would have to come and see the rug. Irene and Burt had been at Aspen where Burt held seminars on "Socialist versus Capitalist Corporative Ethics." I wondered what that might mean and didn't ask. The Yamashiros had heard the entire series of Beethoven Quartets at Aspen and caught tons and tons of rainbow trout. Burt had also gotten an offer from Louisiana State U. The South can use some Japs, I thought, to confuse the Ethiopians. The conversation petered out in pleasantries. I was at a loss as how to dismiss my company and told them about a half-dozen embassy parties I had been invited to during my little European tour. Having topped the faculty wives I was in a hostly position to give them leave to go. We made indeterminate dates for dinner.

When they had turned the corner of the small hall and were out of sight, I closed the door quietly, pulled down my door blind, as if I had gone home, and clawed the telephone. Amazingly, Wanda answered the phone at the Fountain of

Beauty. More amazingly, she said, "I've been trying to get you, Ed. Pick me up at four-thirty." There was no question about that. I sat down in the red chair, then got up and took out my unopened mail, and began to read it.

Most of the letters were manuscripts of poems and short stories with pleas for publication. I thanked God I didn't have to answer these and put them in a pile to give to Oscar Darling. One was a come-on note, with poems, from a young faculty wife in Kentucky who was dying of boredom and a dry husband. She enclosed a picture of herself printed on some amateur ballet program. The leotards expressed her personality and outlined her measurements. Not bad, I thought, but I was tired of wet-nursing remote romanticists and placed this letter on Oscar's pile with the others. There were letters and postcards from hosts and hostesses of my European jaunt but I didn't want to pick up old and fleeting acquaintances. I made a separate pile of those; I'd stick them in the back of one of my file drawers—yes, for Inge Ah-men to read greedily and then file. There was one of my own letters to Wanda which had been returned via some diplomat's "pouch" because it hadn't been able to catch up with me. It was postmarked Berlin, Hamburg, and London, and had some kind of U.S. seal on it. I started to tear it in half when the thought crossed my mind that it had been opened and read perhaps, and I slit it open with my paperknife, a gift from Wanda. I turned the letter-cutter over in my hand.

The handle was an intricately cast piece of bronze which started with what looked like a heart at the end of the handle. It was a thick handle and when you turned it in your fingers the heart became a pair of balls. Above the balls on one side were etchings of hair lines. The rest of the brass shaft was a round staff, three inches long, ending in a lotus shape which was really the head of a penis. Out of the head of the penis the white blade struck like a switch-blade. The blade was steel and unbendable. I never could find out where the letter knife came from, any more than I could find out where the record with the bedsprings came from.

It was the letter about my visit to the licensed brothel in Hamburg. I pocketed it. I would take it to Wanda or maybe read it to her.

I had the afternoon to kill. The horror of having to be alone made me feel seasick. I recited to myself the Camus lines about the Dandy's terror of looking in the mirror. Had I so few resources left that I would rather slurp beer in a student beer joint, hoping for a dialogue with an idiot or opportunist, than go to my apartment and read a book or listen to Mozart or take a nap? And then, where could I go, whom could I see, except by accident, in Milo. Milo? Anywhere. I thought of getting my car washed but the idea of exchanging even a few words with the gas station attendant depressed me. I toyed with the symbolic knife and gazed out the window at the people who had definite destinations. I admired and hated them for having a place to go, a particular thing to do. I was past the stage at which society makes paper-signing demands on a person; I had risen above the quotidian duties of standing in lines or signing documents. Maybe I'll write a poem, I suggested to myself. Like, "I look down with the lostness of a god." No wonder the Greek gods had come down from Olympus to screw the Greeks. Next line, I thought: "Heaven is hell." I rubbed my cheek. I need shaving cream. I'll go to Durd's. I looked around for anything I might want to take with me, saw nothing, and left.

Durd's was a combination drugstore, sundry shop, and warehouse of practical-joke toys. Also it had the only collection of girly magazines in Milo, sexy paperbacks, astrology pamphlets, and even one or two underground papers. It was a nasty littered meretricious hole with aisles so narrow you either brushed merchandise off the counters or rubbed against patrons. The magazines were at the front of the store and at all hours were being pawed over by old men, transients, college students, and a select handful of professors. The floors were uneven shredded boards. I felt a high regard for the place: it was so sincerely, existentially cheap, so low, so sad. I went there.

I found my shaving cream in the maze and went to the magazines. I was looking for one called *Ladder*. I had read somewhere it was a lesbian mag and I wanted to take it to Wanda. I couldn't find it and I looked behind rows and rows of muscle-building periodicals, sex-crime monthlies, plain nude journals, strippy weeklies, photographic annuals, cartoon "oddities," and the stacks of nationally accepted literary organs which carried foldouts of young would-be mistresses of the rich and lascivious. A hand fell on my shoulder and I turned.

"Now, Tremaine," I said to my colleague, "what are *we* doing here?"

"Keeping up with the underground," said Tremaine. We both laughed. I didn't say what I was looking for and finally went to the woman at the counter and asked if they had a magazine called *Ladder*. She thought a while, went to the magazine racks and riffled through stack after stack. She knelt down and opened a drawer at the bottom and came back with the desideratum. I noted that it was a year old. Seasoned, I thought. I stopped to say goodbye to the other professor and had the temerity to ask how Grace was doing on her dissertation. There was no question about her work, said Tremaine Atwood. What a reward it would be if we had ten students like her instead of one or two.

I flicked through *Ladder* in my car. Not a man in the book. Women in the conventional Nazi boots, raising or caressing bullwhips, young "victims" squeezed into bulges by black silk straps, arranged scenes of woman "raping" woman, some dressed in business suits or Marine uniforms. The whole publication had a definitely Spartan atmosphere and I wasn't sure how I would use it on Wanda. I studied the faces of the women, not the bodies. I was looking for traces of—sincere depravity, or something of the sort. But I didn't trust the magazine for authenticity and sighed and drove to my apartment. There I ate an expensive canned onion soup and a can of minced clams out of the can and had two martinis. I took a shower, turned on my FM radio for music. They were playing

Wagner and I turned it off. I lay on my couch under my windows and I looked up through the great elm trees to the sunlight. I dozed.

I have a built-in alarm clock in my brain. All of the actual clocks I have ever had ran either fast or slow. If a clock or a watch runs on time I don't believe in it. My tendency to be early, very early, is legendary. My horror of missing appointments, I believe, amounts to a minor insanity. But my brain-clock works so efficiently that I have developed a cat-nap technique which is infallible. I sleep by fits and starts. I haven't had a good night's sleep for decades and don't think it exists.

I dozed and slept on the couch in the sunlight, yanked to consciousness every five minutes or ten. Once I fell into actual sleep but started awake with such a snap of my back that it hurt. I was in a sweat and had an erection. In the bathroom I doused my face with cold water and peed through my hard-on. It always amazed me that this could be done and I thought that perhaps I was some kind of sexual freak. I'll piss inside Wanda, I thought.

The few times I had picked her up at the Fountain of Beauty I had simply sat in my car until she spotted me. That was the agreement. I saw the operators moving about inside and wondered which one was Milly. Wanda came to the window and waved hurriedly. When she came out she had a black silk scarf over her ashen hair. I leaned over and opened the door.

"Here's a letter for you," I said, driving off. I laid it on her lap. The magazine lay face down on the back seat.

"Listen, Ed, I need a hundred dollars," she answered. I swung the car over to the curb, switched off the motor and took out my checkbook. I asked Wanda for a pen and wrote her a check for $125.

"You really are a good guy, Ed," said Wanda and leaned over and pecked me on the cheek. Ever since my divorce I had more money than at any time in my life. It didn't make sense; I was paying my ex-wife more than half my salary and was living on what amounted to a university assistant's pay. Maybe it was because my surprise money, as I thought of it, was now all mine—the money from poetry lectures and anthologies and reviews. Anyhow I now had a bank balance, something I'd never dreamed of. I only had about five hundred in my checking account but felt I was rolling in wealth.

Wanda had the good taste not to say she was going to pay it back, and how soon. We understood each other well enough to know that money was a gift, or rather barter for fleshly favors. I preferred it that way. Paying for a little of her fleshpot excited me. It was all part and parcel of my whore theory. A pro is somebody who does it for money, I told myself; whether the pro was a golf champion or a scholar of umlauts or a woman who opened her box at the sight of green money. Money doth the strumpet make, I said to myself, making up a line which I immediately blue-penciled as lousy.

"I'm dying for a beer," said Wanda. "Do you know where Biff's Place is?" I had seen it out on a small highway, not far from the Saddle Club. I said I knew the way.

"That letter," I said, "how the hell it got back to me instead of you I'll never know." Wanda looked at the envelope.

"You fucked the address, you jerk," she said. I snatched the letter from her and, driving with one hand, looked at the address and the crayon markings and queries from P.O. clerks and the U.S.I.A. rubber stamps. What I had written on the envelope was:

Miss Wanda Shontz
201 Olive Street, Apt. 1B
c/o U.S.I.A.
Amerika Haus
14 Kunsthalle
Hamburg, Germany

"Good God, I must have been stoned," I said. "And no return address! I know goddamned well it must have been opened at every U.S.I.A. office in Europe." I started to laugh. "I'd make a great diplomat, that's for sure."

Wanda was turning the letter over and over in her hands.

"Right," she said. "There's no return address and your name isn't on it anywhere. I can't tell whether it was opened but it

85

had to be. And here where it gives your address at Milo U.—that settles it. It's written in funny writing."

"Well, read it," I said. I felt a little shaken at my blunder, but being an auto-psychologist, immediately began to wonder why I had "fugued" the address. Did it mean that I wished Wanda was on the tour with me? Impossible. Did it mean that I didn't want her to get the letter, or that I wanted to tell the State Department something about my sex life? Idiotic. But it sure as hell meant something. I said, "It's just a masturbation document." And added to myself, "Part of the wet dream of my life."

Wanda read the letter all the way to Biff's Place, which I got to without wrong turns. She was still reading it when I parked on the side of the clapboard hut. "Let me finish," she said. We sat there. She must have read it six times.

Wanda let out a deep breath when she had finished the letter, put it in her pocketbook and snapped it shut.

"Do you really think you're *kaput*, Ed?" she asked. She leaned against her door and studied me.

"What do you think?" I asked. She pressed down on her door handle and opened the door a couple of inches but sat where she was.

"If you really want to know, Ed, I'll tell you. If you and I had Irma in the same bed, you'd do fine. You're a looker, what you call a voyer." (*Sic,* I thought, giving her the benefit of the transliteration.) "You fuck with your eyes." She opened her door a little more. "And me too," she added, anticipating me. Suddenly she stuck out her silverfish fingernails with one hand and moved them slowly toward my face. With the other hand she drew back her skirt slowly, higher and higher.

"For Christ's sake, Wanda," I said. "You're naked. Who snatched your pants?"

She was out of the car and there was no answer.

CHAPTER VII

The owner of the beer joint greeted Wanda by name and didn't look at me. We found a booth with a curved semicircular back and had draft. "That letter," said Wanda, "why do you want to kiss and tell?"

"Well, for God's sake," I said, "she was only a whore. I thought it made a damn good story."

"*Kaput*," she answered, and drank. I thought of starting on a saga of all the whores I had ever visited since I was seventeen.

"Whores really fascinate me," I said. I decided to try a dangerous gambit. "Did you ever think of being a whore? I mean . . ." I put my hand on hers, seeing the steely glint in her eyes. "I mean, doesn't it have to occur to a woman to want to be a whore and have it over with? If I were a woman I wouldn't hesitate."

"What's your phantasy this time?" Wanda asked. She punched her cigarette down and I lurched on:

"You mean would I like to be a guard in a women's prison? Yes. Would I like to be a lap-dog in a can house? Sure. But would I like to be an Arab sheik and have myself two thousand concubines? No. Not enough tension."

Wanda smiled to Biff, as I supposed the proprietor to be,

87

and he came over with two more beers. I had left some bills on the table and Biff took one and made change silently.

I said, "I've been thinking of making a collection of the faces of prostitutes. Just the faces. Maybe the Janiczeks can start me out. Brom and the chief of the cops."

"You got high ideals," said Wanda. "And just exactly what kind of bang would you get out of that?"

"I got some in the car," I said, and went to find the magazine. It had an article called "The Licensed Women of Mexico" and I folded out the dozen or so pictures for her to see. She bent over them. The women had plucked eyebrows which were replaced by arched pencil lines. Their lips were drawn in the 1920 style, cupid bows. They wore bangles. One or two had missing front teeth. They all leaned out of cubbyholes like the stalls of horses. A few leered, most were stern and mask-like. Wanda whispered "Jesus" and leafed through the periodical. "What the hell kind of magazine *is* this?" she asked.

"Must be for the dykes," I said. "The bulls and the cows."

"Like I said, pal," said Wanda. "You really are a keyhole character. Well? Does that do anything for your rod to look at those poor women's faces, or those women handcuffed to beds?"

"Then felt I like some watcher of the skies," I quoted. "You know, there was a poet once who said the human face was divine. The human face divine. How about that? But I believe in it and I like to see those faces that used to shine with heavenly light turn into mug-shots. They've got character. Those women's faces are all gouged and struck by the lightning of experience. They're in hell and they love it."

"Bull," said Wanda in a deep voice. I was beginning to imagine that she was going to turn into something, like the characters in *Alice in Wonderland*. Maybe a thing with horns or maybe one of those creatures in Hieronymous Bosch paintings which I had studied under a magnifying glass in some art encyclopedia. I remembered a devil with a tongue about two yards long in proportion to his body. It was flicking into a woman's mouth.

"Order me a runza," said Wanda. I did and watched her eat the big gloppy affair as if she were starving to death. I had more beers and I began to feel the enjoyable stupidity of beer-drinkers.

"How about you cook me a steak at your place? I'll buy," I suggested. "I'll get a bottle of . . ." I didn't want to sound too esoteric and said "sparkling Burgundy." Wanda was tempted but of course had plans. My stomach suddenly knotted and I let the beer hit me. "But let's go home for a martini," she offered. That was good enough for me and I left a big tip. Leaving the door, we ran into Bean Harrington, who had stopped at the horse club across the road to look in on a jumper he had stabled there for the weekend try-outs. I introduced Wanda as Miss Shontz and the surgeon graciously shook hands. I admired him for that and my opinion of him went up a notch or two. The doctor was no imbiber and I wondered what he was doing there. Maybe Bean had come to talk to Biff about selling the beer joint to the Saddle Club. I had heard that they wanted to make it into a small supper club for the members of the horsey group, but it would be public, of course.

"Isn't he the handsome dog," Wanda said, going to the car.

"And gentleman," I answered. Driving to Wanda's I told about my morning and Bumpy Harrington coming to the class and about Inge Amen and her proposition to work for me. Wanda thought it was all delightful. I glanced at her, supposing that she was having a wave of lady-likeness. I told what I knew about the Harringtons and their horses and how Harrington, without knowing me, had put up a fight for me to be made a Regents professor.

"Doc Harrington told the Senate at Milo that I was the only person at Milo who had a book written about him, and that did it."

"What book?" asked Wanda. I pooh-poohed it, saying it was some scholarly thing.

I made the martinis by swishing vermouth in the empty glasses and then pouring the vermouth back into its green bottle. I filled the glasses with ice and poured gin to the top.

"*Va bene*," I said out loud. I winced when I took my first swallow and Wanda wanted to know why I drank something that tasted so bad. I answered something to the effect that it was good for my soul. Wanda went and put the chain on her door.

"Need a piece?" she said, kicking off her shoes.

"Lots and lots," said I. I suddenly felt peaceful and sober. The martini hadn't had time to catch up with the beer. Liquor hits me like switching on an electric light, or switching it off. It is a light phenomenon: everything grows bright in an instant, or shifts into some nuance of shade and color.

She was sitting on the sofa, dressed and with her legs propped up and her hairy pudenda showing. She was reading the queer magazine, holding it up to her face, to hide her face, I thought. She was grunting a little, opening and closing her thighs almost imperceptibly. I hoped somehow that she had forgotten I was there, that I was watching her through the window or from a closet where I was imagining I was hidden. I wondered whether she was getting hot or whether she was trying to galvanize me into action. I sat still and watched, feeling nothing.

"Jesus Christ," she said, without lowering the magazine.

"What?" I said. She started to read out loud.

" 'In those days the girls sat at the sewing machines in the tenement loft for ten hours a day, pumping the machine with their feet and legs. They wore ankle-length black dresses which they pulled up over their thighs when the foreman wasn't in the room. The constant friction of their thighs gave them amorous feelings. When a machine sped up faster and faster, its noise of whirring would sometimes be followed by a sigh and panting. The other girls would laugh or make some filthy remark. And just as frequently the girl who had her climax would find Harley, the black-Irish foreman, standing back of her, grinning.

" 'Nice stitching, Ellie," said Harley. "There's a message for you in the cutting room." Ellie rose, still heaving slightly and followed the ugly foreman down the aisle.' "

The age of the machine, I thought, but didn't say it. Wanda

continued to read, growing more tense in the thighs. Once she squeezed them together tight and shuddered a little.

"Does it work?" I asked.

"Ed, get me my electric toothbrush," she said in her deeper voice. I didn't even bother to wonder why but went to her littered and unwashed bathroom and looked around. Jars with their lids off, cologne bottles lying on their sides, towels on the floor with brown stains on them, shoes and slippers to trip over, the mirror grimy, the toilet gray. I wondered why the seat was up.

The toothbrush was a small blue torpedo standing upright on its stand. It sat on an electrical contact button and I lifted it out. I pressed the button on the side and the brush bounced rapidly up and down. I carried it in to Wanda while it was still "brushing" and handed it to her. She switched it off and yanked out the brush part.

"Save the battery," she said.

I took it from her and examined the head. The top was flat and tapered at the sides; switched on, the surface vibrated up and down. I thought I could feel a slight electrical current.

"The mechanical dildo at last," I said, and handed it back.

"I'm reading," she announced. "Find the man in the boat and take him for a spin."

The word "spin" touched a nerve in my genito-nervous system and I knelt to the job. She hiked her buttocks up and spread herself. With one hand she parted her hair in the middle, exposing a stub of clitoris. I switched on the button.

"Higher, higher!" she grunted, continuing her reading. I held the dildo against her, moving it in all directions and now and then inserting it deep. She had begun to wiggle and grind and the blue torpedo was glistening with dew. All at once she dropped the magazine and grabbed the hygienic device out of my hand. She applied it wickedly to all parts of her cunt; she began to sweat and curse, her eyes shut in a wince.

"The fucking battery's running down," she said, and flung the toothbrush across the room.

"*Kaput*," I said, sinking into the chair opposite her.

She heaved off the sofa, flung off her dress, and marched to the kitchen to make a new drink. I stared at the wall. She weaved slightly when she returned. She still had on her black bra.

"What does it take for you to come?" I asked.

"How about you?" she snapped, wheeling on me. She came close to my chair and leaned over me, her jaw forward.

"Cock," she said. "Big fat purple cock with a crowbar in it." She remained in a leaning position, waiting for a reply. The word "purple" as a modifier of "cock" stirred my penis. I remembered the uncircumcised Southerners in the Army who when the doctor told them to peel it back, exposed a purple head. I remembered the head of the flower of a banana plant like a gigantic prick hanging down from its stalk. I touched my zipper and let it slide open. Wanda still hung there pugnaciously. I found my erection and fished out my balls; the talons of the zipper cut into them but it helped the hard-on.

Wanda sashayed to the sofa with a mock-prostitute walk and lay there with open legs. I came over to her and shoved my erection into her face. Her eyes were half open and she had a trace of a smile on her face. I spat in my hand and coated my member with spit, sliding it through my fingers.

"Is it purple enough?" I asked. I climbed on top of her and tried to shove it in. Her hole was like leather but I pushed and pounded until I gained entry. Her hole was so small; it's funny, I thought, I always remember it as big as a cave. My prick felt as if it were being squeezed by a wrestler. She was taking it fine and beginning to pour sweat and pant.

"Crack the whip, you cunt," I told her. Her eyes were shut again and she began to snap her back, heaving into the air and then jack-knifing down. One minute she was clawing at my testicles, another raking my chest with her nails. I reached behind her and unhooked her brassiere and flung it aside. I hoped I was past the point of losing my erection and began to enjoy myself. I saw blood on my chest when I looked down. Wanda's breasts were dyed crimson with my blood. *My blood*, I thought resentfully. Her face had turned from flushed to clay color and she started to mutter nonsense words.

"Agah! Ahnnah! Ahhnahh! Ughh! Oh shit! Aggah! Unnuhh, Ahnnah!"

She was foaming at the mouth, it looked like, and I wondered if she were having a heart attack or a paroxysm of orgasm. She was having a fight with herself; I felt my prick deflate and grow limp and squashy. Suddenly her eyes flew open and she croaked hoarsely, "Fuck! Goddammit! *Fuck!*"

She arched like a car spring with her belly in the air and stayed there shuddering. My penis fell out and began to retreat into my loins. Her body had turned hot again and she was as slippery as melted soap. Then she collapsed as boneless as a jelly fish. She twisted over onto her belly and I got up.

I walked around the room looking for my glass and shearing sweat off my face and chest with the side of my hand. Wanda turned her head and looked at me like a lizard.

"You did a beautiful fuck, professor," she sneered.

"Agahh!" I answered. I picked up the magazine and sat on the floor, leafing through it.

"Why don't you jag off in it, Ed? You rotten son-of-a-bitch," she said.

"You mean you want a hundred million little Lazerows?" I answered.

"You rotten son-of-a-bitch," she said again.

She was sitting up and I suddenly burst out laughing.

"I wrote a poem," I said, pointing at her chest. "I wrote a poem! Look at your tits!"

Wanda looked down and saw her blood-smeared breasts; she touched them unbelievingly, then leaped up and ran to the bathroom, followed by my laughter. It was a phony kind of laugh that snapped off just as quickly as it began. Wanda took a long time and came back dressed in a mauve sweater and a gray skirt. Her hair was combed and she had put on her favorite white lipstick.

"Well, look at us," I said. "Don't you know it's impolite to get all gussied up when your fellow's naked?"

"You're not naked," she said. "Zip it up. Unless you want to try it on Kaz." She said this in a quiet voice, like an elevator girl announcing the credit department. I got up and walked over to her to slap her in the mouth. I drew my hand back a foot from her face but the look in her eyes froze me in position. "Like a basilisk," I said to myself. Her look was so *kindly*. I sat down stiffly on the sofa and she sat beside me and took my hand.

"Fucking is not our strong point, Ed," she said in a schoolteacherly tone.

"Yes, ma'am," I answered.

"Whatcha want out of me, Ed? Whatcha want?" she asked. I felt that she was really asking and that I was going to try to say what. But something clicked in her mind and she didn't pause for an answer.

"Shall I tell you what I think? I'll tell *you* this time, professor," she said. She moved to the far side of the sofa and grabbed a cigarette and lit it and inhaled deeply.

"You know that English poet you told me about who had to get himself whipped by one woman while he was taking another? You're trying to act like him. Only, who's the other woman? Who's the woman who's getting the meat? The trouble with you is you don't know who or what you're trying to—make love to. The bad thing is you're trying to love and you can't. You can't love so you fuck. But you can't even fuck. You're in real bad trouble because you can't even love yourself. You can't even get a hard-on when you jerk off. It was like squeezing toothpaste out of a busted tube."

"For an electric toothbrush," I said defensively. She ignored me.

"And what the hell do you want out of me? I'll tell you. Lowdown common humiliation, what you call degradation. Plain mother-fucking rottenness. You can't make it with a real honest-to-God whore that you pay money to. Hell, you don't have the guts to let a real English whore strap you to death with a belt so you can take it out on the next one. You say you want love. Well, let me tell you something. You can get love from a whore if you deliver. You can get love from a stone if you stick it in. A woman will love Jack the Ripper and Adolf

94

Hitler rolled into one if he gives it to her. And what do you give? A lot of big words and big ideas. And *this!*"

She had fished out the check I had written her and was waving it back and forth under my nose like a little yellow flag.

"What do you think I want this for?" she asked.

I decided on silence.

"It's for Kaz," she said, and subsided.

"I don't care if it's for the Holy Ghost," I said. "Spare me your idealism." I spoke softly, as if to myself in front of a class. I felt pummeled inside my guts, my stomach fatigued, but my mind turning out sentences which had to be spoken.

"I never could see anything wrong about the blind leading the blind," I said. "Nobody else gives a damn. Or drowning twice before you're saved. Or any of that folksy crap. Because if not that, what? Any attraction is its own excuse; also it's mysterious, it's exciting. And if it's not exciting, you make it exciting. When that fails, you're dead. So the little English poet had himself flogged to get a rod on. Big deal. Maybe a lot of guys commit murder so they can be hanged and have a triple orgasm when their neck is broken by the rope. It takes all kinds of people." I paused a little, dissatisfi d.

"If you want to know the truth," I said, not knowing what truth I was going to come up with, "you're what I need and I'm what you need. Okay, call it humiliation, call it perversion or suicide or Mabel, Agnes, and Becky. You can even call it love, dog eat dog and devil take the hindmost. The point being that I'm being the prostitute and you're my metaphorical pimp. We're feeding on each other's spleens or kidneys or ass-holes and sometimes even our hearts. Genitalia-wise, we're way off base. Maybe that's the fascination. You know, Wanda," I turned and looked at her, "I think you're queer and you think I'm queer but neither one of us is really convinced of the queersville aspect of it. But that's quite a fascination. You and I are only alive in a minor sense, minor private criminals, that's what we are. Publicly we are ethical and right, doing what we have to do to work, working not so much for money as for a place in the echelon. I'm doing a deep dig of the sewer of my life" (I saw her stiffen again), "and I don't mean that to apply to you but to myself. I've got to hit bottom and I can't find it. I need a roadmap to the bottomless pit. The point is that we bring out the worst in each other; it's a fatal attraction, a kind of suicide pact. All we're good at is failure, than which nothing succeeds better than. We've got the Void by the balls. We're dead but not dead enough. We still smell sweet; we haven't even started to stink. We're both too decent for the bottom of the cesspool, too—bourgeois. You're still impressed that Harrington is a gentleman; so am I. You Pollyanna, me Frank Merriwell."

"Speak for yourself, Ed," said Wanda, crossing her legs.

"Okay. I know what I fail at. I'm a failed writer, a failed husband, and a failed fucker. But I want the fruits of my failures. I want to crawl. I want to be shit on." (I started to say *shat* but skipped it.) "I want to get low enough to be able to feel again. I can't feel a goddam thing. I'm numb inside and out. I'm dead but not buried. And how about you? Do you know what you've failed at by any chance? Do you know why we can't shake each other? Because you're shot as much as I am. Numb to the core. Do you know why you can't have an orgasm? Because you goddam well don't want the responsibility of having one!"

I was starting to shout a little and Wanda said, "Dimsdale will take care of that."

"In a pig's ass he will. Only you can take care of that. The noble Freudian piggy-bank can lead the horse to water but he sure as hell can't make her drink." Don't get insulting, I cautioned myself. I moved toward her. "Listen, Wanda," I said, "you've always told me Kaz was impotent. You can level with me. Is he or isn't he? Can't he get it up or does he lose it in mid-air? Was his bag shot off in Korea? What's *his* dilemma?"

"He's never even made a pass," she answered. Her face was impassive and her tone steady.

"Just a pure platonic motorcycle love affair," I said. "The Bobbsey twins with Nazi boots."

"It's none of your goddam affair, Ed, so lay off it. And when are you going to get it through your head that I'm not your private property?"

"That's an idea that never crossed my mind," I said. "I'll think it over. I may even pray on it."

I gave her a mock kiss on the forehead and waved goodbye.

Coming up the carpeted basement stairway I met Kaz coming down. We gave each other a grin and a short palm-out kind of wave. Just like a couple of soldiers. Somehow I felt a weak sensation of relief. The minute I got to my house I switched on the FM. They were playing a Razumovsky Quartet and the cello sawed through my bowels. I made a quick drink and lay down on the sofa to listen.

CHAPTER VIII

On Wednesday I put my class through a crash-program in prosody, giving them fifty minutes of what I had spent thirty years trying to master. I told them the four English meters and *apologized* that they were out of fashion. "You can use them if you want to," I smiled, "but you probably won't. In America they are in disgrace. Prosodically you are free, white, and twenty-one." I had wanted not to say "white" but the Negro basketball player didn't twitch an eyelid. He was taking careful notes, as athletes do, on the intuition that they can't understand anything the first time around. But the red beard with the Indian beads wasn't ready to let any casual reference to color go by without notice. He raised a languid hand.

"Would you explain what you mean by prosodically we are free, white, and twenty-one?" he wanted to know.

"You are . . ." I started to say, glancing down my roster.

"Chris Jaffe," he answered.

"Yes," I said, finding the name. "It's that—well—every nation has to find its own rhythms of life, its own *rhythmus*, to use a good old word, and these life rhythms when they are expressed in words have to find a corresponding rhythm. We can't use the great old English meters here because we're not English. Or if we do use them we've got to process them, sort of naturalize them. So American poets are on their own. We have to start from scratch, say with Whitman and Williams. Otherwise we're marking time or just putting on company manners."

Chris Jaffe wasn't satisfied and said without hand-raising, "*But white,* why white?"

I frowned and decided to take cover. "It's a bad cliché. The white part just means the ruling part. Actually, nobody here is either free *or* white, but a couple of you are twenty-one. What I meant was that American poetry has got to free itself from the tradition, break out of the standard forms of the old masterpieces. Colonial psychology has got to go. Like Henry Miller always says, 'Break out or die.' That applies to everything."

I felt I had won, rather than lost the point, though I had given in. I wanted above all to be accepted by the Outsiders, the radical fringe, and to maintain them as a buffer state between me and the Tremaine Atwoods and the administration, the Oscar Darlings and their slimy little hierarchy. Still, I had to keep a distance from these kids with the beads and the beards and the bells and the anarchist crap they talked—crap because they didn't understand it—Zen and the Trappists and guitar-slingers. I wanted them to know that I would godfather them for free, defend them in the university and the Milo courts of appeal, defend them from ostracism, which to me was as bad a crime as lynching. And yet I pined for their reverence, wishing sometimes that they would call me *sir,* the way I had called professors *sir* in the South when I was their age, the way I had called my father *sir.* I sure as hell didn't want to be their guru (one of the stupider terms they had culled from their illiterate publications) but I wanted their loyalty. After all, I thought with a depressed feeling, am I any different from Janiczek, using the fringe to justify myself? And without them, what nexus would I have with Wanda? I had to become a mayor of Limbo, so to speak, in order to survive.

The bell rang and I asked Jaffe to pass out the purple mimeographed poems which they should annotate for homework and bring to the next meeting. Jaffe handed me a stapled set of their first "submissions."

"That was good, sir," he said, as if reading my mind.

"You prick," I thought, but only smiled and nodded. It suddenly crossed my mind that Inge Amen wasn't in the class and hadn't been. I strode to my office, more quick of pace than I liked, but I am no saunterer. When I walked through my always-open door I turned and saw Inge with her hands in my filing cabinet. I just sat down and looked at her back.

"These files are a sin and a shame," she said without turning. "You must have forgotten the alphabet. And, for Christ's sake, half of these envelopes have never even been opened." She sounded genuinely shocked.

"I could either hire you or sue you," I said, examining her behind. "Or maybe you don't understand that I have about as much interest in those files as I have in the archives of Milo County. Less."

Inge rolled the file drawer shut and said, "Not even a goddam lock. You've letters here from every famous poet in the book; editors, agents, reviewers, the government. How do you know you don't have checks in all that unopened mail? You need a wet nurse with a big fat tit." She sat down in the Good Will throne and crossed her thighs. The idea of a bear-trap crossed my mind.

We chatted a long time about what might and might not be in the eight steel drawers, about the autographed books on the shelves, which, I explained pedantically, librarians called Presentation Copies, about the cacti on the window sill, about the few knick-knacks around. Nothing personal or off-pitch. Without any transaction, she was obviously hired, had hired herself, and I was an office-boy, an employee, or at best a colleague.

"Okay," I said, "I'll give you a key to the door. Have to have mine copied. But you are not to lock this door when I'm in the building. Okay?"

She argued the point a little but gave in. Then she went to the filing cabinet and came back with a packet of lavender letters with a fat rubber band around them.

"These are from a dame called Wanda," she said. "You'd better take them home."

"You're the file clerk," I said, handing them back with a gesture of indifference. But I added, "Make a personal file for stuff like that."

Inge went back and tossed them in the back of a file drawer.

"Well, *she* sounds like an interesting piece," she said with her glassy laugh.

I was screwing my office key off my overloaded key ring; I handed it to Inge and told her to have a duplicate made. She took it as if I were a jeweler handing back her repaired watch. I didn't bother to think how *I* would get into my office.

I left her there, in charge. The phone? Well, there were lots of those strewn around the town, if I decided against going home. I felt an overpowering sleepiness out of the blue and decided I would go to my apartment. I took only the purple mimeographed poems from the class, and said to Inge, "Keep the phone-fires burning." She laughed again; it was her kind of punctuation. I would have to learn the keyboard of her humor, if that's what it was.

Driving, I was by turns comfortably drowsy and brilliantly awake. I was glad that Inge had lighted on my doorstep; maybe an omen of change. God knows I needed a change; if *I* didn't change, I was going to cash in. Something about her kept me from being personally interested. "Anyway," I said out loud, stopping for a red light, "I need a housekeeper." I started to improvise: "I need a manicurist (not really), a B-girl, a kindly aunt, a typist. I need a neighborly nymphomaniac who is also the best double-entry bookkeeper in the Great Plains. I need . . ." But I didn't know what came next, any more than I knew what I needed. "All I know is what I don't need," I ended. "I don't need any of this, town, gown, and hayseed. I don't need Wanda. I don't need Grace." I started a recitation of the people I knew or thought I was involved with, but lost interest. I ran the car quietly against the curb in front of my apartment, cursing about the hundred miles of rubber I had just sheared off. I always know by my parking what shape my mind is in. It was in the shape of shearing-off my wheels.

In the apartment I switched on the FM, first things first, and got a gradual blast of Offenbach, which I left on. I looked in the freezer part of the icebox and took out a box of frozen shrimp. I made a gin on the rocks and went and stared out of the livingroom window. I was beginning to feel a blissful distance from what I called my Situation. My fingers were saying to me: Take a nap, bud, give yourself a break. I began to prop pillows behind me. I began to feel a velvety deliciousness of safe sinking into myself. I felt as if I were being held.

Yes, that was it. I always have to identify remembrances about myself. It was the velvet Victorian sofa. It was the Saturday afternoons when I came home from my fileclerk job and lay on the beautiful piece of furniture and listened to the Met. The operas took hours on the radio, the more hours the better. I was always totally alone, then as now. Robinson Crusoe on Verdi-Puccini Island; or Wagner. In those days, before the slaughter of the Jewish nation, I lapped up Wagner too. Verdi mostly. I never knew the operas, plots or libretti, and hated opera in English. The music was all, the arias especially.

Sun shot through the gorgeous elms into my window. It goldened the big houses down the street and fell on the floor. It crept over me and warmed my face. I turned and hid my eyes from the light and went to sleep.

I dreamed that Wanda was standing naked in my office, riffling through my files. She was stuffing purple letters up her ass which ground them up like a Garbage Dispose-All. In my dream I made a mental note of the spelling. Then the filing cabinet doors were closed, glowing red as if they were in a house on fire. Wanda turned around, but it was Inge. Inge had on a black leather apron like a butcher; she handed me a 3 x 5 index card which said SEX CUBES and tore it up and laid it in my lap. My lap was full of ashes and I, or someone, was getting a huge purple hard-on. In the red plush chair sat Kaz, reading one of my books on poems. And Oscar Darling came through the door, flicking his tongue into Kaz's mouth from a great distance; Kaz kept biting it off and spitting it on the floor. The pieces turned into crickets that hopped all over the office.

I shook myself awake and continued to listen to Offenbach. Dreams don't take long. It was starting to be a nightmare, I told myself, but didn't get that far. I took my drink to the kitchen and boiled water for the shrimp. I didn't know how to make decent rice, which I wanted, and took out horseradish and tomato ketchup and Louisiana Hot Sauce. I went back to the livingroom, becoming twilit, and looked up Amen in the phonebook. Should I call her? Why?

Without knowing what I would say or why I was making the call, I was dialing her number. She picked up the phone at the first ring. I had a sudden flash of pure panic and hung up. I didn't know how to *identify* myself.

CHAPTER IX

Thursday was a no-teaching day. I got up to the sound of the FM, which was reciting Dylan Thomas intoning *Fern Hill.* "My God, Dylan Thomas at ten o'clock in the morning," I said out loud. I noticed that I was beginning to talk aloud lately but thought that had a kind of charm. "Dylan Thomas, that phony, that BBC Third Programme ham-slicer, that ass-pincher." Like all the poets of my vintage I had known Dylan (as poet-professors like to call him) for about five days and had admired his "life-style." "The last of the bounders," I said, working myself into a lecture. "Wrote six, maybe seven good poems and staked his reputation on his ability to insult the Tremaine Atwoods of this world by saying *fuck* to their wives and goosing their students. The forerunner of the Beatles, the poet as publicity agent for his little old self." I heard the poem out, however, sitting down to listen. A wild archaic applause greeted the end of the poem, and the announcer, a college student at Milo, said in Hail Mary tones that that was Dylan Thomas reading *in his own voice.* This was followed by a commercial from Myron's Food Mart which was advertising Tid-Bits for the Carriage Trade. I went to the bathroom. I was running low on toilet paper and decided to pay Myron's a visit. "To the schlock-shop," I said.

At Myron's I was always nervous. The checkers and proprietor knew me from my busted marriage and missed the big fat checks I used to send them once a month. They greeted me strangely. I was in such a hurry that I brushed by a tower of bottled prune juice and a quart smashed on the floor. One of the part-owners made his appearance in a white coat. "Sorry, Nate," I said to him. "Put it on my tab."

"You've got to be kidding," said Nate, while a polite Negro did the mopping up. Nate slapped me lightly on the shoulder and went back to another aisle. My hands were shaking. I thought I should buy something expensive and picked out a boned turkey from the freezer. To this I added chrysanthemums, Port Salut, and wine vinegar. As I turned the corner where the paper items were stacked I ran my cart into Irene Yamashiro's, which was overflowing with a rainbow of vegetables.

After our little laugh Irene asked me to stop by her house for the last roses, yellow and tea, but I begged off.

"I'm due at the office," I told her, and began to wonder if Inge was there, digging her arms into my past. I drove back to my apartment and stuck the turkey in the freezer (file it, I thought) and then phoned the office. It felt strange to be calling myself and I had to look up my own number.

"Dr. Lazerow's office," said Inge.

I laughed and said, "I just wanted to see how you answered the phone. I have to come down for something." I couldn't even think of an object for the verb. Might as well take the flowers too, I thought.

"Office flowers," I said, laying the bunch on the desk. Inge seemed a little disconcerted by the gesture and gave her tinkly laugh. It was a strange laugh, a laugh of non-commitment, a little like wind-chimes. She went on her own to the English office and borrowed a vase and filled it somewhere. I saw that my old summer mail now lay open in three neat piles on my desk: personal requests in one pile, stuff having to do with copyrights and permissions in another, and printed matter separately. I riffled the third pile and dropped it in the trash.

"I'm going to bring you up to date whether you like it or not," Inge said, snipping off a couple of the flower stems. I wasn't sure whether I did like it.

"Most people love their mailman," I said. "Me, I could cheerfully shoot the son-of-a-bitch." Inge was keenly curious about this devil-may-care unconcern about correspondence and thought it might be a characteristic of writers. "Not writers, poets," I told her cryptically. I reluctantly and obediently read the letters and scratched notations on the tops. Inge would write the answers herself, I was given to understand.

"Is there anything you *won't* do for me?" I asked. She answered again with her wind-chime laugh. The thought of dialing Wanda crossed my mind but vanished without a trace of a pang.

There was a funny old Victorian hotel near the railroad station, with an old-fashioned bar and grill. "Let's get a hamburger and a martini," I said. Inge seemed pleased but declined the booze. We drove the six blocks almost silently; she tried to cross her legs but the dashboard was too low and she sat sideways, looking at me while I made comments about the Milo campus architecture. They were tearing down a beautiful 1890 Byzantine building, to be replaced by "one of those Bauhaus glass prisons for the well-dressed administrative cockroaches," I informed her. I enjoy acting as a guide and am ready with information, misinformation, and analysis at the drop of a hat.

"*Anyways*, they restored this little old hotel nicely, even if it *is* for their phony centennial. They've got a state bedroom all draped in red velvet, with two fireplaces and a brass bedwarmer. All it needs is Abraham Lincoln and his frigid wife."

I was starting my second martini and Inge was sipping black coffee when the hamburgers came.

"I don't beat around the bush," she said. "Tell me about yourself. I mean you. I'll ask you the standard question; I've heard it a thousand times; what are you doing in Milo? How come you aren't in New York or Chicago or Rome? What are you hiding from?"

"You really come in swinging," I answered. "What the hell

are you up to? Do you want to write my biography? Okay, write it." And I added, "You know, Inge, I've just barely clapped eyes on you, so to speak, but it doesn't strike me that you're making a pass at me. I think you're on the level."

"Are you one of those guys who thinks every woman has got the hots for him?" she asked.

"Not me," I answered. "I've missed too often; I'm even scared of women in a way. You don't seem to mind some straight talk . . ." I almost said *man-to-man*. I leaned over a little and lowered my voice. "Well, Christ, I can't come inside a woman anymore."

Inge's eyes widened. "Who can you come inside of?" she laughed.

"And," I added, "I'm not queer. But," I added with a coy chuckle, "some of my best friends are queers. How about you?"

Inge stirred impatiently. "I'll tell you sometime," she said. "I had a typical nightmare marriage, or maybe not so typical. The bastard forced me into wife-swapping. He even took movies. To sell. We were in Denver when they caught him with the films. He's got another year in jail."

I whistled and asked how she came out on the arrest. It crossed my mind that she was lying to impress me. I was right.

"Don't believe any of that crap," she said. "Now answer me some stock questions. What are you doing here?"

We spent the good part of the afternoon in the bar and grill, me adding up martinis and Inge drinking cup after cup of black coffee. Altogether I felt quiet and fairly sober.

"So on the whole," I said to the table, "I came to Milo to die, I guess, like the old mastodons. What was finished was my happiness. You can't write if it doesn't knock you out. Because it's a process of joy, even of ecstasy. My wife had turned into a battle-ax, I couldn't write poetry, I took up painting and hiding Petri sherry in the woodpile, I played with myself and sent away for verboten books, I was sleepless and had at least one nightmare a night, the house was full of dogs and cats and field mice and faculty wives, I was turning into a phony mystic—mysticism and onanism go hand in hand—I wrote insulting

107

notes to every writer I knew, and wherever I went I hated it, and when I came home I hated that even worse. I was starting to think about suicide actually or even joining the Army if they'd have somebody my age, but opted for sherry instead. Then I tangled with this Wanda bitch." I paused.

"What about her?" asked Inge.

"I wanted to use her for a fucking-block, like the French say, a *machine à plaisir*. With her I could imagine I was in hell, and I was and am. She helped me wipe the slate clean of every value I'd ever had or heard of. Imagine, I felt *grateful* for that."

"I read her letters," said Inge. "She doesn't sound too bad. Just in the usual trouble."

"Usual?" I asked.

"She sounds like one of those females who can give you everything but love, and that's as bad as a dose of clap."

I speculated then on whether poisoned love came ready-made or whether it had to be concocted. The idea of poison impressed me; I sure as hell *felt* poisoned.

"But in a case like this," I said, "I'm not sure I want to be cured. I'm not sure I could live without the pain. Take everything, a saint once prayed, but spare me my suffering. And I'm not normally a sufferer; I love happiness; I have a sensual love of happiness. I like to feel up happiness like it was a woman. Everything makes me happy, or used to. All my life I've had a gift for being idiotically ecstatic over nothing. My God, even this suffering, or whatever the hell it is, makes me feel good. Because at least it makes me feel. I'm scared to death of losing my sense of touch. Everything I've ever known I've *felt*. Maybe my brain is in my fingertips."

Inge got serious. "If you don't shake that woman . . .," she started. "Maybe it's none of my business but she's just a black widow. You know how they handle their mates. It ain't her fault; it's her nature. Your nature ought to have some self-protection in it. Can't you just turn around and walk off? She'd be as glad as you would. You're an artist. You're famous. I sound like a stupid preacher, but people expect things of you. She's like an untrained parrot in a cage and you're the cuttlebone." She stopped and then said, "But if you like it, live it up."

"The black widow image adds up," I said, finishing my drink. "I'll take you back to the office."

"No, take me home," she said. "I'll make you one more drink and send you on your way." Fine, but I insisted on stopping by at the office, without knowing why. Yes, the phone was ringing wildly and I grabbed it.

"Where the hell have you been?" growled Wanda. I felt a release, as if a doctor had just taken a cast off my foot.

"Having lunch and a few with my secretary," I answered gaily.

"Well, blow the man down!" Wanda exclaimed sarcastically. "You sure you haven't been getting a little gash?" I couldn't tell whether she was really upset; she wanted to stop by my place for a drink. "Make it at four-thirty," I said; it was the first time I had ever postponed her.

"Aren't, we, getting, serious," she said with commas and added, "I'll wait for you." She hung up. That must have meant that she would be at my apartment before I got there. I went out to the car jauntily and told Inge about the call.

"Or did you call *her*?" asked Inge.

Milo is filled with tiny frame houses, some with a single room and a kitchen, some with two or three rooms. I theorize that they belong to some pioneer phase of architecture, or maybe the local Slavic influence had been at work. In the winter I would imagine, driving down one of these quaint streets, that I was in Dostoievski-land. Inge owned one of these three-room cottages, painted white with a black trim. The lawn and sidewalk were deep with leaves. We kicked our way to the front door, which like most doors in Milo was unlocked.

The furniture was all a corny, heavy Swiss-chalet type, with two enormous carved chairs which reminded me of the Bismarck Museum I had walked through in the Buchenwald. There was laundry hanging in the kitchen and I brushed under it to help Inge make the drinks. One thing I liked about her, she didn't apologize about anything or make a big deal about her furnishings or her appearance. I sat on the sofa in the livingroom with my drink and she took one of the big carved chairs. She too had a drink and was smoking and looked really feminine, I thought. She started asking my opinion of writers and authors, some of them strange ones: Hergesheimer, Sinclair Lewis, Cabell, Cardinal Newman, Sartre, Gogol, Winston Churchill, E. E. Cummings, Willa Cather. I answered in epigrams; most of my views about writers had become "encapsulated" by now—I had seen that word in the newspaper and was trying to come to a decision about it.

At the door she shook hands with me and laughed. She's a strange one, I thought.

I drove home more slowly than I usually did, more slowly than when I was going to a rendezvous with—the Black Widow; what a tag! Sometimes en route to Wanda's I screamed my tires like a high-school punk. However, I parked neatly and walked casually up the walk to my door. There was Wanda with a home-made club sandwich in front of her and a long brown drink. Quite an oral character, I thought.

"What's her name?" she asked.

"Inge, Inge Ah-men. Like halleluia. Why?" I asked in return. I went and made myself a drink without waiting for an answer.

"I mean," I said, when I had sat down opposite her, "you aren't jealous by any manner of means?"

"How the hell do I know?" said Wanda, settling back with her drink. "But I got a funny feeling about this one. I got a feeling she's going to use you. Like she can give you something I haven't got. You know, Ed, I know my faults and there's lots I don't know how to give."

"She said something like that herself," I said without thinking. Wanda pounced on my sentence.

"Do you mean you were talking about me? If I thought you were talking about me to that whatever the hell she is, I'd rip you to pieces. You blab about every snatch you've ever laid a hand on, but if you do that about me I'll kill you." She got up and started striding around like a ship captain in a TV movie.

I had no choice but to lie. "What I mean is that, certainly, we were talking about *me,* but, for God's sake, I didn't mention names or pass out any lists of my greater and lesser conquests."

I'm not doing too good, I thought.

"Okay, let's have it," said Wanda. "Names or no names, what did you say about me? Did you draw her a picture of our mutual masturbation society or what? Did you tell her your balls are tattooed? You stinking bastard, if you tell that bitch or anybody else about what goes on in private I'll get you for keeps." She came close to me and added, "Me and Kaz both!"

"A little perspective, a little perspective," I said without too much conviction. "Don't go jumping all over yourself. I can talk about *me* without involving others, I hope. I'm not completely inarticulate. And not only that . . ." I tried to raise a little indignation, "I think I'm free to discuss my problems with any goddam soul I please. You'll just have to trust my judgment a little bit."

But Wanda was way ahead of me. "What did you tell her about me? Let's have it." And as a non sequitur she pushed her glass under my nose and said, "Fix it."

She followed me to the kitchen with her hand on my shoulder. It might have been a mock gesture of authority or it might have been the real thing. The Black Widow's pulling her boots on, I thought foolishly.

"Okay," I said. "Okay, okay. I talked about my—what you call it, dilemma. You got to admit I have one of those. A big fat dilemma, with sugar on it. *Mit schlag* and heaps of whipping cream." I was stalling.

"Go on," said Wanda, "I'm creaming all over myself."

"So I told her about my marriage and my screwing around and my multifoliate forms of bankruptcy." I was hiding behind words, words that weren't calculated to amuse her at that. "Ending up with my dream of suicide or drowning in a butt of sack." The literary stuff, I knew, would add fuel to her fire. I was right. She planted herself in front of me and threw the contents of her glass right in my face, hard. One of the ice cubes struck me in the forehead. Just like David and Goliath, crossed my mind, and I slapped her with all my might across the mouth. I thought I saw her unsheathing her nails and I slapped her again. Then again. I heard myself saying, "Get out. Get out of here. Get out of here and don't come back. Get out of here, you, you . . ." but I couldn't think of the proper word to ticket her on her journey, and she sank down on the sofa, sobbing and panting.

Like a somnambulist, I went to make her a new drink. When I came back she had gone. I looked out of the window. The Volvo was gone. I sat down on the sofa, dazed, and began to drink her drink. I'd really socked her; my hand hurt. The idea of striking a woman was so foreign to my being that my mind stood still. I went to look at myself in the hall mirror. No blood. I got up and sat down twenty times. I didn't feel sorry or glad, only amazed, only a little lower than usual but a little firmer too. Manly, crossed my mind; is it manly to hit a woman or manly not to; where do you draw the line? And what's manliness got to do with it, or chivalry, or any of that shit. When a female douses you in the face with a glass of booze are you supposed to stand there and take it? But if you get into that circle of hell, I told myself, you can't exactly expect champagne and roses. I turned on the FM automatically. They were beginning a supper program that turned my stomach. The announcer called it "Candlelight and Wedgwood" and gave the information that Hinsdale & Eisenbray, Milo's fashionable department store, had just received a shipment of Spode and Wedgwood "duplicates" which would be taken as genuine by even museum experts. Then they started to play a soft and highly orchestrated version of the soundtrack of *The Student Prince*. I kept it on, letting my mind unwind and come to a dead stop. I jumped when the phone rang: "Who the hell could that be?"

"I apologize," said Wanda, and hung up.

CHAPTER X

ϾϿ To my surprise, when I entered my class on Friday, Bumpy and Irene were in the first row, flanking Marya Hinsdale. Bumpy got up and said, "Good, good morning, Ed." She was probably the only person in the world who would give you two "goods" for one "morning." "You must know Marya? Hinsdale?" I felt speechless.

"Why yes, we've met." I said it firmly and put out my hand. We shook hands, absurdly, I thought.

"Do you care if I sit in today?" she asked. "I've heard so much about your class." She smiled a beautiful cautious smile while I said, "You come when you like; everybody does in this class. It's an anti-discipline discipline."

Inge came in and sat near the window on the aisle. She flicked me a glance and started writing something in a note-book. I felt nervous and excited; I leaned over my desk and said to Bumpy, "That was at your house where Mrs. Hinsdale was, wasn't it?" I meant the garden party long ago where I had first seen her and wanted her. It was because of that that I had unintentionally frightened her off, because of that that I had achieved my divorce. I knew I was in love with her and knew I could never undo the impression of demonic poet that I had made. But what was she doing here? She was married again to that department store prick, living in an interior decorator's paradise in one of those mansions with a circular driveway and three-story columns and the only swimming pool in Milo. Bored, I thought; she's bored. Okay, I'll bore her in my own sweet way. Everyone had gathered and I went and shut the door. I can't teach with the door open, no matter what the temperature is.

"I'm not ready with your poems today," I started. "I've read them but they didn't fall into a pattern. They will. There were good lines here and there; that happens and it's a good thing. But there's no one poem either good enough or bad enough to single out to make into a sermon. So I'll keep these and wait for the next batch. Okay? So instead of the poems I want to just talk about the Process, about the artist and how he gets that way. This is important. Agree or disagree, that's up to you."

As a professor I am no strider and no blackboard artist. I hate the eccentric professor with a passion. My method is simply conversation, talking until I feel myself being carried away by my convictions or, what is better, by some new idea which gives birth to itself in my head while I am in full career. Standing, I lean on the back of a chair, sometimes because I feel I am trembling, as I was now, either from yesterday's martinis or because of some higher excitement. I was leaning on the back of the oak chair, looking at the wall in the back of the room, over the heads of the class.

"In the first place, this is a room where you turn back the clock. In here your education is practically a matter of indifference. How much you know will never make you write a poem, and the more you know the more you will have to overcome. Now, obviously education is a great and desired accomplishment of the human psyche. But creativity can take education or leave it. That is a shocking fact to some of you who are already highly educated . . ." That was meant for Bumpy in a way. "And to those of you, which is most of you, who are not educated, or *over*educated, you will be in a position to exploit—well, to lay it on the line, your *ignorance*. Because, as every child knows, some of the greatest poets were

114

not educated men, and some of the greatest poetry in the world is anonymous and was composed by people who couldn't read or write. The image of the poet as blind man is essential to you and to everyone who loves or creates it. His blindness is, you might say, self-induced. The poet is a man with the fresh faculties of a child. So of course the world looks at him as childish, especially our kind of world where maturity is measured by material success or athleticism—any kind of athleticism, physical, political, or sexual. But especially financial. Too bad, but we do live in the most brazenly financial culture in all of history. Hence all our phony idealisms; we can't stand to look in the mirror. We are patriotic as much because we are rich as because we are guilty."

I figured that I might be getting a little too lofty and stopped for a second.

"I'm an English professor here," I started up again. "Therefore I teach literature as well as writing. But the two have nothing to do with each other, except at a tangent. The literature process is a history lesson, an accumulation of cultural riches of the past. Every textbook is a museum; there's nothing wrong with that; museums are great as long as you know they are mausoleums, cemeteries. The Greeks called them the necropolis, city of the dead. You have to make sure whether you are in the city of the dead or in the city of the living. Out that door," I pointed, "is the city of the dead. Inside here is the city of the living. I'm talking about poetry, about art, about the artist. Writing is a process of life; it's natural, universal, and absolutely necessary. Any people in history who denied the arts and prevented creativity were writing their own obituary. Look at Nazi Germany, whose only art was massacre, scientific massacre at that. Not one shred of poetry, not one painting, not one phrase of music, not even a statue survives from that cemetery. Killing off their artists was an act of colossal suicide. But in this country, for better or for worse, we've given everybody a screwdriver to take the lid off Pandora's box. We're living in the midst of the wildest artistic chaos in history; ours is more like a lunatic asylum than a graveyard but at least it's alive, crawling with energy, screaming its head off.

We've put the drawings of children, psychotics, and prehistoric Africans on a par with Leonardo and Picasso. This is right. It's got to be. We have erased the time mystique once and for all, as far as creativity goes; child or genius become interchangeable terms; past and present become synonymous. Our only esthetic is that there is no future."

I paused again, wondering how much of this was getting across, and why. If I was talking to Marya, I wondered how she was taking it, whether I was frightening her or making her feel my intensity.

"You weigh what I say. A teacher is always in a minority position in a class anyhow; you've got the drop on me because I *am* a teacher and therefore *you* know better. There's something in that. But don't forget that in this crazy kind of class I am not a teacher, I'm an anti-teacher. When I come into the door I dispute the outside, I'm an enemy of the literati and the professoriat. Maybe there should be no such class. But there is. We're it and I'm the talker."

I stopped to light a cigarette and flicked my eyes across the front row. Marya was looking down; I thought her hands were clenched. I went on.

"The hard thing to say is that as teacher I am not a writer; as writer I am not a teacher. Writing is solitary, absolutely between you and your piece of paper. Not an act of self-expression but of self-love, an act of exclusion, so to speak. Whatever happens to your poem when you are done with it, when you have actually accomplished one, is an afterlife, whether the poem ends in the trash basket or in the most famous anthologies in the world. I am just putting myself on record, to introduce myself and to let you in on this paradox. A literature professor is not a writer in our sense; he may turn out book after book, even great books, but they will never be the kinds of books we intend to write. After all a university is a closed world, a cloister; it is not and can't ever be the world. Only in this room is the world of now let in. Why do universities let us writers in? Don't ask me," I chuckled, "but it's a fine thing for writers that they do."

Chris Jaffe raised his hand, stroking his beard with the other.

"Wouldn't it be better, more authentic, just to be *in* the world, just to be outside?" he asked.

"That's for each to decide," I answered. "You don't have to be here. Neither do I. The prison is voluntary; you can walk out whenever you like. Me too. But I want to be here; it solves certain of my—dilemmas. It may or may not solve yours. What would I do on the street? Well, I could hope for handouts and get a few. I could marry a rich woman or try to write best-seller novels. That stuff doesn't interest me. This more or less monastic life has an—ambience for me. I admire scholarship but can't handle it. I love to be near a library, a real one, and ours is pretty real. And I'd rather hear people talking about Chaucer than about income tax. Anyhow, that's not the point. The point is poetry. Yet that covers two worlds, the inner cut-off isolate life of creation and the outside consequences. Our society is hostile to poets; that's the oldest cliché in the book. And yet it needs them and asks for them and makes them come out in the open, sometimes like vermin. Our friendly hostile society smokes us out. So look at me! *Smoked poet!*"

I am not a great teacher or lecturer but I have the confidence of talking off the cuff, the feeling that I will get through. I toss all my ideas on the table at once, a bad practice for a teacher, I know, instead of letting the class imbibe a little at a time. On the other hand I feel that I have no choice, no other method.

"I'm trying to acquaint you with a real dichotomy, the split between culture and creation. It's the difference between a masterpiece and the person looking at it. The masterpiece may or may not be a masterpiece, because that's for the spectator, the looker, to decide. Society, culture, have already decided. Curators have already paid a million dollars for the picture and have built a special niche in the wall for it. The wall is surrounded with guards with guns and live ammunition. Then some young painter walks up through the crowd worshipping at the shrine and says: 'That painting is dreck.' Is he right or wrong, or does that matter? Of course he is in danger of being rushed off for disturbing the peace of the masterpiece. Maybe he has implanted the idea *in the picture itself* that its time has

117

come and it had better get ready for the journey to the basement or the attic. If you read the history of art you will discover that that is the history of art. And necessarily. Every living generation has the obligation—excuse me for sounding so pontifical—to question the standards of all other generations, and if need be to toss them overboard. And this is the right of the artist, whether he writes or paints or not."

It was Bumpy's turn to raise her hand. "Do you mean that artists—writers—have to be critics?" She gave me a gay prefrontal-lobotomy kind of smile.

"Yes," I said. "Artists are the critics, really. They don't like to write criticism or to put the masterpieces on the spot; but what they create is the ultimate criticism of the past, favorable or unfavorable. The Victorian critic-poet who said that art is a criticism of life was ridiculous. Art is a criticism of art, that's all. Though obviously it's more than that."

I was getting into deep water and was afraid I might lose everybody, and shifted my tack.

"I'm trying to tell you something I think you know but which nobody ever says. I'm trying to tell you the simplicity of the thing. I don't mean that I've made the great discovery that Plato and Aristotle missed—or maybe I do—but I hope to be able to let you take the curse off the cemetery view of poetry, which is that poetry belongs in cemeteries. Let's just say that poetry that has ended up in the cemetery has earned its reward. But for the poetry that walks around like things that go bump in the night, that's another kettle of fish." I enjoy "mixing metaphors" because I don't believe there is any such thing. A metaphor by definition *is* mixed; what else is it? I found myself looking at Marya who this time was looking back at me. She was frowning slightly.

"Now the big discovery is that what you are taught about poetry outside the door is irrelevant. Because you are never taught about poetry at all. You are taught what books the poet read and what stories he heard at his mother's knee. You are taught his similarities to other poets of his time, perhaps. You are taught who 'influenced' him and whom he 'influenced.' You are taught his chapter in the history of ideas—as if ideas could have a history. And you are taught how great a thing it is to be poet, how all nations and cultures have revered poets and poetry above life itself. Most of which is pure scholarly phantasy and moralizing and, shall we say, garbage. What you are never taught is the truth, that poetry is a sub-language, the contents of which are almost universally infantile, trivial, second-hand, and second-rate. But in spite of that, it is and always has been one of the greatest arts and achievements of the human mind."

I thought I deserved a stop after that barrage and went and yanked a window higher, put out a cigarette and lit a new one. I was still using the desk drawer and wished I had brought an ashtray, because of Marya.

Nobody said anything and I went on. "It's a separate language, a language all its own. But do you think what is said in French is any different from what is said in English or German or Swahili or Yiddish? Cultural differences, okay, but meanings, no. Actually there *are* differences in poetry, but *this* is something you are never taught, something that is truly unteachable. But let's skip that for now." I paused to come to my actual lesson for the day. I noticed that the athletes had stopped writing, and wondered what a jumble of signals I had sent them so far.

"Okay," I said, "write this down. It's the only thing you have to write down in this course. It's this: poetry is a sub-language which communicates anything by way of discarded meanings." I waited and I repeated it. "In other words, it doesn't matter what poetry is communicating: I love you, I hate you, God is good, God is a rat, my country 'tis of thee, ripeness is all—anything. You all have to make up your minds that I am not interested in your ideas and that you can have the most platitudinous ideas in history and still write a great poem. Keep your abstractions for your philosophy professor, your math and physics professor, your preacher, your father when he sends you a check. But dig your hands into a bucket of words, fall in love with words, or out of love, as the case may be. And *steer clear of the dictionary*. The dictionary is the cemetery of poetry; that's all it is. As far as the dictionary is concerned,

119

when it comes to poetry, it's a pharmacopoeia for the rational mind. Please leave your rational mind at home when you come to this class; it will only get in your way. This is not a symposium or a colloquium or a Be-In and End-In. It's a place where maybe words can come alive or be reborn. And that depends on you."

I said I would leave it at that for now and asked for questions. The queer lad with the white hair wanted to know more about the "ineffable" which I had passed over mysteriously. I told him to wait; it was a matter of "percepts" and involved a nexus between pre-language and incised language, a question, I said, of the paradox of the child-bed and the cemetery stone. I thought that sounded pretty good and made a certain sense; the lad subsided.

One of the sorority girls asked about the mimeograph stencils.

Irene Yamashiro asked if, because of what I had said, the poet was therefore devoid of intellectual responsibility. "I mean, if I understand you," she said, "can he be totally unrelated to his world and still be a great poet?"

I thought a moment, though I knew what I wanted to say. I should give her the courtesy of seeming to think her question over.

"You see," I answered, "we live in this badly interrelated world, where we are taught to be guilty unless we participate in the newspaper, the TV, education, politics, and so on. And supposedly artists have no choices: to be part of this, what I think of as a bad interrelationship, or to divorce themselves from it and hole up in their ivory tower. But actually, I don't believe in the question because it has hidden premises. Do we have to judge Mozart by his politics or Bach by his religion? We judge their music. Of course it's true that a man is a product of his times, but mostly in unseen, unthought ways. A great artist may be affected more by a piece of furniture in his room than by wars raging all over the world. If I hadn't been vaccinated when I was five maybe I would have died of smallpox; that makes me a twentieth-century man. My literary sensibility is also determined by the fact that I live in an age of freedom of books; I grew up reading what I chose. Well, how can I *not* be related to my own time? It's a logical impossibility. But how I relate, to use the jargon, that's certainly a private affair." I hadn't let her off the hook enough and added, "For example, I'm a Jew. A hundred years ago I would never have been admitted to a university, even an American university. Maybe I would never have seen any book except the Old Testament. Maybe I would have been a poet but I don't think so."

I was not really interested in more discussion and asked Gilchrist, "the monk," to pick up the new manuscripts for duplicating. Then I dismissed the class. I went out first and waited for the faculty wives and Marya. They were going for coffee at the student union and asked me to join them. I looked at Marya and said of course. Could I stop by the office for a minute?

"You have a long-distance call," Inge told me when she came in, and handed me a slip of paper. "It's from Dick Wigglesworth. Is he the poet?"

"God," I said, "I wonder what kind of self-advertising campaign he's putting on this time." I was worried that if I made the call now, Marya might slip through my fingers again.

"It's probably some kind of goddam freedom march or Liberate Pot Week or flag-burning. I'll call when I get back." Inge told me she liked my speech in class and went to her files. I said I'd see her in a little bit.

The huge panes of blue plate glass loomed over us as we tinkered with our coffee in the student lounge. Irene had gone to meet her husband for lunch, after saying that her head was swimming from everything I had talked about in class.

"I've told Marya she ought to take your class," Bumpy said. "She's spending a fortune on that Be A Great Novelist course and getting nowhere."

"Are you?" I asked, facing Marya.

"Am I what?" she laughed.

"Taking the course? Spending a fortune? Getting nowhere?"

"Maybe all three," she answered. "It's discouraging but I may be learning."

"But learning to write for money? It doesn't add up. I know something about that course. You could go to Harvard for what it costs. And they can't teach you anything except how to get into *Feminine Day*. Why seriously, Marya . . ." I paused a second; it was the first time I had ever called her by her first name and she looked at me with a trace of fright. "Don't you know that that kind of writing is really harmful? It can ruin your voice, so to speak. But you have no reason to learn to write bad stuff, if you want to write. Why, it's fantastic."

She seemed uneasy, even harassed, and I looked to Bumpy for help.

Bumpy put on her mock-despairing mask. "That's Marya," she said. "Pulling herself down."

Marya said, "But I don't know that I have any talent at all. And I want to write and publish where I can prove to myself that I can at least get paid for my work. Maybe only to assert myself, to discover that sense of liberation; well, to find myself."

"Oh no," I said, "but not that way. That's not the road. What earthly satisfaction could you get out of writing *down* to the supermarket set. Why those are the readers that *hate* writers. They are your natural enemy. What's the point in trying to appease them? They have fifty thousand kinds of opium already."

Bumpy, the great explainer, took over, showing her prize-winning teeth (as I thought of them) and extending her arm in her mock presidential gesture.

"Marya," she said, "is unhappy. Marya is looking for an ivory tower of her own. She wants to write to keep the country club at bay, and maybe her husband. They'd all be intimidated by her name in print. It's just blackmail. She wants to scare the upper-upper-middle-middle-class-class. Marya?"

"I want to write," said Marya. "I think that kind of writing takes skill and I don't think it's dishonest. Maybe it's not Flaubert or James Joyce but it's the level I'm after."

"Listen," I said in a low voice, "let me read something you've done and let me see what the Great Novelists course said about it. Will you let me?"

"I want to think about it," she said. "I'd be ashamed to . . ."

"I don't mean to brag or anything like that," I said, "but the Novelists course asked me to be one of their readers. I didn't want anything to do with it. I know half the people on their board and I know their work. I'd give you honest criticism and let it go at that. It would mean something to me."

She looked at me quizzically and asked for time to think it over. I apologized for my vehemence and the talk changed to chatter about the faculty. Bumpy announced that she was going to one of Brom's most bohemian parties on Saturday to see if she could hire one of the Jamaicans. "House boys are back," she pronounced, "thanks to the university." Suddenly she flustered to her feet and made a flamboyant goodbye, leaving Marya and me alone.

Marya sat silent and nervous for a while and then said she had to go to the bookstore. I said I had to check on some books I had ordered and asked to walk across the campus with her. She thought and accepted.

"I'd like you to have a copy of this," I said to Marya in the bookstore. I was looking at the poetry shelves; she was looking at short story collections. It was a copy of one of my books of poems that I handed her. "I'll even autograph it," I joked.

"But that is awfully nice," she said, "but I can't accept a gift like that. I just can't; it's ungrateful, I know, but it's too involved. I really can't explain it." She laughed and added, "Maybe I'll have to think about that too. And maybe I'll say yes to both offers. But not today, please."

I was hurt but said I thought I understood and put the book back. Marya had found two books she wanted and said she must leave for some appointment. She put out her hand and thanked me for the class and for the coffee. I held her hand gratefully and a little too long; she had regained her composure now that she was leaving and gave me a full rich smile which made my heart ache. I begged her to come to class again and to think over my suggestion about her stories.

I watched her go to the counter and pay for her books, hoping she would turn around. She actually did and gave me a farewell smile. That does it, I thought. I waited a few minutes and went to the counter and purchased my own book. The proprietor joked about that. I would have to figure out how to send her the book and what to inscribe in it that wouldn't frighten her again. Maybe Bumpy would deliver it to her? I didn't want Marya's husband putting the bite on her, nor did I want any clandestine giving and taking. Not any more. Not ever again.

CHAPTER XI

Be it said that Richard Wigglesworth was a direct descendant of the infamous poetaster Michael of the witch-burning era. Dick Wigglesworth prided himself not so much on the verses of his ancestor as on the physical and intellectual resemblance. I had no particular feeling about Wigg, as poets called him, except envy. Not envy for his poetry, which I thought wooden and fake and lacking in "the poetry of" anything he wrote about, but envy for his genius for publicity. Whenever there was a Cause, Wigg could be seen on the platform, rolling his eyes and dealing out volumes of righteous indignation. He made it a point to become a personal friend, if possible, of every renowned author in the world or at least to mount a massive correspondence with those who ignored his physical presence. He was handy with conversions. When the real news of the German death camps became known after the Second War, Wigg publicly converted to Judaism and wrote Hasidic poems. He even forced his wife, Christine Galloway, the travel writer and bellelettrist, to shave her head and wear a *shaytl*. They were divorced not long after. Following a Fulbright to Ahmedabad he converted to the Jain religion and wore a gauze mask over his face to prevent inhalation of gnats and other more minute insectivora. His picture appeared frequently in the New York papers, partly because of his handsomely tailored dhoti, to which he added a gold-braided Nehru hat. No one could say he was not a striking figure, and his poetry readings, which began and ended with the Hindu prayer-bow, were always mobbed. At the same time he kept two orgone boxes in his apartment, while importing *pan* from Bombay, the scarlet juice of which he spat into marvelous brass Persian spittoons. The last I had heard about Wigg was that he had become a Bahai and was paying special homage to the Moslem altar.

I put the call through and got Wigg immediately. Inge stopped her filing and sorting to listen.

"Wigg, this is Edsel," I said. "What's this I hear about you becoming some kind of health nut?"

Wigg had no sense of humor of any description and ignored the question.

"This is serious, Ed," he answered. "We're putting on a suicide demonstration against the war. Using the technique of the Buddhist monks—burning by gasoline. I even think we can get some napalm! We're working on it. Is your phone on a switchboard?" I assured him it wasn't, though I didn't know.

"It's going to be in front of Independence Hall. Philly. We want every good poet in the country to be there . . ."

"And participate?" I asked, unbelieving. "Who are you going to barbecue?" I asked.

"Listen, Edsel, this isn't funny. It's literally a question of life and death. We've got practically every poet in the living anthology and six novelists and the whole New York School of painters. But the poets are the ones, naturally."

"Naturally what?" I asked.

"For the suicide protest. By lot. The poets' names will be put in a plexiglas Air Force ball-turret from the Second World War. We've already got one. A little child is going to pick out a name. We don't know whose child yet. Do you think it should be a girl? I do. She'll be wrapped in the American flag, like in MacLeish's poem. When the name is picked we'll sing our peace song and the chosen poet will douse himself with gasoline or napalm while all the rest of us light Fourth of July sparklers—you know, children's fireworks—and at a given signal *throw* them at the poet! And that'll be it. We are already alerting the networks. Not about the burning, of course. Gad, are they interested!"

"They *are!*" I said.

"We need you there," said Wigg. "You will come, won't you?"

"Let me get this straight, Wigg," I asked. "Are you going to play this Russian roulette too?"

"Me? It was my idea. I'm putting my name in the plexiglas bubble *twice!*"

I felt slightly insane, as I always did when I spoke to Wigglesworth, and decided to use satire for my refusal. I argued that gasoline and napalm were overstatements, that the *tenor* was out of key with the *vehicle* and that the whole operation sounded like Shirley Jackson and bad rhetoric. I suggested that the heroic victim smoke two hundred maryjanes in a row and die from suffocation. "Or better still," I added, "you know the great classic *The Sexual Life of Savages?* After all, it's love we are trying to push across the line. Let the victim be raped to death by the women in the crowd, the way they do in the Trobriand Islands. Think of the different kinds of messages that could convey. I'm really in favor of something like that, Wigg. My God, man, did you ever smell a burning poet? That will bollix up the whole manifesto. The whole thing needs more *style*, Wigg."

It got through to Wigg that I wasn't about to offer myself as a living sacrifice in front of Independence Hall, and Wigg, who was in a terrible hurry, said goodbye and that he would try again next time.

"I hope he gets elected," I said to Inge as I hung up.

Inge was laughing quietly and wanted to know the whole conversation. I repeated it and then added, "Incidentally, I wouldn't mention this to anybody. I want it to go through. I may even go to the Catholic Church and light a bushel of candles for the kamikaze boys."

The mail she showed me was more of the same except for a small check from some publisher I had never heard of who had used three of my poems. I said I was heading home. Inge wanted to stay. I wished I could have been more friendly or personal with her but I felt nothing about her except curiosity and a touch of sympathy. On the other hand, she couldn't wait for me to leave, it seemed. She was already back in the files, putting in crisp new folders and alphabetical separators. She smiled distantly as I left.

I stopped at the bookstore a second time and bought book envelopes. I would go home and try to think of an inscription for Marya's book. I hadn't thought of Wanda once that day and it amazed me.

There was an envelope under my screen door when I opened it. In Wanda's handwriting it read: "Jack Rabbit." That must be the new me, I thought. She sounds really jealous, or something. Even a month ago I would have treasured a scrap of paper in her hand, studied it, ritualized it somehow or other. Once I had pinned a note of hers on the inside of my shorts and told her about it. She wanted to have a look, of course, that being the point of the whole thing. This time I carried the note to the kitchen while I made a vodka on the rocks. I leaned against the sink and sipped and read:

"About this new life you've embarked on, don't forget you've got an old flame, you might say listening post, who'd like to bend an elbow with you any time you whistle. Is your phone busted?"

I watched myself with amazement as I tore the letter into strips and shoved them into the step-on can. I'm not much of a liar, I thought, but let her think it's Inge. She's going to pump me about her anyway. Have to dust off my lying equipment; it won't be easy.

I was alone with my own book which would soon be Marya's. The delicacy of presenting it was my sole preoccupation. I leafed through the poems looking for some appropriate quotation from myself, but most of the poems were too ironically bitter, too clever or too harsh or too obsolete. My God, I thought, I was nothing but a ball of anger when I wrote all that. The poems are all jagged glass and rusty nails and bile. Can I even give her this book? But I knew I had to, knew I must lead her through the dying-out inferno of my past. She'd best know the worst about me, I said melodramatically out loud. I found a clipboard and paper and started to jot down possible inscriptions:

"These poems are not what I want and hope to write, but have them." Too negative, I thought. "I want you to have a glimpse of a previous life. It will help me." Why can't I stop starting sentences with "I," I thought. I,I,I, has got to go. And stop begging for help! "Because I want to see your work I am giving you this. Please keep it even if you can't or don't want to read it." That's a little more like it but not quite, I thought again. I wrote about six more tries. Finally I decided on a simple complexity, as I considered it to be.

"Marya, please accept this book of poems. It will be a gift to me." And signed it Edsel. I took my old ink fountain pen with a wide nib and practiced the inscription twice on the clipboard. I wanted the writing to be in black ink, very legible and very intelligible. I wrote off the inscription neatly and quickly on the fly-leaf of the volume, changing the period to a dash, signed it, and then decided to add the date. It might be harder to return if it had a date on it. Then I addressed the book sack without a return address and stapled it. I have three staple machines, enough for a post office. Now what? I asked myself.

Making a refill, I decided, as I always decided things in a flash, to deliver the book myself, to place it in her mailbox, not take it to the door. I had seen the Hinsdale mailbox on the street, at the entrance of the big circular driveway; it was one of those foot-high containers that sat on a little black iron jockey who holds it aloft with a hand on the front and a riding crop on the back. I hated these symbols of suburbanite power and nostalgia for the good old days—or so I construed the iron jockey—and I knew perfectly well that Marya probably hated the ikon. The mailbox was so far from the house that there was little chance of my being seen or recognized. I wondered who brought in the mail. In a mansion like that there must be servants. I didn't recall seeing any the day I had come there with my six-pack of beer. As a last precaution I wrote PERSONAL on the book envelope. Just in case Hinsdale was a mail-opener.

I drove past the block behind her house but couldn't see anything through the pine trees and the high white-brick wall. I cruised slowly up the boulevard pretending I was a mailman of sorts, neatly flipped open the front of the Hinsdale box and inserted my package. A lot of mail was in there already.

The phone was ringing when I got back; I could hear it from the curb. I have the idea that phones ring according to the mood of the caller. This one sounded rather lazy, not insistent or hysterical, and I let it ring slowly as I walked to the door. Then the thought struck me that "Maybe it's . . ." and I started to run and flung the screen door back so hard that it stayed open. I picked up the phone and caught my breath.

"Is this Edsel?" asked a quiet serious voice.

"Is this—Marya?"

"Yes. I wanted to thank you for your book. I'm going to keep it. I didn't mean to make an issue of it. And I can't wait to read it."

I was feeling speechless and wanted to quit while I was ahead. I wanted to sit down and think over my triumph. I wanted to write her a wild beautiful letter. I wanted to yell to her to hang up so I could get started. My heart was pounding and I remembered to remind her about the other half of the bargain, that she would show me something she had written and let me have a go at it. She agreed to that too. As she was about to hang up I asked if it would be all right if I sent her things, books or . . . I wasn't quite sure what I was getting at. She laughed a non-committal laugh and said she would see.

I sat back on the sofa and sighed. I got up and turned on the FM. They were playing the fire music from *Don Giovanni;* I turned it up so loud the windows vibrated; I started stalking around waving my arms. As the music reached its crescendo and the Don was letting out his great final groaning scream, I burst into tears and rushed into the bathroom.

CHAPTER XII

The problem, which all the time before had been a desideratum, was to avoid Wanda. *Avoid* her? After doing everything humanly and inhumanly possible to keep contact, to steal from her life and time, to press myself upon someone who didn't want the empressment? I had placed her in a kind of bondage. Mutual insult has its claims, I thought. I was like a man in a cave who had gotten a glimpse of daylight ahead and was equally eager to venture into it and to remain in the dark. It's my strength, I said to myself. I have the strength to walk back into my life and I have the strength to crash through the phony floorboard stage like good old Don Giovanni. But, I said, gird yourself, fellow. You've made the choice of leaving. Now leave. All the same there was the problem of logistics. I knew perfectly well that Wanda was on the warpath, or was about to be. It was a new predicament for me and I decided that I had no alternative but to throw her off the scent. What if Marya were to know about my long affair with Wanda? Should I tell her myself? Should I hope that Marya would never find out? That wasn't likely in a town the size of Milo and with the reputation I had for consorting with the denizens of Blue Town and the befringed students, my sobriquet in the local papers as Colorful and/or Controversial Professor.

I've never done anything like this, I decided, but I'll "cultivate" Inge to keep the Black Widow at bay.

It was almost five o'clock and I hadn't eaten anything all day except a glass of milk. First I'll call Inge, I thought; then Wanda.

Inge was still at the office and sounded delighted to hear from her "boss."

"You know what, Inge?" I said, "I haven't had anything to eat all day but a glass of homogenized milk and four vodka martinis. Are you free for dinner or whatever equivalent we can locate in these parts?"

The wind-chime laugh and an affirmative reply. We decided that I would pick her up in an hour at the office. A workhorse, why? I thought sadly.

I made a new drink before I phoned Wanda. I looked in my bathroom mirror and drank and smiled and said over and over to myself, "Don't fuck it up, Edsel. Don't overdo it, Edsel. Don't blow your luck. Cool, man, cool." I had picked up some of the spade talk, which revolted me but which I felt I could apply to myself if I wanted to.

Wanda had left the Fountain of Beauty; I tried her home number. By the time she answered I was as cool as Little America.

"This is Jack the Rabbit," I said. "How about you come by and bend an elbow?"

"Why?" said Wanda in a bad-weather voice.

"Listen, Wanda," I said, "I'm in a kind of bind with some crazy poets and peace demonstrations and suicide attempts and Christ knows what, so I have to be working later, but come on over and let's have a couple."

"I'm naked," she said. "You come here."

That tripped me. Any such invitation even a week ago would have sent me flying to my car with my zipper open. But I was getting some kind of grip on myself and heard myself saying, "No, it's got to be here. All kinds of phone calls from out of town. I can't leave. Now come on over and shut the hell up."

She'd come, she said, and hung up. In nothing flat, it sounded like to me. I dialed my office again.

"Inge, I know this is cornball but do me a favor. Call me every fifteen minutes during the next hour and keep asking about crazy poets and plots against the government. Do your duties extend that far?"

Inge seemed delighted out of her mind and I settled back like a potentate. The FM was delivering their dinner-type kitchen music and I winced and hoped Marya wasn't a victim of FM.

Wanda rolled in wearing sandals. I heard her slam her Volvo door with a shark-jaw slam but just sat there. She walked past me and went straight to the bathroom and straight to the kitchen from there without looking at me or saying a word.

When she returned she carried a clinking glass and a bag of potato chips and sat down beside me. She took a draught of her drink and ran her fingers through my hair.

"You got a girl, Edsel?" she asked.

I felt myself getting cold and bantered, "I got plenty of nothin'." Ring, phone, I thought one second and the next that I ought to be touching her or talking soldier talk. I waved a hand toward her non-committally and she slapped it down so that it stung from the blow. I felt a wave of pleasant anger.

"A girl?" I asked, turning to her. "Yes, I think so. A girl, a woman, but maybe it's only in my head. Let's call it a poten-tial friend." I decided to add, not sure of the stratagem, "Un-fuckable."

"Right," said Wanda, while the phone started to ring. "I'm the policewoman and you're guilty. What's her name? Give little me the facts. What did you do, import the Kraut cunt?"

"Hold it," I said and got the phone.

Inge had gotten the message beautifully and launched into a barrage about some crazy poet who had called three times already that day and wouldn't let up and what was she sup-posed to do.

"Not again," I said. "I told that lunatic bastard I wasn't in-

133

terested and that I wasn't going to turn him in to the FBI but for Christ's sake to leave me out."

"How many?" I added. I waited while Inge ran off a list of names she was apparently reading out of a poetry anthology.

"Not Carnevalli," I yelled into the phone.

More rigamarole. "Listen," I said, "hold the other calls. I'll get to them as soon as I get there. I'm not going to blow their thing and I'm not going to egg them on their crappy way." Inge tapered off the call and I said yes and hung up.

My blood was up; I was being taken in by my own invention and I turned on Wanda angrily, "And don't think every goddam phone call is an invitation to the bed!" She looked at me as if she had just returned from the vomitorium.

I attempted to explain a little about the mad phone call from Wigglesworth, without going into the suicide plot. I fictionalized and factualized enough to keep her off balance and let some of her anger leak away. But Wanda, as I well knew, put tenacity first on her list of attributes. The second time the phone rang Wanda grabbed it. I started, but then laughed and sat back.

"This is 472-0586," said Wanda in a mock-officious voice. "Who's calling?" she asked after a pause. "Oh, yes, he's here all right," she finished and handed me the phone.

I held the phone to my ear for a moment and then, "Not again!" And then, "Who? Oh yes, Rothenberg. He's a pretty good poet if he'd take his lips away from the jug once in a while. I like him; I hate to see him mixed up in that floating snakepit. What I ought to do, Inge, is to send telegrams to every one of those poets and warn them off. What do you think?"

Inge was laughing enjoyably and said in a mistressy tone, "You'd better come down here, lamb." I said a few things which sounded like decision-making and told her to hang on until I came.

"That's the best way," said Wanda when I had replaced the phone on its cradle, "have her hang on until you come."

I made a misstep. "You really can translate everything into

134

Eff You See Kay," I spelled. I thought I saw her jaw set a little.

"That spells *fuck*," she said quietly. "What's more I want it. My cunt is eating me alive. It's hungry. Wants hot dog with lots of mustard on it. Wants a lube job. Needs a lot of pumping. Needs a lot of plumbing. Got suction. Got a clamp up my ass hole. I feel like I can bite your cock off with six different holes. Wanta make a new hole, Ed?" She yanked her dress up over her navel. "Punch yourself a hole, baby," and she began to poke her torso with her thumb in different places, leaving red weals. I was beginning to feel nauseous; that's a new sensation for me, crossed my mind. How was I going to get her out?

The phone rang and she let me pick it up this time. She had pulled her panties down a little, enough to expose the hair. She was plucking out pubic hairs carefully, one at a time, and flicking them at me. She had on a strange kind of underpants, black, very narrow, with some kind of red stuff over the crotch. Inge was reading off more names from her anthology while Wanda switched her thighs toward me and showed me the panties. Embroidered on them in red was *What's New?* The *What* was on one side and the *New* on the other. Over the crotch was the head of a pussycat.

I kept saying "Yes" to the idiotic list of names and once in a while, "No, not that one" and so forth. Wanda had begun to masturbate, with a dreamy expression on her face. I was saying stock business expressions such as "Pull the file on that one" and "All those addresses are in the black binder in my top drawer." I thought I should end the conversation and said I'd be down shortly. I didn't want to hang up so soon or hang up at all but I was afraid of what Wanda would do next. I hung up. What Wanda did was to stick one callused foot forward and neatly flick the phone off its hook, this while she was plying her hand to her labia minora. She didn't speak. I placed the phone back on the cradle. She kicked it off again, this time a little harder. Again I replaced it. This time she slid over near the phone and grabbed it. I was prepared to have her yank it out of the wall, the way they do in gangster movies, and almost hoped she would. That way I could be released. Instead she applied one end of the receiver to her vagina (it's the mouthpiece, I thought resentfully) and began to turn it left and right against her crotch.

"Give me that phone," I said in a businesslike voice.

"Ugh," she was saying, "little old phone is giving it to *me*."

Better be going, I thought, and got up and went to the bathroom to brush my hair. In a second she had slammed the phone back where it belonged; it started ringing the moment she put it back on its bar. Wanda went straight to the kitchen while I answered it.

"Edsel, this is Inge," she said. "This is for real. The editor of the Milo *Bison* called and wants a statement from you about the protest in Philadelphia. He gave me a number for you to call. Or do you want me to tell him to call you?"

"Jesus," I said and started to think. I knew the editor slightly and had once or twice helped him with editorial opinions having to do with liberal causes, censorship, housing in Blue Town, etc.

"What can I tell him?" I asked Inge helplessly.

"Just tell him what you think," said Inge, "but don't get yourself in dutch."

"What's his number?" I asked. Inge informed me that the editor, Mr. Phil Metzger, had left his office and was on his way to a cocktail party at the Clayton Hinsdales'. I jumped.

"Would he be there yet?" I asked. Inge didn't know and we signed off.

I sat still for a while. It was funny that Inge hadn't given me the Hinsdale number; I already knew it by heart. Wanda reappeared and took her seat beside me, properly clad and demure as a Sunday school teacher. I have a way of memorizing numbers in blocks of integers, by the sound. Or I double and triple the integers, using binary or trinary groups. I dialed slowly; if Wanda were watching, would she have any way to find out whose number it was?

The number rang four times. On the fifth ring Marya answered the phone.

"Hello," she said. My pulse began to race.

"Oh," I said, "I'm really sorry to disturb you. I have a message to call Phil Metzger and I was told he would be at this number." I added, "This is Edsel Lazerow."

"I know," she said with a kind of smile in her voice. "I think he is out in the garden. Can you wait?"

"You bet," I said jauntily, trying somehow to convey something of my feeling about her, without loosing any secrets.

Metzger wanted to know what the Philadelphia rally, as he called it, was all about and what part in it I was going to play, or if I would take a stand against it. I told him that I had had a call from Dick Wigglesworth and that I was not sure of the effectiveness of the protest at this time and wished it luck but that I myself had serious reservations about harassing the government day after day with these histrionics.

"But listen, Phil," I said, "please don't quote me on this thing. I don't want to set up any opposition to a sincere cause, however naive the operation may appear. But if anything turns out to be crazy I'd like to talk to you about it." I was getting an idea that I might start cultivating the upper crust of Milo as a way of being accessible to Marya. When I had moved to the provincial city they, the upper crust, had sought me out in spite of my profession and my "race" but I laughingly declined. "Me in a country club?" I had told some Mrs. Got-Rocks, "why, I'd wreck the place. If I invited three half-breed poets to dinner there, they'd drain the bar in an hour and start firing at the chandeliers with cross-bows!" Somehow I got the point across without doing permanent offense to the society lady. I hadn't even joined the Trenchermen, a professorial snob group that supported the best chef in Milo, so that they—English professors mostly—could have a leg of mutton or prime rib and stout in tankards. Tremaine Atwood had supervised all that. I had even "regretted" the Faculty Club, a ratty little buffet in a pseudo-Tudor ex-sorority house where the professors ate chili or canned spaghetti at noon. Their coffee tasted like warmed-over pencil shavings, I once informed a visiting critic.

I turned to Wanda and told her I had to get down to the office fast. She had a stony expression on her face and I got up leisurely—consciously leisurely—and went to get some papers which I didn't need. Props help.

"Hey," I said to her as I was moving toward the front door like an escapee from my own house, "you stay here and as soon as I get rid of this mess I'll be back."

"Sit down," said Wanda in a basso profundo.

"On second thought," I said, walking over to her, my face burning, "*you go*. I'm not sure what time I'll be getting back. I'll call you tomorrow."

I stood in front of her waiting. She reached out, "gingerly" was the word that crossed my mind, and grabbed my wrist. The vise, I thought. She just sat there and held it. My old Stone Guest, I thought. She stood up and yanked me to the bedroom; I didn't want to let myself be yanked and didn't want to hit her, especially now, when I was feeling the loosening of the chains. How could I get her to just leave, just say goodbye or stalk out, even just march to the rear in a rage, smashing my artifacts along the way? I prayed, "Do a little scorched-earth policy, for the love of God, but beat it the hell out of here!" All of a sudden she lowered her head and butted me in the stomach onto the bed. I gasped a little and watched. She went to the door and slammed it and turned the old-fashioned key. There was an inch crack under the door and she flipped the key under the crack and turned toward me.

"You son-of-a-bitch," I said, "you've locked us in!"

"That's life," she said, and undressed with her fingernails. I sat up. She moved in slow motion toward me and with one hand yanked my shirt so hard that the buttons flew like a spray. Simultaneously she slipped my belt out of my suntans and flung that on the floor. Then with both hands she began to haul down my trousers. It wasn't till then that I socked her with the back of my hand. Her head flipped sideways. I had hit her too hard, I thought, being no expert on the striking of the female. The phone was ringing again, but there was nothing to do about that.

"Get off," I said, for she was straddling me and pretending to do a cowboy act. But she kept her seat, riding higher and higher on my chest until I felt her pubic hair scraping my chin. If she could come, I thought, that would be a help. The way she was leaping up and crashing down on my face I was in fear of my jawbone and my partials. I put up my hands to break the fall of her buttocks on my face. The human face divine, went through my head. I kept an eye open for her nails, not being sure when and if the slashing would begin. Suddenly I gave a sharp twist of my body and was out from under her and on the floor, while she remained in a kneeling-praying posture. She fell forward on the pillows panting and said, "Get out, shithead."

"How?" I said, dressing. I pulled a striped T-shirt from a drawer. Wanda went to the closet and got a coat-hanger and tore it open. With the hook-end she fished back the key from the other side of the door, opened it and crawled back into bed. "Don't forget tomorrow," she said.

"Take a nap," I said inanely and left.

Halfway to the university I discovered that I had left my wallet. I swore out loud, made a wild U-turn and was honked down by a Milo Transit bus. As I got out of the car in front of my apartment I saw that the Volvo was still there. She must have fallen asleep, I thought—until I spied a motorcycle on the lawn. I stopped in my tracks. "Oh no, oh no, oh no," I said, not knowing whether to go in or not, whether to knock or what to do. My house, my bed, I thought, and went to the door quietly. Not even closed, much less locked. No one was in the living-room and I tiptoed to the little hallway. The bedroom door was also wide open and I paused and listened to the rhythm of the bed.

My bed, I kept saying to myself. Then I planted myself in the doorway and watched. They were both naked and locked in the conventional *Ladies' Home Gazette* position. I noticed that both of Kaz's arms were tattooed. "Harder, harder," Wanda was grunting. I saw a water glass half full of a forgotten drink close to my hand. I reached out and picked it up and slammed it accurately against the wall above the bed board, showering the lovers with splintered glass and stale whiskey.

They leapt up to a sitting position, giving me time to take note of Kaz's perfectly normal *Ladies' Home Gazette* erection.

Kaz grabbed the sheet and pulled it over his privates. The expression on Wanda's face was something between pleasurable anger and dubious pride.

"I thought you told me he was impotent," I said preposterously, and turned around and left. I sat in my car, shaking, and once again headed slowly in the direction of the university.

CHAPTER XIII

Inge was typing at high speed; the clicking of the keys sounded almost like a blur. "What did I do to deserve *you*," I said as I came in. She finished a sentence and spun around.

"You've had quite a day," she said. She was serious. "I have lots of questions."

We discussed where to go, someplace where we could sit around and dawdle. There was little or no choice in Milo and for once I wished I had joined one of those eating societies which I loathe, or was even a member of the Country Club. Obviously, I didn't want to take her to my apartment. For all I knew, Wanda and Kaz were still making the beast with two backs, swilling my booze, and washing their genitals with my towels.

"How about Biff's Place, out near the Saddle Club?" I suggested. "It's really a beer joint but they have a version of something called food."

Inge was no particularist about restaurants evidently and she agreed readily.

Getting into the car, she said, "I'm going to grill you," and laughed.

"Grill, but don't eat," I answered. With her straight-at-the-mark markmanship she plunged right in.

"That one who answered your phone, is that Wanda?"

"That's Wanda all right," I answered. "What did she sound like to you?"

"She sounded like she was in the driver's seat," Inge said, and interrupted herself to add, "Edsel, let me say this just once more, about me and my curiosity, I mean. I talk the way I want to and I hope you do. I want to know everything about you that you're willing to tell. And I want you to trust me to keep my mouth shut. I popped in on you off the street. I've got a strong feeling you are in trouble, and I'm sorry about that. I'm not saying I can help you or even that I want to; I'm no goddam nurse. I'm completely and totally selfish about what I'm doing. I've got to know what a real writer is like, what he has to go through to keep being a writer, what stops him and what starts him. I guess you didn't bargain for all that."

"Well, you're in luck," I said. "I'm the biggest blabbermouth about myself you'll ever run into. It's a point of honor with me to shoot my mouth off to all and sundry. You know, I've met women who wouldn't screw because of my reputation for playing back the tape. I always thought that was kind of small-minded." I was trying to banter but felt unhappy about the role.

"Take Wanda, now," I went on. "Could you guess what she's doing at this minute? She is laying a boyfriend, sliming up my sheets and towels in *my* house, in *my* bed. I had to go back to the house and caught them in flagrante delicioso, bare-ass naked and taking five hundred miles off my bedsprings. And what did I do? I slammed a glass of rotgut against the wall, *their* wall, so to say, and stalked out."

"Do you love her?" asked Inge in a timid voice.

"It's what they call a hate relationship," I answered. "She brings out the worst in me, she throws my failures on a giant screen and lets me study the organism Me. She's one step from being a prossie; she accuses me of practically driving her to prostitution for real. I think I'd approve of her more if she did become a whore. Her legs are open to the world; she's got the macrocosmic meat-grinder but love is something she just can't digest. Her vagina rejects it. Do you savor the description?" I asked and glanced at her.

Inge was silent.

"And what do I give her?" I went on, anticipating her silent question. "I give her the power of rejection. I give her back hate, you know, like the carrion of my soul. We feed on the garbage of each other. We eat shit and smear it in our eyes. We are vomit lapper-uppers. The problem is to hit the Low, to make it to rock bottom. And that's the reward of the damned. It all works on the theory that heaven is hell.

"Last year," I went on, "I had a student who went off his head. I've got lots of those; it's an occupational hazard for poets. This guy was a big strong clunk of a man who walked like a zombie, ground his teeth, never smiled, and went on Freedom Marches, always in the front line where he would be hit first by a Mississippi cop's billy-club. Then he disappeared from the ranks of my class—it was off season for protests—and we just dropped him from the rolls. Then one day I was looking out of the window of my office and saw a man who looked like him coming toward the building. Only he was walking with a sprightly walk, carrying his arms loosely and smiling upwards, as if he were looking at the sky and appreciating it. When he got close enough I knew it was that student, and I knew he was coming to tell me something. You know what he said?"

"What?" asked Inge, looking at me. I saw she was disturbed and the car swerved slightly as I turned into Biff's parking lot.

"I'm all right," she said. "Tell me the rest of that story here."

I waited a little, not knowing what to do, and went on. "Well," I started, "are you sure you want to hear this kind of stuff?"

"That's what I'm here for," she answered.

"He had flipped his wig, didn't know where he was, and found himself walking up and down Times Square at night. He never knew how he got there and how he got back. He didn't even remember having any money to travel. But there

143

he was on the Great White Way. *Only it was red!* Every sign, every electric light was *red*. Everybody was dressed in *red*. His world was on fire. He was in Hell on little old hokey Times Square, with the headlines blooping across the big board announcing that General Thomas Q. Dingleberry had just had his appendix taken out on the third floor of the Pentagon. Then he started to *smell* the people. Every person who came toward him was preceded by his smell, and the smell was sulphur. The smell was rotten eggs and paper mills and cancer farts. And the smells were red and the smells were on fire. So my student began to scream and race through the mobs of little old ladies and little old men from Dubuque and Milo until the cops stopped him in front of a taxi which slammed on the brakes, and they held him, fighting like a maniac, until they got him to Bellevue. I don't know how long he was there or what they did but when I sat there in the office hearing his adventure—adventure?—I couldn't believe it was the same man. And you know, Inge, in a way, I felt cheated."

"Does he still write poetry, Edsel?" she asked.

"He didn't mention it," I replied, "and I didn't even think of that till now."

We got out of the car as if by mutual agreement and went into Biff's. We ordered beer and chili and Inge said, "Cheated? Why did you feel cheated?"

"It'll sound cold-blooded," I answered, "but I guess I thought I would never be a poet anymore. But that I had had a walk through my own inferno and then blew it on the conversation with him. Instead of—nursing it, keeping the seed of that fire I had seen and that stink, and blowing on it just enough to keep the seed alive, in case I ever wanted to start a fire of my own."

Inge reminded me that I wasn't a partisan of Hell poets and that my own poems were, well, anti-Hell. She had read me anyway and that was something.

"But here," I said, "with the material—materia human-be-ingcus or something—Hell is the only point of departure. What would this poet write about if he hadn't found his Hell—sorghum? Beef cattle?"

144

She gave her bell-tinkle laugh and sipped her beer. The waiter brought chili in deep soup bowls and a plate of white bread and crackers and butter. It tasted good to me; I found I was starved.

"But that's back to the first question I ever asked you," she said. "What are you doing here? What are you doing with Wanda? Why don't you leave? I know you can. I've read fifty letters offering you professorships all over the country and outside it. Some of which I slit open myself. And here you are and here you stay."

"So I'm trying to be a Hell poet. And don't think I'm not succeeding," I said.

"I've heard people gossip about you, how you are drinking yourself to death, running with the Blue Town crowd, keeping a black girl. Is there a black girl?" asked Inge.

I frowned and then laughed. "My God, that must be Wanda they mean, whoever *they* are. That's a good transliteration, I'd say. Sort of poetic. That reminds me, I was supposed to take Wanda to Janiczek's big bohemian beerbust tomorrow night and that's pretty goddam out. Will you come with me? You'll enjoy seeing the local hippie cell, or do you know people like that?"

"I'll go if I don't have to tangle with your friend," Inge said, seemingly pleased.

"Well, be prepared to clap eyes on her anyhow. She wouldn't miss a party like that if she had to crawl to it. And Janiczek has a particular liking for her; he says she's authentic. Authentic what I wouldn't know. I think those sociology types go around looking for people who have tossed their standards overboard. You get a bunch of people together who have all tossed their standards overboard and you have a bohemian party. It's frightening in a way, all those young punks pretending to be superior because they can't do anything and think it's beneath them to try. Naturally they sneer at an old-timey word like bohemian or avant-garde; in fact they have no vocabulary at all. They are gradually erasing language; maybe they'll subside into silence and leave the world the way it used to be. Creepy but interesting creatures. Ex-people, I call them."

145

"What does Wanda contribute to a party like that?" Inge asked.

"Dancing," I answered. "Marathon dancing; in the dark. It's the only time she doesn't drink non-stop. And her number-one boyfriend, he flamencoes, making pistol shots with his heels while she plasters herself against the Jamaicans. And me, I sit on the floor and watch out for motorcycles."

"For what?"

"You'd never believe it unless you read the papers. Last year at one of Brom's parties two of the cycle set who call themselves the Fall-Outs drove their motorcycles straight into the livingroom, hall, diningroom and kitchen and out the back door. They only knocked over one table but the cops came. Nobody knew who called the police; some people said I did it."

"Well, did you?" Inge laughed.

"I don't really think so," I quipped. "Okay, let's hear about your love life. Husband, brat, all of it."

When Inge was asked about her personal life she clammed up, but with me as her new confidant she felt she owed me some kind of background material. She sat for a while and began to twist bits of paper off her napkin. She looked down while she talked.

"Nothing original about my life," she said. "That's why I got out. I've been separated for three years and he does live in Denver with the boy. What I said about the wife-swapping was partly true. He wanted that and tried every way he could to carry it out. He had already convinced our next-door neighbors but I turned out to be the wet blanket. So Hank, that's his name, had to lay the neighbor's wife on his own. There was all that kind of crap and I just filed and took off."

"Leaving the kid? Why?" I asked.

"I didn't want children in the first place. I got married out of boredom, like most women. I never had any feeling about either of them. The boy is in a Catholic school—Hank is a Catholic—and I couldn't care less. Does that make me a monster? I get enough money to live on and I have time to think and be alone and try to work out my life." She looked at me and added, "When I've learned the editing trade from you, I'm taking off for the big city."

"A fat lot I can teach you," I answered.

"You've already taught me an encyclopedia full," she said. "Just that episode about Wigglesworth is a course in writing and writers. Do you think he'll go through with it?"

"Wigglesworth? He's one of those guys who would blow up the universe to make a point about himself. You wouldn't think any plant as sensitive as a poet would hanker after headlines. The trouble with poor Wigg is that he *is* a headline. He eats, sleeps, and breathes righteous egotism. He really makes me puke."

Inge sat back and looked at me squarely again. "But you're not like that. Are most poets and writers that—infantile?"

"Of course they are," I said. "But it depends on their talent. The less talent the more publicity. It's a Parkinson law. Wigg has a talent but it's nothing to write home about. But he has a genius for making his bit of skill outshine all his contemporaries put together. How? He's not a poet, he's a committee. He's made it his business to sit on every board that gives money to writers and prizes for books. He is on the advisory board of twelve publishing houses. He ghost-writes poetry reviews to keep his claque in line. And he owns and operates *Megalopolis Mind,* the literary review that's in the cursing-business. Then of course his conversions and his soapbox speeches. Now most writers try to steer clear of that kind of nut but they can't. English professors think he's God because he acts like what they think a poet should act like—a burning babe, a firebrand. The trouble is he trades in his firebrand every time a new model comes out."

"Are you trying to discourage me?" Inge laughed.

"It's strange that people have to have illusions about artists," I answered, "but they need them—illusions. They have to believe that the poet is a special breed of cat and not just somebody who got hung up on words. It's the public and the profs that encourage poetic delinquency and urge the poet to drink iodine and battery acid. And the poet, who's not a very bright fellow, sociologically speaking, is only too glad to do their bidding. Okay, maybe it's a primitive Dionysian rite. Maybe the bitches have to tear Orpheus limb from limb. Maybe Hart Crane has to jump off a boat to feed the sharks. Maybe Dylan T. had to drown in a booze bottle. But you can't prove it by me. The Hell poets can have their barbecue; I think it's a goddam sellout."

"That's not what you said about your student in Hell. And what about you, Edsel? You and Wanda and the motorcycle crowd?"

When I am caught in my own trap I try to weasel out with a joke or a paradox, but I had no such inclination tonight. The thought of Marya, for one thing, made all those Hells look silly or sick.

I said, "I feel as if I'm walking away from the city dump. I want to bank those fires, piss on them. I'm beginning to be able to see again, a little; I see a little daylight. I never was a night person really; I love the day. I'm a sun worshipper, even an ascetic, maybe an ascetic of sensuality but an ascetic. A desert Jew. But I'm so goddam tired of slopping the hogs that I could chew nails. Maybe my wallowing days are over. I've got to get out of that playpen of pimps, perverts, parvenus and potheads. Of Wandas, Wigglesworths and whiplashes." (When I begin to alliterate I know I am running out of gas.) "Of the rapturous roses of rupture and lesbian lice."

Screwing up Swinburne, very intelligent.

"Question," said Inge. "When did you know you were a poet?"

I looked at her with an "oh, no" expression but decided that I had agreed to play the game and would go ahead.

"Maybe when I began to hide," I said. "When I discovered that I was alone, that I could never operate in a group, that I couldn't play a game, even a simple game like checkers. That more than one person in a room made me feel nervous or ill. That I was a failure in school. That I cried all the time for no reason. That I could concentrate on a minute object like a pebble until my head swam. That the talk of people sounded crazy or flat to me. That words didn't make sense to me the

148

way they did to others. When I began to read philosophy which I couldn't understand but which sent me into frenzies of delight. When I found Chaucer and then Blake, the little Blake who sang about innocence, and then Shakespeare and Whitman and all the others who came tumbling into my head. And by that time I was caught and was writing my imitations of the poets."

I finished a schooner of beer. "No, there's more than that," I went on. "It was the moderns that got me, they set the hook in my craw. When I read the Eliot poems I was beside myself. I quoted him to people who had never heard of him and they thought I was crazy. I found the esoteric magazines and hid behind them. I lived inside the polysyllable. I took books out of the library stacks which hadn't been touched for fifty years, variorum editions, monographs on prosody, a history of the popes. I was never without a book; without a book, especially walking down the street, I felt naked. I learned to read and cross town on foot at the same time; it made me feel more— *European*. At the same time I was terrified to be a Jew, though I hadn't experienced anything more traumatic than the usual child insults. Sometimes I would panic on one of my walks, imagining I had visible scars from some imagined encounter, some fight or accident or even verbal assault. I had a little study at the back of our apartment; I fitted it out like a ship's library because it overlooked a reservoir and the windows creaked in the wind. You see, Inge, I grew up as a poet during the Great Depression, and it really was *great* for me. There were no jobs to be had and I was spared drudgery. I lay in my ship's library and drifted through those forgotten books, collecting words, words, words. I was wild about archaic spellings and etymologies; I still am. The thing about poetry was that it was a counter-language, an anti-language almost. It contradicted everything everyone thought or said and it belonged to me. It made me unique and independent in myself. It made me arrogant and sensitive at the same time. I was a bastard to my family and what friends I had. But I knew I was acquiring mana, that I had a magic touch and an invisible shield. When I had made that discovery I knew I was a poet. I knew with some kind of primitive intuition that I could always make my way, high or low, that I was a vertical person, not like the rest of the world skating over the thin ice of their rationalistic civilized crust of life. I could be on their level if I liked and when I liked but I could get above them and below them at will. I told myself I was their enemy but also their poet. I would write them the poems they would hate but would know were their truth."

"Why all the enmity?" Inge asked.

"In those days it *was* enmity for me. Well, I was in my teens, when one can see the flaws in the structure of things and say so but can't do anything about it. Sort of an ideal situation for the poet, to be violently helpless. The helplessness leads to vision or at least dreaming and hallucination. I used to recite to myself every chance I got the sweet little lines of Yeats: 'All things uncomely and broken,/ All things worn out and old,' which are the things that wrong the image of love, at least when you're that age. I even had some of the current political enmity of the time, a kid's brand of communism, but I was too selfish and too estheticized to ever join up. The local reds my age called me an esthete, a decadent, a bourgeois and other names. I stuck to my poems and my one-at-a-time friend."

"Your what?" Inge asked.

"Well, I couldn't communicate with more than one person, either male or female. The male friend was my intellectual consort and sounding board and ideological buddy. If a female, she was my poetic victim, the mirror I held my poems up to. That I was in love with her was axiomatic. My love affairs were completely literary, as my friendships were purely ideological. I never had sexual intercourse with one of those girls."

"You? You're lying," said Inge.

"No, I'm not. Kissing games and that was it. I used prostitutes for sex and pretty girls for poetry. Sounds kind of infantile. Besides which I had a terror of marriage and of getting caught with some kid who had such dark designs or who had a tendency to procreate. But actually my motive must have been selfishness again. I wasn't ready or able to give myself to what in those halcyon days I termed my mistress. I don't think I've ever busted a hymen in my life!"

Inge was laughing. "It seems to add up," she said. "And Wanda too. You end up not even being able to give it to her. It's bad," she said seriously.

"At this phase of my life, if life has phases," I said, "I am, you might say, triangulated—sexless, friendless, and loveless. What sex I have is straight out of Krafft-Ebing, documents of the cloacal mind. I actually introduced Wanda to that crazy German book, well, old-fashioned medical tome, if you know it —which you needn't." I added the last earnestly. "I told her stuff about sexual pain and she was a willing student but it never was my dish in the first place. I don't relish sticking hat pins in a woman's buttocks while she's having an orgasm, or whorehouses where perverts fuck ducks, literally. You're interesting to talk to," I said. "Nothing makes you blush." I looked at her and she blushed and we both laughed and ordered more beer.

"Anyhow, sexually, I'm just a minor case history now. Case number 567-B in the fourteenth edition of *Psychopathia Sexualis*. 'Once upon a time,'" I improvised, "'there was this poet fellow who went to the same one-dollar whore once a week and the rest of the time wrote asexual love poems to a high-school girl. Try as he might he could feel no love in sex, no sex in love. To himself he claimed an abnormal capacity for both love and sex but complained that he could never find the proper object of his affections. Later, in marriage, he resorted to wine, mysticism and pornographic hallucination. He noticed that his tool began to shrink and became painfully shy of micturating in public latrines. He sought out philosophies of isolation which he learned to systematize. His real longing, however, was for a magic love partner who would heal his psychic wound and restore the kingdom to potency.'"

"Maybe he was born with the wound," said Inge.

"Possible. Not probable," I answered. "Whatever happened when he was in the playpen, chances are he never passed the auto-love phase and thus was doomed to poetry. Poetry is solipsistic," I said sweepingly. Inge didn't know the word and I explained it.

"It can't be that simple," she argued. "You say yourself it's a way of vision."

"The vision of the concentration of the blind. The eye turned inward. Nothing is more ridiculous or more moving than a poet on the platform. And to poets, awesome. That hollow voice, speaking out of the void of himself, out of a self which grown men and women have long since assimilated and forgotten. Can *they* understand him? Can they possibly know what he is saying? All he can do is lull and hypnotize and stir up the sludge of their forgotten angers and lusts and dried-out dreams. All they can do is listen to the music of his entrapment. You know the old platitude, nobody erects statues to critics. Well, nobody envies a poet, nobody in his right head dreams of becoming a poet, including poets. A French poet said that a poet, when he is born, is about as welcome as a dwarf, or words to that effect. His mother would like to throw him into the fire like an old love letter. How about *that!*" I said gaily.

"And other artists too? Novelists too? Composers?"

"The others may have the curse on them but not as bad," I answered. "The others have to live with non-artists in order to do their work. A composer needs other musicians to play his work, stage hands, actual people. Painters need other painters, schools, apprentices, masters. Even novelists have to know things like law and medicine and how to fix a carburetor. What does a poet have to know? Reactions, impressions, assemblages of memories, and how to imitate feeling, all the feelings. The hardest thing for a poet is to separate his actual feelings from his poetry feelings. If there *is* any difference."

"Your—feelings about Wanda? How can they get into a poem?"

"They could if I wanted to try. Feelings of self-loathing, foulness of intention, failure. After all, Shakespeare had to do all that. Imagine what he felt like when he was Iago or Goneril?"

"Iago and Goneril," she said, as if answering a lesson.

CHAPTER XIV

The day of the Janiczek party I was jittery. I awoke in a sweat; brushing my teeth, my hand shook. Christ, I thought, am I becoming a dipso? I made myself bacon and fried eggs but couldn't touch them and slid them into the step-on can. Passing the hall mirror I noticed that I had nicked myself. "Damn it," I whispered and went and applied styptic pencil. Should I go to the office? I wondered, and decided against it. Inge had had enough seminar last night. I looked at the FM and made a grimace; I was in no mood for whatever might be coming out, good, bad, or indifferent. I looked in my closet, wondering what I should wear to the fray. Inge had asked me about clothes and I had only laughed. "What does the well-dressed woman wear to the Janiczeks'?" I said. And gave her the answer: "Caliban scales."

Since my divorce my closet has taken on the aspect of Joseph's coat of many colors. Splendiferous coloration, I said to myself, leafing through my clothes. But I need something else, I decided, fingering through sports jackets and sports shirts and lumberman's and airman's outer garments. I would go downtown, maybe to Hinsdale & Eisenbray where they had a "salon" called Import Riviera. I could get an Italian shirt, maybe raw silk or stuff like that. I wanted to spend a lot;

I despise salesmen who try to make me save money. Then there was Feldman for Men, a shop that catered to the university boys and carried the latest *Esquire* styles in their windows. Kitsch, I thought. And finally, except for the Army Surplus stores, which I prefer, there was a little shop facing the campus called Mark of Zorro, which favored the psychedelic aspirants and stocked sweat-shirts with luminous paint swirls, and velvety pullovers and trousers so tight that they showed your pubic hair. High-school kids thought it the greatest; I figured that their trade came from the undetermined sexes. I would go to the big department store. I wondered if Marya shopped in her husband's emporium; why shouldn't she? I thought angrily.

It crossed my mind that if I *should* run into Marya—what would I look like? So I selected a pair of well-washed corduroys, almost white, and a black T-shirt. It was a hot day, usual in the September midlands, and I figured I looked slightly apache but not offensively so. I combed my bushy gray-white mop, bringing out a couple of waves. At the last minute I studied my book shelves and picked out a book, "by the color" I thought. It was a thick bright-yellow paperback slashed with jet Chinese characters and called *The Death of the Precise Definition.* It was a tract on the orientalization of American poetry by some overly bright graduate student named Ming-toi Abramovitz. I had leafed through the book and had read one chapter in *Megalopolis Mind;* the author, a paranoid-schiz-ophrenic-with-homicidal-Nazi-tendencies, according to my diagnosis, had already won seven criticism prizes and been knighted by the Icelandic government for translating the *Kale-vala* into both Chinese and Modern Hebrew. I sometimes wondered, or rather hoped, that Ming-toi was either Dick Wigglesworth or Tremaine Atwood. But the cover was beautiful and I tucked the volume under my arm.

A store like Hinsdale & Eisenbray, the best and most palatial mart in a medium-sized town, is a cross between a group suburbia *kaffeeklatsch,* a fashion show, a oneupmanship theater-in-the-round, and a financial success. Traversing the handsome ground floor, past perfume and cosmetics counters, elegant

shoe shops and ladies' leather goods showcases, sunburnt mani-
kins in Island Vacationer bikinis, volcanoes of silken scarves,
real and junk jewelry bazaars, I arrived at the bank of ele-
vators. The ratio of female to male population was twenty to
one. I, one in twenty, was spoken to three times by ladies
whose names I had forgotten, along with their faces. Even the
elevator girl had been a student of mine who reminded me of
how much she had enjoyed my course. *What course?* I thought
furiously; maybe it was home economics or something. I got
out amoebically at the third floor and followed a gilt baroque
sign to the partition called Import Riviera. I felt depressed and
hung over.

I breathed a little easier when I entered the Riviera section.
It was practically empty and I stood against a fake palm tree
and lit a cigarette. You could smoke here, a sign said. Dum-
mies with Japanese kimonos advertised bathrobes; leather-
covered humidors and traveling liquor briefcases and meerschaum pipes proclaimed the masculinity of the cubicle. Alpaca
sweaters in uninvented colors lay in neat stacks on glass counters. Somewhere a gold tuxedo gleamed. Plaid sports jackets
for fall nuzzled each other on an endless rack. Two assegai
spears crossed high up on a wall and an imitation Benin bronze
bell hung from a corner. Tropical, I sneered to myself, as
someone touched me on the elbow. I turned around to face
Marya.

My mind always takes a little while to catch up with the
present. The present presence of Marya, had I known about it
in advance, would have panicked me. But my panic apparatus hadn't gone into action yet, my pulse was even and my
voice steady.

"I have to go to an anarchist party tonight," I said. "I was
looking for a—not a costume—but an appropriate disguise. Pro-
tective coloration, you know. Do you have any ideas?"

Marya laughed. "I wanted to look at the new Italian shirts
myself," she said. "I have a hippie nephew who expects a present because he didn't graduate."

"Shirt," I said, "that's what I came for. How about we help
each other out? I'll buy your nephew's and you buy mine."

We started leafing through Italian real and artificial fabrics. I lifted up a wild heavy silk shirt, a purplish blue streaked with thin red horizontal stripes. *Seta Pura,* it said on one label. *Amadeo Perrone,* it said on a larger one. *Roma,* it said in italics on the third. Marya laughed, "You'll look like a gondolier," she said, "an expensive one." I turned over the shirt looking for the price tag; the shirt slithered through my fingers. "Fifty dollars!" exclaimed Marya. "Too much for your nephew?" I asked. "At least twice," she answered. "I'll take it then," I said and she gave me that simultaneous smile and frown which I was already in love with. Then she selected a soft beige knit sweater but wouldn't disclose the price. That done I asked her would she have a cup of coffee with me. As I did so my panic machine switched itself on.

"Yes, let's do," she said, "but not here. Half the people in this store are friends of mine, or rather my husband's. And the coffee shop is nothing but a gossip column. It's not that I care," she said, as we entered the elevator, "it's that I get so annoyed with their triviality. I hate this town," she added. I was surprised and pleased. "That makes two of us," I answered.

We went to a little bar and café on a side street where the students hung out and a few professors dropped in for a beer. Marya had coffee; I considered for a moment and got a small draft beer.

"Beer doesn't frighten you?" I asked jokingly. She merely laughed.

"Maybe I was foolish in those days," she answered. "I was so frightened of Clay and he kept pressing me to go to a hospital or an analyst. He wanted to make me feel that I was ill and he convinced me that something had to be wrong. He told me I'd forced him into an impossible position because I rejected the position he had made for me in the community. When I told him I wanted to write he said he would burn every goddam book in the house. Those were his delicate words." She looked down into her cup and I thought I saw her hand tremble. On an impulse I laid my hand on hers and her eyes flew open darkly and with a suspicion of anger.

"Don't be offended," she said, and drew away her hand.

"I've decided to trust you, Edsel, and I don't want to disappoint either of us," she said. "I want to learn from you. If it doesn't sound belittling, you are the only person I have ever met in Milo who makes a new kind of sense to me. The kind of sense I've been looking for. I know you are wild and that frightens me; but I know you are—considerate too. I feel now that you won't do anything to hurt—anybody. Would you come to our—*my* house sometime and meet Clayton? Just why I'm not sure but I want you to, at least once."

My head was spinning and I assented to everything. "And about your story? When do I see that?" She said she was retyping it and would put it in the mail. She didn't mention my poems, which disappointed me, but I decided to wait until she did.

She was looking at her watch when I spotted Oscar Darling entering the bar, followed by my white-haired student, the book-clutcher, I remembered. Oscar stopped at the booth and asked to be introduced to "the pretty lady." You fink, I thought. Marya said hello to both newcomers and said for me to stay, that she had other errands. I was furious with myself that I had made no definite plans. "Enjoy your party," she smiled at me. Hurriedly I answered, "I'll phone about the manuscript; all right?" She nodded and gave me what I hoped to be a conspiratorial look. Oscar turned and watched her go and then sat down without invitation. The white-haired student wriggled in beside him.

"Edsel, she is really *stacked!*" was Oscar's comment. The white-haired student tossed his head.

"You're in my poetry class," I said to the student, "but I forgot your name."

"Joseph Amory," he answered with a tight little smile.

"Jo-Jo," corrected Oscar. Oscar wanted to see what was in the Hinsdale & Eisenbray sack and I removed the shirt, which created a flurry of excitement.

"It's just for the Janiczek party," I said, and began to wish I hadn't bought it at all. Oscar wanted to know about Marya but I decided to say nothing. "Just someone I know hardly even casually," I said, while Oscar searched my face for news. We talked about the Janiczek thing. Rumor had it that the famous Beat guru Akiba Mem was heading into Milo after a successful mass rally against war and alcohol which he had just held the past three days in Colorado Springs. Even the Air Force Academy had had him as a speaker.

"It's not his real name, of course," Oscar explained to Jo-Jo. "Mem is a Hebrew letter that Akiba decided stands for Mother. That boy is going to mother us all to death. His real name is Harry Peltz. He's such a smart child. I hope he blows in in time for the party and blows some of his smoke our way. Though I think he's a revolting little animal, he does bring out the general gaiety."

I said I had to get going and that probably we would see each other later. The conversation left me feeling a little wan and tarnished. Why should I go to that stupid collection of freaks at all? I asked myself. It's exactly what I'm trying to escape from. I ought to stay home and try to pick up a pen. I might even attempt to crack a book. I'm becoming practically illiterate. Driving, I tried to picture my encounter with Marya again and felt the same rush of excitement and joyousness that I had while she was with me. I've got to see her, I told myself, but how, where, when?

I knew I would go to the party anyhow, come hell or high water, even though I didn't want to. Inge wouldn't mind if I called the date off, or if she did mind she wouldn't show it. Wanda was past consideration this trip, although a fleeting image of her crossed the horizon of my consciousness. Often I have these waking dreams, or fragments of dream, while I am thinking and wide awake. A face appears before my eye, a real or an imagined face, or at least the face of someone I have never seen. Sometimes the face is ugly or brutal, sometimes plain, sometimes beautiful. I know it is part of my dream mind working overtime because I can't produce these portraits at will. They come of their own volition. Now it was the face of Wanda dressed in gray, with a gray skin, that I was seeing. She stayed a second or two and vanished, "as if saying goodbye, as if with a wave," I said to myself. "Jesus," I thought, "I'm as

158

cracked as Macbeth," though the visions didn't exercise me badly and I rather prided myself on this visionary faculty.

Entering my livingroom I saw, or my dream projector saw, the figure of Marya walking slowly toward me. She was dressed, of all things, in a gold sari, leaving her left shoulder and her midriff bare. Her hair was around her shoulders and the end of the garment was thrown beautifully over her head, framing it in the ancient style. Her right arm was brilliant with glass bracelets of every color. Her complexion was dusty rose and her full delicate lips were painted with a salmon rouge. She had darkened her eyes with—"kohl" was the word that popped into my head—and she looked straight into the middle of my gaze. Her rich breasts and the roundness of her loins, the pride with which she held her body, the "exotic" set of her eyes, all made me weak-kneed with pleasure and wanting. She stayed what seemed to me a leisurely time, a graceful span of moments, suitable for her "rank" or for her aspiration. When she disappeared I gasped. "These are good enough visitations for me," I said to myself. A feeling of confidence followed the encounter. "Part of her," I thought, "is trying to delight my eyes. She is trying out a vision which she thinks I may have of her." I still felt watery in the knees and went toward the kitchen, automatically switching on the FM in passing.

When I came back with my vodka and grapefruit juice—I had run out of bottled mixes—the radio was shattering itself with Beethoven's *Consecration of the House* and I laughed gratefully. One of these days, I thought, I'll consecrate the hell out of a house. I turned down the radio, sat down and dialed Inge.

"It doesn't matter what time we go or leave," I told her after the pleasantries, "but it'll be a liberal education for both of us —so let's."

There hadn't been any question of our going, except far back in my mind where there was a STOP sign in miniature that waggled back and forth. We decided on eight-thirty or so.

CHAPTER XV

ɔɔ When Inge and I parked across from the Janiczek house
ʊ I said, "Sit for a minute." Inge stiffened a tiny bit and
sat still.

"It's only that I've got a crazy feeling," I said, "that in there
I'm going into the waxworks of my life in Milo; that I'm going
to encounter the fuck-up of what they call the best years of
my life. In fact I feel like I'm going to a sacrifice and I'm
the . . ."

Inge relaxed. "Lamb?" she laughed. "Or bull?"

"Prime rib of poet," I quipped, and lit a cigarette. "There
goes Bumpy Harrington and her surgeon," I said. "Followed
by Hugh Gilchrist—you know, the monk fellow who is handy
with a mimeograph and such instruments of total destruction."

The street was getting filled with cars of all vintages and
shadows could be seen making their way on both sides toward the stately little bungalow. No sound could be heard
from the interior, but then, the house was well back from the
street.

"Quiet as a whorehouse," I said.

There was a roar and a wild flash of lights as three motorcycles riding abreast neatly made a right turn and jounced
over the curb and came to a halt against the porch of the

house. With a wild symphony of farts they subsided, and their drivers hunched lackadaisically through the front door. "That's the first echelon of the wave of the future," I announced. I felt nervous and wanted a drink. "Let's go in, Inge," I said. "You know, like the time has come."

"You really take this thing seriously," she said.

"This party has farewell written all over it. Just a prophecy," I answered.

Inge had dredged up a serape from somewhere in her Colorado past and was wearing it like a shawl. I thought it a perfect disguise for the company ahead. Her hair was drawn back into a knot but she wore two-inch-long wooden earrings that flicked when she walked. I still had on my almost-white cords and my fifty-dollar gondolier shirt. I had decided not to shave and wore a salt and pepper stubble on my face. We passed through a spacious vestibule into the semi-darkness of the first livingroom. Since the four Janiczek children (by various marriages) were all ensconced in various way-out schools around the United States, all the former bedrooms had become "other" livingrooms. In fact, the only bed in the house was in the Brom and Karen bedroom where I had watched the flamenco demonstration. "This generation has abolished the bed," Brom had told me at one of the parties. "Part of the tribalism," he added, and jerked his head. "They've rediscovered the floor." "You can say that again," was my reply.

All the rooms were semi-lit but seemingly in different colors. A bluish light leaked from one doorway, a reddish glow from another, a cold fluorescent white from a third. If you whipped your head around quickly it was like the American flag. "Don't say it," I told Inge, "*The Masque of the Red Death*." She laughed dutifully. "Liquor for grown-ups back here," I pointed. "Children bring their own."

We went down the narrow hall toward the back of the house and could hear soul music driving out of an old-fashioned Gramophone horn which had been expertly remodeled to conceal some pretty sophisticated electronic equipment. Brom greeted me and I introduced Inge as "my secretary and defender of the faithful." Brom introduced us to the "adult" liquor cabinet, a scrolly walnut armory which he had rebuilt on the interior with heavy shelves to hold his gallon-size booze bottles, mixing liquids, and a trough in which ice cubes made themselves gaily and plentifully. I asked Brom what the going beverage was; he suggested bourbon and we took large tumblers and splashed bourbon over the blue cubes.

"Let's wander," I said to Inge. She wanted to look first into the room where the music was pulsating. It was a huge glassed-in sun porch at the back of the house and there were no lights at all.

"In this cage," I said sourly, "you don't see; you smell." We stood outside the door and could feel the floor moving in a four-four rhythm up and down—or so I imagined. A strange zoo-like odor filled the room in which we were standing—the diningroom—but there was no dining furniture visible.

"What is the smell?" Inge asked.

"It's a medley," I answered." Cheap Chinese incense to cover up the marijuana, cheap cologne to cover up the sweat, darkness to cover up the Jamaicans, and the sour smell of soul music. Had enough?" Inge shuddered, not at what I had said but because I had said it. We moved toward the more lighted rooms.

We entered the "blue" room and I saw practically my whole Creative Writing Class seated on the floor in a kind of semi-circle. As I entered with Inge they applauded. "Oh my God," I groaned. "One of Brom's goddam *gaietés parisiennes.*" I waved a smily phony wave and asked to whom or to what I owed this honor. I was angry and some of my bourbon sloshed into my shoe.

"Mr. Lazerow, sit down with us," called the white-haired book-clutching person of no known sexual denomination. "We want to—commune!" he giggled.

I looked desperately to Inge who was smiling distantly, as if to say, "Pass your own tests; don't include me in." I sat on one arm of a fat cracked leather chair which had belonged to Karen's grandfather; Inge perched on the other arm, looking at the students.

162

Christ, it really is my class, I thought, as I saw Chris Jaffe
raising his hand in mock permission to speak. He was draped
with Indian beads which he had bought at Durd's Drug, and
around and over them he wore a talith. I bristled at this self-
insult. It was okay to play the Indian bit but to sport the
prayer shawl of the Jew in a hippie outfit—I didn't swallow
that.

"Speak, Jaffe," I said, trying to remain calm and humorous,
"as one must at a party," I counseled heavily.

"Well, it's this, sir," said Jaffe, with a pencil-line sneer
which I hoped I was imagining. "We of the tribe, sir, we teach
as well as learn. We give as well as take, because we are the
believers in the Immediate Present." With his right hand he
began slipping the prayer shawl from his neck, very slowly.
The worn silk tassels dragged on the bare polished floor. "But
one must give slowly, as one must learn by inches," he said.
The talith lay across his lap and I thought this obscene little
clown was going to make me a present of it, with some little
idiotic speech. Instead of which, Jaffe brought one end of the
shawl to his beard and his lips, in an ancient gesture of reverence, kissed it, and then with both hands ripped it longitudi-
nally down the middle.

Inge leaped to her feet and snatched it from him and
slapped him with all her might across his mouth. "You stinking
little turd!" she screamed at him, and began whipping him
across the face with the silk shawl. I had turned to stone and
sat perched on the cracked leather arm of the chair. Inge
caught herself with hand raised and dropped the talith gingerly and catching my eye motioned me out of the "chamber,"
as I thought of it afterward. I stood against the wall outside
the room for a time. I felt icy and somehow clean, as if I had
just passed inspection for cleaning and oiling my .45 which I
had had to carry when I was in the Army. And suddenly I felt
thoroughly drunk, as if all the liquor I had downed since I had
landed back in Milo had risen up at one fell swoop to belt me
in the head. Inge was leaning against the wall herself mutter-
ing, "I hate rottenness, I hate cruelty, I hate it, I hate it." I
looked at her and she was white.

"How did you know what it was?" I asked curiously, coming out of my spin.

"I knew it was some religious thing," she said, "with all that Hebrew writing. And I know you don't give a damn about all that, and I know you goddam well don't go around looking for insults from those spoiled little pricks. Piss on him!"

At that moment the monkish student sidled out of the door.

"Mr. Lazerow," he said timidly, "Chris is drunk, that's what happened. Well, Chris is a Jew—that is, he was born . . ."

"Skip it, Hugh," I said, and walked off with Inge. "Why don't we try the red room," I announced to her, "Krishna only knows what we'll find in that malebolge."

"You're gibbering," said Inge, which was true enough. We moved toward the red glow, the immemorial aura of temptation. A six-foot scarecrow, skinny as a question mark, with watery blue eyes and a wisp of blond beard, collided with me at the door. He leaned over me all atremble and whispered, "She's doing it! She's doing it! Hurry!" And lurched through the hall.

I had stopped at the announcement and Inge asked, "What? Who's doing what?"

"Listen, Inge," I said. "Did you ever go to the carnival?"

"Millions," she answered, getting her laugh back.

"And the sideshows?"

"That's what carnivals are for," she answered.

"Okay," I said, "wait till you see this freak."

We stepped inside the room which was deathly quiet except for one contralto monotone; the voice came from the corner away from the door and about twenty people, sitting and standing, faced a woman in a motionless tableau.

Her name was Catherine House. She was in her late twenties and had the horse-faced handsomeness of an English matron. She was elegantly dressed in a burgundy velvet skirt with a white silk blouse open at the neck. She wore a large gold-rimmed cameo over her bosom and no makeup on her face. Her shoes were what I remembered as "sensible." I had heard rumors of her acts at parties but could never quite believe them. After all, she was a faculty wife; her husband taught scientific classical Greek at the dental college and to pre-meds. Why hadn't she been put away, or why hadn't House been fired for encouraging this termagant? Nobody knew.

"Because," said the elegant Catherine in her throaty voice, "I am the only doer and *you* are all chicken-shit. Male and female the same." She raised her hand and began to point in a manner reminiscent of a regal gesture. "You, Margaret. You, Howard. You, Dale. You, Merle. You, Harlan. You, Clare. You, Marie. You, Scotty. You, Oscar. You, Gustav. You, Miriam. You, Duane. You, Cynthia. You, Ape. You, Cletas. You, Dotsy. You, Emil. You—whatever you call yourself. You, Barb." She had come to the end of the roster and spotted me. "And of course *you*, Mr. Lazerow, Chicken-shit. And I'll include your friend."

"Go, baby, go," said Oscar, who was evidently enjoying the scene immensely. Catherine gave him a withering glance. "You, you—capon-shit!" There was a spatter of laughter but the tableau remained in place like a high-school stage set.

Without knowing I was saying anything I said, "That chair doesn't become you, Mrs. House." It was one of those old over-stuffed chairs which had once been considered the height of posterior fashion.

"I like it," said Mrs. House pettishly, and straddling one of the threadbare arms, began to ride upon it, as it were.

What happened was that she masturbated for the assembled company, cursing them for watching and for not joining in the fray. Her husband Howard smiled and scanned the faces of the audience. Catherine rode her chair under her velvet skirt, modestly concealing her flesh. Her eyes were closed in a squint as her rhythm settled into a jog. The chair creaked and groaned with its unaccustomed load. The company, her intimate audience, began to encourage her with a communal wavelike sound of: "Shhh! Shhh! Shhh!" each time she thrust.

Inge grabbed me by the elbow and whispered, "I'm going to vomit," and rushed through the door. I piloted her to the porch railing and she threw up vigorously and heaved and spat down into the marigolds. I gave her two handkerchiefs—I always carry a spare—and she wiped her mouth with one and her eyes with the other. After a minute of swaying silence she sought out a glider on the porch and sank down. I dropped the handkerchiefs over the rail and sat beside her. Neither of us had anything to say. It was dark where we were and we watched cars parking and unparking, people in curious dress coming and going, but everything in a kind of silence. An ugly quiet, I thought. I suggested another drink, tentatively; Inge wanted to wait a little.

A police car beacon was whipping around a couple of blocks away and we watched it approach and slow down and double park in front of the house. An officer with a good deal of gold on his hat mounted the porch with difficulty and rang the bell. Inge and I sat still. The police officer asked to speak to Mr. Janiczek on the porch "and no cause for alarm" he said, and waited.

Brom emerged with a clinking glass and asked the Chief, as he called him, to come in. "No need, no need," said Slezak. "I just wanted to tip you that the drug preacher, Akiba Maim, is heading for your house with his crowd. We got a call from the state line and you know, Brom, it's our job to give him surveillance. You understand." Brom tried to assure Slezak that everything would be in order, that there were just a bunch of college students dancing in there and that he and Karen were definitely in charge.

"The only thing of it is, Brom," said the Chief, "we have to check his wagon for drugs because there's a report out on him and his crowd. Will you care if we question him here if we can't locate him on the highway?"

"Well, Chief," said Janiczek, "you are as welcome here as always, and I don't think you'll find anything illegal about those boys. They're just religionists, good kids, take my word for it, and wouldn't hurt a fly. You can even wait if you want; they've got nothing to conceal."

The police chief would rather not wait and said he would come back maybe in an hour. Brom offered him a drink which he refused but he took Brom's glass and had a swallow. "See you later, Brom."

Word spread through the house at electronic speed that

Akiba Mem and friends were definitely en route to Milo and would pay a visit to the Janiczeks. Two of the black-jacket motorcycle set sped through the screen door, leaped on their bikes, and vanished down the lawn and the silent street in a roar. I turned to Inge and said, "The message is abroad. Do you want to stay or go?"

"Stay," she said laconically. We sat quietly for about five minutes before Inge decided she was recovered enough to re-enter the den.

"Are you ready for another exhibit?" I asked. Inge apologized for being so squeamish, and laughed, "I never knew little old Milo had so much nightclubbing to offer. From a prayer-shawl-ripping to a public masturbation in two minutes. Lead on, Boss, but get me a motion sickness sack just in case."

"This one won't be so bad," I said, "except for me." She looked at me doubtfully. And I added, "Can you see in the dark?"

Inge took this to mean that we were going to watch, or imagine we were watching, the Jamaicans with the college girls and the faculty wives. We moved toward the throb and wail of the soul music records but the adjoining room was already jammed with spectators and/or auditors and it was hard to get close to the darkened sun porch where the action was taking place. Bumpy Harrington was elbowing her way to the front, her husband standing uncomfortably in the middle of a herd of what seemed to him to be aspiring cowboys and Indians. I spoke to Doc Harrington.

"Have you bonded any yet?" I laughed.

Harrington shook hands and suggested that he had told Bumpy that this was no place or time to get a foreign student to live in, but that Bumpy, "you know Bumpy," said it was precisely and scientifically the time and place and "just you see, Dr. Harrington." By now Bumpy had wiggled into the other room and was in total darkness.

Actually, there were only seven Jamaicans, plus several native U.S. Negroes and two Africans with the embroidered fez. But the dance program was apparently arranged by the West Indians, who always traveled to parties in a body and danced in the same room and with the same ground rules. They picked the records and they set the volume and one of their number had the job of operating the light switch. The overhead lights would flash on before and after each dance, at which time the Caribbeans (I called them The Blues) would crowd at the doorway and leer at the available white meat. Now and then during a record the lights would flash on for a brief second, as if to give the girls a preview of the paradise to come. I wondered how Bean Harrington was taking to this Walpurgisnacht but when I turned to see his face, the Doc had disappeared.

"What do you think?" I asked Inge.

"Just dancing," she answered, and leaning toward my ear added, "with a dry fuck here and there." The music was pounding like the Grand Coulee Dam, and suddenly the lights flashed on in the dance pavilion. In front of the dancers a white girl or woman was standing on her hands, her feet held up by a grinning Blue. The woman's skirt was over her head, making her face invisible. She was naked under her clothes. The lights flashed off so quickly that nobody was sure he had seen what he had seen. Inge had regained her composure and was laughing again.

"For your edification," I said to her, "that was Wanda."

"I wouldn't be surprised," she answered and told me she had seen enough of that side show and why not make us both a new drink. We worked our way back to the armory-bar, where Brom was still hosting the adults, making drinks, and discussing fire rites among the Bantu tribes with a pretty graduate student named Deirdre. She was leaning against the sink, admiring his handlebar moustache and not hearing a word.

"They say you may have a visit from the Dalai Lama," I said, as Brom handed us our drinks. Karen suddenly appeared at my ear like Ariel and whispered, "We arranged it, Ed, *arranged* it!" and gave a *Wuthering Heights* laugh. "And he said he was coming especially to see you, Ed. *You*. So don't get any notions about leaving, Ed."

I laughed and said, "Well, I don't see why I have to have my soul beholden to that phony ex-Hebrew LSD *soixante-neuf* queersville public relations genius with a beard of egg noodles and pubic hair . . ." Karen squealed with delight, Brom chuckled, the graduate student named Deirdre opened her mouth to reveal—braces!—and Inge kicked me playfully on the calf. It was at this moment that Wanda appeared, moving Inge and me just enough apart to confront Brom and demand scotch. "No," she said, "two scotch, one for me, one for Indian." While he was obliging her she turned to Inge.

"Are you the It?" she said. Inge turned a shade pale and said nothing. Whereupon Wanda wheeled on me. "Nice going, Edsel," she said, slightly drunk or dizzy. "Nice fucking going, *Edsel*," she ended in what was intended to be an icy tone, and stalked off with a drink in both hands.

Inge had fair recuperative powers but was slightly flushed from her brief encounter with Wanda. A bit of fire shone from her eyes and I worried what the next brush with Wanda might bring. I toyed with the idea of escaping the party but was too curious about Karen's remark to want to leave so early.

"What time do you figure the Christ and his apostles will descend?" I asked Karen.

As usual, Karen coiled near my ear and whispered, "Gimpy, our faithful fuzz, said they were about fifty miles into the state already. Don't you think that's metaphorical, Ed?" She reared back and laughed at her own joke. "Give or take an hour, they'll be here. And listen to this, Ed. Akiba is bringing the tapes of his mass rally from yesterday and he said he wouldn't play them unless you sat on the floor with him and listened to every last millimeter."

"*Dolce, dolce*," I answered. "You mean I can't wait and read it in *Flowering Banana* or *Pottie* or *All-Day-Sucker* or whatever he calls his magazine?" I began to think seriously of leaving this time and asked Inge her opinion. She flattened an open palm downward against the air and said, "We'll stay. My education is at stake."

I shrugged and we walked off toward the white room.

The white room looked like a secondhand electrical appliance shop. There were beat-up fluorescent desk lamps on the floor and on all the tables, some turned upward toward the ceiling, some facing walls, some turned to shine out of the door. They were all buzzing like trapped New Jersey mosquitoes; I wondered how so many hideous fixtures had found their way together and what message they might be trying to convey. It seemed to be an every-man-for-himself department in here. In a corner sat a drunken Air Force sergeant with his shirt open and out, bent over what looked like a Nazi souvenir bayonet. He was spitting on the blue blade and honing it on his boot. I walked near and spotted the neat little swastika on the hilt. The sergeant didn't bother to look up. In the second corner stood a girl with her face to the wall, as if, I thought, she was being punished for not being able to spell *transcendental*. But it wasn't as simple as that: she was stark naked and was in the process of being painted orange and gold. The huge baldheaded or shaven halfback known lovingly to Milo as The Ape was swabbing her buttocks and legs with wide housepainting brushes, waiting a little after each stroke for the paint to dry. The Ape turned around when we approached and made as if to rise, but, changing his mind, just grinned and went back to his labors. In the center of the room a black-belt Judo real honest-to-God Japanese was demonstrating the graceful art of splitting two one-inch boards with the edge of his hand; his apprentice was a tiny gnome of a student who was actually twenty-one years old but looked nine or ten, a well-known glandular case of some variety. I knew the Japanese, an instructor in geology, and had met him at the Yamashiros'. Rumor had it that he was a nobleman of the ancient regime and had been an aide-de-camp of Hirohito and was even on board the *Missouri* during the surrender to the Americans. His English was practically non-existent, which I attributed to his nostalgia for the good old days.

"I'll hold the other end, Shiki," I said. Shiki turned and greeted me and nodded. Shiki did the expected: let out a scream of *Hai! Hai!* and split the two boards with a clip of his hand.

"You try?" Shiki asked me.

"Me?" I said. "I couldn't break a matzoh." Shiki naturally didn't catch the reference and I amended, "Cracker," and pretended to bite and masticate. We both laughed.

There was a drumming of heels. I turned slightly and watched Kaz flamenco into the room, arms akimbo. "Nice party, professor," he said machine-gunning past me, then circled Inge three hundred and sixty degrees, stopped in front of her and bowed.

"Would you like to dance?" he asked.

"Where?" she answered in a fainting voice.

"Where? Where the action is," said Kaz.

"Thanks. No," she said and took a step closer to me.

"Drink then?" he asked, offering a half-pint bottle from a back pocket.

"I have one already," she said, holding up her glass. He flicked the cap off his little bottle, took a discreet swallow while starting up his heels again, took another, and glided out of the door with the bottle vertical against his mouth.

"What's he want?" asked Inge. She was a little frightened.

"It's not you, Inge," I said. "Just a message to me from the Black Widow." I quoted a few lines from Melvin Tolson:

The black widow spider gets rid of her man,
    gets rid of her daddy as fast as she can.
If you fool around, I know what I'll do—
like the black widow spider I'll get rid of you.

Inge let out a small scream. I jerked around. The Air Force sergeant had lurched to his feet and was stumbling toward Shiki pointing his Nazi bayonet.

"Dirty rotten mother-fucking gook bastard!" he yelled. Shiki stood still and let the soldier come within distance. In one motion he had the bayonet in one hand and had seated the sergeant on his prat with a trick of the foot. The soldier sat stupidly weaving on the floor and began to sob.

I touched Shiki on the back and gave him a wink; I said to Inge, "I forgot. There's a basement as big as a house in this joint. Lots of guitars no doubt, and candlelight. I hope Janiczek has insurance."

But Inge wanted to try the porch again. "Got to process my data," she laughed. We were going through the door and as if by telepathy Brom arrived and wordlessly took the bayonet which Shiki held out to him handleward. The sergeant keeled over with a horrible knock of his head on the wood floor and lay apparently unconscious. As I glanced back I saw Shiki holding the sergeant up and slapping him lightly across the cheeks.

"Love thine enemy," I said. "Not for me. Shiki should have made him swallow the bayonet, swastika and all." We sat down again on the cooling porch. "Pseudo-children," I said and we subsided into our own thoughts.

Traffic was getting heavier up and down the Janiczek front steps and someone switched on the porch light. I saw Grace and Tremaine Atwood coming up the walk dressed normally, as if they were attending a neighborhood cocktail party. They spotted me and came to say hello. "Be careful in there, Tremaine," I said, following the introductions, "it's Durd's Drug come to life. Like *The Nutcracker Suite*."

"Which only goes to demonstrate," said Tremaine, bending gracefully down, "that nature imitates art even in this day and age. Why, where would these drab little citizens get their imagination if not from books? Left to themselves they'd remain the field mice that they are."

"The mice are dead. Long live the mice," I answered.

Tremaine leaned again and said in a stately manner, "Perhaps what we want is the Pied Piper, Edsel?"

"I think he's due here tonight," I said, and mentioned the oncoming caravan. Tremaine raised his eyebrows and gave a smile which might have symptomized delight. The pair entered the house with an air of gravity.

"Poor Grace," I said half to myself. "Always the spectator."

"I hope she gets away with it in there," laughed Inge.

"No danger," I answered. "A woman like that could walk through the fiery furnace and come out without a hair mussed. Cool as a firewalker. Only I always wonder why."

We chatted about virgin immunity until Karen came out wreathed in smiles. "The kids are going to line the walk with candles, Ed, holding them."

"You mean like Rush Week, Karen?" I asked incredulously.

"Maybe they'll bring Akiba in on a bed of nails and we can all throw away our crutches."

Karen laughed at what she thought of as my barbed-wire wit and waved herself back into the party. Pretty soon a line of boys and girls of various sizes and shapes, carrying candle stubs of various sizes and shapes, emerged from the screen door and sat down on both sides of the walk. Karen expected a call from Akiba from the outskirts and had told them she would signal them when to light up. It was a sweet windless night and leaves seesawed down around the young devotees.

"It's pretty," said Inge. Something about the scene touched her.

"And funny," I said. "Those kids would rather be crucified than step inside a church, and here they are starting a religion from scratch. They call it love but it has all the earmarks of hate to me. A little crop of cornball Nazis waiting for instructions from headquarters. Don't think our hosts haven't tipped everybody off about the confrontation between the Cupidons and the Cossacks. Don't think they all aren't dying to be arrested. How else would they have any identity?"

Inge said that I was sounding embittered because of the student who ripped up the prayer shawl. "Yes," I said, "him and the Army killer and the Judo king and the flamenco buff and the I'm-better-than-you-are-niggers from Jamaica and Tremaine Atwood—Dr. Livingstone, I presume—and the whole rotten hick scene lying in wait for the kike Messiah who's going to give them a treat of Hindu wrist bells and maybe even a picture in *Lux* magazine. Look at these denizens of the woodwork who've crawled out tonight to confront what they think is Authority. Tonight their atrophied little imaginations will shine in candlelight and in what Harry Peltz, I mean Mahatma Schlock, calls poetry and love. They've got to make a politic of love too. Like Miss Milo in there getting her ass painted by that Polack mutant."

I started to laugh. "Jesus," I said, "you're right. I am taking this seriously. They all look like cockroaches to me. —I'm in love."

Inge turned and looked at me in the porch light. I felt her look and her tenseness and turned to meet her gaze.

"A woman nobody knows around here," I explained, "and I hope they'll never know."

Inge sighed, with relief I thought and hoped. I patted her gratefully on the hand and said I would go and fix the drinks.

"Pardon the confessionalism," I said. Inge reached out and caught my hand as I was getting up.

"Boss," she said, "I'm so glad. I mean—that you are—in love. Hide it because, you damn well know, in these parts . . ."

"I know," I said, and squeezed her hand gratefully, and went for our drinks. Know *what*, I said to myself as I made my way through the now-excited crowd to the bar. All I know is, Inge is right, if anybody rises above himself in this burg he's clobbered. Definition of the province. Stay in line. Like these stinky little boy-girl-scouts are forming a corporation to keep everybody in line and their boss is coming to give them a Christmas bonus and a few preferential fucks and a few sticks of weed and the gospel according to Saint Smegma.

Brom was again stationed at the bar and engaged in an animated conversation with Bumpy. "They are now superior to equality," Brom was saying. "They don't mind the houseboy bit but it has to be on the condition that *you* are inferior; not at their mercy, mind you, but morally-culturally responsible. You *know*," he ended knowingly.

"Silly man," said Bumpy. "I have three offers already; it's a buyer's market." She garnered two drinks and turned around to face me.

"Aha," she cooed, "there's the man with the blue guitar," and gave me a grin and a buss. Bumpy was proud of her memory of the names of "significant" modern poems and used them to goose appropriate friends and acquaintances.

"How's the hiring going?" I asked.

"It's all but accomplished," she answered. "And the one I want—you'll never guess his name. Rodney William Penn!" She laughed gleefully and announced that Rodney was a direct descendant of the English admiral.

"Pretty unlikely," corrected Brom. "That was the Penn that

chased the blacks up into the hills for a century. He's putting you on."

Bumpy thought that that was perfectly delightful and if she were a Negro she'd give herself a put-on name too. At this moment Karen came floating into the room and announced in a stage whisper that Akiba had called from the highway outside of Milo to alert the party and to make sure that Edsel was still among the company. "It's grand!" she emoted and swept out onto the lawn to tell the welcoming committee to light their candles in exactly four minutes. I made my way back to Inge with our bourbons to watch the candlelighting.

"Nervous?" asked Inge.

"I don't know why I should be, but I am," I answered. "I've never had anything to do with him actually and the last time I saw him was just before the day he woke up famous. He was brought to my house by Hal Beechnut, the Providence poet. I was teaching at Mills that year and Beechnut wanted me to meet this genius named Peltz. Akiba was a later name. Anyhow, nothing happened; Akiba didn't open his trap but just stalked up and down my livingroom, clean-shaven and in horn-rim glasses, looking like he wanted to bite somebody, probably me. Amazing thing was this kid who had never published a line and a few days later he was being seen and heard on TV, radio and every front page in the country."

"I remember something about it," Inge said, "but never got the point."

"The point was," I said laughing, "that Akiba and three cronies, all dressed in pleated Greek military skirts, climbed up inside the head of the Statue of Liberty and found an open barrier and showered the populace below with Akiba's poem 'The Bitch of Bedloe's Island.' The first line was enough to start a riot: 'Imperial virgin whore of Wall Street shore, Whitman and Hart and I Akiba scream no more no more no more to the American gulls of clap and shit,' and such paeans. When they were arrested they claimed that their goal was to remove the bronze sonnet on the statue and replace it with Truth. Akiba meanwhile had lined up thirty English professors over the country, including Beechnut, to pay for an ad for his defense. They didn't need the ad: every veterans' outfit in the country took to the air to denounce the sacrilege; Akiba himself published a book of editorials attacking him or rather pirated the stuff and had to be bailed out by softheaded pinko well-wishers. That poem sold a hundred thousand copies in a matter of weeks and another hundred thou when the California court banned it as obscene. The whole thing was a miracle of planning."

The people on the lawn were standing up and lighting one another's candles. There was a gentle tinkle of Indian bells. Karen had dug strands of little cowbells out of the trunk and passed them around; they were evidently a great hit. I had to admit to myself that it was an attractive scene, reminding me vaguely of Fourth of Julys which I had always loved.

At the far end of the street a car turned toward us flashing its headlights bright-dim, bright-dim, bright-dim. In a moment another car turned behind it, swinging the thick white beacon of authority like a lasso. The candle people rose and lined the sidewalk. The party began to crowd out of the house onto the porch and lawn. Inge and I stood against the rail to watch.

The double doors of the poet's yellow Microbus swung open and the visitors burst out and stood for a moment at the curb. Brom and Karen both marched down the walk while cameras and flashbulbs popped. From the lawn others began popping; I thought I spotted two local newspaper guys with professional stance and equipment. The candleholders meanwhile raised their lights and began to tinkle their bells and sway and chant: Harry Krishna, Harry Krishna! They didn't know what the words meant, but they did know they were Akiba's battle-cry. Akiba would give them the correct pronunciation later.

The police car had pulled up behind the Microbus and switched off its beacon.

"Harry Peltz Krishna," I said, staring.

Nobody got out of the police car and the arriving dignitaries began up the walk. Coming within range, Akiba did in fact look impressive. He wore some kind of faded Russian ballet shirt with billowing sleeves and what might be embroidery.

Long loops of seed-beads hung around his neck, which was wreathed with whiskers. He stopped every few feet and spoke to his greeters, sometimes bowing, sometimes clasping a candleholding boy or girl, sometimes lifting an arm in a gesture of weary delight. Behind him came two tall lads dressed as American Indians, or so I surmised; they wore tightly braided hair which hung down in snaky ropes, and they sported fringed white leather jackets. Bringing up the rear were two college student types in shirts and jackets without ties and with neatly mussed hair, between them a kind of stumbling creature which might have been anything from a trained chimp to a liberated basket case.

Brom and Karen intercepted the delegation as they neared the porch steps and all shook hands vigorously. Suddenly Akiba raised his voice and called:

"Edsel, my friend! I came to see you. Where are you!"

"Go on," said Inge.

"Don't push me," I answered and walked to the steps and down.

The guru stood still and waited until I had made my descent. Goddammit, I thought, why do I have to come down to his level? The holders of the candles had circled over the lawn and made an enclave around the Janiczeks, the new guests and me. Camera bulbs began more popping. As I approached, Akiba spread his arms out like the wings of a totem pole. I walked into them deliberately and we clasped each other like long-lost brothers. A cheer and clapping and ringing of Hindu cowbells came from the audience.

Akiba took a step back and said. "But you look so distinguished, Edsel, like a person of wisdom. The white hair of the suffering. I have come to visit you."

I said, "You too have changed, Akiba." (I wasn't ready to say Harry.) We proceeded side by side up the steps and into the house, saying nothing.

In the back of the house the Jamaican contingent was still holding forth and the beat of the folk-rock had switched to a more intelligible Calypso. Somebody was having fun with

Brom's collection of antique records. Akiba winced as we entered the hall and faced the patriotic-looking lighting and the sound of "camp." He excused himself and disappeared toward the dancing academy. Inge appeared at my side and I beckoned her. "Come with me," I said. I led her to the blue room where Brom and Karen kept their "classical" collection and where the master phonograph was housed. I grabbed an album at random and slapped a record down and turned the volume up full force, then pulled her back into the hall to wait for the guru. As Akiba emerged with his arm around a glistening Jamaican (who was dragging Wanda in tow) they were met with the blast of the *Dies Irae* of the Verdi *Requiem*. The volume was blinding and Akiba, who had just succeeded in turning off the music in the back of the house, seemed to stagger slightly. But Karen had already rushed to the rescue and yanked out the wall plug; she was sweating slightly when she apologized to Akiba. "Some child," she said, "trying for attention." Akiba gave her a mincing smile. He turned to one of his henchmen.

"Govinda," he said, "the tape recorder."

Govinda, of lank braids and fringes of Custer's-last-stand jacket, handed Akiba a leather-bound tape recorder which I judged must have cost someone about five hundred dollars. Karen thought the blue room would be the ideal place for the recital and she led the company through the door. Akiba slipped the handsome machine from its case and plugged it in.

"Sit by me, Edsel," he said, and lowered himself to the floor. "Less light," he commanded Karen, who switched off all but one.

I called to Inge who was leaning against the wall. "Get me a bottle from Brom, please," and gave her a wink with both eyes. She sidled out of the door and returned shortly with an uncapped fifth of blended scotch.

"We don't drink, Edsel," said Akiba, "but with you I drink." He seized the fifth and upended it against his mouth and took a healthy drag, and handed the bottle to me. I took a healthier swallow and set the scotch between my legs.

The room had become crowded with standees and in the hall faces were peering over one another, staring at the university poet and the guru seated on the floor.

"Not only with you but to you I drink," said Akiba, and put his arm around me. "Because I love you," said the itinerant mystic. "Tell me, now, what are you writing?" Akiba said this with air of a creative writing teacher who had just returned from a Fulbright and was speaking in secret to his favorite student.

I in turn had thrown my arm around Akiba and gave him a kiss on the beard. Akiba immediately smoothed it out with his hand. I had the fleeting impression that Akiba had just come from the beauty parlor and thought I could smell the aroma of the hair dryer.

"I've just finished my verse play," I said, "about Snorri Sturlason the skald. He was such a talented bastard, whether more bastard than talented being the subject."

Akiba looked grave. "You know, Edsel," he said, "I follow you, I have always followed you, worried about you. I worry about your joking, your failure of seriousness, your departure from the—well, why can't I say it to you?—the sacred. Our art is holy ground, as well you know. I came to you about this, to return your art to prayer, invocation, to the *semplicità*." I was touched by the music of the Italian word and hated Akiba for having just returned from the Spoleto festival while I had been grinding out lectures in Hamburg and Frankfort.

I laughed and took a swig of the scotch and handed Akiba the bottle. "But there's nothing simple about you, Harry Peltz," I said. Akiba smiled and squeezed my hand.

At this moment there was a kind of rumpus on the outer porch and a shuffling of persons in the hallway, along with a few muffled cries of what might have been indignation or fright; and the chief of the Milo police limped into the doorway of the blue room. Brom Janiczek followed and gave Akiba a pay-no-attention wave.

"Mr. Maim?" asked Slezak. Akiba rose to his feet, handling his beard and smiling.

179

"My name is Mem, Akiba Mem, officer," he smiled and held out his hand.

"Mr. Mam," said Chief Slezak, compromising on the pronunciation. "Sorry to be of bother. May I speak to you privately?"

Akiba leaned over and with one hand behind him lifted the microphone of his Abercrombie & Fitch tape recorder to his mouth like a lollypop.

"There is nothing private between us, officer," he said in a calming voice. "If you wish to ask me anything I want you to ask in front of my dear friends."

Gimpy Slezak lurched back on his short leg and peered at Brom who said, "I told you he is okay, Chief. Just ask him whatever you have to and he'll give you full satisfaction."

The police chief had never been separated from his subject by a microphone except in his own office with witnesses and he asked Akiba why the microphone.

"Sir," said Akiba, "for my rights and for your rights, and no harm done. Besides, I am a traveler, as you know, and I like to keep a record of my experiences."

"Okay," said the Chief. "I have a search warrant for your car. Suspicion of carrying drugs. Have to check that out. Is that all right with you?"

"The car is right there, Chief," said Akiba, "and you have my blessing to search it for whatever you want." Akiba took a step toward the officer, who took a step back.

"Second," said Slezak, "I want to know how long you expect to be in Milo and where you and your passengers are residing."

Akiba glanced at Brom who came forward, put his arm on Slezak's and said, "Chief, these students are my guests, Mr. Mem and the four with him—not the whole party, Chief, for God's sake—and they have my hospitality."

"Thank you, professor," said Akiba. "A day, two days."

Slezak and Brom stepped into the hall and conferred for a few minutes. Brom returned by himself and winked at Akiba and motioned him to resume his sitting posture and to forget the late unpleasantness.

Akiba replaced the microphone in the case and produced a pair of Hindu bells from his pockets. He closed his eyes and began to sway silently at first, then quietly let the little bells tinkle. Slowly he began to chant:

"Hari, Hari, Krishna, Krishna."

Suddenly his eyes flew open and he addressed the assembly. "The word is not Harry, please. It it Harr-ii. You have to roll the 'r.' Try putting a 'd' before the 'r' or after the 'r.' It is difficult to do. But it's definitely not *Harry*—like I'm just wild about Harry." He let his hands flow in the position of a decaying lotus. "Harrdi, Harrdi, Krishna, Krishna," and he let the bells tinkle and his eyes close and his body sway as he chanted:

> "Oh come, oh come, oh dance, oh dance,
> Chanting Harrdi's name with fervor!
> What does it matter that you struck me?
> What does it matter that you fuck me?
> Dance, dear friends, in Harrdi's name!
> Sing the name of our beloved!
> He'll embrace you in his rapture!
> Weep and chant the name of Harrdi,
> Harrdi, Harrdi, Krishna, Krishna,
> And you will see your very moon-soul;
> Harrdi's name is love I give you,
> Give me Krishna, bring my Krishna,
> Krishna, Krishna, Harrdi, Harrdi!"

Akiba's company had begun their tinkling and chanting also and soon the entire group was locking arms and chanting *Harrdi, Harrdi, Krishna, Krishna.* I was being bumped by Akiba's sidewise swaying and shut my eyes and let the music flow over me.

Akiba had the genius of attention and co-attention; he knew when to entrance one person and when to engage a sea of faces. Tonight the house party was of no consequence; he had come to enlist me in some cause or other, or to neutralize me, "sting me into acceptance," I thought. The chanting and bell-ringing stopped abruptly and Akiba gave me a knowing Rama-krishna smile and fished out a huge spool of tape from the pocket of his tape-recording apparatus.

"What, no *samadhi?*" I asked.

"I was close. I am always very close," said Mem. "Like orgasm at will. I know, I know, like wet dream, like bed-wet-ting." I knew, from having read Akiba's poems, his tricks of ellipsis, which was what his style consisted of. It enabled Akiba to sound "oriental" or "foreign" or "with it" all at once, without having to construct anything out of his mind. I thought to myself that Akiba's gift was broken Esperanto.

The tape was in place and Akiba had his hand on the On button. He held his finger poised and lowered his voice and leaned into my face and said:

"I come here, Edsel, to have you hear me. I know you will hear me. That is why you are here beside me. I am nothing. I am nobody. I am a face, a faceless non-entity. Who is there-fore everything. But all over the world I am flocked to. All over the world I am photographed and debated. Why? Why? Now you listen to this piece of plastic tape and tell me why. And tell me who. Or, if you are wise, say nothing or anything. But don't be able to deny that the truth speaks out of me."

He gave me a shy smile and switched on the tape of his last lecture. There was a roar from the amplifier, a mixture of ap-plause and boos. The boos definitely had it. "Listen," said Akiba, "they are booing me. But not for long," and through the crowd noise came the jingle of bells. Akiba leaned his head back and smiled, closing his eyes to slits. When the roaring of the mass audience had subsided, Akiba's taped speech began.

"Resistance is good, resistance is honorable, resistance is authentic," be began. "I respect you and love you for it, even if my presence displeases, even if my appearance is strange and makes you laugh and cringe, even if you would like to kill me. I have come for you, have come to win you, to win with the help of your beautiful resistance, help of your beauty, your and my youth. If you did not resist you would be dead; I kiss my hands to your resistance. I bring your own love to this community, yes, communion of lovers. I dig your youth, you dig my beard, or you would not come at all and you would not cringe with hiss and booings. Soon you will not see my beard and Govinda's pigtails and fringes of the holy Indian of our blood-drenched United States soil. The mystics call it One. I will One with you—it's a paradise verb. I will One you and be your One and together we shall see through and beyond, together we shall resist and together we shall ball the Absolute!"

An outbreak of more boos on the tape and a few obscene shouts of "Beat it out of here, kike!" "Take it off!" "Show us the fur!" "Call the cops!" Akiba smiled at the opposition while the demonstration subsided. His voice reminded them that this was a religious part of U.S. geography, these sacred plains where the food animals and gods of the red-hued owners had been slaughtered and driven into limbo, where punishment religions, as he called them, had grown up and made robots of the white man. He reminded them of freedom of religion, which had made this country great and powerful, and spoke of the universal religion of love and multiplicity which he was about to introduce them to, the vast and ageless wisdom of the high Himalayas, of the Christian martyrs, of the Hasidic Jews, of the Mayan worship of the obsidian knife, of sexual sacrifice and of "the joy of the land of Fuck." "I bring you God," he said, "the god of cock and cunt, of Yin and Yang, of Sin and Bang, holy, holy, holy of nakedness."

The blend of evangelism and fraternity language shut the objectors into silence and Akiba's voice continued in a soft and cajoling tone. "I bring you the freedom to fuck, I bring you the freedom to suck, I bring you the freedom to shit and piss. I bless the holy, holy, holy words and give them back to you and give back their power to your hands and mouths and loins and buttocks." The jingling of bells began louder this time, and Akiba went into his Hindu prayers, chanting wildly, rising to booming crescendos and calling for everyone to join in the Harrdi Krishna refrain. The singing and bell-ringing went on for what must have been twenty minutes, and when it was over, there was a dead silence on the tape while Akiba meditated wordlessly. Now and then a bell would jingle, as in a Catholic Mass.

"You mean the university let that go on?" I asked incredulously.

"That shows what cowardice is," said Akiba. "The power structure is crippled by its own power. Its hands and feet are tied. They preach free speech in the universities but they've preached it once too often. When we get up and demonstrate it, the cops and the trustees just skulk in the corridors, not knowing which way to turn. Yes. They had a warrant for our arrest but were afraid to use it. After what we did at Berkeley you can hardly blame them. All the fuzz did was to search the car and our bodies for grass, as if we aren't better at hiding than the cops at finding. Now listen to this, Edsel; here you can see the total impotence of the Establishment." He bent forward to hear what was coming.

Apparently it was a dialogue between Akiba and Govinda, his favorite lover. The two had taped what Akiba called their love diary, in and out of bed. The tape recorded and described their grunts and curses and positions, their ablutions and advice to each other and to the world about the care and cleaning of genitalia and sphincters. Akiba ran in a little sermon on venereal disease and quoted his slogan: If you love your lover enough to ball him, don't give him V.D.

This chapter of the tape was followed by a noisy and incoherent reply of a daisy chain or gang-shag with much screaming of lines of poetry from Whitman and shouts of "At exactly five o'clock in the afternoon!"

"Louder," said a hoarse voice, which I recognized as Wanda's. Akiba turned up the volume.

The second tape was an elaborate apologia for the use of drugs to expand consciousness, how and where to get them, make them, and use them. Akiba told his mass audience that he was passing out pamphlets at the door which he himself had had printed about the laws of drug use, state by state, "and for the love of God, my resisters and angels, be careful. We need every chick, we need every guy, to stay out of the

Black Maria. We need you, *mes anges,* to help spread total and universal consciousness and to assist in the cure of the disease called America. As we love and adore our land, so must we save her, just as we save our mothers in the flesh. With ancient and godly drugs, with modern test tube and plastic hallucinogens, we shall save our mother Liberty from rape and rapine."

The introduction of the Statue of Liberty led naturally into the "political" segment of the revival and began with another invocation to Krishna, some quotes from *Walden* and the declining Tolstoy, and the recitation of a terrorist poem by the Negro anarchist, Nebuchadnezzar Thomas. The Neb Thomas poem began: "If this America is hell, where are the fires!/ Who burned you black, you spade!/ Burn, hot nigger, your fat is in the fire!/ Light the fires of liberty, hell!/ Shoot off, O Afric cock!/ Shoot off your bleeding balls in Charlie's cunt!"—and such invocations.

Akiba's voice carefully explained the dangers of pure hate but rationalized the poem with a sad shrug of words, "for that is how we freed the chattels," he said. "We must and will suffer with them, aid and abet if need be, and show them our hearts and our sex."

From racial hysteria he moved to a defense of Cuba and the South American revolt. We are all part of the same thing, intoned Akiba: the sexual revolution, the drug revolution, the jazz revolution, all leading to the total and complete moral and political overthrow of the Establishment. "No more university, no more chancellery, no White House, no Black House, no Red House, but love of soul for soul and cock for cock and cunt for cunt and all for all in the Open Air!"

"Aren't you riding Whitman a little hard?" I asked.

"I ride him and ride him," smiled Akiba with a saccharine grin. "Walt is the gland of our movement."

Pamphlets, the machine was saying, were also available in the lobbies for political and race struggle literature, except that these were not for profit. Proceeds were to go to Akiba's foundation which paid for many things: bail for drug users and freedom fighters, but mostly to give scholarships to Kyoto and Benares where the new mysticism was operating full speed ahead. Akiba gave a few elementary lessons on starting an underground newspaper to give the Movement a link with the town and university he was addressing. He asked those interested to meet him and his friends in front of the main campus gate where, as he pointed out, the traffic was heaviest.

There followed a lively rock session by the Liver-Pudds which Akiba had taped himself in England. Tapes within tapes, I thought, drinking from the green bottle and passing it mechanically to Akiba. Mem continued to drink up, contrary to his "principles," and to show good faith with me.

The final tape was Akiba's poetry reading. He had composed new poems on his tape recorder riding through the nights of the Great Plains, labeling each village and farm, hamlet and city, some version of Rome or Carthage or Babylon and reeling off the sins and crimes of the inhabitants. It smacked a little of the *Spoon River Anthology,* but that figures, I thought. The reading was expert, a mixture of recitative and high oratory, plainsong and operatic roaring. Akiba tapered off with the Harrdi Krishna psalm and ended almost inaudibly with a rhythmic tinkle of the Hindu bells. There was a dead silence on the tape and finally the longest and most blood-curdling cheer I could remember. Akiba let the cheer roll on and on until the tape ran out, then leaned over and pressed the rewind button, threw his arms around me and hugged me. "Marvelous," said Akiba about his own performance. He seemed genuinely moved.

"No more," said Akiba, refusing the bottle which I had motioned at him. "I want to meet your friends," he added.

"I don't know them, only a few," I said. "Brom will take care of that."

Akiba rose and smoothed his beard and giving me a cherubic grin made his way to the door, where Brom and Karen stood with arms around each other, enraptured with the performance. As Akiba approached, Karen burst into tears and smothered the mystic with a hug. "Oh, Akiba," she snuffled, you have made this house a holy ground. None of us will ever be the same." Akiba responded silently, detaching himself deftly from the female anthropologist's clutch. The music had started up again in the rear of the dwelling and the bang of guitars could be heard from the basement. The blue room emptied.

"What do you think?" I asked Inge, who had sat on the floor beside me.

"I can't," she answered, laughing. "You do have patience, Boss. What's next on the program?"

"What happens from here on in," I said, "is purely below the belt. Or that's my guess. The Indians will add as many notches to their jocks as they can stomach, the Jamaicans will forsake the dance for the fertility rite, Mrs. House will masturbate on the totem pole, Wanda will solve the race problem in the only way she knows how, the Air Force will start smashing objets d'art while Akiba gives a footnote on the evils of the demon rum, the acid and marijuana will be broken out, the motorcycle riders will pass around their rusty hypo needles, the painted lady will shimmy under the fluorescent lights, everybody under twenty will get the dry heaves, and Kaz will do the Mexican hat dance on the kitchen table. And tomorrow this party will be consecrated as the greatest event in Milo since the James Brothers rode through and killed fifteen alley cats from horseback."

We decided we would just as well leave and I debated whether to say goodbye to anybody. I was afraid that if I didn't Akiba would come rolling up to my house with his cargo of human suffering. As we pushed our way to the kitchen we heard the noise of scuffling and cursing and a bottle smashing. Govinda, who carried an American flag as a handkerchief, had made a point of blowing his nose in it to amuse the admiring students.

"Wipe your ass with your draft card," said Govinda, "like I do this." He had slipped his trousers down and was bending over with the flag scrunched in his hand. But at that moment Kaz grabbed Govinda's arm and twisted it behind his back, snatching the flag with his other hand. From somewhere the

Air Force sergeant appeared and smashed his fist into Govinda's mouth. I thought I saw teeth flying as the braided would-be Indian folded up on the floor, unconscious.

That was the beginning. Akiba was holding Govinda's head and sobbing and kissing the bloody mouth. The Jamaicans appeared from nowhere and started swinging at everything white. Ape Koslow in an effort at peace-making was flinging all combatants against the wall. Karen was screaming and holding her ears. Four teenagers were rifling the liquor armory. "Turn the music up loud, loud!" Brom was bellowing, as all the lights in the house went dark and the pandemonium mounted. "Quick," I said in Inge's ear, "follow me." We edged toward where we had last seen the kitchen door and slipped out onto the back porch. We raced around to the street and got in my car as the police beacon made its appearance around the corner at the far end of the street. I started the motor and made a quick U-turn to head in the other direction and turned down the first cross street I came to. Several blocks away I turned slowly back. "Got to see," I said, looking at Inge who was sitting as silent as an Easter Island image.

I passed within a block of the Janiczek house, which was crawling with police lights. Suddenly, I said "My God!" and saw a burst of flame from the high Victorian window on the side. Simultaneously I heard the fire engines; I started the motor again and slid down the darkened street without turning my lights on.

CHAPTER XVI

℘ The fire, said the morning paper, was not spectacular, but the arrests were. Seventy-five souls of all ages had been booked at three A.M. in the sleepy, bedazzled downtown police station. Milo had never been treated to such a display of orgiastic vice and corruption, especially as it involved the dignity of the university faculty, members of the famous football team, and the Homecoming Princess (charged with nakedness, indecent exposure, and lewd conduct). High-school kids had been found drunk, disorderly, and in violation of the curfew: the Janiczeks were charged with contributing to the delinquency of said teenagers, disturbing the peace, and the possession of narcotics. The Air Force sergeant was remanded to the military police, who had arrived with their own siren-shrieking jeep. Akiba, Govinda and the catatonic boy in their tow were booked for "using" marijuana and for transporting it across state lines. Catherine House was arraigned for using "foul and abusive language" to the police and firemen. Only three Jamaicans were found on the premises, but as they had been discovered in the act of fornication with young ladies on the sun porch, they were charged with "cohabiting in public." Among those named in the latter crime was Wanda Shontz, "employed at the Fountain of Beauty Salon," and one of the

189

sorority girls in my Creative Writing class. There was no mention of Bumpy Harrington, I noted with relief. Kaz Graindorge —so that is his name, I said out loud, and whistled—was booked for carrying concealed weapons (a pearl-handled automatic, of all things) and for displaying a German bayonet— "intention to do bodily injury." Professor Tremaine Atwood and his companion Grace Mendenhall were brought to the station house as witnesses but were almost immediately released. A geology professor whose identity card read Prince Muro Shiki was hospitalized for smoke inhalation. Evidently Shiki had carried a dozen people from the basement when the fire started, and was overcome. The paper listed him in good condition. And the police were on the lookout for four motorcycle riders, all of whom had police records for shoplifting and traffic violations, but who had slipped out of the noose.

Unarraigned but very much in evidence was a Professor Oscar Darling, who stood bail for eleven students and pledged a complete investigation of "provincial police harassment and brutality." I turned on the radio to the local news station and sat back to listen to what must be a great day for Milo newshawks.

"Chancellor Dunstan Irick of Milo U. was visibly shaken as he faced Police Chief Slezak and plainclothes Lieutenant Dave Garvey. The chancellor promises a full and complete investigation and, in his words, full and complete punishment of the infraction of the legal and moral code of Milo by anyone, faculty member or student, or anyone else within his responsibility. Chancellor Irick warmly thanked the police for their vigilance."

I began to chortle. I figured I would have a visit from the authorities myself and was beginning to prepare a kind of brief. My hand fiddled for the phone, but I didn't know whether to call Inge or—Bumpy? The thought crossed my mind that this was an opportunity to call Marya; the *hope* crossed my mind that maybe she would be worrying about me. I removed my hand from the phone and listened to the report.

"The fire started in the rumpus room of the Janiczek residence at approximately 2:30 A.M. this morning. The house was in complete darkness; on investigation, police have discovered that all fuses had been removed from the central fuse box in the basement and thrown into the lavatory basin. Candles used in the basement and first floor of the house during the party ignited draperies and a large pile of excelsior used to strew the basement floor for purposes of dancing. All injuries have been reported minor but damage to the house and its collection of antiques and museum objects collected by Dr. Janiczek and his wife from all over the world is considered extensive."

The reporter was probably going to make a day of it and I got up to turn off the radio when I heard that more than six and a half pounds of marijuana had been confiscated from the party, all of it in little plastic Baggies concealed inside four guitars. The discovery had been made when Govinda tripped coming up the basement stairs, smashed a guitar on the kitchen floor, and began scrabbling for the plastic containers inside the instrument. Over him stood Lieutenant Garvey, who stomped heavily on Govinda's hand and picked up the marijuana and sniffed it. For the lieutenant it was so great a find that he handcuffed Govinda to the leg of an old iron cook stove, and dived down into the smoking cellar for more guitars.

"All the damage in the Janiczek residence is attributed to water from fire hoses," said the announcer, who suddenly began to expatiate upon the weather. I switched off the radio. I decided to wait for the phone to ring and wondered what the protocol would be: the chancellor? Wanda? Bumpy? Oscar? Brom? the police? Inge? Chris Jaffe? Akiba probably, I thought.

There was a knock at the door. I hate doorbells and had disconnected mine in the kitchen when I had taken the little apartment. But before I ever opened a door I peered out the window to prepare myself for the intruder. I spotted Brom's silly Citroën squatting against the curb on the other side of the street and went to open the door.

Brom looked haggard; his handlebar moustache drooped around his mouth, his eyes were bloodshot, there was soot on his face, his fingernails were black, his hair was askew, and there were burnt spaces in his jacket and around his knees. I felt a wave of sadness for him and said nothing, but took him by the elbow and pulled him into the livingroom.

"Shut up, Brom," I said, "I'm making us a drink." I smiled at the anthropologist and hurried to the kitchen. When I returned, Brom was listening to the radio. I handed him his drink and walked to the radio and switched it off.

"Okay, Brom," I said, "what can I do?"

"Goddam it to hell, Edsel," said Brom, his voice raddled, "it's that fucking farmer Graindorge. The cockfight farmer. He thinks I got the cops on him that night and now he got his son to get the cops on me. But Gimpy, you know Gimpy, he's my confidant about this hick police stuff in Milo, Gimpy wouldn't *do* this . . ."

"Wait a minute," I said. "If you keep a zoo, sooner or later you're going to get clawed, right? What proof have you got that Kaz—isn't that the Graindorge guy, your flamenco dancer —what proof have you got?"

Brom looked at me. "His girl, she said so to the police when they hauled us in. Wanda said that Kaz called the fire department when the lights went out. She smelled smoke."

"You're pretty beat, Brom," I said. "You can't tell anything at this point and the best thing you can do is to wait it out for a while and clean up some of the house. Listen, I'll go with you. How bad was it? How's Karen?"

Brom sat stunned and angered and tight as a drum, digging his nails into his hands. After a few minutes he let out a great sigh and began to relax his limbs and let his eyes wander around the room. He looked at me and humphed and said, "You know, Ed, I'm going to be fired."

I didn't know what to reply and made a non-committal remark about premature conclusions. All the same I knew a lost cause when I saw one in Milo. I wasn't about to sermonize the anthropologist but given the occasion I might.

"All right, Ed, what would you do?" he asked.

I turned my drink in my hand as the phone rang. It was Inge and I told her I'd call her in a little while.

"You remember my magazine, Brom?" I said. "It was a good sweet magazine. It had sweetness and balls. It was beginning to be famous, all over the world, as a matter of fact. Then one morning I woke up and found I was fired. By whom? I never knew. Why? I never knew. All I know is that Milo and I get along at bottom like a cobra and a mongoose."

Brom, who was only partly listening, asked to use the phone to see if his phone had been reconnected. There was no signal from the other end. "I've got twenty students at my house, salvaging," he said distractedly. "It's a regular honest-to-God dig. The last days of Pompeii. My manuscript that I've worked on for fifteen years, card files, photos that cost a fortune, were all lying in a puddle of orange and gold paint. Which that football ape was using to swab the backside of that campus prossie . . ."

I wanted Brom to leave; I wanted to let my own mind settle; I wanted to fall into a deep sleep and wake up in a different city, Tucson maybe, or Montreal, somewhere completely foreign to my responses, and find myself walking down a rich street laughing, with Marya on my arm. I wanted to buy her something from a rajah. Instead of which I spoke to Brom, dragging my chair a few feet closer to get his attention.

"You asked me what I would do?" I said. "Should I express myself?"

"Yes," said Brom. "For Christ's sake, *yes.*"

"You've got a crossroads in your life," I said softly. "Right here and now. You came here on your own. You've got to make a choice. Two choices and that's all. One: you patch things up with Chancellor Irick and Gimpy Slezak. You can save what you can of the party-goers and keep your job. You and Karen bow and kowtow and make amends, smile and brown-nose, get the newspaper off your back, keep your kids in expensive schools, play dumb and surprised and horrified at the catastrophe—the fact that your house and your life's work are gutted will weigh in your favor. The Milo administration will back you to the hilt to get you off the hook. Akiba and his rabble will be run out of town; the motorcycle set will get the five years that Akiba has coming to *him;* the sorority girls will be suspended for a semester; the Homecoming Princess will go to Chicago and make a fortune as a call girl; Tremaine will be promoted to dean; Shiki will get his Ph.D. without writing his thesis; the Jamaicans will have more invitations than they can handle and will apply for American citizenship. So if that's what you want, do it."

Brom was giving his begrimed face a dry wash and grinning.

"You're good for a man's soul, Edsel," he said and held out his glass. I went to make drinks.

Handing Brom his new drink, I looked at him and said, "But that's not what you want, is it, Brom?"

"You're so goddam right, Ed," said Brom weakly. I thought Brom was going to cry, instead of which he set his drink down on the little table in front of him with a magnetic click. "That was my party," he said, "that was my invention, that was, you might say, my poem. That's what I'm good at, that party. That's what I'm good at, stupid as it is. Edsel, listen to me, that was a great party; more, invention; it meant as much to me as fifteen years of that book I can't finish. I'm not going to go back on that invention. And Karen, it was like the promised land to her, all those young devoted rebels, the pure primitivism of it, all the beauty!" He leaned over a little and lowered his voice. "Do you know, Ed, that the poets all had peyote and were eating it? Don't you know that the folk guitar in the basement was just a cover for the Indian ceremony! I just thanked God the whole city of Milo didn't burn to the ground."

"Why?" I said, and went to the window and looked out at the great bronzed blazing elms. I fidgeted a while with the venetian blind and then went to sit at a different vantage point from Brom. There was a handsome rattan chair in the room which I liked for its appearance but hated to sit in because it threw my back into a painful obtuse angle.

"Brom," I said. "It's so pointless to give advice, for the simple reason that nobody takes it. I wouldn't take it any more than you would. Still, it's comfortable to hear. Comfortable that someone will want to identify with a friend at least to that extent. So here goes with my advice. Close your ears; listen or don't listen. I can't be you, if you'll pardon the obvious, but in

194

your position, which in a way I envy—I envy the opportunity for a clean and final choice—this is what I would do. Stand up and yell your head off and defend your party. No matter what. Your kids thrown out of St. Marks and Bennington and Reed and Harvard. Screw 'em. House burned down. Fine. Anthropology career ended. *Grazie*. Pick up the pieces and go. But not before you grind down every bastard who has taken you for a ride; and that means not only Chancellor Irick and Gimpy Slezak and Kaz Graindorge but Akiba Mem Peltz and his smegma band; it means all that sub-adolescent scum you've been fathering in your pretty house for years. Okay. It means that you turn the tables on the so-called authorities and on the so-called revolutionaries simultaneously. It means that you speak up and write it down and lay it on the line that you, Brom Janiczek, authority on the sociology and culture and bedbug life of Milo City and University, are going to present your data, whatever they are, and fuck the consequences."

Brom rolled his eyes.

"And if you want, Brom," I said, "I'll back you, whatever that's worth. I'll put my featherweight behind your effort to be free of this crappy town and this never-to-be university. Don't forget that there has never been a man in this school who wasn't fired as soon as he made a reputation outside of the state. It's the rule. Mediocrity or nothing. Genteel poverty or nothing. Cringe or go elsewhere. Eat crow. Die on the vine. You tell me the platitudes and I'll check 'em off."

Brom started to rise. "You're right, Edsel," he said. "I'm going to enlist Karen. You're right. You're right."

I started to ask what Karen had to do with it but kept my peace. Brom rose thoughtfully, thanked me and made his way to the Citroën.

With a car like that, I thought, he'll be here for the rest of his life. He may even be chancellor one of these days.

Brom, pumping up his antique automobile, was thinking the same thing.

195

CHAPTER XVII

ᗡ I had bought a set of colored marking pens, why, I was
not sure. Now I took them out of the box and began to
write words in colors. Maybe it would lead me to a poem. I
wrote "Marya" in bright yellow and my own name in light
blue. Blue is the Jewish color, I said to myself, and the phrase
"blue of Mary's color" crossed my mind. I wrote "love at the
lips" in vermilion, and "done is the battle on the dragon
black" in black. I'm a one-man kindergarten, my mind reminded me, and I crumpled up the paper. I took another sheet
and wrote Marya in all the colors, filling the page. Just a little
sympathetic magic, I thought, knowing I couldn't crumple up
her name. I laid the sheet on the cocktail table while the phone
rang. It rang "amusedly" this time, I thought.

It was Inge. "You have a letter from the chancellor's office,
Boss, she said. "It's sealed and marked Personal. Should I
open it?"

"Open it," I answered, "it must be a summons."

"Chancellor Irick," she read, "would appreciate it if you
would attend a small meeting in his office at 2 P.M. today.
Please inform his secretary if you are not available."

"Call his secretary and tell him I'll be there with wrist-bells."

Inge laughed and wanted to know if I was serious about the message. I assured her I wasn't kidding.

On a hunch I called Oscar Darling. "Listen, Oscar," I said, "I've been summoned into the presence this afternoon. How about you?"

"Natch, Ed," said Oscar. "Also Tremaine has been tapped. I don't know who else. Certainly not dear old Brom."

I volunteered to pick up Oscar at his house at one-thirty.

"And just what does one wear at a Milo inquisition, Oscar?"

Oscar suggested that a tie would be in order. "You do have a clothing complex, Ed," Oscar informed me.

I put on a black Brooks Brothers shirt with white buttons and a button-down collar. I put on a terra cotta tie and a black suit which I had bought to lecture in on my Germany lecture tour. Good, I thought, Humphrey Bogart. I had never owned black shoes and put on the Hush Puppies. Wish I had a carnation or the ribbon of the Legion of Honor, I joked to myself. I made a couple of Bogart grimaces in the mirror. "Play it again, Sam," I practiced, showing my right upper teeth.

Oscar seemed relaxed enough and chatted about the party as if it had been a bridge club.

"That Govinda creep," I asked, "did he come around?"

"He'll need some bridge-work," said Oscar, "otherwise, nothing. But all the visiting poets have been transferred to the County Hospital where they are being sedated and secluded. What worries the chancellor is *national* publicity. That could mean *his* ass. The police confiscated about a dozen cameras, Akiba's tape recorder and God knows how many guitars. And if this silly thing does break in *Lux* magazine I'm going to be the one that has to go to bat for everybody. After all, I *am* the president of the Civil Liberties Club in this district. But actually, the hushing-up process is already working. That's why we are going to meet his holiness."

Oscar told me that the gentle halfback Ape Koslow was the first to be sprung from the local Bastille and that the local newspapers had agreed to keep his name out of the papers. After all—the football team! Muro Shiki was also off the hook because of his heroics, "even though Irick hates Japs," said Oscar.

The chancellor had a private elevator in the hideously modern Administration Building; the elevator floor sported a maroon carpet and there was a generous ashtray in each of the two rear corners; between them a full-length mirror. Oscar and I stepped out into a spacious reception room which smelled of failed air-conditioning. The chancellor's secretary, a stick of an old maid with no mouth and a painful twist of steel hair on the top of her head, motioned us into the room behind her.

It was the Regents Board Room; it contained the usual endlessly oval formica table with its twenty-odd "Scandinavian" chairs, in front of each of which lay great urine-colored glass ashtrays. The only wall decoration was a fifteen-foot painting which abstracted an aerial view of the farms and roads around Milo. The colors were tawny and bisque, and glancing at the thing I felt that I might develop an attack of hay fever.

The chancellor sat at the head of the table "in close collaboration with" Tremaine Atwood, as it struck me. It seemed to me that they had been whispering. Both men stood and all shook hands. I wanted to sit as far away as possible from the little company but chose a chair only four away from the head of the university. Oscar took the one across from me.

"Just one more guest, gentlemen," said the chancellor. "Ah, there he is." To my surprise Dr. Harrington came through the door and greeting everyone good-naturedly, took the empty chair next to me.

"That's all of us today," said the chancellor and gave his half-smile. I had never seen a smile like that: it was from the lower half of the mouth, down. The entire top of the physiognomy was dead-pan and stern: only the lower mouth registered friendliness or pleasure. It was as if the upper half had been paralyzed in some freak accident, or that Irick had had his laughing nerves removed. I hated to face his face.

"I've called you few gentlemen here today because I need your help. I've been administering this university, so to say, for thirteen years, and have solved all kinds of problems, large and small—but this one will take a coordinated effort from our best minds, from our men of imagination." He looked at me, and I looked down into my amber ashtray and carefully ground to shreds a half-smoked cigarette.

"A party and a few minor arrests are of no consequence," he went on. "An everyday affair; routine disciplinary functions that never even cross my desk. But questions of involvement with faculty and sub-involvement with student morale—student morality, if you like—these are definitely within my provenance." I winced at the misusage and lit a new cigarette. I always overload my Zippo and the flame shot three inches into the colorless air. The chancellor glanced at the torch and gave his truncated smile.

"What we have here," he said with his bottom row of teeth showing, "is a bit of encapsulated sociology, in which, if I may mix a metaphor, a few heads might fall. I am not the firing kind," he said, moving his head evenly back and forth across the faces of his guests with an electric-fan oscillation, "but there will most certainly have to be a measure of sacrifice. A party of that order attended by one of our about-to-be Regents, a dozen perhaps of our professors, graduate students, and the assorted riff-raff of any university town, held in the house of a respected faculty member, whose wife is also a faculty member, both highly regarded in their field, attended as well by members of the Camellia Bowl All-Stars, and held, as I am given to understand, for the express purpose of honoring that drug evangelist and, if I may be permitted a very Victorian expression, Anti-Christ, along with his cohorts . . . gentlemen!" Irick had got tangled up in his own rhetoric and no one felt equipped to bail him out. "Gentlemen," he said with a sigh, "I find our university embroiled in no petty peccadilloes but in interstate *felonies*, interstate transport of drugs, sexual perversions . . ." he leaned forward, "possibly even kidnapping. The chief of police has also suggested arson."

He paused a moment and leaned back in his chair and

added that he was open to any advice and stratagem to "ame-
liorate" the situation. He wanted the meeting to be as informal
as possible and he was asking for concrete proposals.

Nobody said anything and the chancellor decided to "go
around the table." He began with Tremaine Atwood, saying,
"Tremaine, if we changed places, what would you do?"

Tremaine placed an enormous Dunhill pipe in his ashtray
(not even lit, I noted wryly), coughed politely and looked at
the chancellor serenely.

"Chancellor Irick," he said, "I gather that the crux of the
matter is the hosting—difficult word. Had the gathering been
held elsewhere, for example at a student's flat or in the barny
outskirts of town, et cetera, there would be no *university* problem surely. However, the party was held in the town and under the auspices of Professors Brom and Karen Janiczek. I
wish to say that in my considered view, both Janiczeks are
eminent members of the clan of cultural anthropologists and
sociologists, that both have contributed deeply to this faculty,
sincere research people, *field* scientists of a quite high caliber,
and that they are both honest and objective scholars, well, a
bit sentimental about their material, as we all are, I hope, but
too valuable to this institution to be made a public spectacle
of."

"You are suggesting what, Tremaine?" asked the chancellor.

"Remove the *onus probandi* from the Janiczeks. Gradually,
of course, until the citizenry get used to the idea. Elevate them
both, if need be, in the British manner."

"Kick them upstairs," the chancellor translated.

"Precisely," said Professor Atwood.

"Bean?" the chancellor asked Dr. Harrington.

I looked at the surgeon. He had an honest countenance, I
thought, that of a craftsman who couldn't afford to make mis-
takes. I am always looking for metaphors for people, and decided that Doc had the face of a mine-sweeper. Maybe that's
why he's so nuts about horses, I concluded illogically.

"It's a tough one, Dunstan," said Harrington to the chancellor. "The drug thing is out of our hands, or that's my under-

standing. The fact that various professors went to a party at another professor's, regardless of what happened, is irrelevant. The football player is in the clear—I don't know about the Homecoming Princess—and the Air Force man is out of the picture. The students and the high-school kids, well, that's up to the schools and school authorities and parents, I imagine. What we're really talking about is the Janiczeks. Is that correct?"

The chancellor ignored the query and said, "Edsel?"

I flinched and answered, "I'll pass for now, Chancellor Irick. I really have no opinions on the party."

Irick gave me the benefit of what was intended to be a stony look and asked Oscar his "judgment." I glanced up at Oscar and saw the same expression on his face that Oscar had worn when he was egging on the auto-erotic Mrs. House in the red room at the party.

"Mister Chancellor," said Oscar in a silky voice, "the idea of the image of Milo being besmirched has a certain charm, a certain advantage for everyone concerned. Crisis is—electrical! Crisis, if I may telescope my thought, is *football!* It occurs to me . . ." he turned away for a moment with a kind of world-weary suggestion of a shrug . . . "it occurs to me that here is an opportunity to provide a certain enlightenment to the community and to *stiffen* the esprit of the university itself."

"Be specific, Professor," said the chancellor with his prehistoric smile.

"I have no specifics, unfortunately, Chancellor," said Oscar, "only theoretics. My suggestion is that the university and its officers especially do everything in its power to shield itself from the high-minded churchmen of our community, from the newspapers and their latter inordinate offspring. I suggest that you, sir, protect this institution from the public enemy."

"And who might that be?" asked the chancellor without his smile.

"The public, sir," said Oscar.

The chancellor sat for a moment and then announced that Milo U. happened to be a public institution, paid for by the public and operated for the public, and that he himself was a public servant, as were all the people in this room. Having said this, he rediscovered his smile.

Oscar had lost his round but wasn't ready to surrender his cause. "I don't know how far the news of the little party has spread," he replied to the chancellor. "All I do know is that the state media are hot on the scent and that Akiba Mem and his friends were being briefed by *Lux* magazine for a national blast-off, and that Milo was one of the key points in their itinerary. And that simply, Chancellor, if illegal charges are made against students or faculty members or householders or whatever, we are all going to be enmeshed in a new Scopes trial from which we may never emerge. Well then, I will give you my specifics, since you have asked for them. Smuggle everyone involved in the fiasco back to where they came from as quickly and as silently as possible. Have the police drop all charges, rush Akiba Mem and his crew back over the state line, ground the Jamaicans and all the other students involved in charges, and start a campaign to raise funds for rebuilding the Janiczek home and its priceless collections."

The chancellor was drumming his fingers on the board-room table and appearing to be thinking. Finally he said, "Do I detect any implied threats in what you have been saying, Oscar?"

Oscar's eyes flashed. "Do me the honor, sir, to exempt me from that charge."

Tremaine Atwood donated a large smile to Oscar and shed some of it on the chancellor. Indignation was something he thrived on.

They sat silently a while, smoke rising. I, who felt drowsy, suddenly shook myself and sat up a couple of inches.

"Chancellor," I said.

"Professor Lazerow," answered the chancellor in his Dr.-Livingtone-I-presume tone. Meeting me on campus the chancellor would call me Edsel or Ed; once he even gave me an "Eddy" while gripping me by the shoulder like an orthopedist, crunching the bones.

"Well, Mr. Irick," I said, wondering whether the "Mister" was a mistake. "This is a strategy meeting, I take it. I mean we're not here to discuss the location of the new cyclotron or extra parking facilities for the stadium. Isn't it our job to outwit publicity, even to capitalize on this situation? Like an intercepted forward pass?" I looked down at the table as I delivered the smile. "I'm sure we all agree on that much, that what we need is a grandstand play."

"If you have a proposal, we are all ears," answered the chancellor, checking his official smile.

"We all know," I said, "everyone knows, in professional circles and in general, that the Janiczek team has been compiling a, or rather *the*, sociology of Milo, that they have devoted their lives to this fine project, and that all reliable informants tell us that the work will surpass *Middletown* or *The Sexual Life of Savages* as a classic of cultural socio-anthropology."

The chancellor closed his eyes for a moment, possibly banning the last-named book in the censorship office of his mind.

"We all know," I continued, "that in this particular undertaking the *field* is Milo itself. And we can be pretty certain that whether Brom and Karen Janiczek are dropped from the faculty or not, whether they sustain prosecution or not, the Janiczeks are going to finish their study. Which means that the Janiczeks will remain in Milo and continue their labors."

"Why Milo?" asked the chancellor.

"Why histology, Chancellor?" I said. "Why systematics and evolution? Why Gerard Manley Hopkins? The Janiczeks came to Milo to study Milo. Maybe they will even put it on the map? I'm not referring to the university, sir, but to the organism of which the university is a part and which in the opinion of the Janiczeks and the graduate council and the university senate is a thoroughly valid subject for scientific probing." I wondered for a moment why I was becoming a defender of the Janiczeks, of whom I felt more tolerant than passionate.

"And you propose?" asked Irick.

"Simply that the university, with its powerful connections among the Regents and the legislature and the multifarious churches, back two of its professors and give them their heads. Let the public fume a little, as when we lose a football game. But, Mr. Chancellor, this proposition of mine is a dead loss unless *you* direct the choir of assent. If you like, I will offer my typewriter to the cause; that is, I am willing to draft a statement giving the university's position, for your emendations and the opinion of the boards concerned." I must be going out of my mind, I thought. What if he takes me up on it? "I'll even dictate it to your secretary," I added.

"Tell us your line of argument," asked Irick, glancing at his watch. I resented the gesture, which I thought was of a degree of rudeness that nobody had deserved.

"A," I said, "the social science departments of the university staged a coordinated experiment which, in the vocabulary of such scientists, is the equivalent of what creative artists refer to as a life study. The project was planned in secret. Certain professors were carefully selected to participate in and supervise the, shall we say, lab experiment."

I saw Tremaine Atwood lean forward to speak and then sit back. "B," I continued, "the cooperation of the police and even the presence of a member of the Board of Regents were thought to be imperatives. The police were especially interested in locating a maryjane—marijuana—session to keep their records up to date. Representatives of various fringe elements of the town, some with criminal records, others with merely 'tendencies' were handpicked by the said social scientists, the police working in close collaboration with the Janiczeks. Chancellor, you do know," I interrupted myself, "that Brom and Karen and Chief Slezak are as thick as thieves. No Slezak, no sociology of Milo is the way Brom puts it. The rest is a matter of details: the Air Force sergeant is being taken care of by the Air Force in person; the petting parties can all be quashed as gross exaggeration, once we line up the police chief, and the arson business is preposterous. Let's give the law and public opinion the motorcycle set and Akiba Mem and his minions. Everybody else goes not only scot-free but in one way or another is advanced in his situation because of his loyalty to science and to the university."

I stopped and flicked my eyes around the table. Oscar, sitting opposite, was studying his fingernails, palms outward. The chancellor was staring at me. Tremaine Atwood was staring at the chancellor, and Doc Harrington suddenly burst out laughing. Good Joe, I thought.

"Despite the fact that none of what you say is true, Edsel," said the chancellor, apparently delivering his opinion.

"Though esthetically highly probable," volunteered Tremaine, to my surprise. The chancellor again looked at his watch, this time apologizing, and thanked each member of the camarilla for his help which he "would earnestly take under advisement." As we rose to go, the chancellor turned to me and asked if I would stay a moment. I sat down again. When the door closed the chancellor went to a wall cabinet and took a letter from the shelf.

"I thought you should see this, Ed," he announced and slid the paper toward me. It was a poorly typed note on a plain white sheet which read:

"Dear Chancellor Irick: This is to inform you that a professor in your university who is a professor of poetry is being accused of bastardy by me. Namely that I have a child by him and that I think the proper persons should be informed." It was signed Wanda Shontz. The address at the top read Kaz Graindorge, RFD 4, Jaeger County.

I felt faint, read the letter over and over, and finally looked at Irick, who was sitting as still as a mouse.

"Do you know a Wanda Shontz?"

"Yes," I said.

"Do you know a Kaz Graindorge?"

"Yes," I said.

There was a pause and then the chancellor said, "Do you know what bastardy is, Ed?"

"At first I thought she was calling me a bastard," I spluttered, "but now I remember the word—something out of Old English law or something."

"Is there any truth in the, uh, allegation—that you have fathered her child?" asked the chancellor.

"Absolutely not," I answered.

"You may keep the letter," said the chancellor. And don't think it hasn't been Xeroxed, I thought.

Aloud, I said, "I'll try to get an admission out of her for your file. I can't begin to imagine . . ." but didn't know how to finish the sentence.

"I am of two minds about this thing," said Irick, "and I'm sorry to say that the letter was opened by my secretary. Otherwise let us keep this under our hat. But I will look forward to another letter from this Miss Shontz momentarily."

I was not so dazed that I didn't register the misuse of "momentarily." The chancellor stood up and offered me his hand. I was surprised at the gesture, shook hands and left.

"Professor Lazerow," said the stone-faced secretary, "I don't believe I have your new home phone number. Is it unlisted?"

"Yes," I said and gave it to her. She thanked me and swung sideways to her typewriter.

I decided not to say anything to Oscar. I noticed that I did look pale in the elevator mirror and bent my head over to draw some blood to my face. I was hanging over when the door opened and two secretaries drew back to watch me. I brushed past them with a coughing laugh.

Oscar was waiting in the car and had turned on the FM radio; he switched it off when he spotted me and leaned over to open the door for me.

"He wanted to know about my trip for the State Department," I said. "Wanted a copy of my report. Stuff like that impresses the managerial set."

I dropped Oscar off at his house. "Why don't you get that crappy sidewalk fixed," I said in parting. Oscar only laughed and waved.

CHAPTER XVIII

I called Inge. "Another one marked Personal," she announced. "Shall I open it?"

"Of course," I said.

"It's a carbon copy. Wait a minute, two of them. The second one has my name written across the top." She paused a long moment and then shouted, "Jesus Christ! We'd better have a drink, Boss." She read the same note from Wanda that the chancellor had received.

"He showed it to me a half hour ago," I told her. "Listen, close up the office and come on over. Maybe two heads will be better than one. And I'm going to call Wanda but I might as well wait."

When I hung up I went for the dictionary. Old French, it said, spelled *bastardie*. Like roses are shining in Bastardie, I thought. Illegitimacy, the book went on. Numeral two: the begetting of a bastard. And what if I did beget me a bastard, my mind went on. I felt weak and silly and my mind was playing with me and was starting a bad poem: I finger-fucked a bastard into time. And what does she hope to gain by this? Getting me fired? Getting me to move out of town? I wonder how many other copies she has spread around Milo? I'd better get a counterattack going. Ten minutes later I saw Inge's jalopy come to a stop across the street and I went to the door.

We discussed the crisis with a bottle of Jack Daniel's between us and got nowhere. At one point I said, "Why don't I ask her to come over?" and Inge objected and then changed her mind. "The bitch interests me," was the reason she gave. I dialed the beauty salon. Sure, she'd be delighted, Wanda said. I made no mention of a third person.

At a little after five Wanda crossed the grass and stooped to break off a marigold. "The pestilence has arrived," I announced to Inge and opened the door and came and sat down. Wanda stopped in the doorway when she saw Inge.

"Sh—it," she stated in one-and-a-half syllables. "Pour me a Daniel's, Ed," she added. She sat down in the rattan chair and crossing her legs exposed a side of gray beef.

When I came back with a glass full of ice I saw Wanda studying a sheet of paper. Christ, I thought, it was the paper on which I had scrawled Marya's name in various colors. As I handed her the glass she handed me the paper.

"I must be losing my grip, Lazerow," she said enigmatically, pouring a generous sour-mash. I placed the sheet face down on a table out of her reach, thinking I shouldn't have.

"We're in agreement on that," I answered. "And why this sudden interest in calligraphy?" I thought I would use a word she wouldn't know or would at least resent. "You're becoming quite a letter writer," I added.

"You're the big word man," she answered with a gruff laugh. "I can only get up to three syllables. Like 'Marya'—or 'bastardy.'" Everyone sat still until she added in a sweet voice, "And who's Marya?"

"What's bastardy?" Inge shot in.

"Since you've gone to the trouble of trying to get me fired, Wanda," I said, "which is a lot more complicated than you think, I imagine you've found out about libel. Would you mind telling me what you are trying to accomplish?" I was surprised that I wasn't feeling angry and that I was discussing this catastrophe as if it were a matter of a slight misunderstanding, like bending somebody's bumper.

Wanda only laughed. I began to feel my temper returning.

"And what's lover-boy got to do with this?" I asked. "Did anybody go his bail?" I added irrelevantly.

"His dad and I bailed him," she answered, "and it took goddam near every cent I've got." She looked at Inge and then at me and said, "The trouble is with the kid."

"What kid?" I asked in a flat tone of voice.

Wanda was already into her second sour-mash and put on her innocent smile which signified that lightning was about to strike.

"What kid? The *kid*. Or should I say *your* kid."

"You goddam liar," I said, "there's no kid, there never has been a kid, and you know it as well as I do," I ended lamely.

"There is always a kid," Wanda answered and stared at Inge, as if making notes.

"How old is it?" asked Inge, rather timidly. She didn't really want any part of the proceedings, but curiosity, anger, and new-found loyalty got the better of her.

"It's a boy," answered Wanda in a bored voice, "fourteen months, dark like his daddy."

"Whoever that might be," I said, setting my glass down with a neat click.

"We named him Arlie," she continued, ignoring the insult.

"And who are *we*?" I asked. I stood up and walked toward her in an arc.

"Me and his godfather," answered Wanda, still in the tone of an applicant filling out an oral questionnaire.

"Godfather!" exclaimed Inge. I wondered if you could baptize a bastard, if there was a bastard. My head began to spin and pound.

"What do you want?" I asked hoarsely.

"Nothing that he's not going to get, Edsel," she answered. "Except I'll raise him and you support him until he's twenty-one. That way it gets us all off the hook. The lawyer says it can be done quietly, the way you like things done, Ed," she said and gave me a sickly-sweet look.

"Lawyer!" Inge and I exclaimed together.

Wanda got up, leaned over and drained her drink and said

she had to leave. When she reached the door she turned around and said, "In exchange for favors done and a long literary correspondence."

I stood frozen in place and Inge kept her eyes on the vacant space where Wanda had last been seen. We heard the Volvo motor start and a squeal of rubber as the car zoomed off.

"Good God!" said Inge.

"He's dead," I said.

We sat in the room a long time, thinking in the coppery light that filtered through my unwashed windows. I felt crushed and defeated in a battle which was not a battle and yet somehow was not a victimization either. It was more like having wandered into a slough of despond, because that was of the nature of things. I didn't take the accusation literally or even seriously but was aware that "on another level," it was both literal and serious. Serious only in the sense that someone or someones would think that I, Edsel, would rise to such bait. I felt an immense boredom with the childishness of the "plot" which Wanda was using, an infinite sensation of withdrawal from my past.

"I seem to be at the age," I said to Inge, "when I meet my second lawyer."

"You are so right," said Inge. And added, "But in that, I can't help."

The conversation narrowed down to finding someone who would find me a lawyer. It couldn't be the one who had handled my divorce, not *that* weakling, I thought. I ran through the roster of friends, enemies, and acquaintances in Milo, leafed through the yellow pages of the phone book searching for a familiar name among the two columns of attorneys and finding nothing, got out the university directory and scanned it page by page. Now and then I would stop over some professor's name and fill Inge in on his reputation or notoriety. The directory was also a dead end.

"It's got to be somebody here," I said. "Even if I knew the Chief Justice of the United States it wouldn't help. Milo is as Milo does."

Inge had to go out that evening and left with the advice that the chancellor wasn't about to expose a new scandal in his bailiwick and that it was up to Wanda to prove her point but that it would be consoling if I could find a lawyer who could keep the Black Widow in her own web. I thanked her for coming and saw her out the door.

I wandered around the livingroom in a daze, turned the FM radio off and on three times, and suddenly developed an overpowering desire to straighten my apartment. I vacuumed, dusted, found oil polish for chairs and tables, made my bed, put soiled laundry in a canvas bag, mopped the kitchen, lined up my jars of spices, swabbed out the refrigerator, took the garbage out to the big can in the back alley, and finally found a spray-can of window cleanser and shined all the six windows of the dwelling. I was feeling better already. I made myself a drink and went back to the livingroom to lay out my magazines symmetrically. I crumpled up the paper on which I had written tags of old poetry, when it occurred to me that the one with Marya's name was missing. I knew I hadn't thrown it out; I never threw away a piece of paper I had written on until I had scrutinized it front and back, sometimes for weeks. Without even telling myself, I knew that Wanda had palmed it—why?

As if I don't know why, I told myself in a fury. The heavy cloud-floor in my head cleared for a minute, the way it does in an airplane when for a little moment a miniature world with houses and farms and a piece of road appears through the hole in the sky and then closes up again. Ask Wanda, my mind said.

I got her on the phone.

"Did you take anything from my apartment?" I asked her, immediately sorry that I had called.

"Only what you call a *souvenir de maison*," she answered, "like you take from my pad. Why?"

I hated myself for not being able to resist asking what it was she took.

"Just a piece of paper with a name all over it," she said, "like a businessman's handkerchief full of ten different colors of lipstick. Want to hear it, Ed?"

I heard a crackling of paper in the receiver that sounded for all the world like a small crackling of leaves burning on a spacious lawn. I hung up the phone with a crash and raced to the phone book to find Marya's number. I waited until my breath quietened and tried practicing "hello" out loud a few times. I didn't want to sound as if I had just lost the high-school hundred-yard dash. When my voice was under control I dialed. Marya answered the phone herself.

"That's a coincidence, Edsel," she said, "I was going to phone you today about your poems. I like so many of them but some are so—angry. They make very strong reading," she laughed.

I interrupted. "Let's have a talk about them. Listen, Marya, I really called about something else. I have to talk with you about something. It's important and as a matter of fact urgent. To put it plainly, I need your help about a kind of crisis, I guess you'd call it. Can you give me about a half hour?"

She seemed a little taken aback and wanted to know if it had anything to do with the Janiczek party. Bumpy had regaled her with some of the more improbable details.

"Only indirectly," I said, "but we can discuss that great historical event also."

Marya agreed to see me and my heart gave a bounce.

"But, Edsel," she said, "I'm not sure you should come to my house. My lawyer advises me against men-friends; I've filed for my divorce and I'm supposed to act the vestal virgin until the case is settled. That means about six more weeks."

"No," I said. "If you agree to see me, it's got to be now, to-day or tomorrow, please."

"Well, I can't get it through my head that I have to live in purdah," Marya said, "and I'd rather you come here than meet in secret. Why don't you come over about eight, and, Edsel, park in the driveway where your car can be seen. If there's any gossip it may as well be honest gossip."

I was becoming breathless with gratitude and wanted to hang up. I managed to keep my voice normal through the conclusion of the conversation, and hung up finally with a medium-sized click. Then I sat back and exhaled deeply, as if I had been holding my breath. I would eat, shower, dress carefully in the informal style, and not drink much. I took my glass to the kitchen for ice and made a moderate bourbon. Drinking it I searched my book shelves for a "mint" copy of my last book of essays—*Essays Literary and Political*, it said—and laid it on the table. I wasn't sure Marya would be interested but if she were I would autograph it in her presence.

It was dark and moonless when I turned into the circular driveway. The big house was also dark except for a row of French windows on the ground floor. An electric lantern that hung from the outside portico was also lit. I left the car directly in front of the portico. When I rang the bell it opened almost immediately and Marya put out her hand and drew me inside. She wore a long black hostess gown swirled over with deep yellow oriental abstractions. She does look oriental, I thought, with her beautiful cheekbones and the suggestion of slant to her eyes. No makeup and no jewelry, I observed pleasurably. "Regal" was the word that crossed my mind.

Marya led me into the livingroom, which was more like a hotel lobby, I said to myself. There was an enormous Tudor fireplace at one end of the room, laid with a fire fit for a king should one put a match to it, I decided.

"Are you living here *alone?*" I asked, puzzled.

"Clay moved out—finally!" she answered, "because that's the law of the land, or this land. There's an old gardener and his wife who live in the back—and me. But I can't stand this place; it gives me the creeps; it's like a miniature department store. So please don't ask to see any of it. It's revolting. I can't wait to leave but my lawyer wants me on the premises. You understand; it's *expensive* and that's all any of them care about. Who gets it. I'd just as soon it burned to the ground."

There was a bar on the other side of the furniture-laden room and I made drinks of scotch and ice and fizz from a silver-laced siphon.

"Then where will you go after the divorce?" I asked.

"Away," said Marya, "only I haven't decided where *away* is."

I remembered that I had left the book on a hall table when I came in, and went to get it. I handed it to Marya, apologizing for adding to her moving bill.

"You may not care for this sort of haranguing," I said, "but I wanted to bring you something and this is the stuff I know best. After all, I made it up," I laughed. She gave me a quick eye-flashing glance and turned to what I thought was the table of contents.

"Will you sign it for me?" she said, while I felt myself deflating with relief. I took my pen from inside my jacket and wrote on the title page: *To Marya—for the ones to come.* I had decided on that inscription during the past two hours and had calculated that it was neither too impersonal nor too intimate. I was right; when I handed it back to her and she read it I thought she flushed slightly. "Thank you," she said simply. I wanted to rush to her and gather her up but was afraid. "Thank *you*," I said. We both burst out laughing.

"And about this urgent business which you've made me a party to?" she asked lightly. I grew wary; she probably thought there was no such business—and what if she were to recoil from what I was going to tell her. Bastardy, the scummy side of Milo, my feelings of total dissociation from everyone I knew in the town and in the school, myself the dregs of myself, crawling on the bottom of the greasy, rusted-out garbage can along with the other maggots.

"I don't know whether I should ask you the simple question I want to ask, which is that I need a good lawyer and don't know any. Because if I ask it, as I already have," I laughed, "you'll want to know why and you might start running . . ."

"Again," we said simultaneously, and stared at each other ecstatically. Or maybe conspiratorially, as I thought of it later that night.

"I used to make a career of washing my dirty linen, or linen that I hoped was dirty, in public," I said. "But maybe my linen isn't dirty anymore, or rather maybe I don't have any more linen. What I mean is that I am climbing out of a rotten world into myself, which I always thought of as a good place, not because I thought I was superior but because I know what happiness is, what beauty and goodness are, even what kindness is, and all those things were dirtied by the people I trusted most, by the people who knew better and who had the good things in their keeping. Administrators, professors, doctors, lawyers, merchants, chiefs. But that didn't matter; I always gave them the benefit of the doubt. What really . . ." I interrupted myself. "Do you know what I'm talking about, or care?"

"I don't know," said Marya, "but I want to hear."

"I don't know either," I said. "If I had, I wouldn't have gone through the various strata of de-idealization and gotten down to the bedrock of the Milo geology. Which I did. And which I'm grateful for in a crucified kind of way. And which I'm coming to you for help about."

"But what can I do?" asked Marya. "You're talking about people who lower themselves when they're supposed to be the cream of the crop. You talk about administrators and professors who are bastards, merchants and lawyers; I know all that. Every fifteen-year-old knows that kind of thing. And it's usually exaggerated. Except in the case of the merchant I happened to be married to. But what's that got to do with you?"

Marya got up to make us both a refill and turned around and said, "Say what it is you want me to help with. I really don't care about the social pyramid of Milo and its intellectuals. I've seen enough of them."

I felt chastised and sipped my drink and set it down and lit a cigarette. "So much for that," I said. "I need a lawyer," I said with a period. "To defend me against a false bastardy charge. Or words to that effect," I added cutely. "On the one hand, Chancellor Irick would like to fire me because I am an 'Eastern intellectual,' and on the other hand, the guerrilla element of Milo which I have been consorting with for some time would like to see me busted down to buck private. Pardon the Army talk," I smirked.

"My lawyer is married to Dunstan Irick's daughter, Edsel," said Marya. "Is that what you want? He's the only lawyer *I* have and the others I've met—I'm afraid I think the same way about them as you do."

"But don't you want to know what *bastardy* is?" I asked with wide eyes.

Marya gave me a big, possibly "knowing" smile. She wasn't

about to embark on a recapitulation of the life and adventures of Edsel Lazerow. I felt cheated. After all, all I have is my past, I said to myself; what else have I to give her? What else have I to give myself? A feeling of animal stupidity overtook me and I sat lumpishly. Marya moved beautifully to a somewhere phonograph and put on a Vivaldi concerto. She's way ahead of me, I thought bitterly.

"Of course I had a lawyer for my divorce," I said, through the music, which was playing at a little below concert volume, "but I had a fight with him and we don't speak, to use an old-fashioned expression." But Marya wouldn't pursue the question, whatever the question was. It began to dawn on me that if Marya didn't consider my problem a problem, then maybe there wasn't a problem to begin with. In any case, whatever it was she was interested in concerning me, it obviously wasn't my anecdotal paleontology.

The evening advanced on a friendly, even footing. We exchanged jokes and rumors about the Janiczek party and speculated about the firing of the sociologists. We discussed "personalities" such as the chancellor and Tremaine Atwood and Bean Harrington. We even tuned in on the ten o'clock TV news and heard that the university faculty scandal was getting down to the fine points of inquiry and that a full report would be released within three days. Police Chief Slezak was apparently ready to release the drug interlopers at the state line they had crossed on the night of the orgy. Irick is pulling in his horns, I thought, and wondered whether this was a good omen or bad.

Marya had gone to answer the phone a few times since I had arrived and I wandered around the big room vacantly. Once, while she was in another room talking, I tossed a cigarette into the fireplace and the paper, tinder, kindling, and what not, started to smoke. I yanked away the fire screen, a brass baroque object of art, and tried to stop the impending yuletide blaze with my hands and a five-foot poker which I could barely maneuver. I was on my knees when she came back and wanted to know what I was doing. "I was going to light it myself," she said, as the logs burst into flame, sending up a sheet of clear red and yellow and blue fire.

"I wasn't trying to light it," I said idiotically. "I was trying to put it out. I was . . ." We sat in chairs near the fire and laughed at each other and watched the conflagration. Again the phone rang and Marya left. "Actually," I yelled to her across the room, "I was hoping it would light."

I waited a long time, I thought, because I had made myself another drink, went back to watch the big logs catch, gazed around the room trying to take it in, trying to formulate my thoughts about Marya and the last surrealist days, trying to visualize some future, even a mere tomorrow; until I felt she must be staying away for some reason I was supposed to know. I got up and walked slowly to the doorway where she had gone to answer the phone. I went down a dim hallway toward what, by the whiteness of the light, must have been a kitchen.

Marya was leaning against a tiled sink staring out of a black window and sipping her drink. She didn't turn when I walked in and said, "What is it, Marya?" She wheeled on me with eyes blazing and her face dark and said, "A woman called me to tell me that you're the father of her child and that—she said— she said she thought that I was supposed to know." I had no answer and Marya had already gone down the hall, I guess to show me the door, I thought. Why else? I followed slowly.

When I reached the intersection of the hall and the living-room I saw her lying face down, stretched out in front of the now roaring fire, and I could see that she was sobbing. I crossed the room and fell beside her and brought her into my arms. She allowed me to.

CHAPTER XIX

℘ She had cried a good deal—we both had—I remembered when I woke up. I cursed having to teach that day and wandered dazedly to the bathroom. She had cried out of proportion to the event, my mind told me sententiously. Both of us had been incoherent, and when there was a lull in the grief, Marya had told me the hour and looked at me plaintively, I thought. I asked to stay but she declined gently. Nothing had been "decided" about anything. I had gone there just to tarnish a few images, I thought. Yet she had agreed to see me today and I decided to call. Nine forty-five ought to be okay, I told myself; besides, it's an emergency. What emergency? I wasn't certain. I dialed.

The phone rang a long time and finally a man answered. It was the gruff inarticulate voice of a person who is unused to phoning, though not impolite. The houseman, or whatever he is, I thought.

"Mrs. Hinsdale is out of town for about ten days," said the voice.

"Out of town! You must be—mistaken. Is something wrong? Where . . ." I was not making much sense, and the voice answered, "Ruba, it's called Ruba. Care of general delivery."

I mumbled something, hung up, and flew to the atlas. Ruba?

Aruba? What the hell would she be doing there? I had wrecked everything all over again; she would never see me again, I boiled, leafing through the index of the big atlas.

"Venezuela! Jesus Christ, she's got to be kidding." I had time to dress and drive to her house to see if the whole thing was a joke or a subterfuge. At least I could tell if the houseman was lying. I was through shaving when the phone rang. As I was equidistant from the livingroom phone and the bedroom extension I stood paralyzed for a minute in the hall; something in me decided for the livingroom. It was Bumpy Harrington.

"Good morning, professor!" boomed Bumpy in the tones of a welcome wagon. "A message for you, Ed," she added. Can't wait to give me the bad news, I thought. "Marya Hinsdale," she said, "called me in the wee hours to say that she had to go to Aruba for a week or so. She has a step-sister there, you know" . . . I didn't know . . . "and she asked me to tell you. That's it, professor. See you in the creative writing snakepit." I thanked her. One thing about Bumpy, she liked delivering messages of crisis, denouement, and the like, but she didn't rub it in. She did it without malice or motive: she was a born vector of the good and the bad.

I felt deflated, rebuffed, punished and sad. I had started a poem for Marya when I had come home last night, but it was such an open declaration of desire that I would be afraid for her to see it until she developed more trust in me. Suddenly I was gripped with a murderous fury for Wanda and Kaz and the whole sleazy Janiczek culture. I decided without going through the necessary motions of cerebration that the minute the class was over I would hightail it to the Graindorge farm and see what I could find out from the farmer about the "bastard."

In class I was, as I thought about it later, "cold and bright." I wore my sunglasses, which were also bifocals. "Impersonal," that's what I was in class, I thought. I had pronounced, "Your ideas, your beliefs, your churches and revolutions, prejudices, and pet peeves are of no possible interest. Your notions about the great and near-great and not-great works of art are immaterial. Everything is immaterial in what you write unless you can translate what you feel into the sub-language of poetry. Poetry is a trick language, a language that lies to give the lie to rational discourse. No matter how rotten and diseased or lofty and sacrosanct your ideas: work with what you have, which are your lousy or your noble thoughts. But this is not a thought-discussion group; it's a studio, a garret where you tinker with the colors of your thought. I advise you to take as your material only the thoughts that you really think, only your worst views, your bigotry, your hatreds. Go along with them; they are your only fuel. Hate or love to your heart's content, but don't bother me with your ideological problems. I'm not your baby sitter. All I am interested in is your skill in translating your strongest feelings into arresting speech. Nothing else."

The usual thing happened: a few females of the art-is-lofty persuasion demanded in hurt tones some kind of equation redeeming poetry from social injustice, "medievalism" and the like. I shot back at them the "greatness" of *The Divine Comedy*, the Sophoclean theater, the Old Testament and *Leaves of Grass*. "Take your pick," I said, "they're all great, but anybody who believes the content of more than one of these at the same time will be taken away in a butterfly net to the Milo Academy of Laughter and Paraldehyde. Listen," I concluded after a look out the window, "you know the corny expression immortalized by Polonius, 'To thine own self be true'—if you want to be a true writer, if you want to write from the top of the tower of yourself, you have first and always to accept the worst, the unspeakable depths of yourself, to not only accept these worst pockets and sloughs of despond but to say them aloud, with clarity. With distinction and clarity, beauty and symmetry, tenderness and truth and urbanity," I quoted from somewhere out of my adolescent reading. "But not confessionalism, not propaganda," I added. "Leave that to the newspapers. As for Idealism and Loftiness, leave that for editorial writers and junior high English teachers. There is no idealism in great poetry, unless it happens to adhere in the mind of the writer. Sometimes it is there, sometimes not; it makes no difference either way."

The athletes were dozing when the bell rasped. There had been time for a few "poems" and a little criticism of their "technique." I did the dozing during that part of the class.

Inge, who had stopped coming to class, having become totally engrossed in my filing mess, had separated more letters with queries written on the top about where to file what, which to throw away, etc. Dutifully, I went through the stack, writing the last names of those correspondents I still remembered. Half of the papers I designated for the trash can.

When I finished I wheeled around in my swivel chair and let out a heavy sigh. "Guess where I'm off to?" I asked. "To the Graindorge place to see my little bastard," I answered, without waiting for her answer.

"Well, don't ask me to be your date," said Inge angrily. "For Christ's sake, Boss, drop it. What are you going to learn from those—Kallikaks!"

"Nothing probably," I answered, "but I want to hear how Graindorge talks. And to see if he or they will really go so far as to produce the fruit of the immaculate conception." I was swiveling hard in my chair.

"Good luck" was all that Inge had to offer.

I remembered how to get there. I stopped for a beer and a hamburger on the way and turned into the dusty country road slowly. At any minute I might switch into a cow-path and turn around and come back; I didn't know. I was already at the Graindorge mailbox before I made a definite decision and turned in and jounced up the rut-road to the lawn. There was nobody visible and I turned around the house to the barn where I had seen the cockfight. Graindorge, apparently having heard a car, appeared at the barn door, rolling an enormous tractor tire.

"What can I do for you, stranger?" he asked.

"My name is Edsel Lazerow," I said. "I came to see the kid."

"Oh," said the farmer, "you're the one. In pretty good time, too." He rolled the tire against the side of the building and walking around the barn motioned me to follow in the car.

"He's asleep," said the farmer, pushing the screen door open for me to enter.

On the second floor, with Graindorge frowning at my elbow, I looked into a crib with rubber wheels. I stared at the blond infant for a long time, trying to figure the shape of its head. "What color are its eyes?" I asked. "Pretty blue," said the farmer. I turned and tiptoed out.

On the stoop I asked the farmer, "Whose child is it, Mr. Graindorge?"

"Wanda had it here," he said. "She reckons it's yours." Graindorge looked at me with a poker face.

"What's your opinion, Mr. Graindorge?" I asked.

"Yours," said the farmer. I burst out laughing, went to my car and drove off. I contemplated busting in at the Fountain of Beauty Salon and announcing in audible tones to Wanda that I had just visited her bastard—or words to that effect—but instead drove back to my office. Inge was typing a mile a minute, making a list of my published articles which I had no recollection of writing. I sank into the red Good Will chair and watched her wonderingly. When she came to the end of a page she stopped and asked, "Did you go?"

"I went," I answered. "I spoke to the farmer and saw a child. Graindorge figures it must be of my manufacture, or so he opined, if you'll pardon the Middle English."

"Well?" asked Inge.

I scratched my head. "It's just a provincial pain in the ass," I said. "There's nothing in it *for* anybody or hardly even *against* anybody. It's just a case of boredom, boondoggling and bullshit. And you're right, secretary. I'll just forget it and go away. Actually, if I had a little bastard I'd parade it down Main Street on my shoulder with a sandwich board on me that says Bastard for Sale—University Blooded." But I wasn't up to the phantasy and slumped into my throne.

"You had a call," said Inge. "It was a woman. Here's the number."

I stared at the slip of paper with its strange series of digits. A small ferment began working in my mind. "She didn't say who or what or anything?" I asked. Inge said that that was all she knew, gave me a genial look and went out. When she turned the corner of the hall I dialed the number.

"Lord and Taylor," boomed a hearty female vocal apparatus.

"Who is this?" I asked angrily.

"Edsel," said the voice. "It's only little old Bumpy," and let out a mild peal of convivial laughter. "With a little news, comrade, which you may or may not want to deposit in your memory bank."

I righted my mind and greeted her and asked what the news was. Bumpy's voice switched to a sincere contralto—like coming in for a landing, I thought.

"Ed, I'm not sure I should do this. I'm doing it on a hunch. Marya called me last night to say she was going to that Godforsaken island. I believed her. She got as far as Chicago and changed her mind. She's back here in a motel and I'm worried about her. And she's worried about you. I'm not *arranging* anything, but I wanted you to know where she is. I think, I only *think*, she wants to hear from you."

"Give me the number," I said. Bumpy gave me the name of the motel and I thanked her quickly and fervently and hung up. I dashed out to the parking lot and hurried home.

With drink in hand and at my lips I leafed through the little phonebook and found the number of the place. With one of my felt pens of many colors I scrawled the number on the front of the book. Then I sat and stared at the number.

I told myself that any call she received she would answer because Bumpy was the only one who knew her whereabouts. I told myself that Marya would know that Bumpy had taken me into her confidence, and that I had a fifty-fifty chance of being forgiven. I told myself that Marya had returned to see me. Then I dialed.

The man at the switchboard connected me with room 14 and on the fourth ring she answered in a sleepy voice.

"Marya, Marya!" I said.

There was a slight hiatus and then she said, "Who is this? Is that you, Ed?"

"Marya!" was all I could say.

"Are you all right, Edsel?" she asked.

"Marya, what in the hell is going on?" I asked. "Please let me see you. Now," I said.

She laughed slightly. "No, Ed. Give me a little time. I'm just waking up. I want to take a leisurely bath to get the kinks out of my neck. Come at—what time is it?"

I looked at my wristwatch. "Five-thirty," I said.

"Come about eight," she answered. "Is that all right?"

"Yes," I said, "but if you want me earlier, I'll be here, just waiting."

"Please make it eight, Ed," she answered. "We'll have plenty of time."

"I'll bring dinner. Soon then," I said and we hung up.

I was twitching and felt feverish. What could I do in two and a half hours? How could I unwind? I could go to the liquor store now or en route. Maybe I should buy some flowers, if they were inconspicuous enough, something she was unused to. I ought to take a bath. Like most men, I hated baths and prefer a whipping in the shower.

"I'll take a bath," I said aloud. "I'll make it a *mikvah*," I joked to myself, not sure whether the word referred to a male or a female ritual washing.

I perched a vodka martini on the soap dish and proceeded to soak. The sun showed no signs of setting, and obviously Marya wanted me to arrive after nightfall. It would be just my luck that the sun doesn't set today, I ruminated, and occupied myself with thoughts of what to wear. Dress noiselessly, I said to myself.

After the bath, I did odd jobs such as snipping the tiny hairs out of my nostrils and ears, examining my genitals for dandruff, counting the money in my wallet, and polishing my car key with steel wool. I pried out my partials and scrubbed them with tooth powder, rinsed out my mouth with Listerine and pressed the expensive dental hardware back in place. I admired my looks and brushed my white hair for the tenth time.

I put on shoes that wouldn't clack, a pair with crepe soles, dark corduroy trousers and a midnight-blue pullover shirt. I selected a worn, once-expensive summer jacket, the remnant of a suit, because it too was dark, dark brown. The outfit reminded me of my tropical Army uniform, dirty motley, and I felt comfortable.

In the grocery store I headed my wire wagon toward the rotisserie ovens at the back of the establishment and stood to watch the birds browning and turning. Rock Cornish hens, said a little marker. Nice and dainty looking, I thought. I wondered whether I should get two or three. Would two be enough? Would three be an odd number? Or four: Wouldn't that be vulgar? I decided on three and the clerk removed them from their comfortable inferno and packaged them, writing the price in huge waxy numerals. So everybody can see, I thought. I wandered over to the aisle where the olives and pickles were stacked. I don't even know what she likes, I mourned to myself, but chose black wrinkly Spanish olives with little bits of condiments stuck to their skins. At the cheese counter I picked up a wedge of Stilton and on the way to the checkout counter, a loaf of pumpernickel.

En route to the liquor store I decided on Lancers for wine. Champagne was corny. Lancers, at least, in its ugly squat stone bottle didn't look elegant and if it was cold and fizzy and dry, what could be better, I argued.

Now I had an hour to wait and nothing to do; nothing more to buy. I went back to my apartment and made a drink. I went into the livingroom and turned on the FM. A Scarlatti sonata was being plucked out on a guitar. I sighed and went to look at my books. They had all taken on a different look, as if they had changed. Maybe it was the slant of light that hit them through the towering elms. The sun is telling me the time, I said to myself. And the books are speaking to Marya. My books. Her books. I brushed my hands across a row of bindings of skinny poetry volumes, "like little ribs," I said. "The ribs of poetry for our hands."

I rushed to find a clipboard, snapped a stack of paper in it, and sat down facing the sunset to write her a poem.

> The sun, my love, is telling me the time,
> The sunset strokes the rib-cage of my books
> My books will be your books and all will rhyme
> And meet in the rhyming couplets of our looks.

No good, I censured, and started to work the idea. My fingers opened and closed. I scratched holes in the paper, keeping one eye on my watch.

The sun is telling poetry the time, I improvised, rubbing the ribs of poets with printed light. Sounds like a barbecue, I commented. No, not now, I thought. As soon as I get home, if it's a week from now, I'll write her a poem. My style, I said, and put down the clipboard.

CHAPTER XX

ꙮ I parked on a side street and walked to Marya's room, avoiding the motel office. The room was brightly lit. She was wearing a sleeveless sharkskin dress of brilliant orange, making her face sunny. Clothes she was taking to the Caribbean, crossed my mind. I placed the dinner parcels on the bureau where Marya had set up a miniature bar: Booth's gin, a small bottle of dry vermouth, even a lemon, part of which she had skinned and cut into tiny twists. I took her in my arms and kissed her.

"Just like a businessman coming home," I said.

"Hardly," she said, and turned to make nine-to-one martinis.

As she handed me one in a bathroom glass, I asked, "Why did you want to go so far away? Was it because of the phone call?"

"Partly, I suppose. I don't really know. It seemed like a good idea at the time. Until I stepped up to the ticket counter at O'Hare. Then I knew I had to come back and face myself here. And I wanted to talk to you—more."

She turned her glass in her hand slowly, watching the ice stand still as the glass moved. "I'll go back to the house tomorrow. To 'maintain residence,'" she smiled. "But now, sit down and tell me about the latest adventures of Edsel Lazerow."

I shuddered. That was exactly what I didn't want to do. It was what had sent her flying only yesterday. And now I wasn't sure of her interest in me at all.

"You have troubles of your own," I said. "What's the point of listening to my chaotics?"

"I'd like to know," she said. "I don't mean to be entertained. Maybe for selfish reasons. I want to know you."

"Well," I laughed, "I could give you the story of my misadventures but it would take longer than the *Arabian Nights* and would, I'm afraid, be just as unexpurgated."

She flushed slightly and I nervously stood up to refill our glasses. Never had I felt so inarticulate. I had to make a decision, for the first time in my life, about talking about myself. For years I had been one of those people who do outlandish things only so they can talk about them. People who make a career of bragging about their mishaps, who create disorder wherever they go in order to take the blame for it. I welcomed blame out of pride and arrogance and peevishness. I expected praise for starting riots in other people's lives. And it didn't matter if I got the praise or not; I could always prove I was right in a poem I wrote. That was the only world of order I ever knew or wanted to know—the poem.

This "confessing" was a deep kind of mischievousness, a vicious kind of clowning that bordered on the criminal. I tried to demonstrate to all and sundry the drabness and meaninglessness of their lives. It didn't seem to matter now, that I was partly right, part of the time. What mattered was that my motives were dishonest. I was trying to prove that I was superior —not better, but more myself, more of a self than they.

I knew that I wanted—I needed—to do it once more. To—for someone who loved me. As a kind of gift; or a burden.

"Well," I began, "it's a domino game. If I tell you about the bastard child, I'll have to tell you about Wanda, the person who called you. If I tell you about Wanda I'll have to tell you about my marriage. If I tell you about my marriage I'll have to recite the roster of my infidelities. I'll have to tell you about my adolescence, even my childhood, my parents. And you can send me a bill for the analysis."

"I think you're dying to tell me how naughty you are," said Marya. Her face was expressionless and I couldn't weigh the remark to my satisfaction.

I was aware of standing at a new threshold and I had a mind to be careful but knew I could not be. I didn't want to lay the same old greasy cards on the table, knowing she wouldn't touch them. I would say the old things but in a new way, so as not to bore myself or her.

"Among the Just be just," I quoted to myself. *"Among the Filthy, filthy too."* But not just yet.

"You glow like an orange in that dress," I said. "I'd like to peel you and bite you."

She smiled languidly and rose to lay out our dinner. Her hair was dark and her complexion peach; for the first time I noticed a little white trench on her ring finger.

"When did you take your ring off?" I asked.

Her hand moved with a nervous gesture of impatience. "The day I filed for divorce. I threw it in the trash."

"I can't remember what I did with mine," I answered, as if we were members of some secret society who had misplaced their badges.

As we cleaned the three birds from their tiny bones, leaving little heaps of skeleton, we talked calmly about bits and oddments, my classes, vacations, air lines, avoiding ourselves. I felt that we were sparring or that perhaps Marya was waiting for me to take the initiative.

Then she said, "What was your adolescence like? Were you happy?"

"No," I answered, "it was somewhere in there, somewhere at the age when boys wake up at night burning with what they don't know is lust—that I began to cry a lot, all the time, without knowing why."

"Just the adolescent Hell?"

"Probably," I said, "but it's always unique, isn't it? It's the time of the flowering of secrecy, when life is just a bad daydream and night is the time for fingering your body. Hell is too mild a word for it. It's the ultimate torture of the damned. The age of blindness and clarity at once. The world suddenly looks

229

misshapen and mismade, a cosmic mistake, a practical joke, while one or another fifteen-year-old girl chewing bubble gum looks like the queen of heaven. I don't see how anybody gets past adolescence without committing suicide at least twice."

"Did you fall in love easily?" Marya asked. I looked at her for a clue.

"In a way, yes," I said. "I had absolute focus on one person at a time. It was all in my mind, of course. The little girl, whoever she was, probably never knew she had an admirer, or shall we say poet. I must have carried phantasy to extremes. But these phantasies were always and necessarily platonic. Her face was all I ever summoned. Other boys my age played with their girls' bodies. Not me. The only bodies I ever looked at or thought of were the photographs in nude magazines. Women. *Bad* women. So of course, when I married, I chose a 'pure' woman who hated bodies."

"You thought that sex was dirty and love was pure."

"Yes," I laughed.

"When did you get over that?" she asked.

I looked at her and felt speechless. She poured us another glass of wine and I thanked her.

"In that case, where do I fit in?" she asked.

The question startled me. "There's a poet, a great poet, I think, who writes about the Virgin and the Whore. An identity, he says, 'both for sale to the highest bidder! and who bids higher than a lover?' Maybe you're neither."

"Or both?"

I was worried and wondered whether I was being made fun of.

"Well, an identity," I said, "an identity I never mastered."

"Did you ever try?" she asked.

I felt nervous, even alarmed, and started to perspire. What was she getting at? I reached out and took her hand.

"I don't want to talk rot," I said, "but you're right. I have never tried—till now. This is my first time. Imagine," I laughed, "at my age!"

I felt a creeping sensation of cold in my genitals, but my face was damp and flushed.

"Kiss me, Ed," she said. I fell to my knees and Marya leaned forward in her chair. I pressed my hand against her breasts. I kissed her face and eyes and hair, returning to her mouth again and again, like a bee that has found an inexhaustible flower. I wondered if I should try to draw her to the bed, but did not make the move. Instead, I sat on the floor and stroked and kissed her hands and arms. Her dress had slipped up to her thighs and for the first time I touched her flesh in a really intimate place. Her skin was warm and dewy and her thighs firm and lubricious. "Lubricious," what a terrific word, went through my wordy head. I felt her muscles tighten and yield by turns. I wondered how high my hands should go.

"Wait," said Marya, and took off her dress.

"Here," I whispered, motioning slightly with my hand toward the bed. We lay down and Marya slid her hand down and unbuttoned the one button of my trousers. Her hand felt for my genitals.

My penis was like an icicle. It was literally as if snow were being rubbed between my legs. Instead of hardening, my member seemed to be disappearing. I began to tremble and my body felt as if it were a torch. I buried my face in her breasts and stroked her belly and her mount of Venus. She opened her legs slightly and my hand reached lower for her clitoris. All of me felt on fire except where the fire was supposed to be.

An image flashed through my mind of a sailor I had seen killed on a ship. He had been carried onto the deck with a hole the size of a fist straight through the center of his body. Otherwise, "He looked perfectly healthy!" I and others had stared at the corpse, so perfect and clean, straight and quiet, with that empty space in his middle.

We continued to stroke each other. I kissed her face and shoulders and nipples and pressed my fingers deep into her secret body. She was moist and a warmth entered my genitals. My penis began to fill and harden and my testicles to tighten. I wanted to yell with relief and happiness. I looked down and watched her fingers gently moving my member up and down, squeezing it tenderly and sensitively. When it had reached its full height Marya whispered, "Put it in."

I wheeled over and mounted her. The sensation of entering her made me intensely drunk; my blood must have been gushing alcohol and adrenaline, hormones and poetry. I reared up proudly over her and pumped deeply and wetly into her vagina. Her thighs opened wider to receive me. I thought I could feel the opening of her womb. "My prick is in her cunt," I said to myself. Would I have dared to use such words out loud? Marya was moving into a deep rhythm, her eyes closed, and a film of moisture on her smiling face.

"Fuck me, fuck me," I whispered in her ear, and as at a signal my penis slipped and began to wither. Marya opened her eyes and looked at me.

I lay on top of her panting, sweat pouring off my body.

"I—I can't hold it," I said, and fell away from her.

I began to tremble and she pulled my damp head against her bosom. She stroked my shoulder as something like a sob escaped me. She murmured, "Hush, hush. It's all right. You're not ready yet. You mustn't worry."

"I'd better worry," I said bitterly.

"You're just shy. You don't feel at home yet."

After a while I sat up and rubbed my tears away with my fist and set my jaw. "I love you," I said bluntly, "and I'm proving it brilliantly."

"We'll have to learn each other, darling," she said. She had never used that word before and I felt an electric shock in my soul.

"I love you," I repeated, "and I'm *in* love. I've never been in both worlds before. I guess that's why I'm scared."

I zipped myself up and arranged my shirt while Marya dressed. She went to the mirror over the bureau and combed her hair.

My God! what a beauty, I thought; what am I going to do with *that?*

She asked me to zip her dress and before I did I kissed her back which was golden and incense-smelling. Simultaneously I caught the odor of her sex on my hand.

"The cedars of Lebanon," I said.

She turned and said, "What is?"

"Your sex," I answered. "You know, like lead pencils. Or as a French poet said, your sex of seaweed and candy."

Suddenly Marya said, "Is it me?"

"Is what you?" I answered.

"Is it my fault that you couldn't keep your erection? Should we try it another way?"

"Good Lord," I spluttered, "where did you ever get that idea? How could it be you?"

"Your friend, Wanda. She certainly satisfied you, didn't she? How did she do it?"

"Marya, for God's sake, listen to me. You've got it all mixed up. She could never satisfy me *or* herself. That whole thing was a blind nightmare, a kind of psychic suicide. It doesn't have anything to do with you or me. It's like a sickness I once had. That's all. It was like a death-bed," I added melodramatically.

"I've never wanted to tell you about Wanda," I said. "I was hoping I could spare you that. And the other females I've been mixed up with in the past. But especially Wanda, the bottom of the barrel. I never wanted her, goddammit; I wanted her *not* to want me. Don't you understand?" I asked desperately.

"No, I don't understand," said Marya quietly.

I felt a righteous indignation rising in me. Then all at once it struck me that Marya couldn't possibly know what my erotic career had really been like. I was a local legend of sorts, the campus Lothario, the rule-breaker, and who was I to damage my own dashing reputation? Not that I had ever particularly tried to conceal my impotence; if it made a good story, so much the better. The failure of sex is as successful in its way as sex itself.

"I beg you to believe me, Marya. I haven't been able to give myself or to take anyone else for years. For, say, seven years, the only orgasms I have ever had have been . . . auto-erotic."

She burst out laughing. "I'll try to believe you, Ed," she answered, regaining the sweetness of her voice, "but it's not easy with your reputation."

"Your husband—Clay—your ex-husband, or whatever you call him—was he like the Beatniks say—good-in-bed?"

Marya gave me a smile but there was a trace of a frown on her forehead, a curiously beautiful expression I was coming to know as a signal that she would speak the truth regardless of the consequences. I had never before known a woman who didn't lie or temporize or subtilize or speak in ambiguities.

"Yes," she said, "I suppose he was good-in-bed, although I haven't much basis for comparison. But there was no love in it. He just fucked me. That was all."

I was stunned to hear her say "fuck." In a way I had imagined that she didn't even know the word. At the same time I felt relieved, as if another door had opened.

"It sounds almost like my story," I said, "either sex or love. A division of labor," I added vaguely. I was annoyed at being sexually outranked by her ex-husband, especially as I, too, had used women that way, as a fucking-block, treating them as Body and only myself as Soul.

"I've never understood marriage," I said, "before, during, or after. And yet I think it must be possible. If only it's selfish enough—I think that's what I mean. To marry and not betray the sensibilities, maybe that's it. Not to give up love for what the politicians and bad poets call Life. Maybe there's something to the pessimism of the marriage vow, which doesn't predict anything but downfall—sickness, misfortune, death—that if love survives there will have been a marriage."

Marya sat quietly, her hand on her cheek, her drink balanced on the arm of the chair.

"Well," I laughed, "shall I begin the Canterbury Tales?"

"Why not?" she said. Her voice was at once distant and close.

"Where shall I begin? There isn't any beginning. No beginning, no middle and no end. I've been in a maelstrom all my life. So? I was in a maelstrom.

"I've told you I'm busted in the places that count," I continued my ramble, "but that can't ring true to you. You know better. Milo knows better. *Who's Who* knows better. I'm the one person in this town that has a book written *about* him. So

234

naturally I'm great. The cocksman of the Great Plains. Whereas the fact of the matter is that I'm ruined as a writer, a husband, a lover, a citizen, a friend, and now, it seems, as what the nineteenth century used to call a suitor!" I was warming to my subject and almost expected Marya to be taking notes.

"I will tell you the story of the Writer's Colony," I said pompously, and was already lost in my theme. Had Marya disappeared before my eyes I wouldn't have noticed it. Had Milo been swallowed up in the earth I would have continued the monologue. Had hydrogen bombs destroyed America, I would have gone on from the great beyond.

"A Writers Colony is an intellectual corner grocery store that's trying to become a supermarket. It's a collection of vegetable bins full of rotten vegetables that are dying to find their way into a salad. Well, they mean well, probably. I was at this Writers Colony a few years ago. I was the Famous Writer. Three quarters of the tuition-paying denizens were women, teachers or assistant professors, eighteen-year-old scholarship aspirants, bearded and unbearded young men and old men, a couple in wheelchairs, one Indian and three Negroes, for the sake of democracy. The locale was beautiful, near Medicine Bow, seven thousand feet, with an ice-blue lake that was icy in an eighty-degree sun. Log cabins, food and booze galore, and screwing under the constellations, just like a travel poster. And the ravenous females beating at my door from sunup to sundown and in the velvet of the night."

I stopped and looked at Marya, who was motionless and without gesture or sign. She was looking at me neutrally and occasionally sipping her drink.

"What I am getting at . . ." I said, uncertainly.

"What are you getting at?" asked Marya.

"Simply that I fell in love." I laughed and went to the bottle. "This is the point. I fell in love with a lesbian." I returned to my seat, awaiting the verdict.

"Did you know she was a lesbian when you—fell in love?"

"I repeat. That is the point. She had a voice like a drill sergeant, she walked as if she were carrying a swagger-stick, and her eyes! I knew she was impossible, but I preferred her to the banshees who were wailing at my door. It would have been too easy and expectable to sleep with the others. Anybody could do that and everybody had. But who but the great Lazerow would fall for a Junker-type daughter of Lesbos?"

"So what was the outcome?" Marya asked.

"Oh, I followed her around like a puppy dog for days. We drank together and talked literary gossip. One night I made a pass at her and she threw me out of the cottage. Bodily. She took me by the arm and propelled me to the screen door. I tried to shake her off but she was stronger than I was. She opened the door, shoved me through, slammed the door and bolted it. I was very offended and I left Medicine Bow the next day."

Marya sighed wearily and rose to make herself a drink. With her back to me she said, "Didn't it ever occur to you that you were playing with that woman's feelings; that your love, as you call it, was an insult to her?"

"I guess I shouldn't have told you that," I said finally.

"What about the child?" she asked abruptly.

"The child? There isn't any child. Or rather, there is a child. But I have nothing to do with it and never did."

"That woman who called me—what was she to you?"

"Nothing," I said. "Well, I was involved with her for several years, along with a lot of other people. She's a kind of erotic mascot of the town and gown. I forced myself on her, I suppose. My worst self. Although, to be fair, she never put any sexual obstacles in my way. But now I'm through. *Finito*. And this wild story of a bastard child is her idea of revenge."

"What do you think she'll do? And what will you do?"

I laughed raggedly. "I'm going to ignore it. I doubt that she'll do anything. She probably doesn't even want money. In any case, she can't do any actual damage. Even to my self-esteem. I guess the only thing I object to is the style."

"It seems to me that the style suits the content, as you professors say."

I sat silently, looking at the carpet. It was a bilious green and there were faint outlines of large stains; spilled drinks or food or vomit? I looked up at the ceiling; there are always stains on the ceilings of motels: squirt of bottles, objects thrown in fury or in drunken fun, mischief? It happens even in the best of motels.

As the night reeled on, I laboriously recited my sins and peccadilloes. Only this time there was no fun in it. It all sounded dreary and cheap and without significance. But Marya listened.

"I used to go to sub-culture parties out of loneliness, but I was out of place there too. I'd go and bring a bottle and sit on the floor and be miserable. Then I'd go home and listen to Scarlatti sonatas or Mozart and cry myself to sleep. The worst places were at students' houses, a teacher trying to be buddy-buddy with the kids who were working on their Master's dissertations. In the daytime when I wasn't teaching, I'd sit on my porch, even in snow weather, and try to write. That's how a lot of it started. The women in the neighborhood started to zero in on me. At first, they just dropped in to visit, or to bring me something they'd cooked—you know," I said.

"Certainly," Marya replied.

"But then, several of them—quite a few actually—wanted a lay. And I tried. But it was never any good. And yet, most of them didn't seem to mind. I used to wonder what they really wanted from me."

"Or you from them. I don't imagine they hurled you to the floor. Why didn't you say no?" Marya asked.

"To tell you the truth, Marya," I answered, "I never thought of that. I guess I thought it would offend them to be refused."

Marya burst into a dangerous laugh.

"Oh, goddammit, what's the point of all this? It's so sordid," I said, making us another drink.

"Stop if you want," Marya said and gave me a smile.

I handed her the drink and continued. "Last Christmas, for instance, there was this ballet teacher dame. Married, like most of them. She had hair that hung down to her ankles, which she wore in one pigtail, like a bellrope. She wore a trench coat, of course, sandals, no makeup, of course, and smelled like a Greek restaurant. She called me up one day and asked me to give her a name."

"A name?" asked Marya.

"Yes. She wanted a professional name and of course I was the one to supply the commodity. So she came over."

"Naturally. Something of that nature can't be done on the phone," Marya said with a straight face.

"All right, I'm stupid. I really thought that's what she wanted. I spent about an hour with her giving her crazy names. Her own name was Zeta Lutton. How the hell can you be a ballet dancer with a name like that? I gave her some good ones: Rosa Lovercheck, Uni May, Trudy Rausch, Patty Firebaugh, Vern Forney. I told her if she wanted to pass as an Indian, Helen Go-Lightly would be nice. I once had an Indian student named Go-Lightly."

"At the Writers Colony," said Marya.

"To make a long story short," I continued, "Zeta also tried to gun me down. She took off her trench coat and began to dance to Barber's *Adagio for Strings* which was playing on the FM. In her leotards, of course."

"Stop saying of course," said Marya.

"Then she said, 'I'm not leaving without a grand climax.' 'What's that?' I said. 'A royal fuck,' she said. Well, I tried. I think I tried. But it wasn't for me. Then this character flew into some neo-Victorian rage and lay there rolling and twisting on the rug, grinding her teeth. It was like I wasn't even there. I didn't know what to do."

"Poor dear," said Marya. "What else did you get for Christmas?"

"Maybe it would have been better if I'd gotten syphilis, if I'd had the wherewithal. So you see, now. I'm a bust. It always seemed to me that I was being victimized, that my hands were clean, that I was being taken advantage of. So, I couldn't make love on demand, like a stud."

"Oh, Ed," said Marya and buried her face in her hands and started to cry. "The way you tell those stories . . . you enjoy them so."

"No," I cried, going to her. "I don't. I don't want to anymore! It will be different with you. You'll see. Let's try, Marya. I know I can make you happy—in every way. I promise you

238

I can. You're what I want. Both of us need a new direction to our lives, and I don't want to start out alone. It sounds like an old-fashioned proposal, but I need your hand. I'm desperate for your love. And for you I'll start writing poetry again. It's been so long—years of desert. If I don't write a poem soon I'll get gangrene!" I felt a wave of self-pity but I felt I was entitled to it. Tears came to my eyes and I held her and we cried together.

"You marry me," I said, "and our nightmares will all be jokes. Like Sunday comics."

Shaking her head slightly, she kissed my face and extricated herself from my arms. She went into the bathroom and bathed her face. When she came back, she dropped fresh ice into our drinks.

"Did you ever notice how gin eats into ice?" she said. "You'd think it had teeth."

"Yes," I answered uneasily. I held the glass close to my eye and watched. "You can see the edges of the cubes pushing down to the bottom of the glass. In little oily swirls."

"You went after a woman like Wanda who didn't want you," she began without prelude. "You ran after a lesbian who threw you out of her house. You made yourself available to housewives and temporary widows and God knows who else whom *you* didn't want. You went where you weren't wanted and you drew females to you whom you had no intention of loving or satisfying."

"Yes," I said with eyes averted.

"So what do you want with me? Where do I fit in?"

"But Marya, you don't! That's the point!" I cried.

"That's right. I don't. From your point of view or from mine." She spoke slowly, sadly, without anger. "How can you talk about marriage to me when you've decided that you aren't worth giving yourself to anybody and nobody is worth giving themselves to you? You've created a vacuum of your life and you expect me to rush into it. I've just left a vacuum and I won't make the same mistake twice. When you're ready to give yourself, if I'm still around, then we'll see. When you start giving yourself some of the esteem you expect others to give you.

239

When you don't hate yourself anymore. How can you love me if you hate yourself? I don't want to be just another audience for your clown act. I'm more serious about you than that. I want your love—not just your poetry."

The word shocked me. It went right to my center like an earthquake. I stared at her unbelievingly.

"Oh, I admire your poetry," she said, "and you, for being a poet. But I want to *love you* for yourself."

"I know," I said, opening and closing one hand like an injured mollusk. "I have to recover—from this freeze," I said, dropping my hand in my lap. "And I think it's possible now, for the first time. It has to be. I want you enough to even love myself," I said with tears in my eyes.

CHAPTER XXI

I was a few minutes late getting to class. To my surprise there were only two students in the room, one of the athletes and one of the sorority girls. Maybe it's some kind of holiday, I thought; I myself didn't keep track of such things. "Where's everybody?" I asked. The sorority girl said that there was some kind of demonstration on campus but she wasn't sure what. I dismissed them and walked hurriedly to my office. I saw Oscar and Inge in deep conversation; Inge was sitting with her hands pressed to her cheeks, listening intently.

"Morning, Ed," said Oscar, "come and join the meeting." I sat down on my desk.

"How about going to the airport with me, Ed," said Oscar, "to pick up Wigglesworth?"

"Good Christ," I exploded, "what's that Savonarola doing wasting his time in Milo!"

"He won't be wasting it," Inge said with a laugh. "Local TV and other parties of the fourth estate are already waiting for his plane. After all he *is* a public figure." I looked at her dubiously.

"What's it all about?" I asked. "Akiba?"

"Akiba and Brom," said Oscar, jerking his head backward, "and the Causes."

"Causes," I said. "Camel vomit. Pardon," I added to Inge.

"Camel shit," amended Inge.

"Akiba is no slouch at getting in touch, Ed," said Oscar. "I have to admire his communicability. Honestly, from the state asylum he organized Wigglesworth in the heart of Manhattan. And Edsel, don't forget that Wigg is effective. He's effective particularly in the originality of his extremism. You know that, whatever you think of his poetry."

"I give him a C for his poetry and a flunk for his brain," I said.

"Let's skip that, Ed," said Oscar, getting serious. He twisted a beautiful star sapphire ring on his index finger. "This is our opportunity to get Irick and the Christ gang. We have what the politicos call a bargaining position."

"What do we get out of the bargain?" I wanted to know.

"Weakening the bastion, Ed," Oscar said. "Throwing them off balance. Simply embarrassing the local nobility. That's all."

"That's all," I said, "but I'll be goddamned if I'm going to put my shoulder to the wheel for that pseudo-martyr who would come to Milo to advance what the publicists call his public image. You can take his public image and shove it up your ass."

Inge guffawed. Oscar looked at me pityingly.

"There will be the first interesting-looking demonstration this town has ever seen," said Oscar. "In a couple of hours. Picketing the Administration Building, a little speech to release Akiba from the county hospital and a little speech to restore Janiczek to his department. The demonstrators will then go to the county hospital by bus . . ."

"Chartered by Wigglesworth?" I asked, standing.

"Why not?" asked Oscar. "And picket the administration building of *their* institution. Meanwhile Wigglesworth is going to see Governor Laska."

"Oh, no," I sneered, "Wigg wouldn't stoop to a thing like that!"

"Ed," said Oscar, leaning over, "you must know that Wigg always goes to the top. You know his poem about it. 'The Top'?"

"Skip the literature," I said, "and do me a favor, Oscar; leave me out of the dung brigade. Why don't you write a monograph or something about this new great liberator of the Great Plains and get me a button that reads Wigg for Pres. That's what the slimy bastard wants anyhow."

"Oh, Ed," said Oscar pettishly, "nobody ever knows what side you're on. You act as if there weren't any issues anymore."

"True, colleague," I said, "but two questions. What happened to Wigg's demonstration in front of Independence Hall? That must not have met the requirements of his publicity agents. And, two, is Brom really fired? Nobody told me about that! I'll tell you what," I added. "I'll delegate my secretary to accompany you to the welcoming committee. Want to go, Inge? Just tell Dick Wigglesworth that I have a bad case of hemorrhoids and it will take me all afternoon to stuff them back."

Inge laughed nervously. "Okay, Boss, I'll go," she said.

I squinted at her briefly. Suddenly I exhaled deeply, leaned over and shook Oscar's hand.

"Don't let your humanitarianism run away with you, baby," I said.

"The manly love of comrades," answered Oscar, giving me a fishy grip.

I went out to my car in the parking lot in a daze and sat behind the wheel for a long time, staring at the aisles of cars in front of me. I saw the white tower of the library—"lantern," my vocabulary told me—and the gray stone tower of the carillon that was playing "America, My Sweetheart," idiotically and out of key. I switched on the FM radio and the ignition to drown out the noise. It was too early to call Marya and there was no place to go but home. If you can call it that, I said angrily and with high self-indignation.

No, I would have to see the demonstration. Without being seen, I decided. Very simple; I would stay in my office, lock the door, and watch it from there. I watched my office window, waiting for it to close. Surely Inge would close it when she and Oscar left. But it remained open. I waited another five minutes and walked back to the office anyhow. I found the door locked and the room empty. I sank into my red Good Will chair and gazed out of the window.

Students carrying placards were beginning to form in little knots. *My* students, I thought. I ought to flunk the little bastards; then they could picket me. It was obvious that they were pointed toward the Administration Building. I studied the hideous rectangularity and modernity of the edifice in which the administrators were hermetically sealed at the upper levels, sealed too in their business uniforms. A wave of disgust for modern achitecture engulfed me. There's got to be something between Gothic and this infantile geometry, I thought, but what? Baroque, Byzantine, Egyptian, Art Nouveau? Anything, anything, I gurgled, working myself into an architectural frenzy.

Three placards passed under my window to the gathering place and I got up to read them. WE LOVE BROM, said the first one. The carrier was my monkish student. POETRY IS GOD, said the second sign. Chris Jaffe, the Jewish Indian, was toting that one. The third one simply, or not so simply, said, HALLUCINATE! The sign-bearer this time was none other than Catherine House, the exhibitionist. I sank back into my chair, snorting and chuckling.

There was a modest rap at the door and I opened it. Tremaine Atwood, impeccably dressed in Harris tweeds, asked to come in. I admitted him and shut the door behind him.

"Watching the show?" asked Tremaine with a twinkle in his voice.

"What do you think it is, Tremaine?" I asked. I was beginning to worry that Wigglesworth was setting a trap for me; I decided to get out of the campus as soon as Tremaine left.

"Something perhaps to be turned to our advantage, Edsel," said Tremaine, crossing his legs primly. He lit a pipe and went on. "I've just come from the chancellor. You know, Edsel, he was impressed by your plan—the scientific experiment aspect of Janiczek's party, you know. Very clever, Chancellor said it was." Tremaine leaned forward and said in an unnecessarily low voice, "He is *encouraging* the demonstration and he very much hopes that you will be in the—uh—procession."

I let out a raucous laugh. "Me with that rabble? I'll stand on the curb with the campus cops. Irick must have flipped his beanie."

"In point of fact, Edsel," continued Tremaine, "Chancellor *wants* you in the demonstration to help give credence to our, shall we say, manipulations."

"You can tell Chancellor that I'm too busy washing the blackboards," I said. "I don't mean to be rude, Tremaine," I apologized, "but I think our dear chancellor is a coward and an idiot. And so do you."

"Ah well," answered Tremaine, "his is a difficult row to hoe." He got up to leave and turned to me again.

"Wigglesworth is a considerable figure, Edsel, and so, for that matter, is the exotic Akiba Mem. You are *our* poet . . ." He didn't know how to complete the thought and added, "The demonstration will be shown on national television, I hear."

"You're goddam right it will be," I exploded. "That's all any of those vermin are interested in—mug-shots."

"The age of the media, Edsel," said Tremaine, and waved himself out into the hall.

In my rage I wanted to hurl a typewriter through the window or set my files on fire. I wished I had a placard which read PHONIES GO HOME but decided that that would be getting down to the level of the demonstrators. All I really wanted was to forget all this childishness; I don't have a damn thing to do with it, I thought. They're forcing me to play their game, all of them, from top to bottom; management and labor in one of their occasional love-feasts. And woe betide the non-participant, I ended ponderously.

Word of the demonstration had sped through the campus, even into the classrooms and fraternities and sororities. Everyone had declared an unofficial holiday, from the looks of things. I was sure that the crowd knew that the demonstrators had the backing of the administration; no chance of a counterattack. Brom was rapidly gaining the status of hero; I watched his crazy Citroën turn the corner and heard a cheer go up; I saw people reaching through his window to shake hands with him. I wondered what would happen when Akiba hit the campus. "I'd better hightail it out of here," I said, and shut my window. As I did so I saw Oscar's car turn into the parking lot, Inge in the back and Wigglesworth's bulky figure and round bald head in the front. They were striding quickly toward my office, Inge in the lead.

"Serves me right," I fumed. I didn't want to be caught sneaking out of my own office and went and opened the window higher. In a second Inge beat a tattoo on the door and then opened it with her own key.

"Hi, boss!" she greeted me gaily. I thought she looked hyp- notized. Oscar came second and pushed the door wider for Wigglesworth. Oscar's expression was odd—pleasure, excite- ment, seriousness all at once. The visiting dignitary lurched in and held out his hand to me as if it were too heavy to hold himself. He gave me a crushing squeeze, bobbing his head slightly, and said, "Good boy, Ed, good work all around."

"How are you, Wigg?" I asked, wondering what I had been a good boy about. Did Wigg think that I, Edsel, had organized this crap? Wigglesworth sat down crushingly in the red arm- chair; Inge and Oscar took the other two chairs, leaving me standing foolishly in the little office. "It's been a long time, Wigg," I said pointlessly. As a trapped host I felt I should say something. The last time I had seen Wigg we had given a double poetry reading at the Cooper Union in New York; during my half of the program Wigg had sat on stage and scraped his chair every few minutes. I had given him a few dirty looks but decided that it was because of Wigg's bulk and his bad coordination that his chair moved like a Ouija board.

Not one for pleasantries, Wigglesworth plunged into the business at hand.

"Oscar is picking up Akiba at two," said Wigg, already giv- ing instructions.

"You mean he's been sprung?" I asked in amazement.

"Just for the demonstration," said Wigg, "and then he and his friends will have a police escort to the state line. Good strategy, Ed. I'm going for the ride. A *Lux* photographer is coming along and the TV people." He turned to Inge and said, "Will you tell the chancellor I'm here and can see him whenever he wants?" Obediently Inge picked up the phone.

"I want to see the chancellor alone, Ed," said Wigglesworth. "You don't mind?" he asked and answered at the same time.

"The chancellor didn't ask to see me, Wigg," I said, "and if he did I wouldn't." They listened while Inge completed her call.

"Mr. Irick's secretary says he awaits your pleasure," said Inge with her tinkly laugh.

Wigg settled back deeper into his chair. He seemed in no hurry. He began to give more directives.

"Oscar told me the parade route," said Wigg. "I'd like the main people up front: me, Akiba, you Ed, Janiczek and Oscar."

"Hold it a minute, Wigg," I said. "Where did you get the idea that I'm one of your gang? I'm not. It's your party. Have fun. Now, if you don't mind, I have to lock up."

Inge looked down, Oscar looked out the window, and Wigglesworth sat quietly staring at me.

"You can't possibly mean that," said Wigg definitively. "You're the poet here. You can't let all these people down. You're even letting your university down."

"I'm not letting anybody down, Wigglesworth," I said, "especially myself. Have your little mob hysteria; only do me a favor, lead the little rats into the mountain and bolt the door."

Wigglesworth unwound from the deep chair and raised his bulk to a standing position. He gave me a sickly grin and extended his paw again. "I'm disappointed in you, Ed, but I respect your right to sit this one out."

"Thanks, pal," I said with an attempt at a sneer. "I'm sitting this one out and all subsequent children's jamborees."

"I'll show you the way to the chancellor," said Oscar to Wigglesworth. A brief goodbye and the pair left. I leaned against my desk and smoked.

"Listen, Ed," said Inge.

"I thought my name was boss," I said, looking at her. "You swung over to the Wigglesworths of this world?"

"No, seriously," said Inge, "I think you should be in on this. It's important—for *you!*" she said.

"I don't give a shit for publicity," I said. "Noble of me, isn't it? Did Wigg offer you a job?"

"Why?" asked Inge. "He's honest, isn't he?"

"He leaves no stone unturned," I said, more to myself than to Inge. "Yes, he's honest, in the way psychotics are honest. Even tying his shoelace is a Cause. And everything that he does is a Cause. Ergo, he's honest."

"He offered me a job on his magazine," said Inge. "In New York. I know I'm not ready for it but it's hard to turn down. It's barely enough to live on but it will be in a place where I'll meet all the writers and publishers."

"You'd better grab it, Inge," I said. "Wigg can kick his way through any door and you'll have writers and publishers and editors running out of your ears. I guess it's lucky for you actually." I felt hurt at this sudden desertion and angry to have been downgraded by Wigglesworth. "Well, I'll be leaving," I said. "And Inge, I don't want Wigglesworth using my office for his headquarters. I want you to lock up for the afternoon. That's an order," I added with a small laugh.

"Okay, boss," said Inge. She looked at me with a guilty smile. I left and closed the door behind me.

A block away, the street in front of the Administration Building was already mobbed. I would have to hurry to get through in my car. It was a one-way street and I would have to honk my way out. When I drew parallel to the marble entrance of the Administration Building I saw Wigg standing on the steps with Oscar, a cheering throng of the bearded and loose-haired set surrounding him like a bodyguard.

"Signing autographs," I said to myself bitterly. "What does he care if he keeps his eminence waiting. Makes him look bigger." Inching my way through the chaos I was spotted by some of my creative writing class. The prayer-shawl ripper pushed toward my car and yelled into the window, "Are you with us, Mr. Lazerow?" I rolled up my window and leaned on the horn. A small group jostled the car and banged on the rear deck. I ought to go full speed ahead, I thought, but only crept forward through milling students. Someone stuck a flower at me through the other window. I laid it on the seat and took the ashtray from the dashboard. I dumped it vigorously out of the window. I shouldn't have done that, I thought. "You bastard," a girl yelled back at me.

Eventually I got to the intersection and moved off the campus. I drove against a small tide of curiosity-seekers. On foot, bicycles and in cars, people were converging on the university, a TV sound truck among the caravan.

"I'll go home and watch it on television," I said to myself.

When I had made a drink I called Marya at her house. Bumpy had already tipped her off about the campus festivities and Marya wanted more details.

"The only detail is me, Marya," I said. "I voted myself out of the action."

"What do you think will happen, Ed?" asked Marya.

"Nothing, I hope," I answered, "unless they send a lynching party for me. Mobs can't stand non-participants. But it's just noise. Which most of the people in the mob call news."

"Bumpy says her husband is furious at the chancellor. He may give up wanting to be a Regent."

"Good for him," I said. "I was beginning to think I was the only one left who makes sense."

We decided on eight for my visit to her house. "Please don't bring anything, darling," she told me. "I have some of everything. I'll have to show you the wine cellar in this hotel." I told her that I was going to watch the monkey-business on television.

The camera showed a large banner in front of Administration which read: PROCREATE PEACE ** POT ** PLEASURE. "All of which spells PUBLICITY," I said out loud.

On TV I saw Wigg emerge from the glass-and-aluminum doors of the Administration Building, arm in arm with Zip Halvorsen, the chancellor's aide-de-camp. The chancellor himself would stay put in his office, I knew, but the appearance of the second-in-command with the visiting rabble-rouser would lend official sanction to the Roman holiday. A TV reporter asked Halvorsen for a statement; he smiled, waved and shook his head. The reporter then shoved a microphone into Wigglesworth's face.

REPORTER: Mr. Wigglesworth, welcome to Milo. What is this demonstration all about?

WIGG: Love. Freedom. The love of freedom and the freedom to love. Look at that sign. (Pointing backward to the banner with the P's, at which point Halvorsen disappears back into the building.) The young are on the march! They are inheriting the campuses, the cities, the rivers. They are taking what they own. God bless the beautiful young! (Cheers from the mob.)

REPORTER: But what's your actual reason for coming to Milo all the way from New York?

WIGG: To welcome the great youth-poet Akiba back into the land of the living. He is on his way here now from that— pest-house. We are all marching together to the state house to speak with the governor.

REPORTER: The governor? What about, Mr. Wigglesworth?

WIGG: Many things. Police brutality, county hospitals, the war in Vietnam, draft quotas, Indian reservations, Negroes, miscegenation laws, pure food and drug laws. You name it! (Wigglesworth waving his hands over his head.)

REPORTER: Has the governor agreed to see you?

WIGG: We'll wait. And wait. And wait. And wait. And wait.

Iambic pentameter, I thought, sipping my drink.

At this moment Wigglesworth must have received a signal from someone on the watch, for he raised both hands straight up in some kind of new salute and bellowed, "The poet Akiba Mem is coming now! Follow us, follow us!" At which point Wigg started to elbow his way through the crowd toward the intersection a half a block away. The TV camera now panned the crowd, which had swelled to twice or three times its number.

"Good Christ!" I said, leaning toward the TV, "the high-school kids are out!" Apparently word had spread to the four high schools and four junior highs that the university campus was jumping. In the distance, as the cameras turned, I thought I could spot the fancy Microbus in which Akiba and his dis-

250

ciples made their raids on what they called the Establishment. Police lights burst brilliantly around the bus, protecting the occupants. "From what," I said, "hay-fever?"

A camera truck had reached the Microbus and the scene came into focus again: Wigglesworth taking Akiba in his arms, the bus emptying itself of its moldy occupants—Govinda and his pigtails, the wretched little catatonic creature and a couple of the would-be saviors picked up en route to Milo before the arrest at Janiczek's party. Cheers greeted the embraces and suddenly a roar began to swell and the mob began to point down the street. The reporter said he wasn't sure what the cheering was about but they would soon know. A pretty bright reporter, I thought, as Brom's Citroën drove into camera view from where it had been waiting.

Wigglesworth's crazy salute—both arms upright and parallel and palms facing inward—had already been accepted as some kind of secret sign, and all the followers shoved their hands up and cheered as Brom edged his way out of his car. Karen, her hair blowing wildly, got out of the other door. Her arms were heavy with bangles and her neck was draped with Indian beads. They were introduced to Wigglesworth rather formally, I thought. They haven't worked out all the protocol of their new religion yet, I ruminated; but look how long it took the Christians to knock the Mass into shape. I was convinced that the whole sophomoric mess might turn into a bona fide religion. But the trouble with this one was that it had no place to go but back; ill-digested gobbets of Zen and the Vedas, acid highs, hepatitic needles, electric jazz, Minoan tit-exhibits, Orphic fucks, Spartan buggering, dung-worship, astrology, Ho Chi Minh and Fidel Castro firing-squads, black Nazi Final Solution for non-blacks, anti-Semitism in the name of the New Left (whatever that is), Art Nouveau, conscious illiteracy, the ineluctable modality of smegma, flag-burning and immolation and masturbation raised to the status of sacraments.

Akiba, aware of the ecumenical character of the occasion, all at once swung into his Harrdi Krishna chant, and before long the entire rabble had metamorphosed into Hindus. Poor little Milo, I thought, where now are your Middle Western

251

sects? I began to rhapsodize: where now are the Seventh-Day Adventists, the African Methodist Episcopalians, the Assembly of God, the Independent Baptists, the Fundamental Bereans; where now the Catholics and the temples of the Hebrews; where the Disciples of Christ, the Scientists, Congregationalists, the Wesleyans, Interdenominationalists, Jehovah's Witnesses, Latter Day Saints; where the innumerable Lutherans, Nazarenes, Pentecostals, Presbyterian Orthodoxes, United Churches of Christ, the Pilgrim Holiness, and the Unitarians? All sunk into the mushy-minded Hinduism of the adolescent. So be it, I said, and formed a benediction in the air. I went, as usual, to replenish my drink.

Wigg had actually procured an appointment with Governor Laska, five blocks away in the state house. Janiczek drove him in the Citroën while Akiba, Karen and the rest of the motley led the procession up the street, chanting and cheering. I wondered what kind of deal the chancellor had worked out with Wigglesworth to get the visiting firebrand such an appointment. The TV reporter also expressed his puzzlement. The programming suddenly switched to an afternoon soap opera, "Country Club Tales," with the announcement that the newscast would return "live" as soon as the marchers reached the state house.

CHAPTER XXII

My timing stinks. If I were political-minded I would get my timing-chain going, so to say, but I cut my teeth on Cummings' saying that a politician is an arse that everybody has sat on except a man. That sort of thing. I never had that low an opinion of politicians actually but I always steered clear of the species. Even when I respected one I feared him. Not that I had met many face to face, but that was probably because I didn't want to. I wouldn't even stand in line at the chancellor's annual shake-hand in the fall when all the faculty had been regathered and new recruits were given the opportunity to pump the arm that fed them. Wigglesworth, on the other hand, suck-assed politicians, the higher the better. It was his way of proving—what? I always suffered for what I thought of as his ignominy. Twice he had made a spectacle of refusing to come to the White House for some art function or other, *after* he had accepted the invitations. A planner.

I was feeling very cool and collected and something decided for me that I would place a phone call, as they used to say, to Governor Laska. The fact that I had nothing to say never entered my mind. I was dialing the operator and asking for the state house before I knew it. When I got the right operator I gave my name as Professor Lazerow of the university and asked to speak to the governor briefly. I was asked to leave my number.

By now the television had switched to the vast steps of the state house, stairs higher than a Mayan pyramid and just as grand. Wigg as impresario had led his leaders halfway up: there were Akiba and the two Janiczeks and, to my surprise, Inge. With Oscar Darling they made five on the stairway. At the bottom surged the mob, some beginning to climb into the surrounding trees. The police were redirecting traffic from the block and all was in readiness for something. A camera focused on Govinda, who was pretending to do Indian leaps for the edification of the mob. A reporter with a microphone staggered back and forth trying to get his attention, but Govinda was too carried away, his pigtails flying at improbable angles.

"Sir!" the reporter kept repeating to Govinda, not knowing how else to address him. Govinda came out of a leap finally in front of the reporter, wiping his face with his braids.

"Sir," said the reporter, "we'd like to get your—uh—views of this—uh—demonstration. What are your views? No, first your name, sir."

"Garbage," said Govinda with a smile.

"Is that your name, sir?" asked the reporter with a brilliant flash of wit.

"Garbage," said Govinda.

"What is this demonstration about—uh—?" he asked, fearing to address the New Jersey Indian as Mr. Garbage.

"Garbage," said Govinda.

"What do you mean by garbage?" asked the member of the fourth estate.

"Garbage," said Govinda, beginning to sound convincing.

My phone rang and I didn't even start. A man's voice said that Governor Laska was ready on the line. I had known Laska slightly and liked him, a raw-boned steel-headed man who stuck out of a crowd like a tree. He never made phony jokes and wouldn't be caught dead kissing a baby. He wanted to go to the Senate but he was against small talk and cheap idealism and would probably never make it. He had asked me once to

254

head a state cultural committee "to elevate the arts"; it was at the time when that sort of dreck was fashionable in Washington, and Laska didn't care for it either. He asked me anyhow and when I declined with a few choice oaths we both had a laugh and he gave me a deep look and thanked me.

"Edsel?" asked the governor. I figured it was his job to give me a *tutoyer*.

"Listen, Governor," I said, "I hate to bother you, but I want to tell you for what it's worth, if anything, that I don't have anything to do with that cornball demonstration on your front steps and that if you ever want any neutral opinions on the subject just let me know." I felt foolish suddenly for calling him but Laska said he understood and appreciated my call. Then he said:

"Where does our chancellor stand on this?"

"I'm not really sure, Governor," I said, wishing I would stop saying *Governor*. "But I have a slight inkling that Irick ain't exactly agin it. That's all I know."

Laska gave me a hearty laugh, thanked me again, and hung up. I turned back to the TV, trembling slightly.

Wigg and his little delegation were mounting the steps again, led by a state house guard; they disappeared into the building. On the street, where the camera was watching, the mob had centered around Akiba's yellow bus, from which poured at window-rattling volume the adenoidal lyricism of Protest. Govinda meanwhile was waving a long-cord microphone in the air and inviting each and every demonstrator to step up, yell his, her, or its name and then shout a four-letter word. In reward Govinda leaned over and licked the ear of the yeller. Long queues began to form to reach the microphone and let go with the magical syllables. I am interested in words naturally and grabbed a sheet of paper and began a tally of frequencies. Until the cops stop the TV camera, I thought. But apparently nobody was going to stop anything.

My *fuck* column took an early lead. At Berkeley it had been the word that started the seismographs going. *Fuck* was to the delirious student mob out there as the cross was to the Christian or the star of David to the Jew. It meant Liberty, Equality, Fraternity, Bitchery, Abomination and Buggery. It meant book-burning, window-smashing, red revolution, grass and the glory of being busted. Activistically speaking, *fuck* is a winner, a two-edged sword that means on the one hand a cold-blooded variety of love, and on the other *begone!* The Fuckers were definitely in the lead.

Shit was a fairly close second, however, but *shit* had become almost as polite as, say, *dowager*. Young humanities professors even used it in class (although taking refuge in the prefix *bull*, and although few of them had ever seen a bull). *Shit* also has therapeutic connotations, my philological mind noted: argot for certain high-voltage drugs. The Shitters tended to run to girls.

One pretty freshman grabbed the microphone and squealed, "My name is Nellie Jamison! Crud!" Menstrual problems, I thought.

My monkish student had his turn and yelled *God!* but was followed by a strapping sorority sister with ironed hair who broke the monosyllabic rule by screaming *Fuck God!* Govinda as master of ceremonies didn't seem disturbed by the breach of etiquette and responded liturgically, *God is fuck!* This precipitated a whole series of variations on religious and sexual signs and symbols, such as *God is shit* and *Shit is god*. By God, I said to myself, they really do understand Hinduism.

The list of four-letter expletives in our language is lamentably brief, but Govinda had made his pitch and had created the consternation which it was his assignment to engender. But suddenly the screen went blank and I was back in "Country Club Tales." At this juncture the soap opera sounded obscene, however.

"Howard, I'm sick of hearing about your new putter," said a sloe-eyed siren, sitting by the club pool. "Your little white balls mean more to you than Chrissie's coming-out." I half expected Howard to answer, "Shit." All he said was, "Oh, Myrna, you can be cutting," and leaned over and kissed her hand. I was afraid to turn the TV off, being in a state of high expectation of disaster. Sure enough, Howard and Myrna disappeared into

256

oblivion and I was back in front of the state house, introduced this time by the wail of fire engines. The announcer, back in the realm of reality at last, reported that an automobile was on fire. "No, two cars are burning!" he panted with relief. "And another is being turned over and the crowd is going wild!" "Touchdown" crossed my mind.

Well, it transpired that the kiddies, hopped up from yelling *fuck* on the media and not knowing what to do for an encore, decided to attack the innocuous state cars parked here and there along the curb. *State* after all is even a dirtier word than *shit* and state cars are veritable symbols of authority and the Establishment. Turning over a car is child's play; as for fire, an upside-down Chevy is practically spontaneous combustion. Ergo, the fire engines.

We were at last having a demonstration of what the kiddies call Participatory Democracy. Everyone was finally doing his Thing, except, of course the bewildered Milo police who were standing around with their jaws open, waiting for word from somewhere.

It suddenly jumped into my mind that all of this was probably being watched on coast-to-coast special news, especially as Akiba and Wigg were playing the heavies in the drama. Milo U. would be read about for the first time since it had discovered the medicinal properties of the hair-ball. An ominous feeling took place in my stomach. What would the governor do? What would Irick do? *Do about what?* kept drumming in my head. What do you do about chaos? And as if in answer to my question I heard the word *looting*. The students were now attacking all cars except the Citroën and Microbus. They started with snapping off radio aerials from hoods and fenders, rifling glove compartments—nobody locks his car in little old Milo—taking packages and ripping them open, popping off hubcaps and sending them spinning down the sidewalks. A few experts made off with the radios themselves or any removables from the dashboard, such as cigarette lighters and even electric clocks. Still the police did nothing but stare. In a way, I couldn't blame them.

One of the reporters was stationed at the top of the state

house stairs, waiting for the emergence of the delegation. They finally appeared, to the accompaniment of the wail of new fire engines and stood still and watched. Wigg took instant command and waved down to Govinda to ascend to the presence. The "Indian" caught the command and without deserting character loped up the long stone steps, weaving from side to side and flinging his braids to the winds. There was a short huddle and he loped down again, entered the yellow soundtruck which is really what it was, and made an announcement.

"Everybody up the steps! Everybody up the steps! Charge, baby, charge! Charge, baby, charge!" and started up a chant to that effect until the car-molesting rabble had picked it up. On my TV it looked like iron filings switching to a magnet. A big swirl of humanity on the left and a big swirl of humanity on the right, forming a confluence and mobbing up the steps. From inside the building state troopers emerged and stood and stared. Wigg was sorting out his delegation, himself in the center, Brom on his right and Akiba on his left and Karen and Inge on the flanks. Oscar was not "placed" apparently, and roved to and fro. Wigg kept pushing the reporter aside and repeating, "Not now, not now; wait a little," until almost all the demonstrators had packed onto the steps and the terraced lawns, waiting for the word from their leaders and heroes, and leaving the fire department to squirt down the last car fire and the police to direct the tow-trucks in.

Wigg raised his arms in his gym-class salute and the crowd went silent.

"Students, countrymen, and lovers!" he began and a cheer went up, maybe for Shakespeare, I thought. "Your governor has given us his word that our dear poet Akiba and his friends are released from the county snakepit as of *now*." Redoubled cheers. "This is our victory! This is our—charisma! And all of you have been a beautiful barricade of love." More cheers. Mobs love nothing better than gibberish; the more the leader gibbers the more they froth at the mouth. Wigg, born politician that he was, knew that a presentation of victory is not enough. You get a roused-up mob, young or old, rich or poor, illiterate or elite, and you have to throw them a fish; more, you have to send them on to what might be called a higher destiny or, at the very minimum, a new endeavor. Was he going to tell them to burn down Hinsdale & Eisenbray, Inc., or to march through Blue Town to denounce Caucasian imperialism?

"I have spoken to your chancellor," he went on. "He understands that inaction is obsolete. He understands that restitution must be made to these two artists of human society, Brom and Karen Janiczek. He understands that *one must take a stand!*" A wilder cheer. A stand? I thought. A stand about what? A stand, the answer came to me, about anything and everything. In other words, if you don't have an opinion about *everything* you are dead. Anybody who says I don't know or let me think about it is dead. If not dead he'll be trampled in the rush. I had a fleeting image of boots a hundred abreast thundering in perfect step up the Unter den Linden.

"And now you know," said Wigg. "Know what?" I said aloud. "And now you know that one must take a stand." He turned to Akiba, who was grinning from ear to ear, and placed him before the microphone. Akiba dug into his pouch, a kind of lady's pocketbook in which he carried God knows what mysterious goodies, and produced his Indian bells. "Not again," I groaned, leaning into the tube.

Akiba merely set up the Krishna hymn and went off into wild wails that reminded me of Yom Kippur at its worst. But the kiddies caught on and managed the four Hindu syllables and the incipient tune rather passably, I thought. They were locking arms on the capitol stairs and swaying and singing. Wigg didn't want this to go too long, of course, and gave Akiba a jab in the ribs with his elbow. Whereupon the microphone passed back to the paw of Wigglesworth. Reporter time, I figured.

Instead of which, I saw Police Chief Slezak limp out of the capitol door and take the microphone.

"This is the Milo chief of police," he said. "You are asked to disperse to your homes or your schools immediately. Any loiterers will be subject to arrest. Go peaceably to your homes or schools." He wheeled around on his game leg, handing the microphone back to Wigg without looking at him. The mob stood still, waiting apparently for a second by one of the leaders of the gathering, or maybe even a corroboration of the police order. The leaders went into a new huddle. Surprisingly, Karen emerged with the mike, shaking her pony-tail.

"We are all going to campus, going for a great sing-in, dear friends, to whom we owe so much of everything," she said. "Let us march together and sing together and love together." She handed the mike back to Wigg, who seemed to own it. The multitude gave vent to a concerted yelp and started down the steps in a body.

"Jesus" was all I could summon up.

The TV reporter finally had his chance. "Mr. Wigglesworth," he said impatiently. "What is this demonstration all about? What are you trying to accomplish here in Milo?"

Wigg handled reporters like hamsters; he fed them, stroked them, and kept them in their cage.

"Idealism," said Wigg. "All over America idealism is awakening. This generation is *fabulous*," he said, waving in the direction of the departing canaille. "This generation has matured before its time; it knows everything and can *do* anything. No more pantie-raids. No more contests in swallowing goldfish. Only contests in reality. This generation is political!"

The reporter seemed bewildered and asked what they were political about.

"The issues," said Wigg. "All basic issues. This generation has discovered the nitty-gritty. It demands the truth about anything and everything."

"What about the burning cars?" asked the reporter. "What about taking the law in their own hands?"

"Civil disobedience, the highest ideal, the ideal of Socrates," said Wigg, laying his hand on the reporter's shoulder. The reporter moved back.

"How long will you be in Milo, Mr. Wigglesworth?" he asked.

"As long as it takes," said Wigg, giving a little shuffle, "and in a sense, forever. The young have taken fire all over the world, and this is just a spark of their power. It is a wonderful thing, sir," said Wigg, "and you are lucky to see an example of idealist action." The reporter switched to Akiba; Wigg followed him.

"Mr. Mem," asked the reporter, "how do you feel about your visit to Milo?"

"A thing of beauty," answered Akiba. "Absolutely super, absolutely mysterioso. Joy has come back to the Great Plains. I am proud, so proud." He beamed at the reporter, who looked as if he were having an attack of facial paralysis.

"Will you be here long, Mr. Mem?"

"We have to be on our way, alas," said Akiba. I'll bet Akiba is the first person to say "alas" since the death of Shakespeare. "We have borders and boundaries to cross, new states of man and new states of mind," he said.

"You mean you are leaving Milo?" asked the persistent reporter. Wigg piped up.

"They are leaving for new engagements on new campuses, you see," explained Wigg.

"Where do you go from here, Mr. Mem?" asked the reporter.

"Only where our instincts tell us," answered the guru. Suddenly he flung his arms around the reporter and gave him a wet smack on the mouth. Wigg looked annoyed; shmoozing didn't fit into his script. The reporter wiped his mouth with his free hand, reared back and announced whom he had been interviewing. He looked around desperately and grabbed Brom; Brom, however, wasn't talking and was looking blissful and above everything. Inge was available and the reporter got her.

"May I ask your name, Miss?" he asked.

"Inge Amen," she said with her tinkly laugh.

"Were you in the delegation to see the governor?" he asked.

"Yes," she said. "I work for Mr. Wigglesworth. In New York," she said.

I felt as if I had been hit by an oak log. "*Et tu,* bitch," I said aloud, but immediately amended it to "poor Inge." I couldn't hear the rest of the dialogue, if there was any. Anyhow, the show was over and it was almost news time on the TV. I sat where I was in my trance.

I am not a news nut, I tell myself, and it is only at critical times that I even give a good goddam about what is euphemistically called the news. I once went for a year without seeing a paper or turning on the radio or TV. Maybe it was because I was working on a book. At other times the news becomes as necessary as going to the bathroom. Since my divorce I had turned on the box late at night, for the blue light it shed and to wash my brain. The thing conveyed nothing to me whatever except in the way a shower does; soothing the exterior man. Maybe I'm not modern; I can't even take movies seriously, even though I go through the Pavlovian reactions of laughing and crying and feeling patriotic. At the end of a movie I might as well not even have watched; it's gone.

This news, however, was different. I was in it, in it in absentia, yes, but I was definitely a character, not a viewer. The whole thing made my flesh creep. I got up and illogically turned off the TV. I went to the bathroom to see what I looked like in the mirror. I looked normal, I thought. And I went to the kitchen and made a dry manhattan, a powerful little thing.

My hand was itching to turn the news back on and it was itching to call Marya. She must have known because the phone jangled as I walked back into the livingroom.

"Yes?" I said.

"Ed," said Marya, "were you listening to the news?"

"All afternoon," I answered. "Were you?" I summoned up a laugh.

"Are you still—listening?" she asked.

"I had enough kindergarten for one day," I said. "*Basta-basta,* as they put it in the old country." There was a pause. "Marya?" I asked.

"Turn it back on, Ed," said Marya. "I'm coming over now. Wait for me." And she hung up.

I went to the TV and looked at it, thinking. My fingers turned it on without my wishing to. I heard the scream of fire engines before the picture came to life. There was that jumping and jumbling of lines and lights before I got the focus, while I heard the voice saying, "They are still battling the blaze, which apparently started in the office of Professor Edsel Lazerow, Milo's controversial professor and campus bard. The fire is now spreading to the third floor . . ."

My fingers, which had apparently become a separate part of my body, switched off the machine. My drink was in my hand and I went out to the porch and sat in a chair. Marya would be here in six minutes at the most.

CHAPTER XXIII

That's another thing about my timing, I was explaining to myself: the delayed reaction. When something rotten happens I go numb; I'm not the type of person who can faint or go into shock; I just seal off. I found this out in the Army. A landing-craft I was attached to got stuck on a beach and we were bombed and strafed for twenty-four hours without letup. From the time of the first strafing to the end of the attack I was opening cases of blood plasma as fast as I could. Dead and dying were hauled into the little shelter where the surgeons were operating—amputating mostly—and all I could hear were the hollow booms of the Bofors outside and the squeak of the nails as I pried off the lids of the boxes with a small crowbar. Explosions now and then sucked the tent wall in and out, but if there were any human sounds I didn't hear them. Those patched up were hauled outside to make room for new casualties; some of the patched-up were wounded or killed as soon as the stretcher-bearers laid them back on the beach in shallow holes. I don't even think I felt fear; I was somehow beyond it, hypnotized by my packing cases marked with the caduceus, and unable to take in so much carnage. I still can't take it in and sometimes feel cheated of my "reaction" to that day and night. At the same time I am soft-hearted and can bawl at a movie or an assassination or even the death of a shirttail relative. Maybe I can focus on tragedy in the particular; abstract catastrophe doesn't reach me at all.

Marya was surprised to see me looking so calm and collected. She herself was nervous. "Shouldn't you go down there, Ed?" she asked. It had never occurred to me to go down there.

"What for?" I said. "To salvage my red Good Will chair? That's the only thing in my office that I like."

"But your papers, your books!"

"It's time those papers went," I said. "Fifteen years of flaky notes, a year of letters I never even opened, the books—" I paused. "Yes, my books, all those poets with all my marginalia. They can go too. The pillar of fire is a sign, maybe. Anyhow," I added, "books don't burn well. I read a poem about it once."

"Darling," said Marya, "the news said that a Molotov cocktail, they called it, had been thrown through your window." I looked at her in surprise.

"And that the office next to yours, the magazine office, is also completely destroyed. Maybe you are right. Maybe you should wait to hear from somebody down there."

"Down there is right," I said. "*Là-bas.* I'll wait for a summons."

It was like a dream, watching TV again, armed with our drinks. The camera was aimed at my side of the building; a huge hose crawled through my window and a fireman was hurling my books out on the lawn. A crazy act of decency, I thought. I must have been losing my mind because I found myself trying to identify some of the books. The unabridged dictionary wasn't hard to spot. A series of little volumes exploded out of the window: "The *Temple Shakespeare*," I said out loud. Marya looked at me curiously. "The *Cambridge History of English Literature*," I said, taking inventory, as ten or so pale octavos hit the soaked grass, now rapidly turning to a mudhole. Armfuls of slim poetry books followed, some of them smoking. A crowd of students had gathered on the sidewalk; now and then one would rush forward and grab a book and retreat. Souvenir-hunters, I thought; well, let them have them.

I was being the perfect spectator and might have been viewing a ball game, for all I cared.

But Marya was impatient for me to do something and I had an attack of laughter.

"Honey," I said, "that's not Rome burning; that's nothing but nothing. I've wanted to do that myself for years. I don't admire the style of it," I admitted, "but the content is passable."

"Ed, stop it," she said impatiently. "I don't see what there is to be frivolous about. You're being idiotic. Oh, I know," she trailed off.

"We'll be hearing about it from the administration before long," I said. "Don't rush the masterminds. They have to convict somebody before they have a trial. It's what Sacco and Vanzetti called *joostice*.

"There's one thing I don't want and won't have," I said suddenly, as it had just crossed my mind. "I don't want Wigglesworth, Oscar and company coming to this house and offering arsenic and sympathy. And Inge, too." I told Marya about Inge's desertion to the enemy. "Let's go to your house, Marya, and avoid the whole mess. Tomorrow will be time enough to rake through the ashes."

She didn't think it was a good idea but she agreed. I figured that anybody who really wanted to locate me would somehow. I wasn't sure whether I was ready or not to join the broil. I turned off the TV as I saw my red velour chair being disgorged from the window. My window, I thought, a beautiful window, a 1920-ish imitation of English Georgian grandeur, wide enough to take a grand piano. The chair, smoldering and undoubtedly stinking, splashed in the mud.

"What can I bring?" I asked.

"Nothing, Ed. Let's go," she answered.

We had quiche Lorraine and salad at her house. "What is this?" I asked, gobbling. "Bacon, cream, swiss cheese, eggs, pie crust," she said laughing. I looked at the wine bottle and picked it up. Green Hungarian. I felt like a duke. We were walking back to the livingroom and I had already forgotten the conflagration on the campus, along with all the other local and personal calamities. We were kissing when the phone rang.

"Come with me," she said, and led me by the hand to Clayton's den. If there is one word that lies at the bottom of my list of domestic euphemisms it is "den." To me it has all the connotations of "Butch," which ex-college-football-players call their sons. "Butch" is short for "butcher" and "Butch" inhabits a "den," as far as I am concerned. Clayton's den was dark and sparkling with real red leather and thousands of brass studs driven into everything in sight. On one low table sat a three-foot hookah. The wall hangings were approximately Asiatic and the book shelves were lined with gorgeously tooled "sets," as if they had been cemented in with a plumb-line.

"Let me ask Ed," I heard Marya say. "It's Bumpy. Bean—Doc Harrington—wants to talk to you and asks us to come to their place, or they can come here." She waited.

"Here," I said. "But, Marya," I asked her when she had hung up, "what about your privacy and legality and all that?"

"Don't worry about them," she said. "They're my only friends; yours too, unless I've made a bad error."

Doc Harrington still had on his riding clothes and didn't apologize. He had been out jumping his beasts when he got a message that Milo and the campus were undergoing some kind of nervous breakdown. He had gone to talk with Chancellor Irick, from whose office, he said, he watched the fire at Hepplewhite Hall (the name of my building). He seemed very upset and clenched and unclenched his fists, bringing white to his knuckles. The four of us were drinking brandy and soda and looking grim, except for Bumpy, who occasionally broke into her raucous and irreligious laugh.

"Dunstan Irick," said Bumpy, "is a cute pusillanimous turd who loves to be visited by flies. He is," she said, expanding the metaphor, "monumentally rotten."

"What has he got to do with anything?" I asked innocently.

Harrington made an irascible move and Bumpy and Marya went out of the den, arm in arm and laughing. The surgeon wanted to know everything I could tell him about my view of the Janiczek party, the campus saboteurs, and the arrival of Wigglesworth. I told him everything I knew, which was little enough, and then he confided what he knew.

"My information is shaky," he said, "but it pieces together. It appears that your colleague Oscar Darling arranged for the Akiba Mem caravan, using Janiczek as the vector. It appears also that Oscar and Wigglesworth were prepared for a public ventilation of the celebration, or whatever it was supposed do be."

"All of which is harmless," I answered. Harrington looked at me a little incredulously. "I mean apart from the fires," I said. Why had I put "fire" in the plural? I asked myself.

"But this piece I can't fit in," said the doctor. "You know I am a friend of the governor's?" he asked. "If you follow the local politics, that is. I helped elect him. A good man. Very bright, very straight." I was pinned down with his gaze.

"And Laska called me to tell me that your Wigglesworth poet had a private session with him in which he, your poet fellow, said he was authorized by the Liberal Party to ask Laska to run for president."

"Of the United States?" I asked, my eyes widening.

"The United States," answered Doc Harrington.

"Sweet Jesus," was all I could come up with.

We sat still for a while. Finally I told Harrington all I knew about Wigg and his venality, betrayals, and fabulous climbings up the publicity ladder, but it sounded like carping and I apologized. "Anyhow," I said, "Wigg is serious, and at any particular time, is deadly sincere. Furthermore, he is effective. Furthermore, persuasive. He is a kind of walking monkey-wrench. Laska can't laugh him off."

"But the political party side of it doesn't concern us, Ed," said the Doc. "Other people will take care of that. What concerns us is—*you*."

"Me?" I said. "Me? What did I do?"

"Nothing," said Harrington, "and that's why you're in trouble."

I guess I know enough about the ways of the world, human psychology, and other popular insipidities to have learned that nothing is more dangerous to a person than neutrality. The spectator is the victim, I started to generalize to myself; a soldier on the battle-line has a better chance for survival than a non-political in Squeedonk. And an intellectual, a writer, a professor, who simply sits and watches, is, well, a sitting duck. Nobody knows where he stands. Ergo, kill the bastard. I was beginning to see the light.

"But Irick wouldn't be so predictable as to accuse me of setting my own office on fire, would he?" I asked, not really joking.

"He has a little polish," was the answer, "barely enough. No, he wouldn't stoop to TV tactics. But he will have his way, and I don't know what he has up his sleeve."

"Do you think he knows?" I asked. We both laughed.

"Dunstan, of course, will want to have his meetings," said Harrington. "And in these meetings he will hew and chisel away at you, Ed. You are a thorn in his side. You wouldn't be on his cultural committees nor even the governor's; you wouldn't attend his levees; you sounded off about federal art stuff. It happens that I agree with you, but that's neither here nor there. Ed, I am staying on the university board because I don't like the looks of things. And I think I'll stick there as long as Irick is around."

We went back into the longitudinous livingroom. Marya and Bumpy had been looking at more local news on the tube and announced that the fires were all out, the campus deserted, the hippies safely across the state line, and the chancellor in intimate conversation with the chief of police and the fire chief. The students were back in the dorms and frat houses and the high-school kids back in their split-levels. We talked about the principals in the case, chiefly Oscar. Harrington wanted to know about the literary review debacle, which he knew pressed on me sorely. I said what I had always said and thought.

"It was a fine old magazine when I got to it," I said, "but it was getting dull around the edges. I was supposed to brighten it up, I guess, but all I did was to print stuff that I thought was worth printing. I had heard about the local taboos but didn't think that anybody inside a university compound would stand for interference from the peasants—without the walls, so to speak."

Nobody said anything. "Drop it," I said, "Go on," said Marya. I shrugged.

"I went to lecture in Hawaii for a semester," I said, "modern poetry and stuff. I'd made up two issues of *Tracks West* in advance, one already in proof, the other all accepted and put to bed, and so forth. When I got back to my office I found that the first number had been held up. Proofs were on my desk and a short story had printed across it in big fat letters, KILL. That's printer's talk, you know. Kill means do not publish. It was some quiet little story whose style I admired. I called in the what-you-call acting editor."

"Oscar?" asked the surgeon.

"Yeah. I asked Oscar what the trouble was, but I knew. There was a little note attached to the killed story which read, 'Ed: this story has to wait for your return. It has a verboten theme, according to the local mores. God knows you understand.' That was the handwriting on my wall."

"I don't get it," said Bumpy.

"Oh well," I more or less yawned, "the story had to do with a homosexual getting fired from a school. As old as *Winesburg, Ohio*, or the Old Testament, for that matter. But Oscar didn't want anything to do with it, even though he wasn't supposed to touch a bunch of proofs ready for the press. Goddammit, it's too stupid to make into a monologue. What happened was that Irick called me in and said that *homosexual*, both word and concept, was the way he put it, was taboo at Milo U. and that that story had to go. I resigned as editor. Oscar became editor *instanter*."

"Why didn't you fight it, Ed?" asked Bumpy. "Everybody asked that."

"It made me so sick; I was so disgusted with the cynicism and degeneracy of it; I was just paralyzed. Editors all over the place wanted to ride to my rescue waving banners of freedom. I hate the hell out of Causes, even if it's my cause. If that's all they think of the magazine, I said, let 'em have it. All the same it broke my heart. I'd never used it for myself, never. To Oscar it was just a rung in a ladder. Oscar and even Chancellor Irick,

270

who wanted a nice clean roll of literary toilet paper to—you know what. Pardon the vulgarity," I said.

"Ed," said Harrington, looking at me with a frown, "Dunstan is going to try to fire you." Surgeons aren't usually practical jokers and I rejoined:

"Me? He can't fire me! I've got tenure!" There was a pause in the atmosphere and everybody, including me, burst out laughing.

The word *fire* began to bemuse me; fire in my office firing me—that sort of thing. Everybody knows that anybody can be fired for anything anywhere and that there are no safeguards against the fireman's ax. Just make it hot enough for the victim; simple as that.

"But Dunstan can only fire you if you want to be fired," said the doctor. "I just want to tell you that I'm on your side, if it comes to sides. And so is Governor Laska, for that matter. He admires you and is very *comme ci comme ça* about the chancellor."

"Doc," I said, "don't think I don't appreciate your feelings. I don't know how to thank you. But I have only one rule that I live by: never stay where you're not wanted. If my colleagues don't want me, if the board doesn't, that's okay with me. I get on my nag and ride off into the sunset." I shot a look at Marya, who said nothing. "Fighting phantoms is not my cup of tea," I added lamely.

The Harringtons left. Marya and I sat close, thinking and not saying much of anything. It all seemed so logical that I was rapidly becoming the scapegoat for all the fools and mischief-makers and campus climbers, the backwoods moralists and the interlopers from the golden west and the rockbound coast of Maine. At times like this I become more interested in the maneuvers of others than I am in protecting myself. I don't *want* to protect myself; it's as if it were beneath me. I was touched by what Harrington had said but felt degraded that it had to be said at all.

"There's something oriental about it all," I said. "It's as if I were the scene of the crime, the ambience, so to speak, and that if I were removed, everything would go back to the status quo. It's interesting the way Oscar works; everything has got to be devious; no straight transactions. Maybe it's because of his queerness."

But Marya wasn't interested in my psychologizing and was visibly worried about my indifference. What if what Harrington said was true? What if I ended up as a case study for the Janiczeks while the rug was being elegantly slipped out from under me? The simplest thing in the world would be to drop Creative Writing for a year or two, for budgetary reasons maybe. I didn't feel that I had any allies in the English Department, God knows. What if I couldn't pay my alimony? I began to see myself behind bars, writing prisoner poems. I had been criticized for publishing some poetry by jailbirds a couple of years ago. The administration thought it was bad taste, etc. etc.

"Guess what?" I said. "I'm going to spend the night at a motel."

"Ed!" Marya expostulated.

"It's a little cowardly maybe," I said, "but I want to think alone and be out of reach of the phone. Irick may decide to have a meeting at four A.M. or maybe he'll even send the police after me or the FBI for . . ." I started to say bastardy but decided against it.

"Darling, you're going into one of your paranoid spins," said Marya and gave me a hug of enjoyment. She enjoyed even the worst of me.

We decided that she would stay home and I would phone from the motel. I hadn't decided which one yet. Marya went to a distant bathroom and returned with a handsome shaving kit with a brand-new electric razor and everything you need for the final ablutions of the day, including a silver flask of scotch. "I feel like I've just been inducted," I said appreciatively and a little sheepishly too. A comfortable wave of self-pity sloshed over me and I kissed her with an unexpected sob. I imagined I could feel the prison walls closing round me, as Wordsworth says in his worst and most famous poem. "I'm just a growing boy sort of thing," I said witlessly.

I blew myself to a double room at the Haddon Hall Motor

Hotel, the one swank hostelry in Milo. I wanted to feel rich. Marya thought I was mad when I called her. I told her that no students were at the desk and that I was as safe as Lenin in his sealed train; I don't think she got the reference, however. We made some tender goodbyes and I lay down on one of the double beds with the lights on and a glass of neat scotch in my hand.

CHAPTER XXIV

Then I leaped up. A clock embedded in the navel of
some kind of caryatid, which was holding up nothing
across the room, said one-fifteen. Maybe there was still time to
catch the news at the end of the late movie. I switched on the
television and lay back on the bed. Before long the screen
cleared and I saw a sea of clouds swimming across the horizon,
from above, a nice airplane shot signifying God, I suspected,
from the hour of the day. It was benediction time and a voice
was delivering some kind of commercial prayer for the close of
work at the studio. A flag took its place in the clouds and, rising in the back in all its Euclidean majesty, the Washington
Monument. I had always noticed that the Monument was in
two colors of stone, I had forgotten why. Something violent
had interrupted its—erection. I looked down at my—penis, also
two-colored. But then I had been circumcised right after my
escape from the womb, and even half a century of wear and
tear hadn't made the two colors one. I don't know why I
thought I should have been one color, but I have always had
the feeling that the thing never healed. Like the Washington
Monument.

I had missed the news and was glad. My hand reached in-
voluntarily for the phone to call Marya again, but I decided

that she wouldn't like it. My mind was as blank as the gray TV glass, which had turned into a mirror. At the margin of my consciousness, as on a far horizon, I saw the other double bed, virgin, untouched, with a graciously baroque bedspread falling to the floor. Man is an esthetic animal, I said to myself sleepily; maybe he'll make it someday. I turned over to sleep, knowing I couldn't.

I am no good at thinking, as I have pointed out. I have never really believed that people think, the way thinking is described. Maybe that's my trouble. It has always seemed to me *dishonest* to think, to plan ahead, to calculate. Calculate: maybe that's why I flunked math all along the line; I always refused to calculate. I never wanted to know the answers. Well, I loved algebra, those beautiful equations and marriages of letters and numbers, but the answers didn't mean anything to me. Answers. I know a little about philosophy; I know enough to know that philosophy begins with answers and ends with mental exercises. My marks in philosophy weren't overwhelming.

Or rather I think in hunches, in atmospheres. I can't ever see anything outside its environment. The mailman out of uniform is a total stranger to me. My own students are strangers to me outside of class; I just don't recognize them. The only exceptions to this are people whose lives have become part of me, after-hours, so to speak, and around the clock. And that washes me out of political thinking as well. It is no mystery to me that the only kind of "thinking" I am capable of and am good at is poetry.

I was so convinced that I wasn't going to be able to go to sleep that I propped up three pillows behind me and sat up like a convalescent, smoking and sipping at the silver flask. I decided to try to think.

What's the Washington Monument got to do with my peter? I asked. *"Good thimking,"* answered the printer's devil in my head. After all, that's the way Freud started out, I rationalized —putting two things together that don't go together, until they add up to a new whole. Patriotism, virility: soldiering, sex: blood, sweat and tears and the roses round the door.

Questions, like faces, come to my mind unbidden. What is victory? a question asked itself. I am poor at asking questions but quick at answering them, right or wrong.

Victory is the triumph of pride, I answered.

What is pride? was the expectable next question.

Next question, I answered beggingly.

I was proud to love Marya; it made me feel so good; I was even proud to know her and couldn't wait for the day when we could be seen together without having anything to hide. What else was I proud of?

Nothing, said the interrogator, switching roles.

Nothing? I asked. I began to think.

My God, that can't be true, not to have pride in anything I've done. I started to recall what I knew of a famous British poet who denied his poetry, who moved suddenly from one end of London to another because somebody recognized him on a tram and said his name in connection with his poetry. A hider; kindly biographers had spoken of him as an eccentric; enemies had hinted at some sexual perversion, passive voyeurism or something of the sort. He had even refused royalties for his exquisite poems, which were also the bitterest of his time. Why had I thought of that?

He was afraid, said my thingamajig. Afraid that if he gave himself he wouldn't get it back. So he pretended that he never wrote those poems at all.

I must confess, though I have been holding it back, that this "voice" or thinking process, or some goddam thing, is no stranger to me, and that for years I have been holding conversations with Thomas Jefferson. That's why I've never mentioned it before; it wouldn't be the most explainable thing in the universe. It works this way.

I've done a lot of chauffeuring ever since I can remember. Like most kids I loved to drive, and driving usually meant driving other people around, waiting at the grocery for mother or picking up somebody or other at anyplace and at an hour they demanded. I did a lot of that in the Army for officers; it was always an escape from camp and a chance to catch a beer on the fly. In other words, I've sat behind a lot of steering-wheels alone, staring down the street through the windshield. And one day I decided to evoke Mr. Jefferson. I arranged it this way.

Mr. Jefferson had died in 1826 on the Fourth of July, my favorite holiday. He had been in total rest and oblivion all that time and on awaking still thought it was July 4, 1826. Whereupon he was given leave to visit the U.S.A. again, with me as guide. Simple.

I had first to arrange in my mind my own credentials and a certain amount of protocol, for it was my pleasure to introduce my favorite American, if I may use a vulgarism, to the shocks and mysteries of twentieth-century life. I made it a rule to volunteer no information unless asked. On the other hand, I didn't want to appear as a mere flunky and would inform the President when he asked that I was a professor and a "member of the tribe of scribblers," thinking that he would recognize the expression.

I carried on my conversations with Jefferson for years and even thought of making them into a book. He was a fine companion, naturally, and never unduly excited except around the eyes, even when I taught him to drive, pointed out airplanes, or showed him skyscraper cities from the Interstate. The biggest bounce I got out of him was when I switched on the FM radio while the car was going ninety and picked up the Mozart twentieth piano concerto. That excited him even more than the consequences of the Louisiana Purchase and the emancipation of the slaves. He pressed me about history since 1826 and I tried to avoid the horrors of the Civil War and the World Wars, putting more emphasis on our world dominance, the magnificent skills of science and the unbelievable prosperity of our people.

Why did you avoid the horrors? asked my voice.

"Well, shit," I said out loud, pummeling my pillows and making as if to go to sleep at last.

You didn't even give yourself to Thomas Jefferson, said the voice. I thought that that was about the corniest thing I had ever heard, but I considered it and felt it was more or less merited criticism. Well, I'm not exactly a historian, I said. This colloquy was getting to be a little too much like *A Christmas Carol*, but nevertheless, like Scrooge, I began to sweat.

You avoid the horror; you cover up, said the ghost. You are phony as hell.

Is that why I have delayed reactions to pain?

There was no answer and no more questions.

I had told Marya I wanted to marry her before I knew her at all. Had flung myself at her before she knew me or what I was about. I had used intensity as a substitute for character, wiping out all pasts like a vandal. I had denied any achievements or accomplishments I had created with my own hands. I had tried and succeeded in being what I was not. I was nothing but a jumping ball of electricity which had escaped from a thunderbolt. I struck down everything I got close to. I had lost contact with myself and therefore everything and everyone else. I had planned for years that everything I bent myself to would end in ruins or mildew. And if I had betrayed myself so scientifically, well, where would it stop? What would stop it?

The voice woke up. The danger of giving, it said. Love thyself as thy neighbor, it said.

That's a switch, I responded with a laugh.

Those women, those whores; those whores I tried to imagine women and those women I tried to make whores, like Wanda. When there was no danger in giving I got my erection. I was a taker, a thief. That word *piece:* to get a piece; that really means surgery, cannibalism. As for me, I wasn't giving anybody a piece of *me.* I was a rapist, hit and run. I chose the right ones all right, the ones that would end in nothing. And after I'd had my piece of skin I could lean back and say to myself: See? it was nothing. It's all gone. As empty as before. And the self-pity would set in. Nobody loves me.

Love thyself, said the old superego.

And because "nobody loved me" I could feel fine, or anyway I had nothing to fear. I had kept myself intactus and could wallow in sewers undreamed of, a kind of untouchable pig. Or a bastard, you might say. So what's a little charge of bastardy, however you translate the term?

278

Guilty, pronounced my interviewer.

I have always told myself that I have no guilt or feelings of guilt. Existential was the word I used, taking my definition from Camus, not from any religious nut. It was a lie: what I called fear of giving was only guilt at refusing to give. Generosity is my middle name but I was only generous about objects, just a gift-giver like an oriental. Giving was only more phony protocol. I made damn sure I didn't give any of the real stuff, my innerness, my quick. Okay, guilty, I conceded to the *vox mei*.

I had played around with my honesty for so long that I couldn't really swear that I had any honest feelings left. No wonder Marya was suspicious, sometimes champing at the bit to escape me. I knew what she loved about me was my being, my selfness, as old Robert Bridges used to say, and she would get nervous to the point of breaking when I was pretending to be my un-self. I had to be who I was really, I thought, and thus came to the most ancient metaphysical question mark: who am I?

Voice? I asked. Who am I?

It laughed.

Okay, I said. I am that I am. I am a part of all that I have known, and all those highfalutin truisms. Okay, I said again, placatingly. When I discovered myself or my ability or my gift or something like that I developed it to the full while I turned my back on the consequences. I cheated myself of my just rewards. I did so (I seemed to myself that I was reciting a lesson to pass an exam) because I hated myself and wanted to fail. I wanted to fail so I could cry. I wanted to cry because it would attract sympathy or even a nerve-wracking lay. And I wanted to attract sympathy and love so I could reject it. This is the house that Jack built.

Love thyself, said my Other.

I got it, I said, sitting bolt upright. I've got to take the chance that Marya won't love me because I am what I am. I've got to take that chance, see? I told my monitor, as if he didn't know it all.

I've got to accept the good of myself and not just the bad. It seemed so obvious I blushed. I've got to be my name.

What's your name? asked the voice. We seemed to be back in kindergarten.

Edsel, I answered.

What's your name? asked the voice.

Edsel Lazerow, I answered.

Keep saying it over and over until you fall asleep, said the voice.

I started counting sheep with my name. I've always thought that that sheep-counting metaphor was a gas and couldn't possibly put anybody to sleep except of course sheep. My name made a little more sense and I started out. The name immediately broke into silly puns:

> Edsel has her, O!
> Oh, Edsel has her! O!
> Edsel Lazerow!

My tendency to versify is a stumbling-block in the real world perhaps.

I'm not sure whether I was asleep and dreaming or awake and thinking. Maybe it's of no consequence. Anyhow I was conducting Thomas Jefferson on a tour of the University of Virginia, which was rather unnecessary, as he had built it. I wanted to show him the slave quarters behind the student rooms. I know about that, said Jefferson. I took him next to the room of Edgar Allan Poe. Jefferson had missed Poe by a hair. This Poe, I said, was one of the greatest American poets but was a very sick fellow. The room was draped in maroon velvet and there was the bust of Pallas over the door with a stuffed raven perched on its head. There was a smell of incense in the room and a poof of smoke and Marya was standing within it. It's all so silly, she said, and pulled down the velvet drapes which disintegrated in clouds of Victorian dust. And that bird, she said, pointing at it and laughing. The raven flapped its wings, screaming *Shit!* and made its way out of the door, grokking and sending up more dust-clouds.

My dreams are always in two acts, as I have noted. In the

second scene Mr. Jefferson and I were in the waiting-room of a brothel. It belongs to the university, sir, I said. I know, said the author of the Declaration of Independence, and settled back in a rattan chair with a magazine. I was on a high Victorian bed with a youthful whore. Look at that, she said, pointing at my privates; you don't even have anything; you're empty; what can *you* do? And she started to cackle and caw and fly around the room, darting at me with long claws and making droppings all over the bed.

It was a nightmare, I guess you'd call it. I woke up shaking and shivering. And I had polluted myself.

CHAPTER XXV

Marya woke me at ten with the news that I was expected at the chancellor's meeting at eleven. Doc Harrington had relayed the summons. I was still thinking of going past my office first while I was shaving electrically when I remembered with a jolt that I didn't have any office. I wondered if I had enough will power to avoid the spot. I didn't.

There was still a fireman on duty when I made my way up a plank to the door and told him I wanted to see my office. He let me by. The concrete floors had kept everything from caving in, on the ground floor anyway, and that's where my office had been. There was some danger of the top three floors caving in but the workmen had already shored up the ceilings and joists. The fireman just cautioned me not to move anything.

I picked my way past Oscar's magazine office; there wasn't much left there and I saw that all the file cabinets had been removed. My own room was a cubbyhole of refuse and stench. My filing cabinets had turned a terra-cotta red from their olive green and I didn't touch them. I wondered if all was ashes inside and didn't check. The desk was char-wood and leaned crazily. On top of it was a paperweight of mine, a small block of marble with two bronze hands clasping: Robert's and Elizabeth's, the Brownings. The fire had cracked the marble but I took it. On the way out the fireman asked if I knew where my books were: they had all been lugged to a warehouse near the campus. I thanked him and went to the meeting.

The Administration Building was humming, the elevator crowded, the carpets muddy. Evidently firemen and policemen had been paying their respects. When I got to the reception desk the chancellor's wooden-faced secretary told me to take a seat and that I would be interviewed next.

"Interviewed for what?" I asked, flushing.

"Just for police and fire reports," she said. "Formality," she said, sparing herself the exertion of pronouncing an article. I sat down and picked up a copy of *Fortune* and held it as if it were a bullet-proof vest.

Soon Oscar Darling emerged, his face bathed in *Weltschmerz*. He clasped one of my shoulders and intoned. "All of your books, Ed! Ed, where were you? I tried to get you all day yesterday, all night!"

I couldn't think of anything to say and shrugged. The secretary said, "Mr. Lazerow," and with her eyes ordered me into a room at her right.

There was a male secretary with one of those silent shorthand writers. The machine always strikes me as being slightly repulsive; the way the fingers bounce on the keys in a rubbery way and the guy's shoulders move as if he were playing at a piano bar. It's usually men who work that machine.

The other two people were Chief Slezak, whom I recognized, and the fire chief, a kind-looking redfaced man whose jacket gleamed with brass and gold.

"Chief Slezak and Fire Chief Brighton," said the secretary. "Professor Lazerow," she added. I sat down.

"Professor Lazerow," said Slezak, "we are asking all the occupants of Hepplewhite Hall to volunteer whatever they know about the fire. You are not obliged to answer any questions. Do you object to answering questions?" he asked rather abruptly.

"No, sir," I said, "especially as some bastard saw fit to throw a Molotov cocktail through my window and I'd sure like to know who." The secretary started rubbering away.

'Were you present at the fire?" asked the chief of the Milo police.

"No," I answered.

"Would you tell us where you were yesterday afternoon?" he asked.

"Home," I said and gave the address. I told them what time I had left the office, the crowd I had to get through to get off the campus and even of watching the demonstration on TV.

"You mean you didn't participate in the demonstration at all?" asked Slezak.

"No, sir," I said. "I can't stand mobs."

"Were you at the party at Professor Janiczek's on the night of . . ." and gave the date. The fire chief asked that one.

"I was there, yes," I said, "and left before the trouble started."

"Where were you when that fire broke out?" asked Slezak.

I bristled: "What's that supposed to mean?" I asked. "I was home, or on my way. With a *date*," I underlined.

"What was her name?" asked the policeman.

I was getting tense and angry and knew I'd better control myself.

"I wouldn't consider it gentlemanly to give her name," I answered. I'd started to say honorable: but nobody uses that one anymore except diplomats who are up to their ears in shady deals.

"Do you have any notion who threw the fire-bomb through your window?" asked the fire chief.

"Not the foggiest," I said, "either who or why."

"Have you examined your property taken from your office and can you give us some idea of the extent of the damage to your books, papers, furnishings, etc.?" he asked.

"I haven't been to the warehouse to look," I said. What the hell was this? They were talking to me like an arsonist or some kind of firebug and I didn't like it.

"Professor," said Slezak, "it would help us to know if you, in your considered opinion, have any enemies or persons you suspect of grudges who would for any reason commit this act against you and fire-bomb your private office."

"I've never known anybody like that and I hope I never will," I answered. I didn't care for that question either. It made a kind of low-lifer out of me. But then. . . . It struck me suddenly that I had blocked the question from my consciousness ever since I had heard of the fire. Another of my evasions, I thought bitterly.

Slezak questioned me about Inge and I gave him the little information I had about her. The chiefs knew that she was the secretary or fifth wheel of the delegation that got to see the governor. She hadn't been on the scene of the fire obviously.

They asked my permission to question me as things developed later on and I assented. Both chiefs thanked me and I returned to the waiting-room.

"Go in," said the hard-core virgin at the desk, giving her head a quick twist toward the board room.

I breathed a sigh of relief when I saw Doc Harrington and took a chair more or less opposite him. I needed to triangulate him with the chancellor. Oscar had taken the chair at the far end of the table, as if he were the hostess. That was interesting, I decided. I am always interested in such trivia as where Oscar sits. Tremaine was at the chancellor's right, and five other chairs were occupied by board members whom I had never met and probably never would again. They were all dressed quietly in prosperous black or charcoal suits, white shirts, and ties tied with small knots. We were introduced informally: I listened for their names; Azbel, McCobb, Crews, Despard, Pulaski. All business guys, I figured, and wondered why I had never heard their names before. I never keep up with the power structure, as the kids call it.

"Gentlemen, as a preliminary," said Irick, oscillating his head around the table and back again to give each person the benefit of his glance, "I will pass these out." Small packets of a report began to circulate around the table. "These are present estimates of damage to Hepplewhite Hall, public and personal property, with estimates for reconstruction, restitution, etc." Everyone began reading busily except me. I can't read reports; if Irick had put a pistol to my head I couldn't have gotten past the first paragraph. But I pretended. "Naturally," he went on, "these are very crude guesses at this stage but they will give us some guidelines." McCobb, who was an insurance magnate, said that his company's investigators were already on the spot but of course had to interview the faculty members who presented claims.

"Gentlemen," said Irick again, as if the word made him feel good, "fires unfortunately are becoming a commonplace on our campuses around the country, as on the city streets. But, as we all know, these disturbances are symbols of socially significant changes in our society." My gorge began to rise. When somebody like Irick, who is a politician of a low order, or a personnel manager of a slightly higher echelon, begins using the language of sophomore sociology courses, I want to begin looking around for exits. Parts of my corpus begin to twitch. My tongue starts to flick at my dentures and my left eyelid droops. Also I chain-smoke. The worst thing about the Iricks of this world is that when they start using the jargon of change you know they have switched positions and are taking a new stance. You know, at least if you are as paranoid as I am, that they are sharpening axes.

"A university is a democracy, as we all agree," he went on.

"I don't," I interrupted. "Pardon the interruption," I added, shifting my Browning paperweight. I had put the paperweight with the Browning handclasps on top of the insurance report, and started moving it around on the paper playfully. The felt had been burnt off in the fire and the marble slid pleasantly to and fro.

"Edsel?" asked the chancellor.

"Excuse me, Chancellor," I said. "You said we all agree—that is, a university is a democracy. I just said I don't agree, but it's of no great moment."

"How do you characterize the modern university, Professor?" asked the chancellor. "Especially the modern *American* university?"

"No quibble intended, Chancellor," I said, "but a university, American or Oxford or Chinese, is, well it's an aristocracy. An intellectual aristocracy," I decided to add.

Irick gave me his knitted brow, laughed a small laugh, and

bestowed his chin-smile on the rest of the company. Whereupon he went back to his message, which I was beginning to
get curious about. That he had something up his sleeve was
written all over his map.

"A minority of feeling can be very utilitarian," he said. I
clamped my jaw. How can anybody mangle English that way;
it had to be deliberate. Why couldn't he at least speak like a
human being instead of a rebuilt tape recorder.

"Utilitarian in retrospect," he said, compounding the obscur-
ity. "However," he went on, "we are dealing with the reality
principle, and we shall face reality with statistics and with
imagination. Let me be specific. Instead of fighting fire with
fire, we shall fight fire with appreciation and discernment."

That specific? I thought, moving my paperweight.

"We shall, in other words," said the chancellor, "overlook
the more or less expectable vandalism of youth and probe at
its underlying hungers." Another big, almost triumphant smile
bathed the faces of the assembly. "I had a fine talk with the
great poet Richard Wigglesworth yesterday and today, a
champion of causes, sometimes a little too enthusiastic, making a wrong turn here and there, but nevertheless a man of
genius, accomplishment and sociologic insight, according to
even *Lux* magazine, who has done us the favor, and to my
pleasure, of explaining the unrest and pointing out the relationship between pressures and values, if I may use the word."

I wondered what that sentence would look like engraved in
bronze. The word "values" for some reason caused the speaker
to fix his gaze on me. But I wasn't looking back. I only
sensed it.

"The long and short of it," said the chancellor, "is that we
educators have to adjust. A fire, accidental or *caused* . . ." he
underlined *caused* . . . "is of no consequence. What is of consequence is the harmonious and democratic explanation."

Gibberish makes me very nervous and I thought of getting
up, making a short excuse, and leaving. But I didn't dare. Besides, the chancellor was warming to his subject and possibly
even coming to his point, which I was sure existed. I almost
knew what it was. I noticed that Oscar was sitting like a stat-

ue, eyes downcast, because, whatever his deficiencies, Oscar loved good speech and precise English and part of him must have been cringing as much as I was, for different reasons. I was even beginning to love listening to the chancellor's gabbling, or so I tried to convince myself. In any case, I too sat still. Doc Harrington was sounding his knuckles very quietly on the table, tense or impatient, I couldn't tell. Tremaine, the impeccable mannerist of speech, was gazing at Irick rapturously. The businessmen sat in studious stupefaction, long-used to the high-sounding illiteracies of board chairmen and knowing that before the cocktail hour, Authority was going to take the world of Milo by surprise. Somehow.

The "harmonious and democratic explanation" went on. "Regardless of who thinks otherwise," he said, "we are a democratic concept and a democratic entity. *We are a land-grant!*" said Irick, actually hitting the table with his fist. "Abraham Lincoln made this kind of higher institution possible all over our once-empty plains. And we intend to justify his gift!" Another gaze around the faces, most of which, for diverse reasons, were studying their fire insurance papers.

Harrington looked at his wristwatch, conspicuously, I thought.

"To be brief, then," said Irick, "and I hope to have your unanimous consent but most certainly your majority, I am going to keep the investigation of the fire under wraps, let bygones be bygones, and turn this great institution toward the direction of participatory democracy, and with all the necessary reforms, gentlemen, appertaining thereto. It is time to recognize that the philosophy of in loco parentis is anachronistic, that the young people of today are adult and mature and responsible and they must be given their head, namely, to help engage in the government of our university, and to push it forward to its outermost limits." He paused, like a Shakespearean actor, for reply.

Doc Harrington spoke up. "Do you mean, Chancellor," he asked, "that there will be no punishment of the arsonist or arsonists?"

I spoke up. "Do you mean you don't care who fire-bombed

my office and also burned up Oscar's magazine?" I turned to Oscar. "Even from an editorial point of view, Oscar," I said, "wouldn't you like to know who incinerated your quarterly?"

"I have no doubt that murder will out, Edsel," said Oscar, "but I think the chancellor is in the best position to handle that kind of affair, don't you?"

"Hell, no," I answered. "That's for the cops."

"I agree," said one of the businessmen.

"Now then, gentlemen," said Irick, "let's keep our lines from entangling. Of *course* the police and the Fire Department are making every investigation. They are doing it now in the next room. Of *course* the guilty party or parties will be brought to justice. But, my friends, the point is bigger than that, much bigger and much more, shall I say, lasting. The point is that we head off even bigger and uglier syndromes of revolution by developing our defense in depth, by letting the soldiers evacuate from the Trojan Horse. Excuse the stag-party joke," he said. Nobody laughed.

The chancellor's face set in what might have been his only sincere expression. He was about to deliver his wind-up pitch. His face looked granitic, statuesque and grained. It seemed to me that he looked the way he would like to look if his picture were on a postage stamp, because he was being honest momentarily and salvaging what shreds of nobility he had. I kind of admired him for a second and felt sorry for him. But I knew he boded no good to the community of men or to me.

"I don't mind telling you, gentlemen," he said, "that since the original fire at Professor Janiczek's house, where so much was lost, that I have been doing some deep reappraisals, of the situation and of myself. And I have had a kind of epiphany." Here he shot a quiet glance of literary-theological triumph around the table. "Here I am on this top floor, so to speak, and here we are, deciding the lives and fates of the future generations of the young. And I confess that I have been out of touch. I confess that I have not known their hungers and their rights. I have been a captain of a ship in a storm and was unaware that my crew was mutinous. And now I know or am beginning to know their discontents. I want to get down in the street with them and demonstrate myself. That is ridiculous, of course, but I wish to express the image, if you understand me. Those students have an intuition of the just. Their recklessness is in a way justifiable. Their vandalism is a cry of help. And I mean to help. I mean to lend them a hand, gentlemen." He paused and spread out the fingers of his right hand and held the hand up to call for strictured silence.

"I mean," he said, "to give them every opportunity to demonstrate their purity of motive; I mean to give them full steam ahead, no matter what the cost. Understand, gentlemen, that my record is purely and for long duration, top-floor, wall-to-wall silence and detachment, administration from above and from afar. That is my record. But my policy from here on in is otherwise. Let us call it mutual freedom, mutual liberation. Or, to make a long story short, let us call it democracy, and let it go at that."

He beamed mightily, and let it go at that.

I should have kept my mouth shut but I spoke.

"Don't you think, Chancellor," I said, "if you are going to be so lovey-dovey with those playschool demonstrators that you might have to deal with a lot more Molotov cocktails?"

He glared at me like Belial and answered, "Those things are not frivolous. Those acts are not the acts of children. They are symptoms."

"I want to say something, Dunstan," said Doc Harrington. "I have to go to the hospital. I'm overdue; there are firemen I have to work on from yesterday. I'm afraid I disagree with you completely. If I were you, Dunstan, if you are going to sanction kid-control, I d call in all the fire engines you can get." He gave a curt nod and left.

"Bravo!" I said, being impolitic.

There was a hiatus while the chancellor got up, went to a book shelf and brought back another sheaf of mimeographed, stapled documents, which he himself personally laid before the committee in person, a bit of noblesse oblige. At a glance I knew I wasn't going to get past the first paragraph which said: *Recommendations from Richard Wigglesworth and Akiba Mem for the Democratization of Campus Life in America and*

290

the Reformation of the Curriculum. I laid my copy down with a slight slap on the table, though I hadn't meant it to be audible.

There was a lot of heavy reading and flipping back and forth of pages and shuffling of chairs. I hadn't the least interest in reading what Wigg and Akiba were transmitting to the insurance executives of Milo or the Chancellors of Squeedonk because I had read it all in their maniac magazines a thousand times. I wasn't even curious to "watch their faces" as the expression goes. On top of which, I felt sick in the stomach.

When the gruel had been more or less ingested and a few heads began to look up in bewilderment, I glanced at Oscar. His face was a study in impassivity, seemingly thoughtful and bemused, but with the necessary trace of cynicism which would pacify any businessman type who might think he was part of a plot. Tremaine Atwood was leaning far over the document, making margin notes, or pretending to. Whatever was going on in his antediluvian head I would never know and would never want to inquire. When everybody had stopped fiddling with the papers and a kind of uneasy silence began to form, the chancellor began again.

"The point being, gentlemen," he said, "that we have to look beyond our immediate boundaries, just as our country has in the broad spectrum of things. This memo from two fabulous poets . . ." I think he meant "fabled" but wouldn't swear to it . . . "is a gentle reminder that we are no longer in the hinterland but are prey to every ill of every part of our American society, whether we wish to or not, and that is our opportunity to capitalize on our defects and those of the militants, or any name will do."

I had a sudden revelation that Irick was the first American poet. How else could he talk like that? I wanted to enroll him in my creative writing class.

"I have taken the liberty, or rather the honor," he said, "to invite Mr. Wigglesworth to sit with our committee and to give us his thoughts." The chancellor leaned forward and added, "as I believe the philosophy of education, of paramount importance from the highest to the lowest, is best put in his mouth. Now, *entre nous,* gentlemen," he went on unbelievably, "top secret, so to speak, we have in this highly recognized man of letters and public figure a key to our situation and to our private dilemma." He beamed. "His analysis of campus unrest and upheavals is very far-reaching. It takes a man of imagination and creativity to point out to us more pragmatic types the hidden lines of force, as he calls them, between our superficial acts of violence and their root causes. I confidently submit, gentlemen, that we shall all profit from our visit of this extraordinary personage. And another thing; I would like you to bear in mind that we are also, in the privacy of our own minds, of course, looking him over for the Flamsteed Lectures for next year."

The Flamsteed Lectures, Milo's only high-paying cultural event, always imported a name and usually a name only. In the early days of the university they had had Billy Sunday, for instance. Blackjack Pershing had lectured on might and right. They had even enticed Baron von Ribbentrop for two lectures on the Leadership Principle. Wigglesworth would be their first poet, a fitting inauguration of letters, I thought bitterly.

There seemed to be no objection to the visitor and Irick said, "Very well, gentlemen, and my thanks." He buzzed for his brittle secretary. "Yes, Chancellor," she said, coming in the door a foot or two. "Have Mr. Wigglesworth come in, Idella," said the chancellor. "Is he here?" he asked abruptly. "He is waiting," said Idella.

I stood up as Wigg walked through the door. I had picked up my paperweight and had my mouth open to speak when the paperweight slipped from my hand and hit the formica table with a loud report. I grabbed it; it had cracked in half, springing loose the little clasped hands of the Brownings.

"Excuse me, gentlemen," I said, "I have an appointment. Pardon the racket," I added, pocketing the little hands and looking around for a trash can for the pieces of marble. I had messed up Wigg's entrance and introduction and I added, "Sorry, Wigg." As I brushed past the visiting dignitary the chancellor said, "But, Edsel, surely you will want to listen in on . . ."

"No, thanks," I said and left.

To Irick's secretary I said needlessly, "Idella," and almost asked if that was her real name. "Would you send the notes of the meeting, if any, to my house. I don't have a new office yet."

She gave me a lipless glare. I leaned over and deposited the marble fragments in her trash can. They hit bottom with a thump.

"Excuse me," I said, "I broke something." I went down the hall jauntily, whistling a theme from Bach's flute concerto in B minor, which was made for whistling.

CHAPTER XXVI

Getting into my car I thought: That little brass thing of the hands of Liz and Bob Browning ought to be made into a pin of some kind for Marya. I took it out and looked at it. Well, it was a little like an insurance emblem, the kind you see on New England housefronts sometimes, but I liked the objet d'art and would have it done. Then I remembered that I had a lot of stray semi-jewelry in my top desk drawer and decided to go back to the ruins and have a look.

The fireman on watch admitted me again with the news that my secretary was in there sorting things out. I started but thanked him and proceeded across the uneven floor to my office. Maybe Inge has relented, crossed my mind, not that I would keep her around anymore even if she had, or maybe Wigg had dumped her, having used her already. I hadn't ever examined the work Inge had done on my files and was suddenly curious. But when I entered the doorway, which now was nothing but exposed brick, it was not Inge at all but Wanda rifling the files. She wheeled around on me with a packet of lavender letters in envelopes in her hand.

"Some things just don't burn," I said, recognizing the letters she had written. She was pretty taken aback and presented a bellicose face, clutching the letters and keeping them more or less to the rear, as if I were going to give combat.

"Letters belong to the writer," I said. "You're more than welcome to them. Unless you want to start a new fire," I added, going to my desk and yanking open the top drawer. There was a rattling and slither of paper clips.

I am probably the only living admirer of the paper clip and place it, as an invention, on a par with the invention of barbed-wire. I have even thought of writing a poem about it.

"You mean you don't want them?" she asked incredulously. I had a hunch that Wanda would never have thought of rescuing her billets-doux; her mind didn't work that way. Kaz or somebody had put her up to this for some obscure reason.

"I'm surprised *you* do," I said, rummaging my drawer. There was nothing there but a couple of arrowheads somebody had given me and a hairball from a cow's stomach. A student who wrote good poetry had once made me a present of it; I never did get the symbolism, if any; this student had told me that the hairball had medicinal properties if worn around the neck. He had given me an article about it. I didn't want the thing around and had tried to palm it off on people from time to time but nobody would take it and I left it in the desk.

Wanda showed no sign of going but instead leaned against the filing cabinet and started glancing through her old half-literate notes. I wanted to go but didn't feel like leaving her in possession of my ruins. My door had been removed, or what was left of it; it was leaning against the wall in the corridor, so I couldn't say I was going to close up.

"I've got to go," I said.

"Do you mind if I stay?" Wanda asked, without looking up.

"I'd rather you wouldn't," I answered, closing my desk drawer.

"Kicking me out, huh?" she said, slapping the letters down on the cabinet.

"Sorry," I said, "it's my office, or what remains of it, and nobody is allowed in when I'm not here."

"Except Inge," said Wanda.

"Except Inge," I answered, feeling a rising wave of anger.

"Just go, Wanda," I said quietly. "You've got what you came for."

"How do you know?" she asked with a forced smile. She sat down or rather squatted on a low stool used for filing in bottom drawers. "How about a goodbye kiss, Edsel?" she asked. "Or better still, how about a farewell fuck for the road? That old fireman wouldn't know and if he peeps in maybe he'll learn something about higher education."

I am no good at man-handling or woman-handling anybody; it's just not in my makeup. But I had no alternative. I went over and tugged at her arm and tried to pull her to her feet. She pretended to tussle, exposing as much of her thighs as she could and wriggling on the stool.

"What if I yell rape?" she said in a whisper. I dropped her arm as if I had been holding a water moccasin.

"You son-of-a-bitch," I said, "you just would. Now get out." I had started trembling and retreated to my desk and sat on top of it. There was nothing to do but wait. Wanda went back to reading her letters as if nothing had happened. I began to study her. How in the name of God had I ever got mixed up with that? How?

Presently she became so absorbed in her reading that I thought she had forgotten me or where she was. A pure primitive, I thought. Once upon a time I had been touched by that and had even called it her "innocence"; in those days I was a preacher of the Noble Savage and the saboteur, the outcast and the outlaw, the fringe case and the psychopath. It was a world I tried to join but which turned out to be as exclusive as a country club. I was never more than a tourist in that realm of mildew and dry-rot. But that it was the grubbiest of bohemias I never doubted; I must confess that the very grubbiness attracted me, but then, in those days, nothing aroused my attention except failure and failures. Wasn't I one myself?

All at once, looking at Wanda became a spectator sport; I was looking at a C movie I had wandered into by mistake or out of boredom. I was in the dark and there was a woman seated on a stool reading lavender letters. She was sitting in a house that had been destroyed by war or bombs or some catastrophe. Her face showed no emotion; she had kicked her shoes off and was wiggling her toes; now and then she scratched some part of her body. Her clothes looked sleazy and her nails reflected the light like little mirrors. Her ashy hair resembled a carving in sandstone. Once she turned her head aside and spat on the floor. Now and then she emitted a one-syllable laugh. She was a masterpiece of a hag.

One should feel sorry for her, said my spectator mind. "One" is a word I never use as a general pronoun but it felt right this time. But I could feel no sorrow or any of the nuances of that emotion. The only thing I could really feel was boredom, with a slight dash of curiosity, and I wasn't even sure of that. I began to wonder what the name of the "movie" was and whether I should leave.

Then the woman got up and snapped a rubber band around the letters. "I think you ought to keep them," she said. "It's a shame they weren't burnt up." And she held them out. But there were no takers.

"Let's burn them here and now, Ed," she was saying, as she produced a man-sized cigarette lighter. That brought me to my senses.

"You start a fire in here and you'll be behind bars for the rest of . . ." I spluttered.

"Oh," was all she said. She looked at me a while and then said, "Well, I guess that's it, friend." She put the letters in her pocketbook. "I mean goodbye," she said, and left. I watched her toil down the corridor and turn out of sight. Her goodbye had had the ring of truth, I decided, and exhaled a long pent-up breath. I watched her rev up her Volvo and shoot out of the parking lot like a racer.

CHAPTER XXVII

One thing that is beautiful and authentic in Milo is the snow. Snow in places like Virginia and Maryland is too much, kind of phony. It will come down in flakes so big they look like movie snow or the stuff you buy in the dime store to put around Christmas trees; it's soaking wet and sentimental snow. It's really slush, the kind that kids eat in the summertime with lemon extract or cherry fizz. In fact, in places where they have that kind of rotten snow, the kids do go out and eat it. It's not snow as much as it's food.

But in Milo the snow comes horizontally and each perfect crystal is equipped with six or eight or twelve razor blades that bite you in any part of your skin that happens to be exposed. Men in Milo in winter wear astrakhan hats and high fur collars. Kids wear wool masks that leave only their eyes visible. It's hard to tell who anybody is. The typical blizzard began New Year's night, and the flakes at my window sounded like a million hornets. Some of the white stuff, as they call it there, worked its way under my livingroom window, where I was sitting, and was so frozen that it didn't even melt. I went out on the porch to check—check what I'm not sure. I was barefooted as a matter of fact, carrying a drink, and had only a light shirt on, unbuttoned, and khaki summer trousers. A big street light across the way looked like a Van Gogh painting: crawls of concentric white and pink and great gusts of more white clouds, sailing up the flumes of the atmosphere. The porch was deep in snow but so dry I couldn't feel the cold for a while. That's the way to freeze to death, I reminded myself, as two figures worked their way up the walk. They were so enshrouded in clothing that I didn't recognize them as my upstairs neighbors. We exchanged laughing greetings and I was reminded that it was ten below zero. I stayed a while longer and went in, feeling exhilarated and happy. Marya would be home in three days.

This time she had gone to the Antilles after all, but without any break between us. In fact, I had taken her to the airport myself, glared at several Milovians who recognized one or the other of us and who disapproved of whatever it was we were up to. She had left before Christmas, waiting out the last days of her interlocutory decree. Her house had reverted to her ex-husband, furniture had been scattered to the winds, and she had bought one of those tiny three-room houses with a mansard roof which the town was full of. It was a particularly good one, facing a little sunken park where children ice-skated in the winter.

And both of us agreed to the extravagance of calling every night to or from Aruba, and contrasting our weather reports, gossip and so forth. Sometimes I would just read her a poem I had written or one I hadn't but liked.

That morning I had met my first class since the holidays. For some reason the Creative Writing group had been transferred to a chemistry theater, as architects call it. That is, it was one of the smallish auditoriums built with tiers of semi-circular seats rising perpendicularly before the instructor, the kind of place where you expect to get a revelation from a Dr. Zemmelweiss, for example. There was no desk, of course, but a slab of slate twenty feet long behind which I could roam, if I so chose. There were four sinks, a collection of beakers, and several high curved pipes leading into the sinks. Behind me was a chart of valences, ten feet high.

It was my same class; nobody had dropped out, even after

the Janiczek fire. I had hoped that some of the students would be behind bars of one kind or another or had lit out for one of their hippie frontiers. No such luck. The student in the wheelchair sat directly in front of the slab, on the ground floor; the athletes were way up in the peanut gallery—everyone had taken approximately the seats that the creative writing tribe takes. Chris Jaffe, the Jewish Indian, was unctuously passing out the purple mimeographed works of art. I suppressed an impulse to vomit into my voluminous sinks.

"There are only twenty of us," I announced. "Everybody down in the first two rows, and close up toward the center. No spacing. Togetherness," I said. They obeyed, a little reluctantly but with no backtalk. Jaffe eventually deposited my pile of the newly created poems on my slate slab. It hadn't gone too badly but I was glad when it was over.

I felt somehow that I was the cause of the Janiczek fire and of burning out my own office. That somehow *I* had to explain myself. It was one of those traps. No, I didn't feel any of that but only that they were determined to make me feel something of their arrogant guilt. No more had been heard of the Janiczek shambles for months, and Brom had been promoted to dean of Social Sciences; his wife was finally teaching all the classes she wanted, namely, his. Oscar's budget had been quadrupled for his magazine, with Dick Wigglesworth as advisory editor from afar. Tremaine had been exalted to vice chancellor, no less. As for me, my office had been transferred to a workroom in the greenhouse. This was supposedly to convey an insult of high order, but secretly I couldn't have been more delighted. I would sit there under the milky glass listening to the snow scraping its fingernails across the roof, listening to the warm clanking and hissing of steampipes, inhaling tons of raw oxygen pouring from half a mile of geraniums, shamrocks, ferns and God knows what. I couldn't have dreamed up a more perfect office. Very poetic, Oscar had remarked one day when he stopped by to see how I was doing. Don't tell anybody, I answered ambiguously.

"Redon," said Oscar, taking a postcard from my table, "dear Redon," and laid it down again. Inge had favored me with a

Christmas card of sorts, one of those reproductions from a museum. Redon with his tinge of the sinister always fascinated me. Sick beauty, I called it. Her message had been: "Dear Boss: Everything going to plan. This is the place, like the Mormons say. Thanks for everything." Maybe I didn't want to do Redon the honor of tearing his painting in half. On the other hand I took the silly postcard as a last leaf fallen from my ugly past. I took the plunge and slid the card in the waste can.

Since all the dinky reshufflings in the university I had been left alone. Rather too much alone, I philosophized. No, I wasn't being made into an experimental leper colony; it was more by mutual consent that I was now peripheral to the institution. From now on I would be just the campus ornament, for what that was worth. Shortly after being made vice chancellor Tremaine Atwood paid me a visit in the greenhouse. I congratulated him in a desultory way.

"One of the first things I had promised myself," said Tremaine, "when all the smoke of battle had cleared, was to thank you, Edsel, for the advice you gave the chancellor and all of us the day after the Janiczek misfortune. Most of the things that have happened since originated from your perceptive suggestions."

"Well," I answered, wondering whether to drop the matter then and there or to try to justify myself. I am a great one for the *arrière-pensée*, dotting the *i* and crossing the *t*; so I had to say, "Well, Tremaine, that was all my little contribution to the art of satire, as I am sure you know. Irick is such a blockhead that I thought I would while away the time to keep from falling asleep, like ye old dormouse." I laughed, "It was just like him to take me seriously."

Tremaine gave a small in-group chuckle which was the equivalent of tut-tut, and took his leave. I don't know; I kind of admired the old stuffed shirt, reminiscent of the days when Rhodes scholarships were actually looked up to, the days when students said *sir* and even *ma'am*, the days when education was considered a privilege and not a biological right. I wished that the modern school would throw all that creative writing garbage down the public drain and make the kids learn Latin and Greek and Hebrew the way the old boys did. Jesus, was I becoming reactionary!

And I had thrown myself into neutral. For years I had sided with and egged on the innocents and the new barbarians, out of boredom, out of mischief, out of my personal unhappiness. How many revolutions have been made in history by the single sickness of a single man? All? Some? Many, I was sure of that. This phony uprising of the so-called young had infected their elders, their teachers, their rulers, and I was a contributor to the common delinquency. Now I had drawn back in shame and even, to be melodramatic, in horror. With nowhere to turn. A mindless rabble is a mindless rabble, I lectured myself, unless it had intellectual sanctions. The treason of the clerks and all that has unfortunately come true. Because of the Oscars teaming up with the Akibas, the Janiczeks with the Wigglesworths, and worst of all the Iricks with the whole she-bang. Everybody is selling the university for a mess of pottage, or just a mess. Nobody even knows what poetry *is* anymore; they call it creative writing nowadays. All values have turned to brown. I went on in this vein until it bored me. I didn't know the answers and it was more than obvious that they didn't. Or rather, yes, they had an answer: tear it all apart and see what makes it tick. Vandalism is all, farewell.

I ought to get out of this racket, is what I thought. But then what? I am one of those people who is trained for nothing but to train others. I've led the sheltered life and the life was suffocating me with foliage. One thing was beginning to dawn on me, however; I had to leave Milo, maybe go to a big city, if Marya would go with me. That would come high on the agenda.

The campus and the main streets had been cleared of snow or had at least been scraped and packed. But most of the side streets had been blocked by the shearing of the snow-ploughs. Marya would be home tomorrow and I had to see if her street was open. It wasn't; in fact the whole entrance to her street was a massive dune of white. I guess we'll have to ski in, I thought. She would like the scene, I knew, especially after the tropics. Tomorrow I would have to get food of some kind or at least flowers. The Milo florists wouldn't have anything but I could raid the greenhouse. Somebody was growing silver-colored roses; they probably wouldn't miss a few. And there were a hundred yards of red and white ones. But how to get them out of there and across the campus to my car? I found myself in a pleasurably thieving mood and drove by my house for an overnight suitcase, a sort of getaway bag. I also brought a pair of haircut scissors, the only scissors I own. Men don't usually collect scissors.

The red and white roses were a cinch; not a soul in sight. I laid them in my suitcase and snapped it shut. The scissors were in my coat pocket. The silver roses were growing in fat pots in a corner. They were more faint lavender than silver and were breathtakingly regal, a kind of moonlight color. I hesitated to snip the stem but did.

"Just one," said a voice behind me. I jumped around so fast I nearly stabbed the man. Then we both laughed. He had on the white coat of the scientist, and I knew him. In the days when I kept cactus all around me instead of the usual greenery one sees in offices he had given me a crazy grafted cactus. It was a fat prickly pulp at the bottom but out of the sides shot yard-long snaky fingers of another species. It was a thing notable for its pure ugliness and everyone remarked on it.

"Thank you, Bunster," I said, "I just needed this one, for a returning friend." I opened the suitcase hurriedly forgetting the other roses. Bunster roared with glee. "There are plenty of those," he said, and left.

I had cleaned out my apartment after the Molotov cocktail had drunk up my office. It had been loaded with multifarious junk because of my propensity to assimilate whatever fell upon my doorstep. I mean that I had been working on the principle of the Beauty of the Ugly for years. Some student would give me a poster and I would dutifully thumbtack it to the wall, no matter what it depicted. The works of art, the loud and vilely printed books, batiks, fragments of art-class sculpture or plain busted brick, poems scrawled in Magic Markers in various colors, hubcaps, hood insignia, ribbons from cattle shows, medals from the Second World War, driftwood, all the waste junk of kitsch, pop, op, craperoo and put-on to which the aspirants to adulthood are addicted. In a rage I ripped it all down —and out. I filled three king-sized garbage cans in the back alley and three more across the way, until a woman stormed out of a back door and wanted to know what the hell I was doing.

Then I started to paint my two rooms but decided, after consulting my checkbook, that I was affluent enough to have it done by a pro. Not being sure about decorating I had the man use buff, not being too certain what buff would look like. Buffalo? Shammy?

It turned out pretty well at that, what with the battleship-gray woodwork I had picked out, looking at a color chart in the paint store. A kind of instinct-shooting. Not bad, I said, when it was done. I had cleaned the hell out of the rooms and lined up all the half-decent furniture in various right angles, with an eye to comfort and also to decorum. So that, if any esthetic sleight-of-hand artist dropped by with an offering of the latest camp fad, he would reel back in revulsion and stagger off, shaking his head.

I had done all this while Marya was in Aruba, as a sort of cleansing sacrament.

The roses looked magnificent. I put them in a large cheap glass vase close to the big window that looked out on the porch. The window was delirious with frost, inside and out. A fall of icy air shed down on them and they stood tall and thoughtful in the vase. They would keep until tomorrow. They better had.

CHAPTER XXVIII

Crossing the snow dune that barricaded Marya's street was work. We slid her two big valises up the bank and left them on the top, returning to the car for her cosmetics case, pocketbook and umbrella. I had dropped the idea of getting edibles and that left only the roses. It was still sub-zero and I had wrapped the flowers in newspaper, making a cone the way I had watched florists do. I even stapled them at the top, against the cold. Then we slid the luggage down on the other side and somehow managed to get everything to her front door in one trip.

We stood a long time kissing and puffing from our exertions and the excitement. She felt cold and hot simultaneously, lightly tanned, windblown and smelling like a perfumed peach. We had laid a good fire before she left and I tossed a match in it and up it went; we made a rum collins at her crowded little bar and flopped on the floor near the hearth. She had brought me a gleaming meerschaum pipe with a pure amber stem; it snuggled in a red leather fitted case with a white fur lining; there was no tobacco around but I sucked on the stem, then rubbed it vigorously on the carpet and picked up tiny bits of paper with the electricity I had made. We did all sorts of aimless silly things, chatting in between, getting acquainted, as it were. We were both a little shy and turned on the FM radio to hear what was playing; classical guitar picked its way into the warm glowing room.

"Darling," I said, "I want to leave Milo. I've had Milo and Milo has had me."

"I know," she said, rubbing my hand on her cheek.

"I won't have any trouble getting the same job at any number of places. But I won't go unless you will come with me."

"Ed, you know I want to be with you but we just can't pick up and ride off into the sunset. At least I can't, not so soon. I'm just not ready."

I said nothing. "I want to," she went on, "desperately, and I know the right time is coming. Start finding out about new places, and I'll help," she smiled.

I was all ready to rush out to wake up a justice of the peace, with or without a marriage license, but I knew that she meant what she said. Besides, I thought, I ought to get out of Milo with a certain dignity of pace and not slink off. Mysteriously, the sins and misdemeanors of Milo had somehow all been shifted to my back. I had committed the high crime of neutrality or indifference, or so it appeared, but thank God I didn't *feel* guilty or *act* guilty. All that I felt was a faint disgust, as when I go into a Good Will shop and can sniff the poverty in the air. Milo had taken on a *poor* smell and it made my nose twitch. Spiritual poverty, and they loved it. We would go somewhere where people were proud of being proud.

Marya wanted to see the snow. We got our coats and ploughed across the street to where the little ice-skating pond lay sunken. The kids had made a path and had actually swept and shoveled the pond clean and were whizzing around on their skates. Under the electric light it looked a Breughel postcard. It was windless in the little depression and you could hardly feel the cold. The tops of the snowbanks were smoky with clouds of powdery white that whipped off into the blackness. Someone had lit a fire in a big trash can and we stood close to it. My boots were full of ice and slush but it wasn't painful so far. A few of the kids greeted Marya. "Hi, Mrs. Hinsdale!" They must have known her from the country club.